Reefs and Shoals

Also by Dewey Lambdin

The King's Coat

The French Admiral

The King's Commission

The King's Privateer

The Gun Ketch

H.M.S. Cockerel

A King's Commander

Jester's Fortune

King's Captain

Sea of Grey

Havoc's Sword

The Captain's Vengeance

A King's Trade

Troubled Waters

The Baltic Gambit

King, Ship, and Sword

The Invasion Year

Reefs and Shoals

An Alan Lewrie Naval Adventure

Dewey Lambdin

THOMAS DUNNE BOOKS
ST. MARTIN'S PRESS
NEW YORK

THOMAS DUNNE BOOKS.
An imprint of St. Martin's Press.

REEFS AND SHOALS. Copyright © 2011 by Dewey Lambdin. All rights reserved. Printed in the United States of America. For information, address St. Martin's Press, 175 Fifth Avenue, New York, N.Y. 10010.

www.thomasdunnebooks.com
www.stmartins.com

Library of Congress Cataloging-in-Publication Data

Lambdin, Dewey.
    Reefs and shoals : an Alan Lewrie naval adventure / Dewey Lambdin.—1st ed.
        p.   cm.
    ISBN 978-0-312-59571-5 (hardcover)
    ISBN 978-1-4299-4133-4 (e-Book)
    1. Lewrie, Alan (Fictitious character)—Fiction.   2. Ship captains—Fiction.   3. Great Britain—History, Naval—18th century—Fiction.   I. Title.
    PS3562.A435R44 2012
    813'.54—dc23

                                                    2011041872

First Edition: January 2012

10 9 8 7 6 5 4 3 2 1

This one is for a dear, longtime friend,
Bob Enrione
February 5th, 1947–June 28th, 2011

We never actually met face-to-face, but back in the misty mid-90s he called me one night to talk about the series as a fan, first, which turned into hours' long almost weekly chats about everything; the Great Age of Sail, naval history in general, social customs and scandals of the times, food (he cooked lobscouse, spotted dog, and sea-pies!), and the eccentricities of the British and the characters of the Royal Navy.

Bob was a U.S. Navy diver and Vietnam veteran who ended up traveling the world with CBS News, knew a bit about anything that caught his mind, so he had a wealth of stories about world leaders he'd met, and the gossip about our media celebrities was priceless, too.

He retired in early 2011 and was looking forward to a lot of things, including a novel of his own and a compendium of his historical naval essays.

I, his wife, Jackie, his family and friends, will miss him most sorely . . . and that voice on the phone.

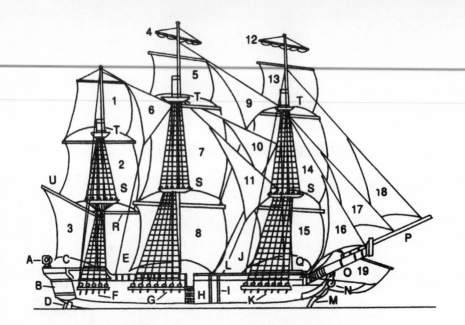

Full-Rigged Ship: Starboard (right) side view

1. Mizen Topgallant
2. Mizen Topsail
3. Spanker
4. Main Royal
5. Main Topgallant
6. Mizen T'gallant Staysail
7. Main Topsail
8. Main Course
9. Main T'gallant Staysail
10. Middle Staysail
11. Main Topmast Staysail
12. Fore Royal
13. Fore Topgallant
14. Fore Topsail
15. Fore Course
16. Fore Topmast Staysail
17. Inner Jib
18. Outer Flying Jib
19. Spritsail

A. Taffrail & Lanterns
B. Stern & Quarter-galleries
C. Poop Deck/Great Cabins Under
D. Rudder & Transom Post
E. Quarterdeck
F. Mizen Chains & Stays
G. Main Chains & Stays
H. Boarding Battens/Entry Port
I. Cargo Loading Skids
J. Shrouds & Ratlines
K. Fore Chains & Stays
L. Waist
M. Gripe & Cutwater
N. Figurehead & Beakhead Rails
O. Bow Sprit
P. Jib Boom
Q. Foc's'le & Anchor Cat-heads
R. Cro'jack Yard (no sail fitted)
S. Top Platforms
T. Cross-Trees
U. Spanker Gaff

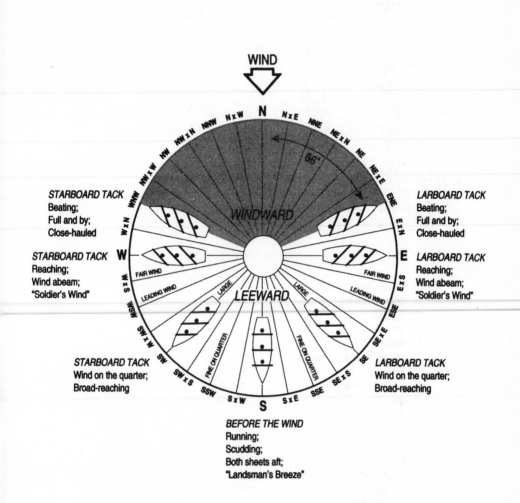

POINTS OF SAIL AND 32-POINT WIND-ROSE

NORTH CAROLINA

Yamboo Inlet

Hatteras Inlet

Cape Fear River

Cape Lookout

SOUTH CAROLINA

Wilmington

Cape Fear

Santee River

Georgetown

GEORGIA

Savannah River

Edisto River

Charleston

Edisto Island

Port Royal Sound

Savannah

Altamaha River

SEA ISLANDS

St. Mary's River

St. John's River

St. Augustine

SPANISH FLORIDA

Mayami Bay

FLORIDA STRAITS

ATLANTIC OCEAN

N

St. George's

BERMUDA

GREAT BAHAMA BANK

Nassau

NEW PROVIDENCE ISLAND

BAHAMA ISLANDS

Havana

CUBA

Santiago de Cuba

HAITI

DOMINICAN REPUBLIC

Santo Domingo

Port-au-Prince

mi.

0   50   100   200   300   400   500

Now let open Justice hear,
Come with killing sword to smite
One who knows no law, no right.
                    -THE BACCHAE,
                    1010-1012 EURIPIDES

PROLOGUE

I wish I were the Bosun, aboard a man o' war,
I wish I were the Captain, aboard a man o' war!
Sam's gone away, aboard a man o' war!
Pretty work, brave boys,
Pretty work, I say!
Sam's gone away, aboard a man o' war!

-SHORT HAUL OR
DRAG SHANTY ANONYMOUS

CHAPTER ONE

*T*o Captain Alan Lewrie's lights, no place was better on such a cold day than to be snug in a warm, soft bed with a toasty-warm woman. A well-stoked fireplace ablaze with a heap of sea-coal, and a brass reflector plate at the back to radiate its heat outward, a brace of candles aglow on the night-stand to create an intimate amber aura, a pot of tea atop a candle-warming stand, and a squat bottle of brandy near to hand, well . . . all those were fine in their own way, but they ran a poor second-best to snuggling close in the after-glow of feverish lovemaking!

Lewrie shifted a bit, digging his shoulder deeper into a pile of pillows and tugged the blankets, thick feather quilt, and coverlet up to his ears, then let out a very pleased "Mmmm!" He lay facing the lone window in the suite of rooms, and the sight of the rime of frost on the inside of the panes, the swirling flakes of snow, stark white against the low, grey clouds outside, brought forth a shiver in spite of the bed's warmth. Early January winds now and then moaned round the corners of the venerable George Inn, al-most whistled cross the fireplace chimney. Like a badly made clock, there even came the irregular *tick!* of tiny, hard bits of sleet against the glass.

"Who'd be a sailor on such a day?" he whispered.

"I do imagine the *smart* ones find a warm inn," Lydia told him with a wee chuckle, and a grin that scrunched her nose. *Rather cutely,* Lewrie thought.

Lydia Stangbourne might not possess the bowed and bee-stung mouth that Society preferred, nor the high brow or the plumpness of form that made gentlemen turn their heads in silent admiration. But Lewrie had thought her oddly fetching from their first encounter at St. James's Palace, the day he'd been knighted, and had grown even more entranced since.

She was willow slim and wiry, with dark emerald green eyes and hair the colour of old honey, hair which she allowed to curl naturally, and scoffed impatiently at the idea of elegant coiffures or wigs. That nose . . . full-on it seemed too wide and large, though in profile, it looked much shorter, almost pug-Irish. And, she was dis-armingly strong for a daughter of the aristocracy, and a sister of a Viscount. That came from vigourous daily rides, fox hunting in season, steeplechasing when not, from brisk walks, hunting with her brother Percy on their estates with her own rifled musket or fowling piece—not when Lord Percy's male compatriots were there, though!—even dabbling at swordplay, she'd gleefully admitted, hiring a swordmaster in for very private lessons when at their main country house near Henley-on-Thames. Her slim upper arms bore more lean muscle than any lady of her age or class might sport! All of that suppleness and strength sheathed in smooth and blemishless flesh as soft, and fragrant, as talc, the feel of which quite made Lewrie's head swim!

"Such good timing," Lydia cooed as she pressed closer to him. "Had I come before Christmas, as we'd planned, you'd have been off with that Popham fellow, but now! I pray most earnestly that the weather stays like this for the next fortnight."

"And I thought I was shot of those damned catamaran torpedoes," Lewrie replied with a groan.

God made women just hellish-fine*!* he thought; *Sleepin' or just layin' close like this, they're better than a warmin' pan!*

The summer before, his frigate, HMS *Reliant,* had been tasked to experiment with a variety of infernal engines designed to drift in on the tides and blow up some of the thousands of French invasion craft. There had been a real attack with them against the port of Boulogne, but the results had been extremely disappointing. Lewrie had thought that would be an end to them, but no . . . Captain Sir Home Riggs Popham, the clever fellow who had invented the Navy's new flag code, had staged an assault on Fort Rouge, a pile-built battery outside the port of Calais, and since

Lewrie knew so much about torpedoes, he had been roped in, despite what he thought of them. Sure enough, of the two launched, one went far off course and blew up harmlessly, and the second did a disappearing act. The lone fire-ship sent in exploded too soon, too, and the whole thing had been a dead bust. After that, Admiralty had given up on torpedoes in general, and since the middle of December, Lewrie, and *Reliant*, had been anchored here in Portsmouth awaiting new orders, and the foul weather had penned them in, fresh orders or no.

For which he was, this moment, *damned* thankful! This was simply a splendid way to welcome in the new year of 1805!

When wakened at 4 A.M. at Eight Bells in his great-cabins aboard ship, anchored far out in St. Helen's Road, it had taken a long look and a hard try to leave his hanging bed-cot. All his blankets and his coverlet, a quilt or two, and the furs he'd bought to brave the cold of the Baltic before the Battle of Copenhagen, and he had *still* been cold! His cats, Toulon and Chalky, had found it too nippy for them, too, and had burrowed under, for a rare once, and would not be turfed out, either. And the long, gusty sail to fetch alongside the King's Stairs in a whistled-up bum-boat had left him chilled to the bone, with his teeth chattering halfway through breakfast and a whole pot of scalding hot coffee!

"Comfortable?" he asked her.

"Blissfully," Lydia murmured back.

"Warm enough?"

"Delightfully so," she assured him, then lifted her lips to his for a soft and gentle kiss. He stroked the length of her back and her flanks; her thigh thrown over his slid higher, but . . .

"Except for your feet, it seems," Lewrie said, grimacing.

"I could say the same of yours," Lydia replied, giggling as she slid her foot down next to his, wriggling her toes as if to grasp, or play at toe-wrestling. "Alan, I hate to ask, but . . . might you mind pouring me a cup of tea, with a dollop of brandy?"

He let out a theatrical groan and a weary "Well, if I must."

Outside the bed covers, the room was merely cool, not frozen solid, but Lewrie made a quick chore of it, pouring tea, adding sugar and a splash of spirits.

"You are a dear," Lydia vowed quite prettily as he handed her the cup and saucer, and hopped back into bed. She slid up to prop herself against the thick piilows, and drew the blankets up to her neck.

"Damned right I am, and I'll thankee t'remember it!" Lewrie hooted, which brought forth a laugh. That was another point in her favour, in Lewrie's books at least, that in private she allowed herself to be raw, open, and genuine, and to laugh out loud when amused.

In public, well . . . that was another matter, as Lewrie had seen early on in London. As late as breakfast here at the George Inn not two hours before, the difference between the private Lydia and the one which wore her Publick Face was as stark as night from day.

She'd been homely as a child, and still thought herself so. In her late teens, her first exposure to the "marriage market" of a London Season had been cruelly disappointing, even for a Viscount's daughter with a dowry of £500 *per annum,* and a future beau's access to more land and property than most people had hot dinners. The beautiful, the giddy, and silly who'd only fetch £100 had ruled the rounds of all the balls, salons, routs, and drums. Years later, at her lovely mother's harsh insistence, she'd been placed on the block again, this time with £2,000 for her "dot", and Lydia had been knee-deep in slavering swains . . . most with the twinkle of golden guineas in their eyes, which had disgusted her to the point that she had treated them all most rudely, which only made the greediest declare her "modern" and delightfully "outspoken"!

And when she'd finally wed, quite late, her choice had been a man most vile, so secretly depraved that she'd run for her life, and had pressed her brother, now the third Viscount Stangbourne, to seek a Bill of Divorcement in the House of Commons. Two years or more of charge and counter-charge, made a scarlet hussy and a scandal in the papers before winning her suit, and she was *still* pointed out as that "Stangbourne mort". No wonder Lydia was so guarded, so icily aloof and imperious in Publick, and preferred the safety of the country, and a *very* small circle of friends, where she could shed her armour.

She was now thirty-two, ten years younger than Lewrie, and most firmly determined never to place herself under another man's control, definitely not as a wife—what man could she trust no matter his promises—or, so Lewrie suspected, allow her heart to be won by a lover's blandishments. Once bitten, twice shy, she was. Yet . . .

Lydia found Lewrie's company enjoyable, right from the first. He was a widower since 1802, his two sons were "on their own bottoms", and his daughter, Charlotte, was with his former in-laws in the village of

Anglesgreen, in Surrey. Lewrie also suspected that the reason that Lydia found him acceptable was the fact that he was in the Navy, and unless the war with Napoleon Bonaparte and France ended suddenly, he would be gone and far away for a year or more between *rencontres*.

Or, maybe it's 'cause I'm nigh as scandalous as she is, Lewrie wryly told himself as he watched her sip her tea with a grin on his face. His father's family, the Willoughbys, had always ridden their own way, roughshod, headstrong, and "damn the Devil." His father, Sir Hugo St. George Willoughby, had been a charter member of the Hell-Fire Club, for God's sake, and Lewrie was his bastard. Like the old adage "acorns don't fall far from the oak tree", he could boast of two by-blows of his own. . . . *Did* one dare boast of such things?

His nickname, gained early in his Lieutenancy, was "the Ram-Cat", and that was not for his choice of shipboard pets!

"What?" Lydia asked of a sudden, peering at him.

"I was just enjoying watching you enjoying your tea," Lewrie told her. "A little thing, but a nice'un."

"I am pleased that you are pleased," she said with a chuckle and a fond smile. "Though it's no *great* skill or social art. What if I slurped or smacked my lips? Might you find *that* enjoyable?"

"I might draw the line did you belch," Lewrie japed, "but, did you, I'm certain you'd do it . . . kittenish." He leaned over to kiss the point of her bared shoulder.

"Oh, kittenish!" Lydia laughed again. "Like a proper lady's sneeze? With a wee mew in punctuation? You are *easily* pleased."

"Well, damme . . . yes I am," Lewrie told her with a laugh and a grope under the covers. She finished her tea, handed it to him so he could set it on the night-stand, then slid back down into his embrace once more, giving out a long, pleased sigh. After several long and lingering kisses, Lydia settled down with her head under his chin.

"I suppose it's too cold to even think of going out to that inn you told me of," she murmured.

"Wouldn't wish that on a hound," Lewrie assured her. "Dinner at the George, here, will more than do, when you feel famished."

"All those senior captains and admirals, and their wives," she hesitantly replied, making a *moue* in distaste. "As dear as I wish the pleasure of your company, I'm surely bad for your repute in the Navy."

"Didn't know I had one," Lewrie quipped, "and if I do, it's as bad as it's goin' t'get. Personal repute, anyways. There's none that can fault me when it comes to fighting, and that's what counts."

He sat up to look down at her.

"Your reputation's more at risk for bein' seen with me than I for bein' with you," he told her. "And I don't give a damn for others' opinions on *that* head. Bugger 'em. Feed 'em thin, cold gruel."

She drew him down close, pleased by his statement.

Lewrie feared, though, that Lydia didn't much care for how the other diners would stare, point with their chins, cut their eyes, and whisper behind their hands and napkins; the matronly proper wives'd be the worst. *They* were respectable, she was not, and they would find a way to make that tacitly clear.

"We could order in," Lewrie suggested.

"And give the inn servants gossip to pass on?" Lydia said with a sour grimace, and an impatient shrug. "They probably have ties to the London papers!"

The many daily publications in London all had one or two snoops to gather spice for their reportage of Court doings, or the appearances of the famous and infamous. The morning after Lydia had dined out with him, there'd been a snarky item about them in several papers. No names were printed, but anyone who had kept up with Society reporting could make an educated guess about ". . . a recently divorced lady often featured in our pages the last two years running . . ." and the distinguished Naval Person she'd been seen with, ending with a smirky ". . . will the lady in question teach her Sea-Dog new tricks, or has our Jason found himself a fresh Sheet-Anchor?"

" 'Which infamous divorcee was seen dining, clad in nothing but her shift, with a dashing naval hero, similarly *sans* his small clothes at an inn in Portsmouth,' d'ye mean?" Lewrie scoffed.

"Exactly so!" Lydia snapped.

"Then we'll dress, and dine publicly," Lewrie decided. "Much as I'd admire t'see you gnaw a chicken leg, nude." He drew her back into a snug embrace and stroked her hair to mollify her.

"Do I live to eighty, they'll *still* find something delicious to write about me," Lydia groused in a small voice.

"Nonsense!" Lewrie hooted. "They've Nelson and Emma Hamilton t'write about, or the doings of all those damned Bohemian poets."

"Well . . ."

Lewrie yawned and slowly stretched against her.

"Lady Caroline Lamb," he added. "*There's* a road smash, and good for daily scandals." He yawned again, louder and longer.

"Now you'll get me started," Lydia said, covering her mouth as she snuggled closer, and lower down the bed.

"Let's try something novel," Lewrie suggested. "Ye know, we've never . . ."

She stiffened and slid away from him a few inches, bracing herself on an elbow. "Something novel? Something un-natural? Bind me to the headboard posts? Just what perversion do you desire, sir? Do you drop your pretense, at last, like the beast I foolishly wed?"

"Lydia . . . Lydia, I mean nothing at all like that!" he gently insisted. "*Reliant*'s in Channel Fleet, and no officer is allowed to sleep out of his ship. We've never had the time before to just cuddle up, nod off, and *sleep* together. Take a long, snuggly nap?"

Rumour had it that her ex-husband had been driven by scandal to his country estates, wore a bell round his neck like a leper to warn off objects of his beastly desires, and would bugger ducks, geese, and stray sheep if he couldn't run down anything bipedal, male or female, young or old.

"Just . . . sleep?" Lydia mused with her head cocked over, and a wry look on her face. She screwed her lips to one side as if biting her cheek for a moment. Then, with a rush, she was back close beside him, snuggling under the heavy covers. "I'm sorry I mistook . . ."

"After *that* bastard, you'd be right t'suspect," Lewrie allowed. "Said it yourself, though . . . I'm so easily pleased," he japed.

It'll be like bein' married to a parson's daughter, he thought with a well-stifled groan; *and goodbye to fellatio forever!*

For all the innuendos and charges laid during Lydia's two years of waiting for Parliament to grant her divorce, and what a scandalous bawd she'd been painted, she was surprisingly shy and "conventional". He could only caress, stroke, and kiss so low down her belly, then no further. She might slide atop him and "ride St. George's lance" now and again, but anything more *outré* was right out.

It was not that Lewrie was a *devotee* of the *outré*, but now and then some rare variety, some surprise, was pleasing, he'd found.

That's why men keep mistresses, or go to brothels, he thought with a secret grin.

"Yes, let's . . . what do sailors call a nap?" Lydia agreed.

"They 'caulk off', take a 'caulk'," Lewrie softly whispered. "Do two sailors board a coach, one'll ask the other does he prefer to 'caulk or yarn': nap or trade stories."

"Caulk or yarn, sir?" Lydia asked with an impish tone.

"Caulk," Lewrie said with a chuckle.

Dodged another bullet, Lewrie congratulated himself after some minutes, when her breath against his chest became slow and regular, right at the edge of sleep himself; *Ye cheated death, again!*

CHAPTER TWO

*T*he old George Inn did set the best table that Lewrie knew of in Portsmouth, which made it the favourite destination for those Navy officers who could afford to dine or lodge there, and their mid-day meal was no exception. After a good two-hour nap, a slow and languourous awakening with much snuggling, caressing, fond mutual regardings—and a delightful if conventional bout of lovemaking—Lewrie and Lydia had risen, dressed, and come down to the dining rooms, he with his sash and star of a Knight of the Bath, at her insistence, to dine.

Hopes for a good salad in mid-winter were moot, but there was a hearty and hot tarragon chicken soup, followed by servings of haddock in lemon and drawn butter, then a course of sliced roast beef, all with roast potatoes and peas, sloshed down with glasses of Rhenish and one shared bottle of claret. Lewrie went for pound cake with cream and raspberry jam, whilst Lydia settled for sweet biscuits and coffee. She was a light diner, Lewrie had noted before, always leaving portions of her dishes un-eaten, and ordering only a few items, not the usual ritual of fish-fowl-swine-roast beef or beefsteak that could take hours to put away. "But I've always had a light appetite," she had explained once, and to Lewrie's cocked brow when she'd passed on cheese and nuts this time, she leaned over to put her head close to his and said, "You must know, Alan, that I am so *easily* pleased," which made the both of them laugh, no matter who else dined with them, or what they thought of their intimate moment.

"More coffee, sir?" a servant asked.

"Aye," Lewrie agreed.

There was a bustle in the entrance hall as someone new arrived, accompanied by a blast of cold air. It was a Navy officer, a Lieutenant in his early thirties, and a pleasant-enough looking young woman with him, both swaddled in travelling cloaks. Behind them came a civilian servant bearing the woman's luggage, and a sailor loaded down with the Lieutenant's. Once the door was shut against the snow, they shucked their cloaks and embraced.

"A fond reunion, do you imagine?" Lydia asked him.

"Seems so," Lewrie agreed. "Hell's Bells!"

"Do you know him?" Lydia asked him.

"No, but his man," Lewrie told her, plucking his napkin from his lap and dabbing his mouth, ready to rise. "He's off *Aeneas,* my son's ship!" he quickly explained.

Atop the sailor's head was a wide-brimmed and low-crowned flat tarred hat with a long black ribbon band trailing down his coat collar. Painted in white lettering on the front of the hat was his ship's name.

"Excuse me for a moment," Lewrie pled, getting to his feet and going to the opened double doors from the dining room to the entrance hall.

The Lieutenant and his lady—revealed to be husband and wife, once their gloves were off and their wedding bands in plain sight—were lost in joy to be re-united, oblivious.

"My pardons, sir," Lewrie began. "Ahem . . ."

The young wife spotted him and inclined her head to direct her husband's attention from rapt adoration.

"Captain Alan Lewrie, sir. Hope you'll forgive me for intruding on your moment, but you are off the *Aeneas* seventy-four, Captain Benjamin Rodgers?"

"Aye, I am, sir. Allow me to name myself to you, Captain. I am Robert Stiles. My wife, Judith," the officer replied. She dropped a passable curtsy. "We came in just yesterday afternoon, from the Brest blockade. Do you know Captain Rodgers, sir?"

"Happy t'make your acquaintance, Mister Stiles, Mistress Stiles. Captain

Rodgers and I are old friends, but more to the point is the fact that my son Sewallis, is one of your Midshipmen."

"Oh, *Mister* Lewrie, aye!" Lt. Stiles said in a gush, laughing. "Forgive me for not making the connexion at once, sir. He's one of ours, right enough, right Carter?" he said to the sailor who'd borne his shore-going traps.

"An' a fine gennulman 'e be, sir, is Mister Lewrie," the sailor assured him. "As smart as paint," he added with a grin and wink.

"Glad t'hear it," Lewrie said, a bit relieved. "I'll attempt to get in touch with Captain Rodgers, at once, treat him to a shore supper, perhaps go aboard to see Sewallis. Thankee, Mister Stiles, and I apologise again for interrupting you and your wife. My very best wishes for a long and joyous stay in port!"

"The officer is from your son's ship?" Lydia asked once he was seated with her again, and getting a warm-up of his coffee.

"Aye, he is," Lewrie happily told her. "God, I haven't seen Sewallis since May of 1803, and damned few letters from him in the meantime. Haven't seen Benjamin Rodgers, his captain, in a dog's age, either! The Adriatic, in '96!" I must buy him at least *one* supper, with lashings of champagne, and hang the cost. He's *mad* for the stuff. Won't sail without a dozen dozen bottles in his lazarette store, ha ha!"

"And treat your son to something better than salt meats, too?" Lydia asked, looking a touch sombre.

"Of course!" Lewrie declared, his head full of plans.

"Captain Rodgers knew you early on, I think you said. When . . . when your wife was alive," Lydia continued, fiddling nervously with a coffee spoon. "Perhaps I should not be present when . . . if they've kept up with the papers. I might bring bad feelings. . . ."

He peered at her gravely, taking a long breath, then reached to take her free hand. "Lydia, I don't give a damn what they've read or what they've heard. I'm done with mourning Caroline's passing, and I'm fortunate enough to have met someone new who's become dear to me. I'm not the sort t'sneak about, or shove you into an *armoire* 'til company's gone, either. We've nothing t'be ashamed of."

Well, in certain circumstances, I have! he remembered; *Mostly the sneakin' about bit.*

"You've become very dear to me, as well, Alan," Lydia told him with a fond, almost shy smile. "If you wish me to meet them and be with you, then I shall. Gladly."

"Such a grand lass!" Lewrie congratulated her.

"Know who that was?" Lt. Stiles was telling his wife once they had gone above stairs to their temporary lodgings. "'Black Alan' Lewrie, the one who was tried for stealing slaves to crew his ship, and got away with it! A real fighting frigate captain, knighted and made Baronet last year. The 'Ram-Cat', some call him. Oh, he's made a name for himself!"

"The 'Ram-Cat'?" his wife asked, puzzled.

"For the scrapping way he goes after England's enemies. Or for keeping pet cats since his first command." Lt. Stiles breezed off.

"Well, which is it?" Mrs. Styles asked.

"I'm *pretty* sure it's the scrapping," her husband answered.

"I'll write a quick note," Lewrie was planning. "Two, really, and find a bum-boat t'bear 'em out to *Aeneas*. Or, long as I'm there, I might as well go out to her and see 'em both, first! If Benjamin has any fresh stores aboard, or the pedlars get to him quick enough, I might even get dined aboard."

"So, you may be gone 'til dusk," Lydia speculated, "and not be back 'til tomorrow morning? Since you cannot be out of your ship at night?"

"Oh, well, there is that," Lewrie said back, deflating. "You would be twiddlin' yer thumbs, with the weather too foul for shopping. Not that shopping in Portsmouth's got a jot on London, hey?"

"Surely there are art gallerys that feature nautical paintings," Lydia mused. "Something realistic depicting a frigate, to remind me of you when you're gone. And realistic enough to allow me to lecture Percy on every detail," she added with a mischievous grin and another impish wrinkle of her nose. "He's bored *me* to tears with the details of cavalry saddlery, fodder, and Army drill manuals!"

"You'd go out in this raw chill? You'd catch your death!" he objected.

"And you won't risk the same?" Lydia scoffed. "Go then, and I'll see you on the morrow. I'll dine in alone this evening. And I will tuck myself in with a good novel. And sleep by myself," she said as she leaned closer, her lips curled in secret amusement. "Though I will confess that that will not be as warm, or as blissful, as that nap of ours."

"I wish I could kiss you this instant," Lewrie told her in a hoarse mutter, after a quick peek round the dining rooms.

"One to warm you just before you go out into the cold," Lydia promised.

"With expectations of more, tomorrow," Lewrie wished aloud.

"Most assuredly," she vowed.

CHAPTER THREE

*W*ell, damme!" Captain Benjamin Rodgers boomed as he barrelled up to the starboard gangway and entry-port of his two-decker Third Rate to greet an un-looked-for arrival. "Will ya look at who turns up? I haven't clapped eyes on ya in ages, and here ya are. Hallo, Alan, and how the Devil do ya keep?" he hoorawed taking hands with his old compatriot from the Bahamas between the wars, and the Adriatic.

"Main-well, all considered, Benjamin, and how the Devil are you? It *has* been too bloody long!" Lewrie beamed back. "You're lookin' . . . prosperous, and fit as a hound."

"The word you're looking for is *substantial*, ha!" Rodgers said, slapping his girth. Even as a young, up-and-coming Commander in 1786 at Nassau, New Providence, Benjamin Rodgers had been a stoutish fellow, and even years of sea duty had not managed to lean his physique. He'd been as dark-complexioned as a Welshman, with thick and curly ebon hair . . . hair which now was salted at the temples beneath his cocked hat.

"A sight for sore eyes, no matter," Lewrie assured him.

"Let's go aft and get out of this bloody raw wind," Rodgers insisted. "What say ya to a glass or three of hot punch?"

"I say lead on, soonest!" Lewrie laughed.

⚓

Once out of boat-cloaks, hats, swords, and mittens, and warming their hands and backsides near a Franklin-pattern iron stove, Rodgers let out a slow whistle. "Knight of the Bath?" he said, jutting his chin at Lewrie's sash and star. "I may have to bang my head on the deck in *kowtow*. When did *that* happen?"

"Last Spring," Lewrie said with a grimace. "S'posed t'be for a squadron-to-squadron fight off the coast of Louisiana, but it's my belief that it was for Caroline. Some cynical bastards used her murder t'stir up war fever. This is the reward. I don't like wearin' it."

"Then why do you?" Rodgers asked, cocking his head over.

"A lady's insistence," Lewrie told him, heading for a leather-covered chair by the settee grouping.

"Life does go on," Rodgers said, joining him. "Punch, Dugan," he called to his cabin servant. "Truly, I'm sorry I couldn't come to Angles-green and attend her funeral, but I was too far off when I got word of it. God, I can picture the two of you to the life, newlyweds at Nassau. What a grand house she made of that gatehouse cottage off East Bay. She was a grand girl, and damn the French for killing her."

"Your letter was most comforting, all the same," Lewrie replied. "Did you ever marry?"

"Aye, I finally did!" Rodgers boasted, pointing to an oil portrait that was hung above the sideboard in his great-cabins dining coach. Lewrie turned to peer at it, discovering an image of a pert-faced and blue-eyed woman with masses of dark brown hair. "Susannah and I met in Reading, just after I paid off my last ship after the Peace of Amiens, and hit it right off. Imagine, a 'scaly fish' like me, well into my fourties, turned 'calf-eyed cully' over a lady of twenty-seven, but . . . it's been grand. We even have a boy, he's two, now. I've even had to re-learn dancing, can you feature it, haw?"

"I'm glad for ye, Benjamin," Lewrie was quick to say. "Though, it's hard t'be a father in our trade. Or a husband, either."

"Miss her and little Ben something sinful," Rodgers confessed in a soft voice. "Ah, the punch! Scalding hot, I trust, or I'll have ya at the grat-ings, Dugan."

"Scaldin' 'ot, sir," his servant said with an easy grin.

"And, I doubt ya got yourself rowed out this far in the bloody blizzard just t'see me," Rodgers laughed. "It's your son, too, I'd wager."

"Right in one," Lewrie agreed. "Is he aboard?"

"Sent him off with the Purser and a working-party about three hours ago, so he should be back soon," Rodgers said, blowing on his tall china tankard, cupping its warmth against his hands.

"How's he doing?" Lewrie asked, doing much the same as Rodgers with his own tankard. "Shapin' well, is he?"

"Oh, he's settled in satisfactorily," Rodgers told him. "Once he found his sea-legs. About in the middle of the pack . . . some older, some younger than he is. A dab-hand at mathematics, sun sights, celestial navigation. He can reef, hand, and steer as well as any."

"Bags sharper than me, most-like," Lewrie japed, thinking that his old friend's assessment of his son's nautical prowess and progress was grudging at best; as he had feared, Sewallis might not be suited to the rough-and-tumble of the Royal Navy.

"Best way to describe him'd be . . . earnest," Rodgers went on between tentative sips of hot punch. "Earnest and diligent, attentive to duty, as smart as paint, all told. Has a mind like a snare trap, and learns quickly. Once he's learned something, he'll not forget it, either. A bit sober-sided."

"He always was," Lewrie said, "Reticent, sometimes. Shy?"

"Well, if my Mids pulled a prank, he'd be the last I'd suspect of it," Rodgers hooted. "The one that *schemed* it, more like. He ain't a sky-larker, like most of the lads his age. He strikes me as a lad closer to one ready to stand for his oral exams, a Passed Midshipman. Bless me, he ain't idle, nor possessed of your sense of humour, but . . . he's the dependable sort. Give him charge of something and it gets done. And the ship's people respect him, and obey him chearly. That goes a long way in my book, and damn the likable ones."

"Sounds like he's prosperin, then," Lewrie concluded.

"The lad'll most-like *never* tell a good joke, but prospering?" Rodgers said with a chuckle. "Aye, right nicely, I'd say."

"I'm glad t'hear it," Lewrie said, smiling at last. "And from a man I trust t'tell it straight, too."

"A *lady* made ya wear your baubles?" Rodgers prompted. "It'd be about time ya dipped back into life after . . . ya know."

"Met her at Saint James's Palace, the day it happened," Lewrie told him. "Rather complicated, really. . . ." And he made a grand tale of meeting

Eudoxia Durschenko and her one-eyed father off Daniel Wigmore's circus ship, how Viscount Lord Percy Stangbourne had met her in London and had decided to woo her, how Eudoxia had spoken so highly of how he'd saved their bacon on a return convoy from Cape Town, and how Lord Percy had dashed up to meet the fellow who'd saved his "intended", dragging his sister along to greet the new Knight and Baronet.

"Shit on a bisquit!" Rodgers exclaimed. "You're a Baronet, too?"

"King George was havin' a bad day," Lewrie explained. "There were a couple o' baronets made before me; he'd picked up someone else's glasses, or . . . it stuck in his head, and out it popped. I *thought* it would be corrected, but the senior palace flunkies said that the Crown don't *make* mistakes, so there!"

"Swear to Christ, Alan, but you could fall into a lake of shit and come up with a chest full o' guineas," Rodgers whooped. "So the lady, Lydia, insists ya wear your honours? All the way from London?"

"Ehm . . . she coached down to Portsmouth a few days ago," Lewrie confessed. "We were dinin' at the George when I saw your Lieutenant Stiles and his wife, and a sailor with them with the ship's name on his hat, and . . . here I am."

"Going to wed again?" Rodgers asked, looking happily expectant. *He'd* found wedded bliss, after all his years as a bachelor and—like all who had, and as a good friend to boot—was eager to rope others in,

Like a slum missionary, Lewrie cynically thought; *He's found salvation, and won't let ye go 'til ye've enlisted, too!*

"Early days," Lewrie hedged, busying himself with his tankard. "Lydia, ah . . . was married once before, so she may be shy of touchin' a hot skillet a second time."

"Ah, a widow, is she? Any children?" Rodgers asked.

"Divorced," Lewrie had to admit.

"Uhm. Ah!" Rodgers replied, his face becoming a puzzle.

"No children," Lewrie offered, with a hopeful note.

"Well, ha," Rodgers flummoxed, shifting in his chair so hard it squeaked most alarmingly, clearly torn between joy for an old comrade, and his sense of the Conventions. If Lewrie had announced that Lydia was a Hindoo *nautch*-dancer he'd picked up in Bombay, a swarthy Hottentot maiden from the Kalahari, or a pox-raddled whore he'd tripped over in a Portsmouth alley, Benjamin Rodgers could not have been more stunned.

Should I have called her an actress, or a circus trick-rider? Lewrie asked himself; *There's a lotta that goin' round, these days!*

"You might've read about it in the papers, two or three years ago," Lewrie went on, to fill the awkward silence. "Her husband was an utter beast, with the morals of a *drunk* monkey, but he could wear a good face in Publick, and fooled everyone. She's well shot o' him."

"Oh, I don't keep up with all the scandal-mongering newspapers," Rodgers scoffed. "Gossip, rumours, and slurs don't signify to me."

"Unfortunately, Lydia suffered at their hands, even though her suit was . . . righteous," Lewrie further admitted. "He's ruined for all time, and she's free, and didn't deserve a jot of it. More innocent than me, 'bout that trial o' mine for stealin' slaves."

"Oh, that 'Black Alan' thing," Rodgers snickered.

"The worst was 'Saint Alan, the Liberator'," Lewrie said with a long sigh. "Even though Wilberforce, Hannah More, and their Abolitionist crowd are done with me, I'll most-like never live *that* down. Ehm . . . I told Lydia I owe you a hearty shore supper, with *magnums* of champagne. If you'd care to meet her?"

"Damme if I haven't *earned* one, after four months off Brest," Rodgers exclaimed, "and I'm down t'my last four bottles o 'bubbly', to boot. Good God, stick with frigates, Alan, long as ya can. Once ya get a ship of the line, you'll die o' boredom, if the shoals and rocks and the Bay of Biscay don't get ya first! You're offering, and I'm accepting, gladly. And I'd be happy to meet your lady."

"I probably owe ye *more* than one, just t' make up for old times and a too-long absence," Lewrie told him, glad that Benjamin *seemed* open to meeting Lydia, and waiting to form a first-hand opinion.

The Marine sentry outside the door to the quarterdeck rapped his musket on the oak-planked deck. "Midshipman Lewrie, SAH!" the sentry added with a stamp of his boots.

"Aha!" Captain Benjamin Rodgers said, rising from his chair. "About time, too. Enter!" he called out.

The door opened, admitting a gust of icy wind and a swirl of snow. Mr. Midshipman Sewallis Lewrie stepped in, hat under his arm and his boat-cloak dripping moisture.

"Captain, sir, I beg to report. . . ."

"Look who's come calling, Mister Lewrie!" Rodgers boomed out.

"Hallo, Son," Lewrie said, rising from his chair.

"Ha . . . hallo, Father," Sewallis managed to say, his eyes as blared in surprise as a first-saddled colt.

CHAPTER FOUR

*S*ewallis was certainly surprised, but so was his father. At their last supper at the George Inn in the Spring of 1803, as Lewrie had been fitting out *Reliant*, Sewallis had just turned sixteen, and had been dressed in his usual dark and sombre style; well-tailored and neat, with his hair brushed and combed in close order, and his complexion had been the sort sported by those who lived mostly indoors, in libraries and schoolrooms. Now, he looked . . .

He looks like the poorest Mid ever born, Lewrie told himself.

His errant eldest son's uniform looked as if it had been plucked from a discard pile, or off the used rack, and had not been made from the best broadcloth to begin with. His white waist-coat and breeches were streaked with tar and slush stains. He'd done some growing, too, for his wrists showed below his coat cuffs, and the knee-buttons of his breeches were undone so his longer legs could bend without popping them off. Plain white cotton stockings, clunky and cracked shoes with dull pewter buckles, a linen shirt that was going pale tan . . .

Boy always was *tight with his money,* Lewrie thought for an awkward moment, groping for a way to begin.

"Well, lad . . . how d'ye keep?" Lewrie said at last, stepping up to shake his son's free hand.

"Main-well, Father . . . sir," Sewallis replied with only a faint smile on his face, as if unsure that one was allowed.

"It's good t'see ye alive and well, I'm bound," Lewrie went on. He went so far as to embrace him in a brief hug, and clap him on the back. "Christ, though, I'd've thought Captain Rodgers'd feed ye more victuals. Buyin' 'millers' from the bread-room, are you, t'make ends meet?"

"The Captain feeds us quite well," Sewallis replied, grinning. "I've *tasted* bread-room rat, but I'm not partial."

"I'd just promised your captain a grand shore supper, and I intended t'sport you to one, too, but . . . you look in more need of one, first," Lewrie declared. "And a spell at a good tailor's, to boot," he added, stepping back to give his son a head-to-toe examination. "The wear-and-tear o' blockade duty's not done your kit any good."

"I . . . I did not imagine that continual sea-duty would require grand rig, sir . . . Father," Sewallis flummoxed. "We've seen no need of silk shirts and such . . . no port calls."

Didn't know he could dissemble, or dance round the truth, quite so well, either, Lewrie thought; *He can't claim that I kitted him out so poorly, or that he did it on his own.*

"*Told* ye that ye needed better," Lewrie lied to help him out. "The lad looks like Death's-Head-on-a-Mopstick, hey, sir?" he asked as he turned to grin at Rodgers. "Ehm, I wonder if there was somewhere we could, ah . . ."

"Well . . . ," Benjamin Rodgers said, considering the matter. His great-cabins were *his,* not to be usurped, even by an old friend.

"No matter, we'll go on deck," Lewrie offered. "I won't keep him from his duties long."

"You'll dine aboard with me, Alan?" Rodgers asked.

"My own cook'd be heart-broken if I let his efforts spoil," Lewrie said, declining, "and, you're short of champagne. Let me dine *you* out tomorrow afternoon, then I'll be glad to accept your invitation. Once your stores are replenished, hey?" he added with a wink.

"Most suitable," Rodgers agreed.

"Shall we go get snowed on?" Lewrie bade Sewallis.

The most exposed place to the raw weather was atop Rodgers's great-cabins, on the poop deck aft of the mizen mast trunk; it would also be the last place *Aeneas*'s crew would be found at that hour.

"What in the world got into your head, lad?" Lewrie demanded. "Damme, don't ye know the penalty for uttering a forgery? They *hang* people for it! Had ye been discovered, you'd have sunk your brother's repute in the Navy, along with yours. Lied to your captain, lied to *Admiralty* . . . a legal document, your—!"

"So, you've come to snatch me back, is that it, Father?" Sewallis interrupted, looking pinch-faced and miserable.

Lewrie glared at him, locking eyes with his son for a long bit. Sewallis must have gained *some* gumption in the Fleet, for the longer his father frowned, the firmer and more determined the son's face became.

"No," Lewrie relented, after another long moment. "It's much too late for that. If I dragged you ashore by your ears, it would all come out, and you'd be in the 'quag' up to your neck. You *could* pass it off as a lark, back at your school, but . . . I doubt the authorities would think so. 'Least said, soonest mended'. Or, as your granther says, 'you've made your bed, and now must lie in it'."

Sewallis did not say his thanks aloud, but his countenance brightened, and he nodded his head as he took in and released a long breath.

"Why the Devil *did* you do it?" Lewrie asked. "The one letter ye wrote me never explained."

"For Mother," Sewallis baldly stated. "I told you why I *wished* to serve, at that last supper we all had, the night before you sent Hugh aboard *his* ship. The Navy, the Army, in a line regiment or the Yeomanry militia. For a bit, I even considered finding a recruiting sergeant's party, and going as a volunteer . . . or signing aboard for the first ship that would have me."

"Oh, for God's sake!" Lewrie blurted. "As a bloody *soldier*? Or a Landsman lubber? Were ye *completely* daft?"

Even my *father wasn't that* cruel t'me. . . . *I went to sea as a Midshipman!* Lewrie recalled his "pressing" into the Fleet in 1780, so his grandmother Lewrie's expected inheritance could be used to pay off Sir Hugo's creditors, with him thousands of miles away and unknowing.

"I *told* you all, I wished to avenge Mother's murder. I wanted to fight the French and make them pay," Sewallis said with some heat.

"And, have you, so far?" Lewrie skeptically asked.

"Well, not so far," Sewallis admitted with a shrug and a shy grin. "The cowards sit at anchor in Brest, and won't come out to face us. Do they assemble in the outer road, we stand in within sight and they slink back to the inner, letting a good slant of wind go to waste. Then the Westerly gales come, and we have to stand off windward."

He talks *like a sailor, at least,* Lewrie considered.

"Are you disappointed by life in the orlop cockpit?" he asked his eldest, as they paced from the taffrail lanthorns to the railings and ladders that led down to the quarterdeck and back.

"It's much like school, really," Sewallis told him, opening up, now that he was sure that he would not be exposed as a forger and sent ashore as a fraud. He even sounded "chirpy" and amused. "I was John New-come, but I've been that before. I've learned to shrug off all the japes, or find ways to get my own back, d'ye see, sir. I paid heed to the cautions you told Hugh, to ready him for sea, so . . ." He heaved off a shrug and another brief smile. "Like any dormitory, there will be dullards, clever ones, spiteful ones, bullies, and victims. I get by."

That *don't sound rosy,* Lewrie thought, frowning to imagine that Sewallis was too mild-mannered and reticent to stand up for himself.

"Any real problems? Anyone who gives ye special grief?"

"We have made our accommodations," Sewallis cryptically replied, returning to his usually grave self. "Call it a truce, if you will, sir. There's only the one—I name no names—but, he is beastly to one and all, to the ship's people as well, and the Captain has his eyes upon him. He's failed two Post-Captains' Boards already, so he may not be long in the Navy," Sewallis said with a wink.

"That, or the oldest Mid going," Lewrie replied with a laugh. "I've met a man, fourty or more years old, and *still* a Midshipman. Stood your ground . . . faced him down, did ye?" Lewrie asked.

"Something like that, aye sir," his son said, rather proudly.

"Damn my eyes, Sewallis," Lewrie said with a sigh, coming to a stop in the back-and-forth stroll. "When my father wrote and told me you'd run away to sea, I didn't think you'd be up to it. You always struck me more suited to the Law or something suitable for the eldest son, and the heir to whatever I leave. I didn't *want* this for you. A second son, like your brother, Hugh, aye, but that's what *he's* always wanted. I thought you'd be happier ashore, in your books, or . . ."

"I know, sir," Sewallis glumly agreed. "I've known for a long time that I'm not as . . . rambunctious as Hugh. Not as suited to be like you. That you never quite knew what to do with me, when you were back from the sea, and . . ."

"Damme, d'ye think I loved ye less than your brother?" Lewrie exclaimed, aghast that Sewallis felt that way; aghast, too, to confess that sometimes, yes, he had. Hugh had been so much "all boy" that he had been so much easier to understand, and to relate to.

Sewallis said nothing to that; he just stood erect, shivering in the cold snow, and frowning.

"Hell if I did, Hell if I *do*, son!" Lewrie declared, flinging his arms round his eldest and pulling him close. "I love both of you, and I'm *proud* of both of you. I can't say that I *understand* you, now and again, or approve of ev'rything you do."

He stepped back, still gripping Sewallis by his upper arms.

"No father wants t'hear his children've gone and done something daft, Sewallis. Knowin' how hard life at sea is, d'ye think I wished *both* my boys t'be at risk? D'ye think I don't worry and fret over all that could harm either of you? When you see your first horse to the gallop, you went off to your first school . . . !"

"Thank you, Father," Sewallis said at last, looking happy and relieved. "Thank you for that. I can stay aboard?"

"Benjamin Rodgers thinks you're shapin' well, and I trust his judgement, so, aye. You're on your own bottom. And when he gives ye leave t'come ashore with me for a day, you'll come back aboard much better dressed. We can't let ye continue on so 'rag-tag-and-bobtail'."

"I must admit I look forward to a larger coat," Sewallis said with an outright laugh.

"Let you stuff yourself at the George Inn, again, and fill up your seachest with goodies, too," Lewrie promised. "Have scones and tea, or a *huge* breakfast before, with me and . . . uhm. With Mistress Stangbourne."

"With whom, sir?" Sewallis asked, checking his pace.

"Lady I met in London last Spring, at the palace when I was presented to the King and got knighted," Lewrie said, though he winced to have blabbed her existence. "Sister of Viscount Percy Stangbourne, and quite nice. I'd saved Lord Percy's intended aboard one of the ships in that convoy in the South Atlantic, years ago, when I had *Proteus*, and we took the *L'Uranie* frigate. Didn't know either of 'em from Adam, but . . . up they popped at the *levee*, and . . ."

Damme, how much o' that can ye tell, without mentionin' that Eudoxia Durschenko, the circus, and how she made cow's-eyes at me? Lewrie thought. That part of his life was *terra incognita* to his children . . . so far. They might even still believe that he had been a faithful husband to their late mother!

"They reside here in Portsmouth?" Sewallis queried.

"Uh, no. Their country seat's near Reading and Henley," Lewrie tried to breeze off, "but they have a grand house in Grosvenor Street. You'd like Percy. He raised a cavalry regiment, all on his own, and got it taken onto Army List last Summer, and posted to the Kent coast. *Damned* fine horseman, it goes without sayin' . . . her, too. Huntin' and steeple-chasin' . . . God only *knows* how many acres they own, or where." *Stop babblin'!* he silently chid himself.

"You are *seeing* her, sir?" Sewallis asked, looking stricken.

"We've become friends," Lewrie cautiously allowed.

"Oh. I see," Sewallis replied. "It has been three years, now, since Mother . . . even so . . ."

"I'd not wish t'hide her under a bushel basket, but . . . if you don't care to, we won't."

"Well, ehm . . . I'd . . ." Sewallis said, groping to express his true feelings. After another deep, pent breath, he, very gravely, added, "This comes as most surprising, sir. Had you written about her . . . the lady's existence . . . first, to prepare the ground, as it were?"

"It's still early days, and 'til lately, there wasn't much to write *about*," Lewrie lied, a bit rankled that one of his sons would even think to dictate his personal life, or enforce the lack of one. "Perhaps a brief hour over tea? After we've had you at a tailor shop, of course. Can't have the heir of a Knight and Baronet showin' up in rags, now can we?"

"No, sir, I suppose not," Sewallis answered. "If you wish, then I would be pleased to meet your Mistress Stangbourne."

No, you bloody aren't! Lewrie scoffed to himself.

"Fine, then," he said, instead. "Damme, but there's a tale to amuse ye, the how of gettin' a title t'boot."

"I look forward to hearing it, sir," Sewallis replied, *seemingly* in better takings.

"Damme, but it's cold up here! Do I keep you any longer, after all your boat-work in this foul weather, you'll catch your death. And I should be going back aboard *Reliant,* anyway. Thaw yourself out in the fug of your Midshipmen's cockpit. Your fellow Mids'll have a bowl of hot punch, surely."

"I expect so, sir . . . Father," Sewallis said, grinning at last. "And, in port at least, Captain Rodgers allows us the use of a Franklin stove. For a few hours each day."

"Oh, don't get me started on bloody Franklin stoves!" Lewrie cried. "There's another long, sad tale that ended up costin' me dear! Well, then, 'til I make arrangements with Captain Rodgers for a shore liberty for ye, I'll take my leave."

"'Til then, Father . . . sir," Sewallis said, doffing his hat in a formal salute, with a slight bow from the waist.

Lewrie doffed his own cocked hat to his son, as well, a grave exchange from one naval officer to another.

Even if Lewrie still thought his son had made a bad decision, one that he might come to regret.

CHAPTER FIVE

The "hour over tea" with Sewallis, Lewrie, and Lydia had become a late second breakfast that had lasted a bit longer than two hours. Not that it could be described as a resounding success, for Sewallis had had his "grave face" on, like a wary investor offered a "fail-safe" stock. He'd been polite, and had *seemed* to thaw when Lydia had shown interest in his seafaring life, so far, but the wheels had come off when Lydia had ventured into talk of her brother, and his engagement to a "circus person," Eudoxia Durschenko.

"You saw her, Sewallis, when we all attended Daniel Wigmore's circus," Lewrie had breezily reminded him. "Met her face-to-face when they paraded through Portsmouth, too. Eudoxia rode her white stallion right up to us, remember?"

"Oh, that was she, sir?" Sewallis had said, "Rather racily and scantily clad." He'd been purse-lipped and dis-approving of *that*.

"She is fearless, I've come to learn," Lydia had chimed in, "and a crack shot. When Percy brought her up to the country in the fall, we all went birding, and she out-shot me every time. Quite sweet, too."

"You . . . hunt, ma'am?" Sewallis had all but gasped, though he'd kept his tone level. He'd dis-approved of women with guns, too.

Their long tea-time had gotten chillier and stiffer from there on, and it was with a shared sense of relief that Lewrie had seen his son to the docks, and back to his ship.

"Dear Lord, Alan, but I think you've reared a *parson*," Lydia had chuckled when he'd returned. "A Methodist dissenter, at that! So far, I gather that he's a 'down' on Percy's gambling, Eudoxia, bawdy women, and my having guns! Such a stiff young man!"

Supper with Benjamin Rodgers went much better; at least *he* had kept an open mind, and when Lydia, who had been studying and reading every book she could find on seamanship, ships, and their handling since being dined aboard *Reliant* at Sheerness the previous Spring, could converse somewhat knowledgeably with two senior naval officers, Rodgers had become the soul of geniality and jollity. He'd listened with glee to tales of Percy's amazing luck at gambling, and the doings of the rich and titled. He'd almost sounded as if he *did* devour the "Tattler" columns in the papers, despite what he'd said about them.

"Reading and Henley?" Rodgers had exclaimed. "Why, that's in my bailiwick! My father's an attorney in Reading, and I grew up there. Punting on the Thames is what led me to the Navy. Good Lord, yes, now I recall your father, too. Big, tall, rangy fellow . . . Your pardons, Mistress Stangbourne, but we children used to dread the Viscount for how fearsome-featured he was. Not the handsomest man in England, he was, Alan. Splendid rider, though, and a grand sportsman. We used to ride by Stangbourne Park quite often, though, on the way to a day of shooting at my uncle's . . . an estate he called The Hermitage?"

"Gabriel Rodgers, of course!" Lydia had gushed quite animatedly. "I knew him well when I was a girl."

They were "neighbourly", knew the same people, no matter their class, and Lydia had met Rodgers's new wife, too. All in all, they'd gotten on like a house afire.

"Quite like her, Alan," Rodgers had said on the long cold walk back to the boat landing. "And, if the war ever ends, I'd be delighted to have a chance to shoot over *their* fields. Matter of fact, it's good odds the house Susannah and I bought in Reading got run up with Stangbourne money and labour. The old Viscount dabbled in rents and real estate in a *huge* way!"

Lewrie had been delighted that Benjamin had sounded approving, too, if Sewallis didn't. And the sea-change in Lydia's manner with Rodgers had been a fine thing to see. He *knew* how guarded and leery Lydia was about how people took her, and to have seen her at ease and open, how "chirpy" and quick to laugh, had been a marvel.

Unless Benjamin had put on a complete sham, of course! Lewrie didn't think him capable of such duplicity, but . . . oh, surely not! Lewrie had never detected a *speck* of guile in bluff, hearty Benjamin Rodgers!

That next morning had dawned cold, but clear. The thermometer in the great-cabins stood at fourty degrees by the end of breakfast, and the liquid barometer's pale blue fluid had sunk down the long tube neck to indicate a coming high-pressure spell. One more cup of creamed and sugared coffee, and Lewrie would make an inspection of the ship in slop-trousers and his oldest coat, then change to go ashore for another delightful dinner, and a long afternoon with Lydia in her lodgings at the George. But . . .

"Midshipman Warburton, SAH!" the Marine sentry loudly cried.

"Enter," Lewrie bade.

"Pardon, Captain, but there is a boat approaching," Warburton reported. "And there appears to be an official fellow aboard her."

"Admiralty pouch?" Lewrie asked, peering at the Mid, who had sprouted much like his son had, in the two years he'd been aboard the frigate; Warburton had been a cheeky sixteen-year-old when fitting out in 1803, and was now a *slyly* cheeky eighteen.

"I could not see one, sir," Warburton replied, "But . . . !" The fingers of his right hand were held up crossed for luck.

"Very well, Mister Warburton. Show the visitor aft when he's come aboard," Lewrie ordered.

Sailin' orders, at long last? Lewrie mused while he waited for the caller to show his face; *But orders for where?*

Mid-January was a miserable time to be ordered to sea, and if it was their fate to join the blockade of the French or Spanish coasts and harbours, even the most-Sutherly latitudes would make little difference. Gales and storms off Cadiz or Ferrol would be as fierce as those found off Brest. Lewrie found that he'd involuntarily crossed his own fingers for luck . . . of a different kind of hope than Warburton's!

He fought the urge to gulp down his coffee and rush to the deck with impatient curiosity, but there were times to *act* like a captain in the Royal Navy; he forced himself to sit and sip slowly.

"Admiralty messenger, SAH!" his Marine sentry cried.

"Enter," Lewrie answered, striving for a bored drawl.

And won't that perk up the ship's people's ears! he thought.

"Captain Lewrie, sir," the newcomer, a youngish and ill-featured fellow in dark blue "ditto" suitings began, "Daniel Gower, from Admiralty, with orders for you and the *Reliant* frigate."

"Thank you, Mister Gower," Lewrie said, rising to accept them in a sealed envelope. "Are they 'Eyes Only', or 'To Be Opened Upon Attaining a particular Latitude'?" Lewrie japed, rolling his eyes.

"Why, no, sir. Quite straightforward, I assume," the man said with one brow up in puzzlement.

"Hmph," was Lewrie's comment. "We've had our share of 'cloak and dagger'," he explained. "Thank you, Mister Gower. May I offer you anything? Coffee or tea?"

"No thank you, sir, but I've others to see," the clerk said, tapping the large leather pouch slung at his side.

"Very well, sir."

"Good day, Captain Lewrie."

S'pose I can rip it open, right here and now, Lewrie thought, and did so. He sat back down at his dining table to read them over, just as soon as that Gower fellow had left his cabins.

"Good God," Lewrie muttered. "Privateers? No profit in that."

> *Making the best of your way, you are to take HMS* Reliant, *sailing under Independent Orders, to the Bahamas and Bermuda, there to conduct operations against Spanish and French privateers engaged in predations upon convoys bound from the West Indies to Home Waters, specifically directing your efforts upon the Eastern coasts of Spanish Florida, where said privateers are believed to base themselves since the Declaration of a State of War by the Kingdom of Spain on December 12th of last year.*
>
> *Upon arrival at Bermuda and the Bahamas, you are further authorised to take under your command any and all naval vessels Below the Rates which you deem suitable for such operations, and for this purpose you are granted the right to display the inferior Broad Pendant for the duration of the expedition.*

"Pick and choose, lead me own little squadron? Whew!" Lewrie muttered, louder this time, and wondering what sort of minor warships could be had at Bermuda or in the Bahamas.

He would not be promoted to Commodore, nor would he be assigned a Flag-Captain to run *Reliant* for him whilst he mused, schemed and plotted the ruin of Frogs and Dons. His red broad pendant would bear the large white ball in the centre which would mark his frigate as a squadron flagship. But, to cover the Spanish port of St. Augustine, along with the many smaller settlements from the St. Mary's River, the Northern boundary of Spanish Florida, to the great Tamiami Bay and the Keys to the South, Lewrie rather doubted that the little vessels of his putative squadron would ever be sailing in formal trail formation behind him, and that flying broad pendant would be more a sop to his ego, did he bother to look up and gawk.

> *In the course of your operations, you will not consider yourself strictly limited to Spanish Florida. You will also make a diligent effort to ascertain whether privateers of those nations now at war with Great Britain exploit the neutrality of the United States of America, and whether the authorities of the several states, and the authorities of the ports of Savannah, Beaufort and Port Royal, Charleston and Georgetown, Wilmington and the Cape Fear River, and the ports of New Bern and Beaufort round Cape Lookout shelter privateers, or may succour and support them in violation of neutrality laws.*

"Christ, I don't need a squadron, I need a *fleet!*" he gawped.

There was also some blather about calling upon the Consular officials who represented Great Britain to get their informations, to use their good offices to make the acquaintance of local American officials responsible for the enforcement of strict neutrality regarding the visits of belligerents, the frequency of said visits, and how long they could remain at anchor before being shooed out to sea.

> *. . . in this regard, you will do your very best to diplomatically impress upon said American officials the importance of a strict observance of neutrality laws between two nations now in amity. . . .*

"Now I *know* they've lost their wits in London," Lewrie said with a long sigh, and a wee *yap* of dis-belief. "Diplomatic? *Me?* Do they even know the first thing about me? Bull in a bloody china shop!"

Finally, there was a paragraph or two about taking soundings and up-dating the charts of the approaches to Bermuda, and marking the entrance channels to St. George's Harbour, Castle Harbour, the navigable limits of the Great Sound and Grassy Bay, and the approaches to the settlement of Hamilton . . . so long as he had nothing else going!

To aid him in his diplomatic endeavours, and to snag himself a few small warships, enclosed was a thick packet of letters of introduction to the various British Consuls, and orders directed to "Whom It May Concern". And, if he did discover gross violations of American neutrality, included was the name and address of His Britannic Majesty's Ambassador in Washington, the District of Columbia, who, upon receiving an information from Lewrie, would make the strongest remonstrances to the United States government on His Majesty's behalf!

"At least Hercules got t'take on his twelve labours one at a bloody time!" Lewrie fumed, sagging lower in his dining chair.

One bell was struck by a ship's boy up forward at the belfry; half past eight in the Forenoon Watch, and the time that Lewrie had appointed for his officers and senior mates to muster in the waist for his inspection. He rose and placed the thick packet of orders in his day-cabin desk, then shrugged into a well-worn grogram overcoat to go out on deck.

"Good morning, gentlemen," he said to one and all.

"Good morning, sir," was returned in a rough chorus, punctuated by yawns from some who had been up since the 4 A.M. change of watch which roused all hands to lash up and stow, swab and sweep decks, and partake in breakfast. *Reliant*'s three Lieutenants, Geoffrey Westcott, Clarence Spendlove, and George Merriman, looked blearier than most; officers stood no watches when anchored in port, and they'd most-like returned aboard the evening before just in time for their supper, then shared a bowl of hot punch, liberally laced with spirits, before a late retiring, sitting up in the dark after Lights Out at 9 P.M. to "fathom" the bowl's depths.

"Damn my eyes, no one's curious?" Lewrie teased.

"Well, sir . . ." Lt. Merriman said, sharing a glace with the rest, and making a speculative grin.

"We're bound for warmer weather," Lewrie told them. "If we survive the winter voyage to get there, that is. It's the Bahamas, for us, Bermuda, and the coast of Spanish Florida."

"Bermuda," the Sailing Master, Mr. Caldwell, said. "Brr!"

"It's in the mid-Atlantic," Lt. Spendlove pointed out. "It cannot be a cold place, can it?"

"Ah, but Bermuda is surrounded by miles and miles of banks and shoals, coral reefs, and submerged rocks, sir," Harold Caldwell contradicted with a gloomy look. "There's been ships wrecked twenty miles or more from there, in what they took for deep, open water. Captain, sir, I'll be needing the use of a boat to go ashore to obtain charts, for I have none but the sketchiest and oldest at present. In point of fact, I've never been to Bermuda, but I've heard tales. Brr, I say, for good reason."

Who at Admiralty hates me that *damned bad?* Lewrie asked himself.

"Neither have I, Mister Caldwell," Lewrie admitted. "When you do seek the latest charts, pray obtain a set for me. Part of our new orders directs us to survey and make soundings while we're there, do we have time to spare for it. They mention the principal harbours and a bay or two, not the distant approaches, but . . ." He ended with a shrug.

"My mates, Nightingale and Eldridge, could stay aboard for your inspection, sir," Caldwell said, "whilst I could go ashore now."

"Very well, Mister Caldwell. Mister Warburton?" Lewrie called out to the senior Mid on the quarterdeck above them. "A boat for the Sailing Master."

"Aye, sir!"

"Well, shall we begin, sirs?" Lewrie posed to them. "And, as we look things over, let's make lists of anything needful before sailing. Start at the bows, shall we?"

"Aye, sir," the Bosun, Mr. Sprague, agreed with a firm nod. "I think you'll find the ship in top form and well-stocked for sea, so far as *my* department goes."

"But not your private rum cache, hey, Mister Sprague?" Lieutenant Westcott, the First Officer japed.

"Don't know what you're talkin' about, Mister Westcott, sir," Sprague replied with a twinkle in his eyes, "when ev'rybody knows it's Mister Cooke what hides rum in his galley."

"Then we'll look over the galley damned close," Lewrie quipped. "*And* the nooks and crannies in the carpenter's walks."

That made the Bosun swallow hard, and look a tad guilty!

CHAPTER SIX

$\mathcal{T}$he other side of the ocean?" Lydia sadly mused once Lewrie told her of his orders. "Oh, God."

"We both knew it was bound t'come," Lewrie said, taking her by the hands as they sat together on a settee in her lodgings.

"I'd hoped . . ." she said, looking down for a moment. "Foolish me. I did know you'd have to sail away sooner or later, but I hoped . . ." She shrugged and seemed to be biting the lining of her cheek for a second as she looked back up. "I'd hoped that you'd be assigned to the blockade, like your friend Captain Rodgers. Somewhere closer, and come back every few months to . . . what do you call it? Re-victual? I should have known better," she sighed, slumping.

"I don't like it any more than you do, believe me," Lewrie said, putting an arm round her shoulders. "You've quite spoiled me."

"Have I?" Lydia skeptically asked, bracing back from him.

"Utterly and completely," Lewrie assured her. "I should have known better, myself. Just as soon as I begin t'feel pleased, old Dame Fortune *will* kick me up the arse. She always has."

Lydia relaxed her arms and sank into his comforting embrace.

"You may not be the only one that Dame Fortune picks on, Alan. Here

I finally meet a man whom I *think* I can trust, and the Navy will send him halfway round the world, for years on end," she mourned. "I will feel so alone, again, with you gone."

"I've grown hellish fond of you, too," Lewrie whispered in her sweet-smelling hair. "But, t'wish me on the blockade, after all that Benjamin Rodgers told us of it, well . . . !"

"It *will* be warmer, where you're going?" she asked.

"Much warmer, even in January," Lewrie told her. "The Bahamas and Bermuda, I expect, are vivid green and surrounded by blue-green seas. In the old days, we sailed little *Alacrity* over waters so gin-clear, or the palest blue, and could see the bottom and fish swimming, ten fathoms down, as clear as day."

"It sounds like the fabled Land of the Lotus Eaters," Lydia commented, chuckling,

"Isles of the dead-drunk rum-pots, more like," Lewrie japed.

"Even so, they sound heavenly," Lydia said, then looked up at him sharply. "Take me with you."

"What?" Lewrie gawped.

"I've learned enough of the Navy and ships to know that some captains take their wives with them, even in wartime," Lydia animatedly said. "God knows, I brought half a year's worth of gowns and such when I came down to Portsmouth. I could be packed and aboard by the end of the day!"

"Lydia, I can't," Lewrie told her, though wishing he could.

"Did not your wife sail with you to the Bahamas when you were first there?" she pointed out, cocking her head to one side.

"To be settled in a house ashore, in peacetime," Lewrie said. "We'll be up against French and Spanish privateers, might even cross hawses with some of their frigates, and I can't put you at such risk. Besides, there's . . ."

"If I *accept* the risks, then why not?" she pressed.

"There's the matter of *Reliant*'s people, Lydia," Lewrie continued in a sombre but soothing tone. "They can't take their wives and sweethearts with them, and for them to see their captain enjoying the privilege they can't . . . rubbing it in their faces everytime you took the air on the quarterdeck? The Navy won't even give them shore liberty, unless it's a damned small island, and there's an Army garrison t'help round 'em up do they run . . . take 'leg-bail'. The best we can do for 'em is to put the ship Out of Discipline for a few days in port and let the . . . women of the town come aboard. Some of 'em might even really *be* wives, but that's a rare ease. You wouldn't wish to see it. When you toured *Reliant* last summer, she was in full discipline."

"Whores, do you mean," Lydia said with a scoffing smirk.

"Aye, whores," Lewrie admitted. "And, finally . . . there *are* some captains who'd take their wives to sea, even in wartime, but . . . they're *wives*, not lovers. Admiralty has a 'down' on that."

"Hmmm," was Lydia's comment to that. She put one brow up in quizzical thought, eying him over quite carefully.

"What?" Lewrie asked, wondering if she was contemplating . . . ! "What are you thinking?"

"Well, in the first instance, I was wondering what poor Percy would say, did I dash off with you, married or not," Lydia confessed, a grin spreading. "Secondly, I was wondering if I were brazen enough to propose to you, and lastly . . . I asked myself what I might say *did* you propose to me!"

Oh, shit! Here we go again! Lewrie told himself, hoping that his phyz didn't mirror the stricken feeling inside him. He'd been in "Cream-pot Love" with his late wife, Caroline, and had admitted "there's a girl worth marrying . . . someday, perhaps, *maybe*!" before circumstances anent her future had dragooned him into proposing, to give her an out from the beastly attentions of her neighbour Harry Embleton, or her only other options: marry a much older tenant farmer, or take a position as governess to someone's children, far from family.

"And, did you come to some conclusions?" Lewrie whimsically asked, wishing he could cross his fingers.

"God, the look on your face, Alan!" Lydia said, laughing out loud. "Have I frightened you into next week?"

"Astonished, not frightened, really," Lewrie breezed off. "You have a knack for that," he added with a teasing smile.

"As for Percy and Society, I don't give a toss," Lydia said with a cynical jerk of her head. "I'm *already* scandalous, so what else would they expect? And, no . . . as fond as I've become of you, I am not *that* unconventional, at bottom. The man must do the asking. Lastly . . ."

"Hmm?" Lewrie prompted.

"Fond as I am, I would refuse," Lydia told him, turning sombre.

"Mean t'say . . . ?" Lewrie flummoxed. Not that he *would* be asking, but it irked that she would have spurned him if he had!

"After all I've been through, Alan, my dear, I've too many fears to be settled, before I place myself, and my heart, at the mercy of *any* man again, without knowing him so completely that I could overcome my trepidations. I told you once, remember?" she slowly explained.

"At the Cocoa Tree, wasn't it?" Lewrie replied. "Tea and scones in a quiet corner, while Percy was in the Long Rooms, gambling. You told me you'd never willingly re-enter such a slavish institution as marriage. And what did I tell you?"

"To suit myself, and enjoy my life," Lydia replied, grinning, pleased that he could recall.

"*Do* you enjoy your life?" Lewrie asked her softly.

"I began to, that very night," she answered, "and 'til now, I must own that I have, immensely. But I would not marry you. Even for a sea voyage to the splendours of Cathay. Not yet."

"Call it early days?" Lewrie fondly teased.

"Early days," Lydia whispered back, beaming at him, though he discerned the rising moisture in her eyes. Before her tears came, he scooped her to him and kissed her long and gently.

"I will pack and coach back to London tomorrow," she told him, her face pressed to his gilt-laced coat collar. "You will have many things to attend to, and I would be in the way . . . at the best, quite ignored, so . . ."

"I'll settle your lodgings," Lewrie offered.

"You will not!" she chuckled for a moment. "You, as you said, are 'comfortable', but *I* am rich. Consider it my gift to you."

"Your being here's been the real gift," Lewrie assured her.

"That night at the Cocoa Tree, later that night," Lydia teased. "Recall where we went?"

"Your house in Grosvenor Street," Lewrie supplied promptly.

"And what did I ask you there, dear Alan?"

"You said . . . 'Make love to me'," Lewrie quite *gladly* recalled, leaning back to look her in the eyes, knowing that he was beaming like the hugest fool in the Universe.

"Such a *keen* memory you have!" she praised him. "Do, please?"

CHAPTER SEVEN

Whether HMS *Reliant* had received sailing orders or not, all the business of provisioning and victualling for sea was continual. Spare spars and replacement sails, huge bolts of cloth from which to fashion or repair the existing ones; livestock for fresh meat issue in harbour, and for the first week or so on passage . . . Captain Alan Lewrie was in sanguine takings that only a day or two more to take aboard last-minute items, and he could take his frigate to sea just as soon as the winter winds swung round to a favourable quarter. Then . . .

"Currant jam, of course, sir?" his cook, Yeovill, suggested as he went down a long list of "necessities" to be purchased for Lewrie's comfort from a chandlery.

"I've developed a taste for raspberry," Lewrie mused aloud with a grin. "Those tarts and popovers o' yours? Dried currants and raisins for duffs, aye, but . . ."

"Midshipman Houghton . . . SAH!" the Marine sentry shouted, with a crash of his musket butt and his boots on the deck planking, beyond.

"Enter," Lewrie bade.

"Good morning, sir!" Midshipman Houghton said, right cheerily, as he stood before Lewrie's desk in the day-cabin, hat under his arm, and all but rocking on the balls of his feet. "I fear I must depart the ship, sir. My Lieutenancy's come through."

"Good God!" Lewrie gawped. "Well, congratulatons, of course."

When Lewrie had fitted *Reliant* out for sea in May of 1803, when the war with imperial, Napoleonic France had broken out again, Midshipman Houghton had been his senior and most experienced at twenty-one, and had already faced one board of harsh Post-Captains' grilling for promotion. Houghton was very competent, in a stolidly quiet way, but not the sharpest nail in the keg; he'd always struck Lewrie as rather dull. Whilst *Reliant* had been at Sheerness the previous Spring, he'd finally become a Passed Midshipman, but no immediate commission. The secret nature of their work with catamaran torpedoes that Summer might have been the factor.

"Where are ye bound, and how soon, Mister Houghton?"

"I'm to be Fifth Officer aboard the *Victorious*, a Third Rate, sir, just in with a Spanish prize sloop, and her First was promoted to Commander, so there's an opening, and, well . . . my uncle's one of the civilians on the Board of Admiralty, so . . ."

I'd known that, I'd've cultivated the fart a lot hotter! Lewrie told himself.

"Immediate, is it? Well, if you must," Lewrie said, rising to shake Houghton's hand and offer him a parting "stirrup cup" of brandy, though pondering how he'd fill Houghton's experienced but dull shoes. Could he advance one of the Master's Mates? Eldridge and Nightingale were in their mid-to-late twenties, and were good at their trade, but . . . might he be able to cultivate a little "interest" from stuffy old Admiral Lord Gardner, Port Admiral of Portsmouth, or from Admiral the Honourable Cornwallis, head of Channel Fleet, of which *Reliant* was yet a part 'til sailing?

"Sorry to place you a fellow short, sir, but . . ." Houghton said.

"Oh, tosh!" Lewrie quickly assured him. "That's the Navy's way. Never can be sure of anything, one year to the next. And, when a man gets a shot at promotion, he'd be a fool t'turn it down outta sentiment. We'll send you off in my gig, with my boat crew, to make a good show for your new captain. A brandy with you, *Lieutenant* Houghton?"

"Ehm . . . thank you most kindly for the offer, sir, but, I'd not wish to report myself aboard my new ship with spirits on my breath, if you see my point, sir?" Houghton hedged.

"Coffee, then, t'warm yer long row," Lewrie decided. "Pettus, a coffee for Lieutnenant Houghton, and a top-up for me," he bade his cabin steward.

"Accepted most gladly, sir," Houghton brightened. "And might I say that the last two years aboard *Reliant* have not only been most instructive, but . . . delightfully exciting, Captain Lewrie, sir. I shall consider serving under you one of the . . ."

"Hoy, 'ware . . . !" came a shout from on deck, followed by a loud series of thuds and bangs, as if a large sack of potatoes had slipped from someone's grasp and was tumbling down a steep ladderway.

"Oh, ow! *Gottverdamt!*" came a painful howl, and then a curse or two. "*Sheisse, meine arm, meine beins! Sheisse!*"

"Mister Rahl!" Lewrie said. There were very few "Dutchies" in *Reliant*'s company, and the raspy voice of the Master Gunner, Mister Johan Rahl, was easily recognised by one and all.

"Passing word for Mister Mainwaring!" a muffled shout demanded from the gun-deck, forward and below.

"Let's go," Lewrie urged, dashing for the forward door.

Master Gunner Johan Rahl *had* fallen down the main companionway hatch, and lay sprawled on his back, grimacing and growling bear-like to keep from howling in pain, and un-manning himself before his shipmates. Even as Lewrie knelt beside him, the Ship's Surgeon, Richard Mainwaring, arrived with his kit-bag, closely followed by several loblolly boys from the forward sickbay, with a carrying board.

"What happened, Mister Rahl?" Mainwaring asked.

"I trip unt fall . . . down der fockin' *verdamnt* ladder, *arrhh!*" Rahl shot back, his long and stiff-waxed grey mustachios wriggling. "*Heilige sheisse*, but it hurts!"

"A tot o' neat rum for Mister Rahl, smartly there!" Lewrie ordered. "Stand back and give the Surgeon room t'work, lads."

"*I'd* take a tumble for a tot," Patrick Furfy whispered to his mate, Liam Desmond, Lewrie's Cox'n.

"Oh, hesh yerself," Desmond hissed back. "Is it bad, sor?"

Lewrie shrugged his answer, looking into Mainwaring's face as he glanced up from his work.

"It seems you've broken your left arm, Mister Rahl," Mainwaring said at long last. "It seems a clean break, and it's good odds that it will heal, but your legs . . . hmm. The right one feels like a clean break, as well, but the left . . ."

"You cut it *off*, sir?" Rahl asked, almost incredulous. "I vill *not* be der ein-legged *cook, nein!*"

"We must get you to the sickbay, up forward," Mainwaring said. "That'll be easier on you than being strapped down and bumped down to the or-lop cockpit. More light and air, up forward, too. Get Mister Rahl onto the carrying board, you lads. Easy, now! Don't jostle him too much."

"Der doctor heff to take *meine* leg, Captain Lewrie, do not make me a cook," Rahl insisted, rasping, gasping, and spitting his words as the lob-lolly boys gently shifted the carrying board under him, causing him sheer agony.

"I swear I won't, Mister Rahl," Lewrie told him, shaking his hand for a moment. "Served with ye before, and I never saw a sign ye could even toast bread."

"*Ja,* d'ose were *gut* times, sir," Rahl replied. "*Sheisse,* you are *trying* to kill me, you bastards?"

"Slowly and gently, there!" Mainwaring snapped, before his hands started the carrying board down the length of the gun-deck, between the mess-tables, stools, and sea-chests, and the horde of curious onlookers.

"Desmond, Mister Houghton'll need a boat so he can report aboard his new ship," Lewrie told his Cox'n. "Best turn-out, and see him to the *Victorious* in my gig."

"Arrah, you're a Commission Officer now, Mister Houghton?" Liam Desmond exclaimed.

"He is," Lewrie assured him, and the rest of the nearby people.

"Huzzah fer Mister Houghton!" a sailor cried, raising a cheer from the rest.

"When you're ready to debark, Mister Houghton, pray do inform me, and we'll see you off, proper," Lewrie promised.

"Thank you, sir. Well, I should go pack my traps," Houghton said.

"Can I have your second-best silk shirt?" Midshipman Warburton, one of *Reliant*'s cheekiest, asked tongue-in-cheek, razzing him.

"Uhm, pass word for the Gunner's Mate, there," Lewrie said. "I will be in my cabins."

"Acres, you're now Master Gunner," Lewrie told that worthy when he reported to him.

"Thankee, sir. Though 'tis not the way I'd o' liked t'get it," the burly

Gunner's Mate replied, fidgetting with the wide brim of his hat that he held before him. "Poor old Rahl. Th' Surgeon think it's bad for 'im, sir?"

"No word, yet, Mister Acres," Lewrie said, shrugging his lack of information. "His left leg looked damned bad, though. Old Rahl, well . . . Lord, he was 'old' Rahl when we served together, years ago."

"An' stiff'z th' guards at Saint James's Palace, sir," Acres said, chuckling. "Or one o' those Prussian grenadiers, where he came from, in the Kaiser's artillery."

"Does Kemp look likely to take your place?" Lewrie enquired. The current Yeoman of the Powder was fairly young in his position, up from a gun-captain of short service before *Reliant* commissioned.

"Well, sir, I'd prefer Thorn, the senior Quarter-Gunner. He's older and more experienced," Acres said. "Shift Kemp t'be a Quarter-Gunner, and bring a good gun-captain on as Powder Yeoman."

"Your choice, then," Lewrie allowed, "and we'll see how they work out. Congratulations, Mister Acres."

"Thankee, sir, and I'll see ye right when it comes to gunnery."

Half an hour later, and it was the Sailing Master, Mr. Caldwell, who stood before Lewrie's desk, to settle who might be promoted into Midshipman Houghton's position.

"Are either of your Master's Mates promotable, or should I send ashore to the Port Admiral, Mister Caldwell?" Lewrie began. "Sit, and have some coffee, do, sir."

"Thank you, sir," Caldwell said in his usually cautious manner, even giving the collapsible leather-covered chair a good looking-over before entrusting himself to it. "I expect either of them would leap at the chance to be made a Midshipman, but . . . ah, thank you, Pettus. Very good coffee, I must say," he said to the cabin steward after one taste. "Nightingale's a tarry 'tarpaulin man', a bit rough about the edges, but he's been in the Navy eight years, off and on, and he can hand, reef, and steer, and can lay a course as good as any. Ehm . . . there *is* the problem that he's not what you'd call . . . gentlemanly. He came out of the fisheries, and that life's coarser and rougher than where most Mids come from."

"You think he might not fit in?" Lewrie asked, frowning. With Houghton all but gone, he had Mr. Entwhistle, now twenty, the "Honourable" Mr. Entwhistle, as the oldest and most experienced, a lad to the manor born. There was Mr. Warburton, now eighteen, Grainger, who was now seventeen or so, then Munsell and Rossyngton, both about fifteen. All, like most Mids, were from the landed gentry, the "squirearchy". He could not see any of them turning top-lofty to a much older, rougher John New-come, but . . .

"There's that, sir," Caldwell said with a nod. "Now, Eldridge. He's younger and quicker, and just as experienced as Nightingale, and I *have* noted that he *might* be a bit more aspiring, though he's never mentioned becoming a Midshipman. Eldridge comes from Bristol, son of a ship chandler, so I expect he was raised better off than most before he volunteered, back in '98. Better-mannered?" Mr. Caldwell added with a shrug. "Eldridge's family could send him the funds he'd need for new kit, whilst Nightingale might have to go deep in debt to cover the expense."

"And, which'd be more *jealous* of the other, Mister Caldwell?" Lewrie posed to the Sailing Master, with one brow up. "It don't signify to *me* as to which is more polished, and if it does in the Mids' cockpit, then there'll be some boys at the mast-head, but . . . I'd not cause you and your department too much aggravation. If promoting one and passing over the other won't serve, then I might as well send for a 'younker' from the Port Admiral, and take whichever Tom-Fool they have on the shelf, some ten-year-old ninny-pate."

"Uhm . . . perhaps it'd be best did I *ask* them, sir," Caldwell suggested, shifting his bulk in the chair, and crossing one leg over the other. "Sound them out on their ambitions?"

"We don't have long, Mister Caldwell," Lewrie pointed out. "A sudden shift of wind, and we'll have to be off, instanter."

Crash-bang! from the Marine sentry beyond the door.

"First Orf'cer, Mister Westcott . . . SAH!" *Stamp-Bang!*

"Enter," Lewrie shouted back.

"Good morning, sir, Mister Caldwell," Lt. Geoffrey Westcott said once he'd entered the great-cabins. "I've spoken to the Surgeon, sir, about Rahl, and it don't look promising." There had been but one brief flash of his teeth in greeting before Westcott's dark-tanned and hatchet face went glummer. "Mister Mainwaring had to take off Rahl's left leg, above the knee. He's made it through the surgery, and he's resting quietly, but . . . he needs to be gotten ashore to the naval hospital as soon as he's able to be moved."

"Christ, that bad?" Lewrie grimaced. "I *saw* how the bone was snapped, and stickin' through his skin, but . . ."

"Evidently, sir, his arm and right leg were clean breaks, and didn't jut out, but the left was not only broken, but his knee joint was so badly wrenched that it couldn't be saved. Like a mangled turkey leg."

"Damn," Lewrie said with a long sigh, drumming his fingers on his desk. "Pardon my manners, Mister Westcott. Take a pew and have a coffee t'warm ye. Faulkes?" he called to his clerk and writer. "Do up a Discharge form for Mister Rahl, and a petition for him to be sent to the Pensioners' Home at Greenwich Hospital. See the Purser to get his pay and debts cleared, would you?"

"Of course, sir. Poor old fellow," James Faulkes sadly agreed.

"He pleaded that I'd not make him a cook," Lewrie mused. "Now, at the least he'll have a good retirement, in sight of Deptford Dockyard and traffic on the river."

"With no kin that I ever heard tell of, sir, I suppose that'd be the best he could expect," Lt. Westcott agreed. "And the best we can do for the old fellow."

"There'll be dozens of old gunners to trade yarns with, aye," Caldwell chimed in. "He'll not be slung onto the beach to starve and beg on the streets. *And* get his rum issue 'til Eternity."

"Word has it were losing Mister Houghton, sir?" Lt. Westcott asked after Pettus had gotten him his coffee, with sugar and sweeter goat's milk, the way he liked it. "Good for him."

"Aye, we were just debating who'd take his place, Nightingale or Eldridge, or should I request some Admiral's favourite idiot, hah!" Lewrie informed him with a sour bark of humour.

"Well, there's your son over in *Aeneas,* sir," Westcott said. "Your friend Captain Rodgers would surely oblige you."

"Uhmm, perhaps not," Lewrie said, making a gruesome face. "I've seen that before, and I never cared for it, no matter it's so common in the Fleet. Cater-cousins, sons and nephews? Hell, the *Cockerel* frigate was the worst. Half the ship's *company* was named Braxton! One could *not* dote, sooner or later, and make the rest of the Mids grit their teeth. Sewallis is best off where he is, among familiar faces, and on his own bottom, without me lookin' over his shoulder."

I'd scare what little he's learned clear outta his head, did I haul him aboard!

Lewrie told himself; *Fragile as I still think he is, that'd be the ruin of him. And, he'd not thank me, and end up resentin' it!*

Lewrie busied himself with creaming and sweetening a fresh cup of coffee, to cover his dread that what really motivated him was fear that he would witness Sewallis should he fail!

"Suggestions, Mister Westcott?" Lewrie asked. "Nightingale, Eldridge, or a sprat?"

"Well, sir . . . I'd go with Eldridge," the First Lieutenant said. "I've stood so many watches with both that one can't help but natter, here and there. Nightingale's ambition is to become Sailing Master, someday, he's told me. Mister Eldridge joined as a Landsman, but he's shot up like a rocket . . . Ordinary, then Able, Quartermaster's Mate to Quartermaster, and now a Master's Mate. And, he's still young enough to hope for a Sea Officer's commission. Nightingale's married, with a child, and promoting him would most-like sling him into debtor's prison. Midshipman's pay's not much improvement on what he earns, now . . . the cost of uniforms and such'd do him right in, sir."

"And, he'd not be the one t'pick his nose at table, or use the wrong fork?" Lewrie joshed.

"God, they *all* do that, sir!" Westcott laughed out loud. "Mids have the manners of so many pigs."

"Mister Caldwell?" Lewrie asked. "Sound right to you?"

"Aye, sir," the Sailing Master slowly intoned, nodding solemnly. "I'll advance Quartermaster Hook to Eldridge's place, if I may. . . ."

"Good man, he was aboard *Thermopylae* with me," Lewrie said.

"Then move Malin up as a Quartermaster, and ask about for one who wishes to strike for Quartermaster's Mate, sir," Caldwell agreed.

Crash-bang! "Midshipman Munsell, SAH!" Slam-crash!

"Enter," Lewrie bade. "Busy as a *tavern* door today, ain't it?"

"Beg pardon, sir, but Mister Houghton is ready to depart, and the Surgeon sends his duty, and a request for a boat to bear Mister Rahl ashore to hospital, as well," young Munsell reported.

"My hat and sword, Pettus," Lewrie asked. "Let's give both of 'em a proper send-off. If you gentlemen will join me?"

"All Hands" was piped to summon the ship's company on deck to see Houghton off, with three cheers raised. A bit of a dullard that Houghton was, he was recognised by all as a competent officer-to-be, and a "firm but fair" disciplinarian who'd treated everyone the same.

The Marines turned out with the side-party to render honours, the bosuns' pipes blew, and Houghton's fellow Mids and the officers shook hands with him and wished him well.

"Make us proud o' bein' a *Reliant*, Lieutenant," Lewrie urged.

"Thank you for everything, again, sir, and I shall!" Houghton vowed before doffing his hat at the entry-port, and beginning to make a careful way down the boarding-battens to the waiting gig, where the boat crew were turned out in Sunday Divisions best.

A few moments later, though, and it was a much sombrer send-off for Gunner Johan Rahl. Strapped to a carrying board, and swaddled in blankets, he came up from the forward companionway hatch, rolling his head with his eyes half-glazed from doses of laudanum to smother his pain. The ship's people parted to let the loblolly boys through, and many reached out to give him goodbye pats and reassurances, though he was all but oblivious. "Take care, mate!" and "Bye, ye old son of a gun!" and "Get well an' back on yer pins soon!" were called out.

"Greenwich 'Ospital'z good'z Fiddler's Green, Mister Rahl. Ale an' rum, they flow like warter, an' niver a reckonin'!" one hopeful older hand assured him. "Music an' fetchin' girls visitin' round th' clock, they say, ye lucky ol' devil!"

It wasn't the entry-port for Rahl, though. Bosun Sprague had rigged a lift for the four handles of the carrying board, The main-mast course yardarm was fitted for hoisting out, with hands standing by at braces and clews to raise him up and out-board of the starboard gangway bulwarks, then down into a waiting cutter. Rahl's battered old sea-chest, has hammock, rolled up into a fat sausage with all of his bedding and spare clothing, and a pale grey sea-bag sat amidships to be lowered down, too . . . meagre as it was, that represented everything that Rahl had amassed in decades of spartan Navy life.

"I've his Discharge papers, and pay chits, sir," Mainwaring told Lewrie, who had come down from the gangway to shake Rahl's hand one last time. "I'll see him ashore, myself, if that's alright?"

"Perfectly fine, Mister Mainwaring," Lewrie agreed. "Will he . . . make it through?" he asked the Surgeon in a softer voice.

"Touch and go, sir, touch and go," Mainwaring said with a sigh. "He's old, but he's a tough old bird. Assuming he gets good care and sepsis does not set in, he stands a decent chance of surviving, but at his age, what life would be like, well . . ." he wondered, shrugging.

"Hoist away, handsomely," Bosun Sprague ordered, and the course yard began to tip upwards, bearing Rahl aloft.

"Don't let your fellow pensioners talk you into cookin' for 'em, Mister Rahl!" Lewrie shouted to the departing burden. "Three cheers, lads. See your shipmate off with a cheer!"

Bosun's Mate Wheeler began a long call on his pipe; the Marine boy-drummer rattled the Long Roll, and a fiddler and fifer began a gay tune, "The Bowld Soldier Boy", the air that was played aboard *Reliant* when the rum keg was fetched on deck, that usually brought joy.

"Sway out, easy!" Bosun Sprague directed, and Rahl's sling-load slowly swung out-board, above the starboard gangway bulwarks. "Aft a bit . . .'vast hauling!" as Rahl hung above the open entry-port.

Just before Sprague ordered the yardarm to dip, the last that Rahl's shipmates saw of him was his right hand feebly raised above his blankets, giving them all a goodbye wave and a "thumbs-up".

"Bit more . . . a bit more," Midshipman Entwhistle called, standing in the open entry-port, looking down into the waiting cutter. "A foot of slack, there."

"We have him!" Midshipman Warburton, in charge of the cutter, reported. "Carrying board's secure, and the lines are free."

The cheers and the happy tune faded away as the Surgeon left the ship to descend to the cutter, and his patient, with only the customary honours.

"Ship's comp'ny, on hats, and dismiss," Lt. Westcott ordered, and the men fell silent, drifting off in threes and fours, or idling on deck despite the cold in eight-man messes, gun-crews, or mast-tender groups. Mostly looking very glum.

"Rather a lot of change, of a sudden, sir," Westcott muttered as he and Lewrie mounted to the quarterdeck together. "Perhaps too much for them, in one morning."

"Promotion, departure, people discharged," Lewrie mused aloud. "Happens all the time in the Navy. At least six of the people gettin' promoted, and more pay. I should think there'll be some celebrations, by supper this evening."

"Might I suggest talking to them before supper, sir," Westcott said, leaning close. "And 'splice the main-brace' to give them *cause* to celebrate?

The people brood on it, and they might take this morning as a bad omen, right before the start of a winter sailing."

"A bad omen, Mister Westcott?" Lewrie asked, frowning heavily. "D'ye really think so?"

"They already know we've sailing orders, sir," Westcott went on, standing close with his hands in the small of his back. "And it's sure to be a stormy passage. That's gloom-making enough, but now . . ."

"It ain't like the ship's rats're leapin' overboard," Lewrie said back, with a disparaging laugh, but then thought better of that.

They could *take it as a bad omen,* he realised; *and damme if I ain't feelin' a bit fey, myself! Now where's a good-luck seal that I can whistle up?*

"Hmmm . . . you may be right, Mister Westcott," he told the First Lieutenant. "Aye, we will 'splice the main-brace' at the second rum issue, and see that the people get fresh roast meat, *and* a figgy-dowdy for supper . . . damned near a Christmas feast. I'll speak to the cook, and see to the arrangements."

"So they can congratulate the newly promoted, and see the upset as an opportunity, aye, sir!" Westcott said, baring his teeth in one of his nigh-savage characteristic grins.

"Just so long as the officers don't mind making some *minor* contributions to said feast, hey, Mister Westcott?" Lewrie japed. "Can't be expected t'foot the bill all by myself. Hmm?"

Westcott looked close to a shiver; whether it was the wintery wind that caused it, or the loss of nearly a pound from his purse in pursuit of his aim. "*Touché*, sir."

"*Touché*, Hell, Mister Westcott, I barely *grazed* ye!" Lewrie said with a satisfied smirk.

BOOK I

LETTER OF MARQUE
A commiſſion granted by the lords of the
Admiralty or by the vice-admiral on any
diſtant province, to the commander of a
merchant ſhip, or privateer, to cruize againſt,
and make prize of, the enemy's ſhips and
veſſels, either at ſea, or in their harbours.
                    -FALCONER'S MARINE DICTIONARY
                    1780 EDITION

CHAPTER EIGHT

*T*he *Reliant* frigate left Portsmouth on the last Monday in January, after four days at anchor in the Sutherlymost protection of St. Helen's
Patch, near the Isle of Wight, waiting for a slant of wind, and taking
aboard the last necessities and luxuries for a long winter voyage. An icy
shift from the Nor'east came at last, and she hoisted sail and raised her
anchors, severing her last, slightest connexion to England, and pounded
out into the riotous Chops of the Channel.

The first day and night, she could bowl along under reduced sail,
pushed by the forceful following winds. Her top-hamper, all her t'gallants
and royals—masts, sails, yards, and stays—had been brought down and
stowed alongside the spare ones even before she left harbour, in expectation
of storm conditions that might prevail right across the entire Atlantic.

The second day at sea, the winds blew just as strongly, shifting more
Easterly, allowing a slanting course closer to the Lizard and Land's End
than the French side of the Channel, and Cape Ushant, letting them stand
out further to the West with the winds fine on the starboard quarter, with
the frigate booming and thudding through the heaving, churning waves.

By the third dawn, though, the fickle winds changed direction, howling an Arctic blast down upon them from the Nor'west, pushing the seas slamming against *Reliant*'s starboard sides, starting a sickening, wallowing heave and roll that had even the saltiest hands gagging at the lee rails. It was the roughest sort of beam-sea, and maintaining a beam reach required hands aloft to take reefs in the courses and tops'ls, reduce the spanker, and take in upper stays'ls completely. The only good thing that could be said for that day was that *Reliant* could still steer roughly West, gaining even more of an offing from the dangerous lee shoal of the French Bay of Biscay coast. Lewrie could turn into his swaying bed-cot that night a bit before midnight cautiously satisfied that they were making decent progress West'rd.

When he rolled out at 4 A.M. on the fourth day, though, his hopes were dashed, for the winds had veered ahead into West by North, half North, and Lewrie had to lay his ship onto a close-hauled "beat to weather", steering no closer to the wind than Sou'west by South, heeled hard over onto her larboard "shoulder" with the bows rising and plunging and shipping great bursts and avalanches of cold white water over the forecastle to swirl and pool and slosh from bow to stern almost knee-deep, before gurgling and gushing out the lee scrappers, and every seam in the deck planking, no matter how firmly packed with tarred oakum, then paid over with more tar with iron loggerheads, dripped chill misery onto the off-watch hands on the mess-decks.

"One would think that some damned fool was whistling," Mister Caldwell, the Sailing Master, gruffly muttered as he peered at their pencilled-in track in the chart-space in Lewrie's cabins. "Or, someone's snuck a woman aboard."

The Westerly winds had churned up the sea nigh to a slow boil, with vast grey-green rollers nearly as tall as the main course yard, a sickly snot-green sea that shed stinging blizzards of spray pellets from every wavecrest, even foamy dollops that tumbled and flew from wave to wave like fleeing rabbits. The smell of fresh fish was prominent, the reek that came from storm-wrack, as if the sea below them was stirred right to the bottom.

"Bosun Sprague didn't sneak *his* wife aboard, did he?" Lieutenant Westcott asked, striving for amusement, though his lean, harsh face and four days of stubble showed nought but grimness and a lack of real sleep; especially so in the eerie, swaying glare of the overhead lanthorn which cast long shadows over the chart.

"I have it on good authority that the official Mistress Sprague resides in Chatham . . . and the Bosun can't abide the harpy baggage," Caldwell told Westcott with a nasty cackle. "So, whoever that doxy was he had aboard as his 'wife' in Portsmouth, she was young enough to be one of his daughters."

"Mistress Sprague's presented the Bosun with nothing *but* girl children, Mister Westcott," Lewrie stuck in. "Half a dozen now, or so I heard. No wonder he stuck with the Navy so long. Hmmm . . . we are in need of a backin' wind. Does the current one veer into Due West, we'll be on a good course for Spain."

From the moment that their frigate had cleared the Isle of Wight into the Channel, while they still had clearly visible sea-marks, the chip log had been cast each half-hour, and an officer of the watch had pencilled in the course and the rate of knots recorded. The skies had been solidly overcast when they departed England, and they hadn't seen even a brief glimpse of the sun since, so their progress and position were pretty-much By Guess and By God, all by Dead Reckoning.

The recorded course was a staggering, stuttering series of X's strung along a jagged line, some close together, some X's further off from each other where they'd had a good run and turn of speed.

"Not to borrow trouble, sir," Westcott glumly said, "but does the wind veer close to a Sou'wester, we may have to wear, even in this, else we fetch up somewhere East of Corunna and Cape Finisterre."

"It could go Sou'westerly, sir," Caldwell cautioned. "So long as this Arctic gale rules, another day or so with any luck, we're making ground West'rd, but does it blow out, a Sou'westerly's not unknown in Biscay."

If that happened, *Reliant* would have no choice but to wear. A Sou'westerly would smack them right in the mouth, and paying off would drive them even deeper into the "sack" between the long right-angled trap of the French and Spanish coasts. Square-rigged ships could not sail closer than sixty-six degrees to the true wind.

"We're too far North at the moment to meet Sou'westerlies," Lewrie said after a long moment, in which he used a ruler to measure from their latest cast of the log to the edge of the chart. "We're still round the fourty-seventh latitude, so we've bags of sea-room, but it's *longitude* that's wanting. Now if . . ."

Their frigate smacked into yet another wave with a deep hollow boom, and rolled back onto her larboard side, then rose up, shedding tons of sea-water, and wriggling a bit more upright with a sickening twist, making them all cling to the flimsy chart table and shuffle their feet to keep upright.

I won't gag, or spew, Lewrie commanded himself, though he had a feeling that he was damned close to doing so. He tried to recall when it was that he had been in such foul weather, and in such a predicament, and realised that it had been years.

I'm worried . . . worried and scared, he admitted to himself, alone; *I wouldn't trust mine arse with a fart, right now. Nor a gag, either! Why didn't Father shove me into the bloody Army, instead? Oh, aye . . . 'cause he was too cheap!*

Lewrie looked to his liquid barometer for inspiration, but the blue-dyed water in the fat lower flask was still rather high up the upper tube, about as high as his last peek at it an hour before, when he had made a chalk-mark slash upon it. The storm's pressure was still low, allowing the fluid to creep upwards; no higher yet, thank God!

"About all we may do for now, sir, is ride this out and hope for the best," Mr. Caldwell concluded.

"Even with bare yards and storm trys'ls," Lt. Westcott added.

"Midshipman Grainger, SAH!" the Marine sentry outside the door to the great-cabins shouted, his usual piercing cry almost swallowed by the din of wind, rain, and the working of the hull. With luck, he might have been allowed a tarred tarpaulin coat with which to tolerate the elements.

"Enter!" Lewrie shouted back, louder than usual, too. He and the others staggered out from the tiny chart space, clinging to light deal-and-canvas partitions. Grainger entered, sopping wet and looking as miserable as a drowned rat.

"Mister Merriman's duty, sir, and I am to report that several of the fore and main-mast shrouds are slackening," Grainger said.

"Well, damn," Lewrie spat. "It seems we must wear, after all."

There was no safe way to adjust the necessary tension of the mast shrouds unless the immense load was taken off them, even on good days. Their weather shrouds must become lee shrouds, if they wished to keep the masts standing.

"Aye, sir," Lt. Westcott regretfully agreed.

"My compliments to Mister Merriman, Mister Grainger, and he's to have 'All Hands' piped," Lewrie ordered. "With your able assistance, of course, Mister Westcott . . . Mister Caldwell?"

"Of course, sir."

"I'll fetch your foul-weather rig, sir," Pettus, his cabin steward, offered, staggering from one piece of furniture to the next, and looking a tad green. Lewrie looked aft into the gloom of his cabins. His cats, Toulon and Chalky, were curled up on his bed-cot's coverlet, like two furry loaves of bread, bristled up and moaning in misery. To larboard, his young cabin servant, Jessop, was on his knees inside the quarter-gallery toilet, with only his shoes and shins showing, bent over the "seat of ease" and making offerings to Neptune; rather loudly.

"Carry on, Jessop!" Lewrie called out.

"Ah . . . aye, sir," the lad muttered back, between gags.

Once bundled into tarred canvas coat and hat, Lewrie staggered forward, steeling himself for a second or two before opening the door to the weather deck. When he did so, it was like barging out into utter chaos: the force and howl of the wind, the sudden chill of it, and the stinging volleys of sea spray that pinpricked his hands and face. Here, too, was the full sound of the storm, and the hiss and thunder of the waves, and the alarming groans of the hard-pressed masts, and the booming of the hull as the frigate fought the sea.

Off-watch sailors were swarming up from the relative warmth and security of the gun deck where they berthed and messed, adding to the sense of confusion as Lewrie managed to clamber up to the quarterdeck.

"Sorry about this, sir, but we *must* wear," Lt. Merriman said, his mouth close to Lewrie's ear.

"Aye," Lewrie shouted back. "If you think the weather shrouds will hold 'til we've got her round on larboard tack!"

"I believe they will, sir," Merriman hopefully replied.

At present, their frigate laboured heavily, even though the mizen tops'l had been taken in, as had the main course. The fore course and fore and main tops'ls were close-reefed, and the jibs up forward had been replaced by the fore topmast stays'l. Above the quarterdeck, the spanker had been reduced, and the mizen stays'l had been rigged.

Leave the tops'ls, for now, Lewrie speculated; *they're higher up than the wavetops, and can still catch wind. The fore course'll get us round the quicker.*

Send up the main topmast stays'l, again? Hmm. Oh God, all these bloody years at sea, and I still feel like a total fraud!

He'd not wished to go to sea and be all "tarry-handed", but his father had seen to that, "crimping" him into the Navy at seventeen, and *years* behind his peers in experience—for God's sake he could not even *swim!*—and even the ten-year-olds in his first mess had known *bags* more than he had, and his bottom had paid the price for not "knowing the ropes" from expasperated officers; and all his career he felt as if he had never quite caught up.

There had been a series of small ships, where things were much simpler, where little was expected of a lowly Midshipman. Surely, he had had no business at all becoming old Lt. Lilycrop's First Officer in the *Shrike* brig, where his first few months had been an embarassing pot-mess of ignorance and re-learning of his trade. There had been a whole year of shore idleness between the end of the American Revolution and his assignment aboard *Telesto*, and the jaunt to the Far East and China in '84, and when he'd come back and gotten his first command, the little *Alacrity*, in '86; just enough time to forget almost everything! By 1789, after paying *Alacrity* off, there had been years of bucolic peace ashore, with wife and children on their rented farm at Anglesgreen, and once more all he'd learned of the sea had sloughed away 'til 1793 and the war with France. When he'd reported aboard the *Cockerel* frigate as her First Lieutenant, he'd felt as overawed and unready as the rawest fresh-caught landlubber, unable to recall the proper names for things without long hours secretly poring over his frayed, illustrated copy of *Falconer's Marine Dictionary*, just as he had done when first aboard a warship in 1780!

God help 'em all, he thought; *lookin' to me t'keep 'em safe!*

"All hands are on deck, sir," Lt. Merriman reported.

"Very well, Mister Merriman, have Bosun Sprague pipe 'Stations for Wearing Ship'," Lewrie said, after a deep breath and shrug into his foul-weather rig. "Let's be about it. The men are getting cold."

"If I may, sir?" the Sailing Master, Mr. Caldwell, intruded before Lt. Merriman could raise his speaking-trumpet to his lips. "I've been studying the set of the waves, and believe they're coming in sevens, with the seventh the most forceful. Once that one is past, we'll have an easier go."

"Very well, Mister Caldwell. Carry on, Mister Merriman, but do you wait to issue your first order 'til the seventh has passed, as the Sailing Master directs," Lewrie said.

"Here it comes, Mister Merriman," Caldwell warned.

"Stations to Wear!" Merriman bawled out the preparatory orders. "Main clewgarnets and buntlines . . . spanker brails, weather main and mizen cro'jack braces! Haul taut and stand by!"

Reliant butted through a creaming, humping wave at a slant with a *thrum* and groan, surging upward toward its crest as the wave billowed under her keel, hobby-horsing upwards, then pitching bows-down into the trough with a roar.

"This is the one, sirs!" Caldwell shouted excitedly, as if he enjoyed heavy-weather sailing. His seventh wave marched down to the frigate, humping higher like a steep hill, its crest fuming white and its lee slope mottled with rippling circular eddies. "Whoo!"

"Up mains'l and spanker!" Lt. Merriman screeched once the ship had staggered up, over, and down into that great wave's trough. "Clear away after bowlines! Up helm!"

Reliant fell off quickly, shoved by wind and waves to lie abeam the sea for a bit, slowly, so very slowly falling alee and taking that howling force on her starboard quarter.

"Overhaul the weather lifts! Man the weather headbraces! Rise, fore tack and sheet!" Merriman cried.

Further, further off the wind, 'til it was coming just about dead astern, and . . .

"Clear away head bowlines!" Merriman howled. "Shift over the headsheets, and lay the head yards square!"

Now the wind was clawing at their ship's larboard quarter, and she was coming round, wallowing and rolling, but on larboard tack.

"Man main tack and sheet! Clear away the rigging! Spanker outhaul! Clear away the brails!"

"Haul aboard! Haul out!"

"Mind yer helm, there!" Lewrie cautioned as she swung up closer to the wind and seas.

"Brace up head yards!" Lt. Merriman ordered, looking and sounding calmer than when he began the evolution, now that *Reliant* had crossed from one tack to the other. "Overhaul weather lifts, and haul aboard!"

"Nicely done, sir!" Mr. Caldwell congratulated.

"Thankee, sir," Merriman replied, quite pleased and relieved, then turned to deliver his last trimming-up orders. "Steady out the bowlines! Haul taut weather trusses, braces, and lifts!"

"And, here comes the bloody seventh wave, again," Lewrie said just as the larger, fiercer wall of water humped up before them. The ship heaved up and over, then down into the trough, where she wallowed as the wave stole the wind from the tops'ls for a moment before bowling astern.

"Clear away on deck, there!" Lt. Merriman ordered.

"Mister Westcott," Lewrie bade. "Let's go forrud and see to the shrouds. Rhys, how's her helm, now?" he asked the Quartermaster of the watch at the wheel. "Can you hold West-Nor'west?"

"Aye, sir. Fair balanced, she be. Not too crank, nor griped."

"Very well," Lewrie said with a firm nod. "Full and by, and none to loo'rd. Ready, Mister Westcott?"

"Aye, sir," Westcott replied with a brief flash of teeth. "I'm as wet as I'll ever be. Bosun Sprague? Hands to the lee bulwarks."

The shrouds, the main portion of the standing rigging, ran from the outboard channel platforms down the sides of the ship, the thick and stout oak "anchors" that jutted out to ease the steep angle of support to keep the masts standing, and un-moving. Each thick rope shroud was further supported below the channel platforms by metal fittings bolted into the hull, called the chains. For each shroud there were two massive blocks, the dead-eyes, with lanyards running between them in four-part purchases. To ease or tighten the dead-eye lanyards, sailors had to go overside—the steeply angle *lee* side—where the heaving waves that creamed down *Reliant*'s flanks could surge up over the channels, turning every hand-hold or precarious foot-hold ice-slick with chill water. Even with the slackened starboard shrouds now eased by being on the lee side, it would require gruelling manual labour to set the tension to rights. For every man going over the side, there were two to anchor a shipmate with safety lines.

"Handsomely, now, lads, and have a care," Lewrie urged them as the first clambered over the gangway bulwarks to work on the foremast shrouds. In better weather, they might have seen to all three masts at once, but not now.

Lewrie was shivering with cold, his clothing soaked with spray, and his face felt like a bad shave with a dull razor as the icy droplets kept stinging. Despite a wool scarf, cold water trickled under his tarred canvas coat, too, but he was determined to remain on deck as long as the work took; if the ship's people were miserable, then he would be, too. At least he could comfort himself with the thought that he was on the gangway, not on the weather deck below, where the icy surging waters showered down each time the bows soughed deep into the sea, and left shin-high floods sluicing from beam to beam with each roll of the ship!

"Think that's got it, sir," Lt. Westcott reported, at last, an hour later.

"Very well, Mister Westcott. Dismiss the working party below," Lewrie replied. "Let 'em thaw out, and dry out, as best they can."

"Aye, sir."

Lewrie went back forward from the mizen stays, steeled himself, and waited for the hull to roll upwards before making a dash for the hammock nettings and stanchions at the break of the quarterdeck. Then it was a slow ascent, clinging to the nettings, to the weather side, where a captain was supposed to be. He hooked an arm to the shrouds of the main mast to stay upright as *Reliant* heeled far over to starboard with the next roll, and stood there, scowling at the fury of the sea, and wishing for a cup of something boiling hot; coffee, tea, or cocoa, it made no difference. Even hot water would suit, but with the ship pitching, heaving, and rolling so violently, everyone was on cold rations, for the galley fires could not be lit in such weather. Lewrie let out a long, deprived sigh.

Eight Bells chimed in four double-dings from the foc's'le belfry up forward; it was 4 P.M., and the end of the Day Watch and the beginning of the First Dog. There were happy and relieved smiles upon every hand's face, for they could go below for two hours. Far glummer were the faces of the men of the fresh watch, some of them the spare hands who had just gotten below for a few minutes, and would face two more hours of misery before the Second Dog Watch.

Lieutenant Spendlove was mounting to the quarterdeck to replace Merriman, so Lewrie timed a (fairly) level-deck dash down to the helm, and the binnacle cabinet as those worthies exchanged salutes.

"I relieve you, sir," Spendlove was intoning.

"I stand relieved, sir," Merriman answered. "Course, full and by to West-Nor'west. The last cast of the log showed five knots."

"Gentlemen," Lewrie intruded.

"Sir," they chorused.

"I'll go below with you, Mister Merriman, and leave the watch to you, Mister Spendlove," Lewrie told them. "Should the wind shift a touch more Sutherly, alter course as near as you're able. If the wind veers ahead, summon me at once. Nicely done, by the way, Mister Merriman."

"Thank you, sir," Lt. Merriman said, grinning.

"Aye aye, sir," from Spendlove.

Once below and aft, in the relative warmth of his great-cabins, Lewrie peeled off his hat and canvas coat, both stiff and soaked with half-frozen spray, and wound off the useless scarf. He hugged himself and shivered, blowing on his chilled fingers as he slid into the chart space to plot the last few hours' progress, and the change of course.

"Might you care for something warming, sir?" Pettus asked. "I could heat up some of your cold tea over the candle warmer."

"God, yes, Pettus, and thank yer kind soul!" Lewrie boomed out with a quick laugh. "How's Jessop doin'?"

"Crop-sick as a hound, sir," Pettus said with a shrug.

Lewrie looked aft, and found Jessop in pretty-much the same position he'd been in when he'd left to go on deck, hours before.

"Aye, some warmed-up tea, Pettus, with lots of milk and sugar."

Lewrie returned to peering at the chart, speculating with brass dividers and parallel ruler that if they could maintain at least five knots over the ground for so many hours going West-Nor'west, the ship would have made . . . Pah! He tossed the tools aside in frustration, for that course would carry them further North into even colder seas, and gained them nothing to the West.

As much as he detested the idea, they would have to wear about once more, right at the time that the second rum issue of the day was doled out, in the midst of preparations for what meagre cold rations would be served. Before sunset would be best, but . . . it was better than standing on 'til they struck Iceland!

Lewrie managed to make his way aft to his hanging bed-cot, to check on the cats. "How ye copin', lads?" he gently asked them.

He was answered by low moans and the flicks of bottled tails. They had not moved far from where he'd last seen them, either.

"Tea's almost ready, sir," Pettus informed him. "A few minutes more, and it'll be nigh scalding."

Thud! came the Marine sentry's musket butt on the deck without, and the cry of "Midshipman Munsell, SAH!"

"Enter!" Lewrie called out, the fingers of his right hand most firmly crossed against more bad news.

"Mister Spendlove's duty, sir, and he says that the winds are veering ahead, West-Nor'west, to Half-North in gusts," Munsell said, his teeth chattering.

"Steadying on West-Nor'west, or more Northerly, young sir?" Lewrie asked.

"Ehm, it seems to be shifting more and more Nor'westerly, sir," Munsell speculated.

"Very well," Lewrie said with a sigh. "I will come up. Give my compliments to Mister Spendlove, and inform him he's to summon all hands and be ready to wear about."

"Aye, sir."

"The tarpaulins, Pettus," Lewrie said, looking for his sodden scarf. Once dressed again, he took time to duck into the chart-space and stepped off six points of sail from their present course, then suddenly smiled. Six points off the relative wind would be Due West, did they continue sailing "full and by", but . . . did they fall off to a "leading wind", two more points, to West-Sou'west, he could ease the ship its tortuous twisting and pounding, *and* not only make bags of Westing, but much more progress to the South, as well, where surely the weather might be a *touch* more moderate!

It might be a tad warmner, too, by God! Lewrie thought; *And we might not be blown ashore on Cape Finisterre, either!*

Feeling more hopeful of their immediate prospects, he headed for the door, with but one longing look at the mug of tea on the warmer, which was beginning to steam most nicely.

Damn, and bloody damn! he mourned.

CHAPTER NINE

*T*he harsh Nor'westerly gales continued to blow fiercely for all that night after wearing, and all through the next day, allowing the frigate to trundle along "two points free" headed West-Sou'west, and making a goodly Westing, as Lewrie desired. The force of the gales was too great to bear more canvas than they already had spread aloft, and the great rolling of the troubled sea's wavecrests still robbed wind each time that *Reliant* sagged down into the deep troughs, so it was still hard to exceed a snail-like five knots, but it was still progress.

It couldn't last, of course. The Nor'westerly blew itself out, the storm driving it spending its wrath on the French and Spanish coasts as *Reliant* reeled onwards. To replace it came a fresh gale, this one from the West-Nor'west at first, requiring the tautening of sheets and braces a bit at a time 'til they were back on a beat to weather steering West-Sou'west, then ceding one point, then another, to Sou'west by South. If there was a moderation of the fierceness of wind and sea, it was only a matter of degrees, with only a slight rise in barometric pressure, and a fresh chalk mark on the neck of the liquid barometer perhaps a quarter-inch below the others. There had still been no sun sights, but the communal agreement on their Dead Reckoning had them near the 43rd line of latitude, and a safe one hundred miles West of Cape Finisterre.

By that point, the temperature *had* warmed a bit, so that the spray droplets that got flung like bird-shot stayed liquid, and the seas shipped over the bows were no longer icy. What sloshed or dripped below was no longer frigid misery, but cool, damp, soggy misery.

"Nine days . . . about nine hundred miles made good, sir," Lt. Westcott commented as Lewrie came to the quarterdeck for the second time at Four Bells of the Morning Watch at 6 A.M. Lewrie grunted his acknowledgement as he looked at the chart which Westcott had spread by the compass binnacle. "And it's not raining, for a wonder."

During the night, the seas had abated a bit, and the wind had backed more to the North, and had lost some of its fierce strength.

When Lewrie had first come up at 4 A.M., at the end of the Middle Watch, there had been a steady rain, driven by the wind at a slant to drum and hiss on every flat surface, sometimes thickening in squalls, then easing off to a sullen downpour.

"It's easing, at last," Lewrie replied after a long lookabout the ship, the sea state, and a deep sniff of the wind. "Our course?"

"Back to Southwest by South, sir, and the wind's still backing. We could be heading Sou'west by the start of the Forenoon," Westcott said with a brief, savage smile.

"A rough guess below," Lewrie said, nodding in agreement with his First Officer. "I placed us about on the same latitude as Lisbon, or thereabouts. We might've made enough Southing to pick up a hint of the Nor'east Trades."

"And if the weather continues to moderate, sir, we may even light the galley fires and have a hot meal!" Westcott enthused.

"Keep yer fingers crossed, Mister Westcott," Lewrie said as he paced over to the starboard side of the quarterdeck, hooked an arm through the shrouds, and leaned out for a better look at the sea. He saw hopeful signs. Though it was still blustery, the waves no longer towered over the ship. They were still steep, but spaced further apart in long rollers, cross-fretted and dappled with large white caps and white horses, and in the pre-dawn greyness, no longer seemed quite as green as they had the day before.

The reek of storm-wrack and the smell of fresh fish was not as noticeable, either. The raw wind was tinged with iodine and salt.

Reliant battered along "full and by", but her motion was less tortured, her decks less canted to leeward, and her shoulder set more firmly without that sickening deep rolling or twisting. Aloft, what remained of the commissioning pendant shivered and fluttered less frantically, too.

Damme, it's muggy! Lewrie realised, taking off his tarpaulin hat and opening the tarred coat to let the wind in; *It's becomin'* warmer, *at last!* He had not looked at the thermometer in his cabins, but it felt like it might even be near sixty degrees, or so.

"Dawn Quarters, sir?" Lt. Westcott asked.

"Aye, carry on, Mister Westcott," Lewrie agreed.

It was a habit long-engrained in him, in emulation of former captains more cautious than most, to go to Quarters before the false dawn ended, and the risen sun might reveal an enemy ship, or a possible prize, above the horizon.

A drummer began the Long Roll, the Bosun's calls started the pipe to Quarters, and the off-watch crew came scrambling up from the mess deck. Lewrie passed the keys to the arms chests to one of the Midshipmen, should muskets, pistols, boarding pikes, and axes need to be issued. The on-deck lookouts quit their posts to go aloft to the fighting tops and the cross-trees for the furthest view as the guns were cast loose and the ports opened, the tompions in the muzzles removed, the flintlock strikers fitted above the touch-holes, powder charges fetched up from the magazines, and roundshot from the shot racks and rope shot-garlands selected by gun-captains.

"Sunrise should be when, Mister Caldwell?" Lewrie asked the Sailing Master, once the bustle quieted.

"My best guess would be twenty minutes past six A.M., sir," Mr. Caldwell crisply answered, "though without a firm position of latitude and longitude, all I may swear to will be . . . soon."

Lewrie smiled at him, then pulled out his pocket-watch to see the minutes tick by; eighteen minutes past, then the estimated twenty, then twenty-five. The false dawn grew lighter, revealing more of the ship from bow to stern, the night-softness more stark. The horizon that could be seen from the deck expanded from a mile or two to five or six miles, and the sea began to take colour, the white caps and white horses, and the foaming wavecrests turned paler, rather than a dish-water grey. The sea became a steely blue-grey, almost a normal hue for deep ocean, and the line of the horizon was no longer the heaving, rolling waves close aboard, but a real, far-off line.

"Damn my eyes!" someone whispered loud enough to be heard, for there off the frigate's larboard quarter, in the East, the sun burst like a bombshell above the horizon. It was weak, watery, and hazed by clouds, but the first up-most loom of the sun shone yellowish in promise of a clearing day! Everyone with a pocket-watch snatched it out quickly, to note the minute of the sun's rising; Mr. Caldwell's ephemeris had tables which could give them a clearer idea of their position.

With much hemming, hawing, and throat-clearing, the Sailing Master played "shaman" for a bit, consulting his ephemeris, scribbling with chalk on a small slate, uttering a "damn" or two when the damp slate and damp chalk refused to co-operate, then ordained that they were a full fifteen minutes of a degree further West than they had initially reckoned. "Now, perhaps the discrepancy is due to being further South than our Dead-Reckoning guesses, sirs," Caldwell went on. "A decent shot at the sun at Noon Sights should reveal all," he concluded as he made an X mark on the chart a tad West of their first estimate. It was only a few miles, but . . .

The rippling horizons were clear, and the disturbed seas were empty of threat. "Secure the hands from Quarters, Mister Westcott," Lewrie ordered at last. "Have the galley fires be lit, and pipe the hands below to breakfast. I may dare to shave this morning."

"Aye, sir." Westcott replied. "And I must say, sir, that you would decently resemble a pirate, do you give the stubble another day or two more."

"Arrh," Lewrie sham-growled, returning to the starboard side, daring also to smile for the first time in days.

Conditions did not prove quite as hopeful as they might have wished, though. By the middle of the Forenoon Watch, fresh banks of grey clouds loomed up from the Nor'east, destroying any hope of a sun-sight. They were feeling the fringes of the benign, the dependable Nor'east Trade Wind, yet it only brought more gusts, and a raw and chill rain! The winds settled on *Reliant*'s starboard quarter as she was driven South by West, ploughing and hobby-horsing through the swells. Lewrie at least had enough rainwater with which to sponge-bathe, for a rare once, and a ship steady enough under him to lather up and shave!

CHAPTER TEN

*I*t was two more wary days of scudding South by West 'til the sky showed even a hint of blue, still mostly lost in blankets of clouds—clouds paler and whiter than any they had seen since leaving Portsmouth, which at least were promising. Gradually, ragged holes and clear-sky streaks appeared in those clouds, like ripped and torn curtains, or an old blanket that the rats and moths had been feeding upon. *Shadows* appeared, and here and there round the ship, in large patches, waves glittered in actual sunlight!

Lewrie was aft in his great-cabins, as the Forenoon of the third day of their South by Westing wore on, pacing to peek out the transom sash windows, then go forward to the door to the weather deck to stick his head out and scan the sky. The ship's drummer and fifers began to "play" the rum cask up at Seven Bells, and it began to look promising, at last. His sextant and Harrison's chronometer were safely stowed in their protective boxes in the chart-space, and he gave them an intent look. Hoping for the best, he clapped his hat on his head and picked the boxes up by their brass carrying handles.

"Cap'm's on . . . !" the Marine sentry cried, for the tenth time since Lewrie's first peek, turning his head to see if Lewrie would appear for real this time. "Cap'um's on deck!" he cried in full.

Lewrie trotted up the windward ladderway to the quarterdeck, to discover that the Sailing Master, his officers, and Mids had brought up their
own sextants, slates, and paper scraps for reckoning.

"Damned nice," Lewrie said, after a good look about and a sniff of the
wind. The Trades no longer gusted, but were steady, and this late morning's temperature, while still nippy, was pleasant enough to be stood without shivering. "Good Lord, what's that in the sky?" he japed. "What should
we name it? Should we worship it, d'ye wonder?"

"There's still thin clouds and haze, sir, but . . . we'll soon see," Lt.
Merriman said.

"Close enough for naval work," Lt. Westcott snickered.

They compared chronometers, then waited for the last grains of sand
to trickle through the hour, half-hour, and quarter-hour glasses at the
forecastle belfry, bringing their sextants up to their eyes as ship's boys
turned those glasses, and chimed the first stroke upon the ship's bell.
Then, as Lt. Spendlove relieved Lt. Merriman, they wrote down their
sights and began their calculations. A few minutes later, the officers co-
vened to compare, results, which caused smiles all round, and a communal gathering by the now-ragged chart.

"Twenty-five degrees, twenty minutes West," Mr. Caldwell summed
up with un-accustomed glee, "which places us about . . . here. Five hundred miles Sou'west of Cape Saint Vincent, and only a few minutes North
of the thirty-third latitude," he said, making a tentative X upon the chart.

"Do we stand on this course a few days more, we could fetch the Madeiras," Lt. Westcott pointed out. "Anyone thirsty for some wine?"

"Or, we stand on West-Sou'west a bit longer 'til we strike the thirty-
second latitude, then follow it the lubberly way, right across the Atlantic
to Bermuda," Lewrie countered. "Perhaps thirty-two degrees twenty minutes, just in case."

He and the Sailing Master had pored over another chart of Bermudan
waters for hours, the night before, and both of them had gloomed in unison
to note how quickly the Atlantic's abyssal depths shallowed and shoaled,
the nearer one got to shore. Even more fearful were the many and great
expanses of rocks, shoals, flats, and banks indicated all round the North,
Northwest, and West of the chain of islets that made up the wee archipelago . . . and the ovals that marked the wrecks of ships that had gone down
on those myriad underwater perils. It was not a place to approach unwarily;
Bermuda's old name among sailormen was "The Isle of the Devils"!

"Now your results, young gentlemen," the Sailing Master asked of the Midshipmen. Some showed blasé calm, one or two even beamed in confidence, whilst the two youngest, Munsell and Rossyngton, displayed more trepidation.

"Uhm-hmm, very good, Mister Eldridge," Mr. Caldwell droned on as he studied each slate or sheet of foolscap. "A few minutes out, Mister Warburton, but close. Uhm-hmm, Mister Entwhistle, Mister Grainger. Well, well, Mister Rossyngton, despite the First Lieutenant's jape, we are not as close to the Madeiras as you make us. Now then, Mister Munsell," Caldwell said, expecting the worst, as usual, with a grave phyz on, and a demanding hand out for the lad's slate. "Well, my word. My word, indeed!" the Sailing Master marvelled, glancing quickly from Munsell to his slate and back again, so "all-aback" that he looked as if he would inspect the backside of the slate, or turn it upside down.

"Mister Eldridge has been tutoring us, sir," Munsell said with joy. "Me in particular, really," the lad confessed.

"Not half a degree out, either in longitude or latitude!" Mr. Caldwell exclaimed, holding Munsell's slate for all to see, to prove it. Even Lewrie, who had struggled for ages with the formula, and admittedly still not a dab-hand navigator, could see that Munsell had worked it properly, with very few side-scribbles, and had not cribbed it from the others. He was all but gape-jawed in amazement, too; Midshipman Munsell could usually place them on the far side of the ocean from where they really were, or somewhere in the jungles of the Amazon when in West Indies waters!

"Congratulations, Mister Munsell," Lewrie said in praise.

"Well, there's always tomorrow," Rossyngton teased.

"Perhaps Mister Eldridge should now concentrate upon tutoring you, Mister Rossyngton," Lewrie suggested, pulling a face. "It's rare t'have an experienced Mid for the others to learn from, but . . . that's what a congenial and co-operative Midshipmen's mess should be, hey? Very good, Mister Eldridge."

"Uh, thank you, sir," Eldridge replied, a tad embarrassed to be pointed out. Lewrie gave him a reassuring nod and a smile, also taking note of Eldridge's kit, and wondered how he was fitting in in the orlop cockpit. Eldridge normally wore slop-trousers (did he have a pair of breeches? Lewrie wondered) or a snugger pair of dark blue trousers, linen or cotton shirts, a waist-coat that had gone a light tan from age, black neck-stock, and a plain uniform coat with dull brass buttons, and the white collar patches of his rank. If he had a cocked hat, no one had seen it; his head-gear day in and day out was a black felt civilian topper with a narrow brim and a tapering crown.

His fellow Mids ranged from fifteen to twenty-one years of age, whilst he was in his mid-to-late twenties when suddenly promoted into their compact little world, with all its lame jests, pranks, and general igno-rance, shoulder-to-shoulder with Entwhistle, an "Honourable", and the rest who had been reared in the comfort of the landed gentry, and the "squirearchy", whilst Eldridge's father was a Bristol chandler, a man in "trade"; a lot in life usually scorned by "the better sorts".

Lewrie had been too busy with the last-minute lading, the alteration of muster lists, the sailing from Portsmouth, and then the weeks of foul and threatening weather, with not a minute to spare for thought over the matter.

Have t'get Westcott t'look into it, Lewrie told himself; *That's what First Officers're for, ain't it? The weather relents, start dinin' officers and warrants in, again . . . with Eldridge in the rotation.*

"One more thing, young sirs," Lewrie said. "Mister Munsell, do you know the longitude and latitude of Bermuda?"

"Ehm . . . sixty-four degrees, fourty minutes West, sir," Munsell piped up quickly before the others could open their mouths, "and Saint George's Harbour is at thirty-two degrees twenty-three minutes North."

"The highest sea-mark visible from offshore?" Lewrie posed to them. That made them share quick looks of worry, and took the wind from their sails; there were several dumb shrugs.

"The Sailing Master has the pertinent charts," Lewrie said with a wry *moue* over their lack of knowledge. "I'd suggest ye all take a good, long gander at it, and familarise yourselves with the island and its waters . . . and all the cautions, right, Mister Caldwell?"

"Aye, sir," Caldwell replied, back to gruffness.

And damned right, so shall I! Lewrie vowed to himself.

"The off-watch lads are dismissed," Lewrie ordered, turning to secure his chronometer and sextant in their cases. "Carry on, Mister Spendlove."

"Aye, sir!"

CHAPTER ELEVEN

*H*MS *Reliant*'s landfall at Bermuda was hardly an auspicious occasion. The lookouts aloft, and the watch officers, spotted a few dim lights from far offshore, in the wee hours near the end of the Middle Watch, Unfortunately, those few low-on-the-horizon lights were spread to either side of the bows. A quick peek at the chart, and a hidden gasp later, and Lewrie ordered an immediate turn-about to stand away Sou'east, into deeper water; there to stand off-and-on 'til daylight.

"What I feared," he told Lt. Merriman and the Sailing Master, "that we'd fetch the bloody place too far North of it, and end up on the reefs and rocks. Once we can see where we're going, we'll come to anchor in Five Fathom Hole . . . assumin' we can find it without rippin' her bottom out."

The previous day's Noon Sights had placed their position close to Bermuda, close enough for Lewrie to order the t'gallants to be reefed and gasketed, the tops'ls reduced to the second reefs, and the fore and main courses shortened down to first reefs. After a light supper, a most informal one with Lt. Westcott, the Sailing Master, and a chart spread over the dining table, Lewrie had taken a three-hour nap, then had gone on deck at the beginning of the Middle Watch, at midnight, to slouch in his collapsible canvas deck chair, pace the deck, and fret for the first cry of "land ho", hoping that their navigation was accurate enough, their course correct, so that they would fetch the islands to their Sou'east, well clear of Kitchen Shoals, Mill Breakers, Great Breaker Ledge Flat, the Nor'east Breakers, and Sea Venture Shoals, so named for the *Sea Venture*, which had wrecked upon them, setting the first English colonists on Bermuda . . . whether they wanted to be, or not. They *had* been bound for Virginia, but, once succoured with fresh victuals, most had stayed to make the best of a dangerous serendipity!

"I daresay we've been bitten by the mysterious magnetic variations hereabouts, sir," Mr. Caldwell said with a scowl. "Bermuda's infamous for them, sometimes up to six degrees or so, and no explaining why. They're not seasonal, nor tied to the phases of the moon, tides, or weather." Caldwell shrugged and gloomed in perplexity.

"Sounds spooky," Lt. Merriman commented.

"Let's not let the ship's people hear any of that, hey?" Lewrie muttered to Merriman, laying a finger upon his lips for a moment. "We have enough superstitions amongst 'em already. Carry on Mister Merriman. Now we believe we're in deeper, safer waters, I'll take a short 'caulk' in my deck chair."

"Very good, sir, aye," Merriman replied.

The dawn did not bring an auspicious landfall, either. As the Forenoon Watch began at 8 A.M., the winds began to freshen once more, and the inshore waters fretted and chopped in white caps and white horses, with ruffling cat's paws over the surface. There was a heavy, scudding overcast that made the early morning shadowless and gloomy, and there was a strong smell of rain in the offing, to boot.

Oddly, though, Bermuda could not have been a more welcome sight if they had stood in in bright daylight, for, as their frigate cautiously neared St. David's Head, the shoal waters turned lighter and clearer blue, the shores fringed in aqua green with pure white waves breaking upon almost pinkish-tan beaches, beneath the ruddy limestone headlands. And the island was so brightly green! There were trees, some fronded or spiky like palms or palmettos, flowering bushes, and open grassy spaces, perhaps lawns or croplands, and all the *flora* lush and verdant in an entire palette of green. Quite unlike some islands in the West Indies that could look brown and shrivelled in the sun and talced with dust, Bermuda appeared as if everything had been freshly watered and washed for their arrival.

The Sailing Master, his Mates, and the trusted senior Midshipmen busily plied their sextants to take the measurements of the known heights and prominent sea-marks, working out the distances from shore, and the known dangers of the shallows and submerged reefs noted on the charts.

"Do we stand on as we are, sir," the Sailing Master said after a long, grim musing over the chart pinned to the traverse board, "we will enter Five Fathom Hole. There is an anchorage area just North of there, where we can find six or seven fathoms, and firm sand and rock holding ground . . . or so the chart promises."

"Right there?" Lewrie asked, pointing a finger at the chart. The area that Mr. Caldwell was recommending lay close to the infamous Sea Venture Shoals . . . uncomfortably close, to his lights! He took a long look about to judge the wind direction, worrying that it might be foul for entering St. George's Harbour proper. "Mister Westcott? Best bower and stern kedge, the kedge to be let go first as we crawl on. Unless a pilot takes pity on us."

"Aye, sir," the First Officer replied.

"Speak of the Devil, sir," Mr. Caldwell said, pointing towards Town Cut, the very narrow entry channel into harbour. "There's one of the harbour pilots coming to us, just now."

Lewrie fetched his telescope and spotted a singled-masted boat coming out of the channel 'twixt St. George's Island, tiny Biggs Island, and St. David's Island which formed the Southern shore of the harbour. Its jib and gaff-headed mainsail did an uncertain shiver as it left the Cut, a sure sign to Lewrie that it would be a right-bastard set of swirls and back-eddies in there, too uncertain a wind to risk *Reliant*, this day at least. Once clear, the boat's sails cracked wind-full, and she began to bound over the choppy inshore waters like a running stag, bound for his ship. As she drew closer, Lewrie could espy three occupants; a lad about twelve or so to handle the sheets, one even younger at the tiller, and an older man in the boat's amidships.

"I say, that looks fun," Midshipman Munsell tittered. "Should we ever have the time, we could stage boat races."

The pilot boat—if that was what it was—passed ahead of *Reliant*, swung about in a wide turn, and jibed about to swan close to the starboard main chains, and the opened entry-port.

"Hoy, what ship, there?" the older man shouted up, using an old brass speaking-trumpet.

"The *Reliant* frigate, Captain Alan Lewrie!" Mr. Caldwell called back for them. "You are a pilot, sir?"

"Warrick, and I am!" the fellow replied, beaming broadly under a wide-brimmed straw planter's hat. "Shall I come up, sir?"

"Aye! Come alongside."

The lad at the tiller, no older than ten, deftly put the tiller over and brought the boat to within inches of the channel platform as the slightly older boy hooked on with a gaff. A second later and Mr. Warrick was scrambling up the boarding battens, and the boat sheered off to stand alee.

"Good morning, all," Warrick said, doffing his hat to the officers gathered on the quarterdeck.

"Good morning, Mister Warrick," Lewrie said, stepping forward and doffing his own hat in salute. "Your servant, sir."

"Nay, I'm more yours, Cap'm Lewrie," Warrick replied, "if you wish to enter port. Though the wind's not good for that, today. We can find you a good anchorage, just off yonder, 'til the morrow, and guide you in then. What's your draught, sir?"

"About eighteen feet, right aft," Lewrie supplied.

"Good, long scope, to a bower and kedge, I'm thinking? Good," Warrick said, noting that the hawse-bucklers had been removed, a kedge was already attached to a stern cable, and the best, larboard bower anchor was swinging free of cat and fish lashings. "There's many the cautious masters that'll anchor out, anyway, and send their boats in through the Cut for provisions. Do you not have need of lading cargo, or landing goods, the anchorage'll suit you fine.

"Mind, sir, my fee's the same for either," Warrick said with a smug grin, naming a goodly sum for his services, one which made every officer, and Lewrie, wince. "These are dangerous waters, gentlemen, more so than most. Without a pilot aboard, you'd be lost and wrecked in a twinkling."

"Carry on, Mister Warrick," Lewrie said. "Do you require cash, a note of hand, or an Admiralty chit?"

"Cash is topping fine, Cap'm Lewrie," Warrick breezed off, then turned his full attention to the sails, the course, and the sea-marks. "Hoy, lads. A half point loo'rd, if you will," he said to the men on the helm, bypassing the watch officers. *Reliant* was now wholly in his hands.

The frigate swung off to starboard a bit as she came level with Little Head, standing out to avoid a shoal noted as the Spit. To the West was revealed a maze of islets; Paget and Biggs, the larger Smith's Island, and behind that, in the harbour proper, little Hen Island, all in clear green waters as shallow as six to nine feet, and even the Town Cut entrance looked suspiciously shallow, to Lewrie.

Damned right *I'll not move without a pilot aboard*, he vowed to himself; *no matter* how *much they charge me!*

"Cap'm sir," Warrick said at last, "do you let go your kedge and let it pay out half a cable about here, then you're good to swing up to windward, go flat a'back, then drop the bower on a short scope for the nonce, 'til you've balanced between them, you'll find good holding ground."

"Very well, sir, and thankee. Mister Westcott? Let go the kedge, half a cable scope."

"Aye aye, sir."

"Do you wish to enter port proper tomorrow, sir, it's good odds that the wind'll shift astern of you, and you can trust your kedge to hold you at full scope whilst you take up the bower," Warrick suggested. "Then, it's smooth sailing right up the Cut, holding Sugarloaf Hill fine on your bows. You hoist a flag for a pilot, and me and my boys'll see you right."

"I'd not try it on without you, Mister Warrick," Lewrie said, which seemed to please the man. "Once we're anchored, might I offer you a glass of something, and ask you a few questions about Bermuda? This is, I believe, the first time any of us have put in here."

"That'd be right kindly of you, sir," Warrick replied.

It lacked half an hour 'til "Clear Decks and Up Spirits" by the time *Reliant* was safely anchored, and all her sails at long last brailed up in harbour gaskets or handed and stowed. The crew would get the rum issue a bit later, but Lewrie's wine cabinet was open, and he kept a stone crock of rum for just such a purpose.

Warrick's boat had come alongside, and the two lads, his sons, had scrambled aboard to peer about and josh Munsell and Rossyngton, the ship's youngest Mids. They were bronzed by the sun, bare-legged and shoeless, in faded old breeches with the knee buttons long gone, open and sleeveless linen shirts, and straw hats much like their father's.

"Ah, but that's fine," Warrick said after a tentative sip from his glass of rum. "Navy issue's stronger than most, Strong enough to make a man's ears itch, har!"

"We noted some compass variation," Lewrie began to probe, and Warrick let go with a plethora of local lore. "Mistifying, that."

There was no explaining the variations, for one thing. With a chart spread on the dining table, Warrick went over the string of islands. Some were so close to each other, like North and South Ireland, Boaz, Somerset, and Watford Islands on the West end of the chain, that if the Crown ever thought to spend money on bridges, the distances between could easily be spanned. Inside the shoals to the Nor'east there was a vast expanse of deep, somewhat sheltered water, Murray's Anchorage, and there were at least two good deepwater channels that led to a very good sheltered anchorage in Grassy Bay, and the Great and Little Sounds, out to the West.

"During the Peace of Amiens, the *Leavder* anchored there, sir," Warrick said. "She's an old two-decker fifty gunner, and draws more than you. But, there's not much in the way of provisions, or entertainment, for your sailors from Somerset, or Sandys Parish, either. Nor is there much joy in Hamilton, do you send your ship's boats through Two Rocks Passage into Hamilton Bay. 'Tis a sleepy little place. You can send your people ashore with little fear of desertion, though. You will note there's several forts, and a sizeable garrison, on Bermuda.

"Not that there's much call for them," Warrick went on, holding out his glass for a top-up. "Keeping order, and rounding up the drunken sailors, mostly."

"Is *Leander* still here?" Lewrie asked. "Is her captain senior officer present?"

"Depends on who's in port, sir," Warrick said with a laugh at that notion. "Right now, *you're* senior naval officer present. Does one of the brig-sloops come in, then it'd be a Commander in charge of the island for as long as he's at anchor. If both brig-sloops are out at sea, then it might be one of the Lieutenants on the small sloops. There's no real dockyard, no Port Admiral or much organisation."

"How many warships are there, then?" Lewrie further asked.

"Like I said, two brig-sloops, and two smaller sloops, more like two-masted tops'l schooners, around eight or ten guns apiece," Warrick prosed on. "Much like the Bermuda or Jamaica sloops that the old pirates

like Blackbeard and Stede Bonnet sailed in the long ago. Ever hear of
Stede Bonnet?"

"No, I haven't," Lewrie replied, pouring a tot of rum for himself to be
companionable.

"Oh, he was a 'fly' fellow," Warrick happily related. "He was a gentleman, an officer in the island Army garrison, married with two or more
children, respectable as anything. Came of a French Protestant family,
what they call Huguenots, that were massacred or expelled long ago?
Well, upright as he seemed, one day he up and boarded ship for Nassau,
the old pirate haven, and turned sea rover! S'truth!"

"A total 'lubber'? I'd not imagine there's much future in that," Lewrie
said, chuckling.

"Now, no one ever said he was anything close to a 'tarpaulin' sailor,"
Warrick went on, "but he was a gentleman, and a leader, a man with
some style about him, so he ended up captain of a small ship faster than
you can say 'Jack Ketch'. Ran with Blackbeard, 'Calico Jack' Rackham,
Mary Read, and Anne Bonny, and so long as he could keep order and be
backed up by experienced mates, he did right well.

"They caught him, though, in the end," Warrick added, turning
wistful-somber, as if telling of the end of a tragic hero. "Got him at anchor in the mouth of the Cape Fear River over in the North Carolina
colony . . . 1715 or so? They took him down to Charleston for his trial.
Now here's the oddest bit: Were there women aboard a prize he took,
they took up with *him,* husbands, lovers, and families bedamned, and in
all his captures, there never was a single murder, nor even all that much
resistance, so . . . the judge says since Bonnet's hands are clean of killing,
he's of a mind to pardon him, so long as he swears to give up piracy and
return to his family. Know what he said?"

"Pray, do tell," Lewrie urged, encouraging the pilot, whether he really
cared or not; it sounded promising, though, for Mr. Warrick was almost
wheezing with impending wit.

"Bonnet says to the judge, 'Well my lord, if that's my only option, you
might as well go on and *hang* me!' Damned if he didn't, hee-hee!"

"She must've been a *real* shrew," Lewrie said, laughing.

"And damned if they didn't . . . hang him, that is," Warrick said.
"They say Stede Bonnet went out with style, pirate or not."

"No piracy round here, since, I trust?" Lewrie japed.

"We don't get the great trade convoys to attract much of that," Warrick said with a shrug, sounding as if he might wish that there was some piracy to liven a sleepy mid-Atlantic island's days.

"Privateering?" Lewrie asked.

"Ours, mostly, preying on the French and the Dons, but after the war began again two years ago, not much of that, either, Cap'm Lewrie," Warrick admitted, sounding as if that was a let-down, too. "Our two brig-sloops prowl round the island, an hundred or more miles off, and stay out nigh three months before coming back in to provision. The small sloops patrol closer in, but it's rare that any enemy ship turns up, and they're mostly bound for more important places."

Can't commandeer the brig-sloops, just in case the French do turn up, Lewrie thought; *I need small ships t'make squadron; it'll have t'be one of the little'uns.*

"None of the small sloops are around, at present?" Lewrie asked, making free with the crock of rum. While rum was not his preferred aged American corn whiskey, it was a decent substitute. Lewrie was one of the few officers in the Navy who would even admit to liking a spirit issued to the common seamen.

"Well . . . there might be Lieutenant Bury," Warrick told him, a scowl on his face.

"Berry?"

"Bury, like a funeral. B-U-R-Y," Warrick corrected him. "He's the *Lizard* sloop, though a fish name'd suit him more. Fellow might as well be covered in scales and fins. An odd bird, altogether is Bury."

"How so?" Lewrie asked, topping up both their glasses.

In vino veritas, he thought; *He knows the truth, and I don't.*

"He likes hydrog . . . hydrography," Warrick carped; perhaps it was the rum that was tangling his tongue. "Swans about the shoals and reefs, taking soundings and making charts. Bury's got it into his head there's channels through the flats that nobody's found yet, or *wants* found!"

Which'd cut into yer trade, and yer earnings, Lewrie cynically speculated to himself.

"And, when he's not doing that, he's out in a small boat with a bucket on his head," Warrick scoffed.

"Beg pardon? A bucket?" Lewrie gawped.

"Had himself a bucket made, with a glass-pane bottom," Warrick explained, shaking his head in wonder. "Like an old tavern tankard in the old days? Wants to see the bottoms, watch the fishes, study the coral and such, and catch samples so he can gut them and pick them to pieces and draw pictures of them. Spends more time in the water, upside down as a feeding duck, hee hee! Last anyone saw of him and the *Lizard,* he was off for Grassy Bay, dropping Vickers, one of the other pilots, soon as he got out of The Narrows and into the South Channel cross Murray's Anchorage, the silly sod!" Warrick huffed up like an adder in revulsion, and in defence of his "guild". As dangerous as Bermudan waters were, the pilots had been making a killing for years, and anything that threatened their income was stealing food from the mouths of their children!

Don't sound like the sort I need, Lewrie thought.

"And the other small sloop, and her captain?" he queried.

"*Primrose?* Lieutenant Percy's more sensible, but he's been out the last two months, entire, and most-like won't come back to harbour 'til the rum runs out . . . another month or so," Warrick speculated.

Damn! Lewrie thought; *I may be stuck with 'Mister Minnow' after all! Not much choice, really.*

"Well, then. I intend to idle at anchor at least a whole day, through tomorrow. Give the hands a well-earned rest after the voyage *we've* had. Allow the chandlers and bum-boats alongside?" Lewrie idly said. "After that, the wind permitting, I'd be much obliged to you, did you pilot us up through, The Narrows, and into Grassy Bay, so that I may speak with Bury."

"You have it, Cap'm Lewrie!" Warrick quickly agreed. "Now . . . if you'll be ready, and if there's not a scramble over a new ship coming in, there's no need to make a hoist, asking for a pilot, see?" The man actually winked at him! "I'll come out to you, and we'll be off!"

"That would be most agreeable, Mister Warrick," Lewrie replied.

Once Warrick and his sons had tumbled down the battens into the boat and had set off for Town Cut, Lewrie returned to the quarterdeck.

"We'll be entering port, sir?" Lt. Westcott asked.

"I think not, Mister Westcott, sorry," Lewrie told him. "We'll hoist the Easy pendant to whistle up the bum-boats, and let the Purser go ashore for fresh victuals, but Saint George's doesn't look that promising. Did they send out *all* the doxies, I doubt they'd make a corporal's guard."

"I see, sir," Westcott said, sounding a tad disappointed.

"I doubt there's more than a half-dozen *decent-lookin'* girls on the whole island, and the men of Bermuda most-like guard 'em like the bloody Crown Jewels, anyway," Lewrie told him, smiling and chuckling. "We're ordered to visit all the major ports in America, from Cape Fear to Savannah, Mister Westcott, and Nassau, to boot, so you will have your . . . opportunities, hmm? Take joy o' *that!*"

"Oh, very good, sir!"

"Anything needful t'see to, sir?" Lewrie asked, turning back to ship's business.

"Over the last few days of decent weather, sir, we've re-rove all the frayed or snapped rigging, patched or replaced all the torn sails, and replaced the odd broken spars in the topmasts, so there's not that much to see to, really," Westcott reported, more crisply.

"Summon all hands, if you will, sir," Lewrie ordered.

Bosun Sprague plied his silver call, piping the hands up from below, summoning the on-deck watch to gather in the waist or on the sail-tending gangways. Lewrie stepped to the top of the starboard ladderway to the waist to address them.

"Men, we've reached the first stop of our voyage, and it's been a hellish chore t'get here, as well you all know, hey?" Lewrie began. "We've put the ship to rights, as the First Officer informs me . . . and now it's time to put *your* things to rights.

"We'll not put the ship Out of Discipline, but we will allow the bum-boats alongside for fresh fruits and victuals," he went on. "By tonight's mess, I hope to obtain fresh meat and shore bread for your suppers, too. Right, Mister Cadbury?"

"Right, sir," the Purser, who was standing by to go ashore in one of the ship's boats, heartily agreed; though how much it would cost him out of his slim profits he would not express, even by a tiny frown or wince.

"We'll have 'all night in', tonight," Lewrie continued, noting the smiles breaking out, "and the second rum issue for the day will be 'splice the main-brace'. Tomorrow . . ."

Lusty cheers interrupted him for half a minute.

"And tomorrow will be 'make-and-mend' to dry out and repair your kits," Lewrie concluded. "Mister Westcott? Dismiss the hands."

"Aye aye, sir!"

And I'll sleep the bloody clock round, myself, at long last! Lewrie promised himself.

CHAPTER TWELVE

I think I'm beginnin' to regret this, Lewrie thought in trepidation as the pilot, Mr. Warrick, conned *Reliant* across Murray's Anchorage towards Grassy Bay, two days later, after the winds had come fair. The Bermuda Islands lay too far North of the tropics to own reliable Trade Winds, and too far South of the North Atlantic Westerlies, in the belt of the Variables, to trust from which quarter the wind would blow, two days running.

Likewise the islands' weather, the garrulous Mr. Warrick imparted in the idle moments between dashes to either beam of the deck, and many consultations of the ship's binnacle-mounted compass. One could count on fairly mild weather, even in high summer, with temperatures rarely above the low eighties, but only a few degrees of relief after sundown. It could rain at least twice a week, and blow up a stronger quarter-gale at least every ten days to a fortnight. All that precipitation was welcome, though, for Bermuda was not blessed with all that many springs, and the rain was funnelled down into stone cisterns from the rooves, which every private house possessed, for later.

Taking pity on a new-come, Warrick piloted *Reliant* along the North Channel, which was deeper and more open, rather than the South Channel, which even Warrick admitted could be very tricky. Even so, Lewrie felt it quite enough un-nerving to look overside and see just how clear the waters were, and how close they were to the Three Hill Shoals, and how gin-clear and knee-deep the flats to the North were!

Near the Chimneys Shoal, Warrick directed the frigate into a turn to the Sou'west to stand well away from Devil's Flats, then into a welcome "lake" of deep water, before threading a channel through the White Flats, a passage even narrower than The Narrows, which had been harrowing enough, just thankee! Well West of the vast expanse of Brackish Pond Flats, and with North Ireland Island off the starboard bows, Warrick reckoned that they could round up into the wind and safely anchor just about anywhere; they were in Grassy Bay.

There was only one other vessel in sight, a two-masted sloop anchored off Long Shoal to the Sou'east, with a rowing gig idling at the edge of the shoal.

"They don't seem to be paying much attention to our arrival, sir," Lt. Westcott said, after a long look with a telescope. Upon his face there sprang one of his brief, feral, tooth-bearing grins, in anticipation of somebody getting a strip torn off his arse. "Perhaps we should fire a gun to wake them up?"

"Bring my gig up from astern, Mister Westcott," Lewrie decided, "and pass word for my boat crew. I think I want t'see what this Bury fellow's like in his own element. Who knows, he might offer me a fine fish."

Someone had been awake aboard HMS *Lizard*, for a small jolly boat had set out for the shoal and the gig a bit before Lewrie's gig began to row over. There was a flurry of activity, a scramble of people into the far-off gig, and a furious row back to *Lizard* before Lewrie's boat could arrive.

"Permission to come aboard?" Lewrie shouted up to the deck as his boat crew hooked on to the sloop's main chains and began to ship oars.

"Aye aye, sir!" a flummoxed Lieutenant, a fellow in his early twenties, quickly replied, whilst hastily mustering a side-party fit enough to receive a Post-Captain. Feeling devilish, Lewrie did not stand on ceremony, but scrambled up the battens and man-ropes before the sloop's Bosun could even begin a call.

"Captain Alan Lewrie, the *Reliant* frigate," he said, doffing his hat to the flag and the young officer.

"L-lieutenant Rainey, sir. Welcome aboard the *Lizard*. The captain, ehm, Lieutenant Bury, is aft at the moment, sir, if you'll pardon . . ." the young fellow babbled.

"We could be seen entering the bay from quite a way off," Lewrie casually commented.

"Harbour watch, sir, and a 'Make and Mend' day, and some of the people off with the Captain, and . . . a thousand pardons for being so inattentive, Captain Lewrie," the lad replied, all but wringing his hands. "Normally, we . . . but here's the Captain, sir!"

HMS *Lizard*'s Captain, Lt. Bury, appeared from an after hatchway between the transom and the helm, looking anxious . . . and guilty. He was also sopping wet, dressed in faded and stained old breeches, with the knee buttons open and no stockings on his lower legs. He had not had time to don a fresh shirt, tie a neck-stock, or find a waist-coat, and had hurriedly donned a plain undress coat that had seen better days. Lt. Bury also sported a straw hat, much like pilot Warrick's, which he quickly doffed in salute.

"I beg your pardon, sir, I have no excuse," he baldly said.

"Alan Lewrie, the *Reliant* frigate," Lewrie told him, doffing his own hat in reply. "I've come to summon you from your duties here in Bermudan waters, Mister Bury. I am to lead a small squadron able to go into shoal waters, and hunt and harry French and Spanish privateers, off to the West, and am in need of vessels such as yours."

Lt. Bury looked at him most solemnly, blinking his pale blue eyes a time or two, as if stunned by that announcement, or pondering whether such duty might cut into his soundings and fishing.

"We would be delighted, sir!" Bury said at last, beginning to display a slow, equally solemn grin. "Ehm . . . might I offer you some refreshments, Captain Lewrie?"

"Lead me to it, sir," Lewrie agreed.

Down the steep ladderway through the square hatch they went, with Bury offering the usual caution to mind the overhead deck beams. His quarters were tiny, almost a cuddy. There was a transom settee beneath the stern sash windows, piled with books, piles of foolscap notes, and a wood-and-twine fishing net. There was an open chest of clothing, a wee desk hooked to the larboard side to serve as his day-cabin, a slung hammock (not a bed-cot) to starboard, and a wee dining table right forward with only six wobbly old collapsible chairs. The rest of the cabin was draped with things hung on pegs. Most of the deck was taken up by wooden tubs made from cut-down kegs. They were full of fish!

"Pardon the mess, sir, but even were I expecting company, there is only so much room," Bury said, going to a wee wine-cabinet for two glasses, then fetching a bottle of hock from out of one of the tubs, where it was slightly cooled in water. "If you will take a seat, ah . . . there, Captain Lewrie," he added, indicating a chair by the dining table. Lewrie sat down, noting that the top of the table bore a few odd, and wet . . . things.

"My viewing devices, sir," Bury explained. "None of them all that effective so far, but one hopes to discover a solution someday."

"Viewing devices?" Lewrie asked, picking one of them up. It was an odd sort of spectacles, with two round glass lenses set into a wood frame, each lens as round-about as a mug, with tarred canvas attached, much like an executioner's hood, with some light line so that it could be bound behind the head and knotted.

"At first, I thought it possible to slip the hood over my head and bind the spectacles snug enough to allow me to float face-down in the water and see the marine life," Lt. Bury slowly explained, "but I found that the salt water still gets into my eyes . . . and the tarred canvas makes it hard to draw a breath whenever I turn my face up to the surface, do you see. Now the other . . ."

This one was a rectangular box with an eight-inch piece of window glass set into it, without the canvas hood. Lewrie picked it up, eying it most dubiously.

"The box frame cannot be bound snug enough to my face to keep out the salt water, either, sir, though when I turn my head, I am able to draw breath," Bury said with a shrug, and a look of disappointment that his inventions had so far not been of much avail. "For now, the bucket with the windowpane in the bottom works best, though after a minute or so, it fills with water and has to be emptied out, else the view is no better than peering down from above the surface, alas."

Christ, who still says 'alas'? Lewrie sourly thought.

"Just no way to tar it waterproof?" Lewrie idly asked, just to see what else Lt. Bury would say; he was an odd bird, indeed! "Maybe an iron or brass coal scuttle would work better."

"Perhaps one might, sir, thank you," Bury said, rising to the suggestion. "Now, the best solution might be to construct a glass ball, much like the one that Alexander the Great was reputed to use to look at the sea-bottom, though my readings of the classic histories shed no light on how to *construct* one."

Bury looked sad that he could not conceive a way, either, as he took a morose sip of his wine.

"Have t'be a big'un," Lewrie commented, "else you run out of enough air."

Is he daft as bats? Lewrie asked himself, half appalled.

"Perhaps a helmet of some kind, that could be strapped under the arm-pits to keep it in place, with soldered and tarred glass panes set into it," Bury enthused a tad, "with a flexible canvas hose led to the surface to renew one's air, sir? I've sketches, but . . ." Bury broke off with a sigh, and took another abstemious sip of his hock.

Must live on his Navy pay, Lewrie thought, after a sip of his own, for the hock was really the usual thin and slightly sour purser's issue white wine, dismissed as "Miss Taylor".

"When you're not . . . studying sea-life," Lewrie posed, "what is *Lizard* up to?"

"We patrol about fifty or so miles offshore, sir," Bury said, "doing circumnavigations of the islands. The brig-sloops, able to be on station longer, usually scout an hundred or more miles beyond our range. Several laps, if you will, before putting back in to victual."

"Sounds dreadful boresome," Lewrie commented.

"Oh, it is, sir," Bury agreed, lighting up in agreement. "We rarely see anything but for vessels bound to or from Bermuda, and with so little trade hereabouts, there's not much to entice French or Spanish attention. And when not patrolling, there are my secondary duties of hydrography—taking soundings, up-dating the old charts, and making new ones from scratch. *Trying* to mark the known channels, but I've run into a lot of op-position to that, sir."

"The local pilots," Lewrie said, nodding in understanding.

"At any rate, I've no funds for such, and my letters to Admiralty go un-answered on that head, sir," Bury said, looking miserable, again. "I've tried using painted empty wine bottles, bound with tarred line to stones for the most hazardous spots, such as the narrows through the White Flats, which you just entered, sir, but . . . damned if they don't dis-appear a day or two later . . . completely."

"I knew officers in the Bahamas who tried to erect buoys and range-line pilings," Lewrie said, chuckling. "Soon as they sailed away, the local wreckers and salvagers tore 'em down, so they could keep their livelihoods."

"Much of the same thing, sir," Lt. Bury sadly agreed.

He seemed completely at ease to sit there and dry out in his wet clothing, with his shins bare. Lewrie pegged Bury as one inch taller than his own five feet nine inches, very slimly and wirily built. With his straw planter's hat set aside, Bury wore his pale blond hair as short as a fellow who feared bugs in his wig, snipped to within a quarter-inch of his scalp. He had a round head, but a long, lean horse face, a prominent upper lip that dwarfed the lower, and a receding, weakish chin. He didn't look like the sort to serve in the Royal Navy; he was more the don or tutorial type, more suited to the library. Could he count on him, Lewrie wondered?

A fish flopped in one of the tubs, drawing their attention.

"They don't live long, poor things," Bury mourned, "and it is a pity, but . . . at least I've been able to dissect them once they pass, and make coloured sketches of their anatomy. I've amassed quite a lot of interior drawings, as well as to-the-life paintings of them as they would appear in the water. Would you like to see some of them, sir?"

Hell, no! Lewrie thought.

"Aye, I would," he lied, instead, steeling himself to display great interest, and cautioning himself not to yawn, or let his eyes glaze over.

"Damme, Mister Bury, they really are remarkable," Lewrie had to admit after a few minutes, though Bury's explanations of what the fish were named, both in local argot, dry scientific Latin classification, and general terms went right past his ears, heard and flown in an instant. "You should get together with my First Officer, Mister Westcott. He's a dab-hand artist, and draughtsman. The two of you could produce good, up-dated charts to send to Admiralty, and copies for our use while here. Have you always been interested in marine life?"

"Since I was a wee lad, sir," Bury shyly confessed. "We lived near Plymouth, close enough to go down to the water and the beaches to fish almost daily. There, and the fish-markets, well . . . I always was curious about what it was like under the sea, and how they lived before being landed."

"You eat 'em, too? You don't feel . . . ?" Lewrie posed.

"A good fish is more toothsome to me than roast beef, sir," Bury said, coming close to laughing in real amusement for the first time. "The crew think my interests, odd, sir, but they eat well as a result. Might I send you over something for your table tonight, sir? Grassy Bay's shallows abound in pompano."

"My cook and I will be delighted, thankee!" Lewrie enthused. He had not had more than two fresh suppers of anything since leaving Portsmouth, and those only in the last two days. Fresh fish had not been among them, and the idea made him salivate.

"So, we shall be off soon, sir?" Bury enquired.

"As soon as dammit," Lewrie told him, "and bound for Nassau in the Bahamas, to beg, borrow, or scrounge up a few more shoal-draught vessels. I'd suppose you must victual, and take on firewood and water at Saint George's, before we can do so?"

"Aye, sir, a few last-minute items," Bury said, almost by rote, gazing off at the middle distance—or his foul-weather tarpaulins on a peg—to muse upon their departure. He then turned to face Lewrie with a quirky expression on his face, and said, " 'And he saith unto them, 'Follow me, and I shall make you fishers of men'. And they straightaway left their nets and followed him'. Matthew four, nineteen and twenty."

"Ah . . . something a *bit* like that, Mister Bury, aye," Lewrie managed to say, wondering what to make of the Biblical quotation, and if it might be blasphemous to be compared to Jesus.

An odd, odd bird, indeed! he thought.

BOOK II

PRIVATEER a veſſel of war, armed and
equipped by particular merchants, and
furniſhed with a military commiſſion by the
admiralty, or the officers who superintend
the marine department of a country, to
cruize againſt the enemy, and take, ſink, or
burn their ſhipping, or otherwiſe annoy
them as opportunity offers. Theſe veſſels
are generally governed on the ſame plan
with his majeſty's ſhips, although they are
guilty of many ſcandalous depredations,
which are very rarely practiſed by the
latter.

-*FALCONER'S MARINE DICTIONARY*
1780 EDITION

CHAPTER THIRTEEN

*R*eliant's First Officer peered upwards at the mast tops to study the winds as the frigate ghosted into West Bay of Nassau Harbour on New Providence, in the Bahamas. Satisfied, he turned to look at his captain and cocked a brow as he said, "You will not hoist your broad pendant, sir?"

"Bugger the broad pendant," Lewrie growled back, though in good humour. "One sloop don't make a squadron," he added, jerking one arm out in the direction of *Lizard,* which preceded them by a full cable.

"It would seem a suitable number to justify *that* fellow's broad pendant, though, sir," Lt. Westcott pointed out, indicating the bit of red bunting which lazily curled to the light winds atop the main mast of an older 64-gun two-decker anchored between Hog Island and the town's main piers. They were close enough for Lewrie to make out, as a faint gust spread the pendant, that the officer allowed to fly it was much like him; it displayed a large white ball, indicating that whomsoever the officer was, he was still a Post-Captain without a Flag-Captain or staff approaching admiral-hood. Further East in East Bay, Lewrie could espy at least two more Royal Navy vessels no bigger than *Lizard.*

"Hmm, seems at least two will suffice, Mister Westcott," Lewrie japed. "Give the man another pair, and he might style himself a Rear-Admiral. If he has twice that number out patrolling the down islands, he might sign his letters as Lord Nelson!"

"Do your orders name him, sir?" Westcott asked.

"No," Lewrie replied, "just 'senior officer present in the Bahamas'. Don't think Admiralty knew just who that was back in January." He shrugged, as if it really didn't matter. "The old'un t'be called home, the new'un not yet appointed? No matter. You may begin to fire the salute to Captain Thing-gummy now, sir, and be ready to round up into the wind and let go the bower, once done."

"Aye aye, sir! Mister Acres . . . begin the salute!"

The new Master Gunner who had replaced old Rahl jutted an arm at the forrud-most 18-pounder's gun-captain, who jerked the lanyard of the flintlock striker, and the first shot of the gun salute boomed out, creating a thick jet of yellow-grey smoke. Mr. Acres paced aft, to all outward appearance mumbling to himself before halting and jutting an arm at the second 18-pounder of the starboard battery for their second saluting shot. Acres was reciting the ancient ritual for timing under his breath; ". . . If I weren't a gunner, I wouldn't be here. I've left my wife, and all that's dear . . . number-two gun, fire! If I weren't a gunner . . ." and on aft, repeating himself 'til thirteen guns for a Post-Captain with broad pendant had been delivered.

"Lee helm, and flat her a'back, Mister Westcott," Lewrie ordered. "Four-to-one scope on the cable should suit."

Right in the middle of coasting to a stop, letting go the anchor, and the lowering of jibs and stays'ls, the clewing and brailing up of the squares'ls, Mr. Eldridge, their newest Midshipman, announced the appearance of a signal hoist which had soared aloft on the two-decker. It was "Captain Repair on Board".

"Impatient sort, ain't he, Mister Eldridge?" Lewrie said as he settled the fit of his waist-coat and shirt cuffs. "Cox'n Desmond? My gig, d'ye please."

"Aye aye, sor!"

The gig was led round from towing astern and his long-time Cox'n, Liam Desmond, "stroke oar" Patrick Furfy, and the other hands of his boat crew quickly went down the battens to take their places with oars held vertically aloft. Lewrie made his own, slower way down to step from the main-mast channel to the gunn'l of the gig, then quickly staggered in-board and took a seat aft. "Make for the flag, Desmond."

"Aye, sor. Ship oars, starb'd . . . shove off, forrud. Make way, starboard. Ship oars, larboard . . . and, stroke t'gither!"

"Natty-lookin' t'day, sor," Furfy dared comment. For this occasion, Lewrie had donned his best-dress uniform, and had included the sash and star of the Order of the Bath, as well as his medals for the battles of Cape St. Vincent and Camperdown, for a rare once. He had yet to accept the fact that he had been knighted by the King the past year. Lewrie knew he'd *earned* the medals, but still suspected that he had been knighted and made Baronet in sympathy for his wife's murder by the French in 1802, and the outrage and increased patriotism which her death had engendered, and not for his part in the brief but conclusive squadron-to-squadron action off the Chandeleur Islands of Louisiana in late 1803. To be called "Sir Alan" or "My Lord" made him squirm in embarassment!

"Stuff and nonsense, Furfy," Lewrie told the fellow, bestowing a brief grin and shrug.

Damme, that diplomatic shit in my orders. Lewrie thought; *All up and down the American coast, I'll have t'wear all this flummery! Show the flag . . . show* me*! Gawd!*

He turned to look aft over Desmond's shoulder to see if *Reliant* was safely anchored, and if her sails were finally brailed up and put in harbour gaskets, that the yards were tidily level and not "a 'cock-bill'" and disorderly. When he turned back to look forward, his gig was passing under the high jib-boom and bow-sprit of the two-decker, bound for her starboard entry-port, and almost close enough to touch. The 64-gunner's figurehead was a ubiquitous crowned lion, giving not a clue to her name; at least it was brightly gilded, revealing a bit about her captain's attention to detail, and his relative wealth. Gilt work came from a captain's pocket; the Admiralty wouldn't pay for such!

"Stroke, larboard . . . backwater, starboard," Desmond snapped as he put the tiller hard over to swing the gig about almost in her own length before calling for a few strokes of both banks together, just enough to glide her to the main channel and battens. "Toss yer oars! Hook on, forrud!" and the rowers hoisted their oars from the tholes.

Using mens' shoulders for bracing, Lewrie went to amidships of the gig, stood teetering on the gunn'l for a second, then stepped onto the chain platform to swing to the battens and man-ropes. He tucked his hundred-guinea presentation sword behind his left leg and climbed up quickly. As the dog's vane of his cocked hat peeked over the lip of the entry-port, the Bosuns' silver calls began to *fweep* a salute. And, once in-board on the starboard sail-tending gangway, there were Marines in full kit and sailors in shoregoing rig presenting arms.

"Welcome aboard *Mersey*, sir," a Lieutenant with a plummy and top-lofty Oxonian drawl said in welcome, his bicorne fore-and-aft hat doffed.

"Captain Alan Lewrie, of the *Reliant* frigate, sir," he replied, introducing himself even as he doffed his own hat.

"Sir Alan, sir. Lieutenant Hubbard, your servant, sir," the fellow said. "Second officer into *Mersey*. Captain Forrester is aft in his cabins. If you will come this way, sir?"

"Francis Forrester?" Lewrie gawped. "'The Honourable' Francis Forrester, is he?"

"He is indeed, Sir Alan," Lt. Hubbard told him. "Do you already have the honour of his acquaintance, sir?"

Christ, that *pig-faced bastard!* Lewrie thought.

"Served together, long ago," Lewrie said, leaving it at that.

He'd come down with the Yellow Jack and had been put ashore, to most-like die, from the *Parrot* schooner, had spent some time on staff to Rear-Admiral Sir Onsley Matthews at Antigua, then had finally won a sea-going berth aboard the HMS *Desperate* under that daft lunatick, Commander Tobias Treghues. Francis Forrester had been cater-cousin and "pet" to Treghues, and had made life for the rest of *Desperate*'s Mids a pluperfect Hell. Forrester back during the American Revolution had been a fubsy, crusty, *round* young fellow, and an arrogant, sneering pig to boot. Lewrie and the other Mids had once gotten some of their own back by obtaining some royal blue lead paint and had given Forrester a goatee, a fat and curling mustachio, and blue cheekbones as he slept, snoring like a stoat. Treghues had been outraged, and, being good paint, after drying in the overnight hours, it had not come off for weeks, no matter what Forrester used to scrub at it!

I read in Steeles that he'd been made Post, Lewrie told himself as they went aft; *but I never expected t'see him in the flesh . . . of which he had* very *much . . . the rest o' this* life!

Lt. Hubbard spoke in the Marine sentry's ear. The Marine private jerked his head in a short nod, then stamped boots, slammed the butt of his musket on the deck and bawled "Cap'm Sir Alan Lewrie, SAH!"

Music to Lewrie's ears, it was, for instead of the usual calm return cry of "Come!" or "Enter!" from within the great-cabins, there could be heard a startled "Wha'?", a long pause, *then* an "Enter!"

Lt. Hubbard slightly raised one brow in surpise, then opened the door for Lewrie to step through. He ducked his head to avoid the overhead deck beams, then made his way aft past the dining coach, the chart space, into the spacious day-cabin.

Lives well, Francis does, Lewrie thought as he took in all the finery. Captain Forrester's furniture was exquisitely made and shining with bees-wax polish, and there was a faint tinge of lemon oil as if freshly buffed that morning. The black-and-white painted canvas deck chequer looked spanking new, where one could see it past the edges of several colourful, and expensive, Turkey or Axminster carpets. All the settee area furniture was of gleaming cherry wood, upholstered in dark brown leather; collaps-ible and stowable at short notice, certainly, but looked more substantial than most sea-going pieces. All the interior bulkheads above the wain-scotting were painted in a soothing mint green, with mouldings added in cream and gilt. There were satiny drapes for the windows in the transom in a cream colour, pale green cushions and contrasting throw pillows for the transom settee, and a satiny coverlet for Forrester's hanging bed-cot, and the flimsy deal and canvas collapsible partitions were done in that mint green, with white louvred shutters in the upper halves.

Forrester himself sat behind a long and wide day-cabin desk of cherry, one that rested on X-shaped folding frames, with lots of well-polished brass accents. Forrester, well . . .

By God, we once said he was battenin' like a hog ready for the fall slaugh-ter, Lewrie gleefully thought; *and damned if he ain't gone fubsier since!*

Captain Francis Forrester's uniform was elegantly tailored, of the fin-est broadcloth wool for the coat and waist-coat, of the finest and softest cotton denim sailcloth for the breeches, and the whitest cotton or linen for his shirt, but . . . he did put a strain on it!

Lewrie walked up to the desk, hat under his left arm, and gave For-rester a nod. "Francis. It's been a long time. How d'ye keep?" Captain Forrester did not at once reply; he seemed dumbstruck, as if pole-axed like a beef cow. His face looked flush, and his cheekbones were even redder . . . putting Lewrie into a fond, blue-tinged, memory. Forrester's eyes were glued to the medals, the bright blue silk sash, and the gleaming star on Lewrie's chest. At last he looked up, with a faint scowl blossoming,

"Captain Lewrie," he gravelled. "You are come as re-enforcement to my squadron?" Forrester asked.

"Sorry, no," Lewrie replied with a grin. "In point of fact, I am come to borrow a few small sloops from you, so I may break out my own broad pendant."

"The Devil you say!" Forrester snapped, turning tetchy. "Come for some of *my* warships?"

"Only a couple or three," Lewrie said, trying to sound assuring. He reached into the breast pocket of his uniform coat and drew out the orders. "This is addressed to the Senior Officer Present in the Bahamas . . . perhaps your appointment here was only a few days after? If you give it a looking over, you'll see what Admiralty intends. I'm to put together a small group of shoal-draught vessels able to go close inshore, poke into inlets, bays and rivers in Spanish Florida, to hunt down French and Spanish privateers."

"The suppression of privateers is properly *my* duty, Lewrie!" Forrester snapped, turning a tad redder in the face, if such was possible. "Florida is not an hundred miles West of here, and the vessels of *my* squadron, few as they already are, have their hands full patrolling the Florida Straits, not to mention making regular rounds of the whole of the Bahamas, down to the Turks and Caicos, and the Inagua Islands . . . protecting the salt trade. Why . . . these orders are impossible to fulfill! I've nothing to spare! Not even that little sloop that just came in."

"Uhm, the *Lizard* sloop is with *me*, actually," Lewrie told him, striving for a mild tone, and chiding himself not to gloat. "I drug him off from Bermuda, where he, Lieutenant Bury, *was* the senior officer present at the moment."

And damn yer bloody eyes, but are ye ever going t'offer me a seat, or a glass o' somethin'? Lewrie inwardly fumed.

"Good God!" Forrester spat, like to shake himself to wake from a *very* bad dream. He looked as miserable as a hanged spaniel.

"If you'll look over the orders, sir," Lewrie prompted, holding them out once more. "And, might I sit down, sir?"

"How remiss of me," Forrester said, dead-level in his tone of voice, for it was nowhere near a sociable apology. "Do, sir, sit." He looked over at one of entourage of cabin servants and snapped his fingers. "Some hock?"

"Most welcome, sir," Lewrie agreed. Reminding Forrester that his Post-Captaincy predated Lewrie's, and that he was higher up the Navy List, *seemed* to mollify him . . . somewhat.

The wine arrived whilst Forrester continued to read the orders over, several times, it seemed, his piggy eyes darting and squinting as if in pain. The cabin servant was tricked out in immaculate white shirt and slop-trousers, wore a black neck-stock round his collars, and white gloves, nigh as grand as a waiter in a London chop house! The bottle stood in a shiny pewter bucket, dripping water as it was removed, and Lewrie definitely heard the sound of ice chunks as the steward did so. Aye, the wine *was* iced!

"Yankee Doodles," Forrester disparagingly commented. "Come to buy salt, and sell lumber and New England winter ice. Pity, for this lot may be the last 'til next November or December."

"Yes, I recall the ice-houses of Nassau," Lewrie replied, "and how hard it is t'pick all the straw and sawdust off before you could use it in a cold punch. Had the *Alacrity* sloop in the Bahamas, from '86 to '89. Ketch-rigged sloop, once a bomb vessel, really, but it was fine duty in those days."

"The Bahamas?" Forrester scoffed, looking up with the orders in one hand and a wine glass in the other. "Well, perhaps you would appreciate it, but I find the islands a dreary, boresome place, lacking the basic rudiments of proper civilisation. Barely a cut above a Cornish fishing village. Or a smuggler's inlet," he added.

"Best place t'shop for the rudiments of civilised life, the smugglers' dens," Lewrie japed. "Like 'Calico' Jack Finney's emporium that used t'be on Bay Street."

"Yes, I heard of him," Forrester said.

"I'm the one who chased him to Charleston, South Carolina, and killed him," Lewrie told Forrester with a tight little grin.

And what've you done since we were Mids t'gether? Lewrie asked himself; *All 'claret, cruisin', and bum-kissin'?*

"Ahem! As I said, Lewrie, this request from Admiralty is just impossible for me to fulfill," Forrester, fussily announced, re-directing the conversation. "I've but two brig-sloops on station, and eight small sloops.

Given the fact that Spain has been an enemy since the first of the year, I cannot spare a one. Their colonies in Florida and Cuba, just South of here on Hispaniola, on Puerto Rico? The risk of invasion is too high to despatch even the smallest to you.

"Hmmm . . ." Forrester pondered, a sly smile blossoming on his face. "Given that threat, it might make more sense did you and your frigate come under *my* command. Then, when I may spare you, you may prowl round Florida to your heart's content. The presence of a two-decker sixty-four, and a Fifth Rate frigate would surely give ambitious Dons pause, hey?"

"Hmm," Lewrie replied in kind, taking his own sweet time with his wine glass, as if really considering the proposal. "Actually, I fancy that our ships at Antigua, Barbados, Trinidad, and Jamaica are keeping the Dons awake at night, so the risk of invasion from Spain is negligible, sir. The *Spanish* are at more risk.

"Secondly," Lewrie drolly went on, quite enjoying himself, "Admiralty did not *request,* but *ordered* you to supply me with a few shoal-draught sloops or cutters. Thirdly . . . ," Lewrie said, pausing to let that sink in, "a refusal on your part would hamper the fulfillment of *my* original orders. And, lastly . . ."

Stick it up his bum-hole, yes! Lewrie thought, feeling like he could barely keep from chortling out loud, and delighting in the puce colour of Forrester's full face; *Here it comes, ye gotch-gut!*

"Lastly, am I shackled to the Bahamas under your command, I'd not be able to execute the rest of my duties of surveying Bermudan waters, or calling upon our consuls in neutral American ports to see if enemy privateers may be operating from them covertly."

"As I recall, you were made 'Post' in the spring of ninety-seven, whilst I . . ." Forrester shot back, eyes as lidded as a cobra.

"That don't signify," Lewrie quickly dismissed with a wave of one hand. "I've 'independent orders' to form a punitive squadron and root out privateers . . . from Admiralty, sir."

"I will consider your requ — the matter, Captain Lewrie," Forrester sputtered, as "sulled up" as a bullfrog, "and will send you my decision by letter . . . when I've completed my deliberations upon it."

"Oh, when you do," Lewrie quickly rejoined, "ye might add Baronet t'the heading." Well . . . I shall take my leave," he added, finishing his wine, and rising.

He *knew* that would gall the man even worse! Francis Forrester was an "Honourable", but so were all his brothers and sisters as sons or daughters of a baron or viscount, and he was not the eldest son due to inherit . . . else he'd not have gone to sea in the first place, and made a *career* of the Navy!

"Good day to you, Captain Lewrie," Forrester was forced to say, *not* rising from his seat behind his grand desk, and *not* offering his hand, most un-graciously and sulkily.

"Good day to you, yer servant, sir," Lewrie replied, making a sketchy, polite bow from the waist before departing.

Damn my eyes, but maybe bein' a Knight and Baronet comes in handy, *now and again!* Lewrie told himself as he gained the deck and the open air.

CHAPTER FOURTEEN

*L*ewrie was back aboard *Reliant* just long enough to remove the sash and star, warn his cook, Yeovill, that he'd take his dinner on shore, and ordered the Purser, Mr. Cadbury, to take a ship's boat to seek out fresh victuals. Then, he was off in a whistled-up bum-boat for the docks of Nassau.

Captain Francis Forrester might not care for New Providence Island, or the Bahamas, but Lewrie still liked it . . . somewhat. Nassau *was* a raw and rowdy place, sleepier than grander ports he'd visited, and might lack the refinements of the symphonies, opera houses, or theatrical halls of London, and yes, its miniscule attempts at Cultured Society might be provincial and "chaw-bacon", but Nassau had a bustle to it. The shoreside streets teemed with push-carts and waggons and vendors. The piers were lined with merchant ships, and thronged with stevedores landing and carting off cargoes, or lading exports. Lewrie found a Free Black with a push-cart from which he sold ginger beer by the pint and half-pint, right off, and savoured the sweetness and the sprightliness, along with the sharp bite of the ginger.

And there was the chop-house where he and Caroline had dined so many years ago, where he'd first met his friend and fellow officer, Benjamin

Rodgers. Where they had politely declined the clumsy invitations of "Calico" Jack Finney, the rag-seller turned privateer, then local hero, then rich entrepeneur, and secretly, pirate. He popped into its coolness and dined on jerked pork and crisp-fried, breaded grouper, with white wine and a fresh salad, finished with the very same key-lime pudding he'd relished in his early days.

On a tour of remembrance, he later idly strolled Bay Street, noting the new houses and stores that had sprung up over the years. Where he'd first "bearded" Finney, in his massive, sprawling emporium, nigh a whole corner block once, with all the various shops opened to each other and to the streets through grand doorways, Lewrie found it changed, the interior pass-throughs now walled back up and divided into at least a dozen new concerns.

He made a courtesy call on the island governor at Government House, spent about twenty minutes there, then made his way back East towards the piers, beyond Fort Fincastle that loomed above them, and, on a sudden whim, hitched a ride on a passing empty waggon further to the East out towards Fort Montagu, on East Bay Street.

He alit by the gate house to the old Boudreau plantation that had been his and Caroline's shore residence once. And, from the first moment, he was sorry that he'd come. It had had a tight cedar shingle roof once, but that had gone to seed, and was littered with reddish-tan detritus blown off the many pines and palmettos. Their little cottage had been an ambitious stab at grandeur, an un-needed stables or overseer's cottage, all of stone or coral "tabby". There had been the main section with two bedrooms, a parlour, and space for dining to one side, then a breezeway— Caroline had called it a "dog run", he sorrowfully recalled—separating the main house from the smaller kitchen, pantries, and storerooms, the bathing facility, and "jakes". His late wife had had the exterior painted a startling but cool mint green whilst he had been away on his first patrol down the island chain to the Turks and Caicos; his teasing about the colour had lit their first real argument!

Now, though . . . it had been painted and re-painted, then neglected for so long that it was hard to choose which pastel colour it was now. The deep front and back porches, and the dog-run breezeway held rickety tables and mis-matched chairs, occupied by off-duty soldiers from Fort Montagu, jaded doxies, and scruffy, ill-clad civilian topers, all of whom peered cutty-eyed at him, or found the presence of a naval officer amusing.

He looked past their old house up the drive towards the manse that had once been a sedate and solid home; even if it had been painted the colour of boiled shrimp with glaring white trim. It, and the rental houses, the wood "salt boxes" that the Boudreaus had run up had gone to seed as badly as the gate house, the wooden houses reduced to greying, weathered, tumbledown shacks.

The Boudreaus had refugeed from Charleston, South Carolina, at the end of the American Revolution, Low Country planters and grandees who'd upheld the Loyalist cause. Like so many "Torys" who had fled to the Bahamas, the West Indies, or Canada, they had faced sudden poverty, and the wrenching shock that if they *could* afford to purchase land, or slaves with which to work it, the island colonies could not support them for long. The sandy "white lands" were only good for truck gardening, and the richer "red lands" further inland were deceptive. Without livestock and their manure, the "red lands" gave out after two or three good crops; and Nassau could never have the grazing land large enough to support livestock herds.

The Boudreaus had quickly given up the idea of a plantation and had gone into housing, supporting themselves at a modicum of their old lifestyle from rents and the running-up of modest lodgings. They had stayed in the Bahamas, whilst so many others, heartbroken, fled.

Warily, Lewrie went to the front porch of his old home and ordered a pint of ale. "Have you ever heard of the Boudreau family?" he asked the tapster, who looked very much like a retired pirate.

"The who, Cap'm?"

"They owned all this, once," Lewrie said. "I rented from them, my wife and I, back in the eighties."

"Ye lived up there, ye did?" the old fellow marvelled.

"No. Here, This was our rented house. The Boudreaus lived in the house, yonder." Lewrie corrected him. He took a peek inside the tavern, and was sorry that he did. The gleaming white woodwork, the pale tan-painted walls, had gone as scabrous as a basement dive in the worst London stew.

"Never 'eard of 'em, Cap'm. 'Tis a boardin' house now, when it ain't a whorehouse, hee hee. Th' doxies board there, an' all th' soldiers foller," the tapster supplied with goodly mirth.

"Ah, well. Ye go away a few years, they'll change things all round," Lewrie sighed, with a sad, philosophical shrug. He finished his ale, then

went back to the road; he'd seen enough. He was certain that the Boudreaus were both dead and gone by now, and as French-born Huguenots—
French Protestants turned Church of England—their graves could be
found in some parish's churchyard, but . . . he felt by then a dispiriting
langour, and a desire to be away.

To make matters worse, it was a long, warm walk back to town and
the docks, and no wheeled traffic from which to hitch a ride. By the time
he was there, he needed another ale to quench his thirst and cool him off.
He took a seat on a covered porch off the side of the public house, fanned
himself with his hat for a while, and looked at the harbour and up Bay
Street. The flowers, the flowering vines and bushes, and all the planters
all about him! How could he have forgotten? Once more, he felt a pang,
recalling how scrofulous and weedy the grounds about the old gate house
and mansion were.

With help from Mrs. Boudreau and her old Black gardener, Caroline
had created a new Eden, nigh a jungle! Their house had been awash in
greenery, and blossoms of the most vivid and exotic colours. There had
been tamarinds and flowering acacia, Tree-of-Life bush, cascarilla and
red jasmine, bright yellow elder and bougainvillea vines growing up the
trellises, poinsettias and poincianas, angel trumpets and flamingo flowers, graceful bird of paradise, and Jump-Up-and-Kiss-Mes in planter
pots and beds. To screen their front gallery from the road, and the rear
gallery from the main house, they had had palmettos, sapodillas, sour-
sops, and guava saplings, and their own lemon or key-lime trees, their
candlewoods and sea grapes, and Caroline had been so *very* proud of her
fragrant and colourful handiwork!

Ghostlike, there was a shift in the breeze that brought scents of flowers
from the nearby gardens, as sweet and intoxicating as the sunset breezes
off Potter's Cay and Hog Island had come to their old house so long ago,
forcing Lewrie to recall the sweetness, the contentment, and lazy satisfaction of sitting with a young wife at the tail-ends of tropic days, and he
had to squint and grimace in pain. To cover his public un-manning, he
pulled a handkerchief out to dab at his eyes before even slight tears of
grief came.

Thought I was beyond all that, he chid himself.

He finished his ale quickly, for he really needed to be back aboard his
frigate, in the privacy of his great-cabins . . . where he could hide for a
while.

CHAPTER FIFTEEN

To Captain Sir Alan Lewrie, Bart.
Aboard the Reliant *frigate*
Sir;
After giving the matter due Consideration, and pursuant to Admiralty
Orders received from your hand, I deem myself able to second to you
only two Vessels, to wit; the hermaphrodite brig Thorn *(12), Lieu-*
tenant Darling, and the sloop Firefly *(8), Lieutenant Lovett, now*
lying at anchor in East Bay. Orders to the officers commanding in re-
gards to their Transfer to your flag are issued, and . . .

"Take those two and get the Hell out o' my sight, hey?" Lewrie chortled as he read the letter. "The sooner we're gone, the better Forrester'll
sleep!"

Of course, Forrester made that conditional, referring to the transfer of
the two ships dependent upon whether the Spanish threatened the Bahamas or Turks and Caicos and he needed them back, further claiming that
if such occurred Lewrie would simply have to ignore his original orders
and place *Reliant* under Forrester's command, and if he, Lewrie, stepped

into the "quag" up to his neck over in Florida waters and found himself over-matched by the Spanish, he'd best place himself under Forrester to, in essence, pull his chestnuts out of the fire!

"I take it that your early days with this fellow were not all that jolly, sir?" Lt. Westcott asked once Lewrie had read the orders aloud to him.

"Forrester and the *Desperate*, and Commander Treghues . . . ah, what *splendid* memories!" Lewrie said, the sarcasm dripping. "Well, it's of no matter, Mister Westcott. We've a squadron. Don't know what *sort*, yet, but it's a start."

"I asked about when I was ashore yesterday, sir," Lt. Westcott told him with a sly look. "People in the taverns, civilians and Navy sorts alike, say that Captain Forrester's *Mersey* has been at anchor so long, she's not aground on beef and pork bones, but he'd have to send people overside to chip her off the coral reef that's built up under her keel!"

"If he don't much care for Nassau or its lacks, ye'd think he'd at least put to sea and sail round the islands," Lewrie supposed, as he tossed the letter atop his desk. "But that might take him too far off from his fresh tucker. Hmm . . . while you were ashore, you didn't pick up anything about *Thorn* and *Firefly*, or their commanding officers, did you, Mister Westcott?"

"No sir, sorry," Westcott told him with a shrug. "Didn't know we'd be getting them, so . . ."

"Oh, well. I s'pose I should go call upon Lieutenants Darling and Lovett and introduce myself . . . before Forrester changes his mind and snatches 'em back," Lewrie said with a short laugh. "You see to an hour's drill on the great guns, then the rest of the Forenoon with cutlasses and boarding pikes, and I should be back aboard by the start of the rum issue."

"Very good, sir," Westcott replied, preparing to rise and leave the great-cabins. "Uhm . . . not *live* firing, sir?" he japed.

"And wake all of Nassau's drunks? Lord no, sir!"

Lewrie had himself rowed over to HMS *Thorn*, first, assuming that a 12-gun ship would rate the senior of the two. As his gig came to a stop under her boarding battens, he could see that *Thorn* was alert and ready to greet him with the proper side-party. He had served in a schooner, a ketch, then three-masted ships, but never aboard an hermaphrodite brig, which was neither a real brig-rigged vessel, nor the usual fore-and-aft-rigged schooner or cutter, but a bit of both.

"Welcome aboard, sir," her "captain" said once the salutes and the Bosun's calls were done. "Lieutenant Peter Darling, sir, commanding. My First Officer . . . the only'un, really . . . Lieutenant Child . . ."

"Your servant, sir," Lt. Child said, doffing his hat once more.

"Alan Lewrie, sir . . . Mister Child," Lewrie said, naming himself. "You've received Captain Forrester's orders, transferring you and your ship to my squadron?"

"I have, sir," Darling replied. "Might I ask if our transfer may involve some special duty?"

"You may, and I will gladly reveal all to you over supper this evening, say . . . half past six?" Lewrie offered. "Ye never can tell who might blab in the meantime if allowed ashore. Nassau's bung-full of un-trustworthy people, so I'd feel more confident did your people see to last-minute victualling if they don't know much right now."

"I see, sir," Darling said, looking a bit happier that his new duties might bode of some mystery, and the prospect of action.

"Tell me a bit about your ship, sir," Lewrie said, "and give me a brief tour, if you would."

"Gladly, sir!" Darling said, leading the way forward. "*Thorn* was Spanish, a merchant ship taken as prize off Mayaguana just after we learned of our declaration of war against Spain. The previous officer on station decided that she'd make a useful cruiser. We think she was built by an American yard, for the split rig's rare back in Europe, so far. Quite handy, though, sir, on almost every point of sail."

And how'd you find favour enough t'have her? Lewrie wondered, suspecting that Darling might be one of Forrester's *protégés,* pets, or catercousins. They certainly resembled each other. Lt. Darling was two inches shorter than Lewrie's five feet nine, but outweighed him by at least two stone. Lt. Darling had a round, cherubic face, a stout upper body, and short bandy legs; he had an odd, scissory strut when he walked about his decks.

Lewrie looked aloft at *Thorn*'s masts. Her foremast was rigged with course, tops'l, royal and t'gallant yards, *and* a large pair of gaff booms so she could set a fore-and-aft lugs'l behind that mast, or hoist a very large main topmast stays'l in its place, depending upon whether she was working to weather, or sailing large off-wind. Her main mast, aft, featured a very large spanker, the equivalent of a schooner's main sail, but had no yards crossed above.

"You've carronades?" Lewrie asked, noting the short, stubby guns mounted on slides ranged down either beam of her deck.

"We've two six-pounders for bow chasers, but twelve eighteen-pounder carronades, sir," Lt. Darling said with a wry *moue*. "It will be quite the shock to anyone our size who closes with us and offers us a fight, sir," he hopefully declared.

"Unless he has nine-pounder long guns, hangs back and shoots you to pieces," Lewrie dryly replied, pulling at an earlobe.

Carronades were much lighter than long guns of the same calibre, required smaller gun crews to man them, and threw much heavier shot . . . unfortunately, not all that far; anything over three hundred yards was iffy.

If he's one o' Forrester's pets, he didn't get all that much of a plum command, Lewrie thought; *Still, beggars can't be choosers, and she might've been the best Forrester could offer him.*

"You came off *Mersey*?" Lewrie asked, trying to make that sound mere idle curiosity.

"Oh *no*, sir," Lt. Darling countered. "I was Fifth Lieutenant aboard our previous senior officer's two-decker sixty-four, *Aquila*. Mister Child was her senior Midshipman, and we scrounged up a brace of lads off other ships for *our* Mids."

Lewrie took late note of the presence of two young Midshipmen; that meant that *Thorn* had at least one hundred crew altogether; one Mid for each fifty hands was the norm.

"What's your draught, Mister Darling?" Lewrie asked.

"We draw ten feet, sir," Darling said, looking as if he hoped that would be useful. "She'll go very close inshore, if needed."

"That'll be most satisfactory, sir," Lewrie told him, smiling with delight at that news. His smile engendered one upon Darling's face, too. "She handles well?"

"Quite well, sir," Lt. Darling proudly said. "Under fore-and-aft sails, with stays'l and jibs only, she'll go about quick as one can say 'Jack Ketch', and she's tolerably fast, to boot."

Lewrie put his hands in the small of his back and went stoic and silent for a moment, taking in *Thorn*'s material condition, as if judging her. In reality, he was counting up supper guests:

Me, the Sailing Master, Mister Westcott, Bury, Darling and his First Officer, that Lovett fellow yonder on Firefly, *that makes seven,* Lewrie tallied up; *Whoops, there's* Lizard's *other Lieutenant, Rainey, that'll make eight. I'll place him or Child at the foot, "below the salt".* Somebody *junior's got t'give the King's toast!*

"I'd admire did you and Lieutenant Child both dine with me this evening, Mister Darling," Lewrie said, as if coming up from the depths of a serious musing.

"Delighted to accept, sir!"

Lt. Oliver Lovett's HMS *Firefly* would be the smallest of their squadron. *Thorn* was about ninety feet on the range of her deck, *Lizard* about eighty-five, whilst *Firefly* barely managed to attain seventy feet. She was fore-and-aft rigged, with only one crossed yard on each upper mast to spread square sails. Her armament was made up of eight old 6-pounders, with only 2-pounder swivel guns on stanchion brackets for bow or stern chase guns. Unlike *Thorn* or *Lizard,* which had a Commission Officer to assist their captains, Lt. Lovett had only one Midshipman, and was his own sailing master or purser. None of them rated a Marine complement, either, and all had but two small ship's boats, a gig and a jolly boat each. That would have to be rectified, somehow, Lewrie determined, if they came across a privateer encampment, though he did not know how to whistle up suitable boats at short notice, right off. He could not afford them out of his own purse, might spend years explaining issuing Admiralty chits, and doubted if Forrester would allow them a spare bailing bucket. Could he *steal* some, he wondered?

Lt. Oliver Lovett was another "odd bird", though nowhere near as solemn as Lt. Bury. Lovett was an inch taller than Lewrie, slimly built, but leanly muscular. He had a large "beak", as big and cranked as a Cornishman, dark brown hair that he wore long and curly on both sides of his head, in an un-manageable mop over his forehead, with the "surplus" bound at the nape of his neck in an old-time sailor's queue as thick as the tail of a border collie. When Lewrie went aboard, Lt. Lovett was dressed in stained breeches, Hessian boots, and a weather-tanned linen shirt with the collar open and the sleeves rolled up to his elbows. Give him a waist sash and an eyepatch, and Lovett could do a fair impersonation of a pirate; the young fellow nigh-vibrated with pent up, and boundless, energy.

"Bless you, Captain Lewrie, sir, for you bring deliverance from utter drudgery!" Lovett loudly exclaimed, with such eagerness that he seemed impatient that they would not be off, instanter. He would also be delighted to be dined aboard *Reliant* this evening, though he did make apologies for how shabby his turn-out might appear, and hoped he would not disappoint.

"It's more a working supper, nothing grand, Mister Lovett," Lewrie assured him. "Come alongside a bit before half past six."

After a quick tour of *Firefly,* Lewrie had himself rowed back cross the roadstead to the deeper anchorages in the West Bay, and his mid-day meal, feeling quite satisfied, so far. He had two vessels of ten-foot draught, and one, *Firefly,* that only drew nine, all of them able to prowl quite close inshore, or into the many inlets and rivers too shallow for his frigate. He had a slew of 6-pounder guns available, did they operate together, and even if *Thorn*'s carronades could not reach out very far, or aid in the bombardment of privateers' shore camps, when put up against the light wales of a privateer at the usual range, Lt. Darling and his stubby guns could shoot clean through them!

Lewrie turned his attention back to his oarsmen, instead of musing on the shore, and noted that they seemed . . . antsy, constantly looking over their shoulders towards *Reliant.*

"Anything wrong, lads?" he asked.

"Oh, no sir!" one replied.

"Well . . ." Patrick Furfy carefully spoke up. "If ye wouldn't moind, sor, might ye be tellin' us th' time?"

Lewrie pulled his watch from his pocket and opened it, grinning as he twigged to their concern. "It's twenty minutes past eleven . . . and I do believe we'll all be back aboard in time for 'Clear Decks and Up Spirits'. If we get a goodly way on, that is."

"Hear the Cap'm, lads?" his Cox'n, Liam Desmond, snapped. "Git a way on, ye lummoxes. Set a hot stroke, Pat."

"Pull!" Furfy cried, digging in with his oar. "And . . . pull!"

All in all, a good morning's work, Lewrie happily told himself.

CHAPTER SIXTEEN

*W*ith his cook's, Yeovill's, help Lewrie aimed to make the supper a succulent and filling affair to introduce his new subordinates to each other, and to himself. Though the various courses were toothsome, he had promised a working supper, so, over the spicy shredded chicken broth soup, the grilled shrimp and vegetable medley, the mid-meal vinaigrette salad, and the requisite roast beef, roast potatoes, and peas, he quizzed them on their backgrounds and past experiences. Darling was the most loquacious and amusing, Lovett gruffer and more modest, and Bury the most enigmatic, but Lewrie was secretly satisfied that all three younger men had come up from the orlop cockpit at slow paces with years as Mids or Passed Mids before gaining their Lieutenancies. Both of the Lieutenants off *Thorn* and *Lizard*, Child and Rainey, mostly kept proper and deferent silence, much like Midshipmen allowed to dine aft with their superiors; though they did tuck the victuals in heartily, and knew enough to laugh or smile when past merriment was mentioned.

"Clear for the sweets, sir?" Yeovill asked, taking note of the empty plates and crossed tableware. "'Tis a key-lime jumble, though I fear the meringue's a failure." Yeovill gave Pettus and Jessop the nod to begin serving the light white wine to accompany dessert.

"Thankee, Yeovill, aye," Lewrie agreed, dabbing at the corners of his mouth with a napkin. "Now we've come t'know a bit about each other, gentlemen, I think it's time to fill you in on what we're to do together. One hopes ye'll find it more exciting than patrolling the Bahamas."

"Anything would be, sir," Lt. Lovett exclaimed.

"Come across many French or Spanish privateers among the islands, do you?" Lewrie asked.

"Uhm, hardly any, sir," Lt. Darling said, "for there's not all that much to prey upon, with the bulk of the shipping American or neutral."

"Not much in the way of really valuable cargoes, either, sir," Lovett added.

"There's not much prize-money in hunting privateers, but somebody's got t'do it," Lewrie said, after a sip of his wine. "Head or Gun Money on crew and armament, and perhaps, if a vessel's big enough and in good shape, she *might* be bought in after surveying, to do the sort of duties *you're* performing, but . . . there's little profit in it. Which explains why our Navy doesn't put much effort into chasing them," Lewrie said with a faint grimace.

"More glory in close broadsides, frigate to frigate," Lt. Bury almost gloomily agreed with a slow nod.

"Why even stir out of, port, if there's not fame in the offing?" Lt. Darling cynically asked, and Lewrie noted the secret grins shared between Darling and Lovett, and their junior officers.

Can't *abide Forrester either, can you?* Lewrie thought; *It's no wonder!*

"Unless one guards something precious?" Lewrie posed, tongue-in-cheek. "Protection being the greater duty than seeking battle, and letting the foe come to you?"

Lt. Lovett could not hide a wry snicker.

"Yayss, one never can tell when a mighty Spanish armada comes up over the horizon," Lewrie derisively said, dismissive of Forrester's dread of invasion. "But, perhaps do we go nip at the invaders' heels, stir up a spot o' bother, the Spanish'd be too busy with us to try it on. Mister Caldwell, you've brought the chart I requested?"

"I did, sir," his Sailing Master said.

"Then, soon as we've had seconds of this marvellous jumble, we will spread it on the table top and get down to business," Lewrie said with a grin.

⚓

They had to stand to gather round the dining table and the sea-chart, taking their sweet biscuits and shelled nuts from bowls on the sideboard, and passing the port bottle hand-to-hand for top-ups in a larboardly direction.

"Do we sail directly from Nassau to Spanish Florida, past the Berry Islands and Bimini, it's good odds the Gulf Stream'd sweep all of us as far North as Saint Augustine," Lewrie sketched out, using a dessert fork for a pointer. "Better we head South, down the Tongue of the Ocean past Andros, and prowl our way down close to Cuba to see what we can see, before heading West up the Old Bahama Channel, into the Florida Straits, where our large trade convoys pass."

"Ehm, where Spanish merchantmen pass, too, I've heard, sir," Lt. Lovett stuck in with a wolfish, expectant look. "Then, do we just happen to come across one . . . ?"

"I'd think that Spanish trade would've dried up," Lewrie said with a frown. "We shall keep our eyes on the main chance, of course, Mister Lovett, but the reason we'll be going the long way round is so we may scout the Florida Keys," he went on, tapping the tines of the fork on the string of cays. "I lost a prize to Creole pirates out of New Orleans a few years ago, and it always struck me that the Keys'd be a capital place for pirates or privateers t'lurk . . . like Blackbeard did behind Topsail Island in the Carolinas, waitin' for passin' ships. We'll probe into the bays behind the Keys, from Key West up to this 'un called Islamorada, then into this great bay . . . the Tamiami, or something like that. The chart shows a huge natural harbour. Have any of you ever been there, or had a look inside to see if there were settlements?"

None of them had; once ordered to the Bahamas, their duties had leashed them to the island chain's inner waters.

"If I may be allowed to opine, sir," Lt. Bury said in his usual solemn mien, "I was given to understand that the Spanish settlement system of *encomiendas,* the awarding of land grants to the original *conquistadors,* required their farms, mines, or *rancheros* to be profitable, and the native populations to be their slaves. Yet . . . from what I've read of Florida, it does not appear there's anything *worth* settlement South of Saint Augustine. No mines, no riches, no gold and silver as there are in New Spain, or Mexico, or whatever one may call it. And, no natives to enslave, either."

"Hence, no settlements?" Lewrie asked. "Damme, we know that the Dons are a lazy race, but *that* lazy?"

"During the brief time I was allowed ashore, sir," Lt. Westcott spoke up, "I asked the locals of what they knew of Florida. Despite the strict rules the Spanish have about trading only with Spain, only in Spanish bottoms, and very little inter-colonial trade, there *was* an illicit trade 'twixt Bahamian merchants and Florida, so long as Spain was neutral."

What I should've *done,* Lewrie chid himself; *but I was sunk deep in the Blue-Devils, lookin' up the past!*

"In the twenty years that we owned East and West Florida after the Seven Years' War," Lt. Westcott went on, "most of the aristocrats and wealthy landholders moved out, to Cuba or other Spanish colonies, leaving only the poor to remain. And, even after Spain got it back at the end of the American Revolution, not all that many returned. What remains are gathered round Pensacola, Mobile, perhaps a few in Tampa Bay, and Saint Augustine and San Marcos. If you will note this great swamp on the chart, sir? There's a huge shallow lake, the . . . Okeechobee," Westcott had to lean close to read the name, then made a stab at its pronunciation. "Below that, is the Everglades. The local Bahamians told me there's not ten Spanish to the square mile above the lake, and but one or two along the coast. A Catholic mission, a pig farm, and a few wild cattle or so, and all of them as poor as church mice. Spanish trade monopolies'd support them, did the system really work. Traders from here ship over shoddy goods, and the Spanish settlers in Florida are glad to get them, for they've little else.

"Now, down here along the coast, sir, behind the barrier isles and perhaps in the Tamiami Bay," Westcott continued, running a finger down the Sou'east shore, "there are very small, and incredibly poor, fishing *rancheros*. Portuguese, Spanish, runaway Black slaves from up in American Georgia, even some half-breed Indians, living day-to-day off what they catch or truck-garden. All they have to trade is fish, and they can't do that without smoking them . . . or curing them with Bahamian salt. The locals said some Cubans have set up shop in the Keys, but they don't know if their settlements are permanent or just seasonal."

"The sort of people who'd *leap* at a chance to go privateering, or turn outright pirate if they had decent vessels?" Lt. Darling said with a laugh.

"All the more reason to go have a look," Lewrie agreed. "And obtain

ourselves a few more boats . . . by hook or by crook. Between us, we've
only jolly boats, gigs, and a pair of launches. Last year in the Channel, I
got some cutters and barges for work close inshore to France, and the
dockyards didn't get 'em *all* back, but not enough to go round. You'll
each need something larger to tow astern 'til needed, if we have to land
armed parties. We'll keep an eye out for them. Now . . . once we've done
that, my orders require me to sail on Northwards and go into *supposedly*
neutral American ports . . . show the flag, all that, to the people who *might*
be victualling enemy privateers, or even arming them, and buying their
prizes on the sly.

"Once we've made our sweep up the coast as far as Saint Augustine,
which of you is senior?" he asked. "What are the dates of your commis-
sions?"

It turned out that Lt. Darling of *Thorn* pre-dated Lovett by seven
months, and Bury by more than a year.

Hope you're worth yer salt, Lewrie thought, while putting on a gladsome
face as he named Lt. Darling to temporary command of the rest in his
absence, while wondering if the portly, idly-aired fellow would prove
suitable; he still put Lewrie too much in mind of Forrester!

"Victualling and last-minute supplies, tomorrow, then, weather permitting, we sail the day after," Lewrie told them. "Hopefully, we are off on
a grand and successful adventure."

"Amen, sir!" Lt. Lovett exclaimed.

"Port, pass the port, and top-ups all round!" Lt. Darling cried.

"A toast, aye!" Lt. Westcott eagerly proposed.

"Ahem . . . if I may, Captain Lewrie?" Darling asked. He held up his
glass at Lewrie's nodded assent. "Confusion and death to the foes!"

"Confusion and death!" they chorused before tossing back their drinks.

"Here, I've another!" Lt. Lovett insisted as the bottle made its way
round again. "To close broadsides, blood, and prize-money!"

"Broadsides, blood, and prize-money!" they roared.

"And here's mine," Lewrie said. He topped up his glass and let the
bottle go past him, then held his glass chin-high, as the others looked to
him expectantly; Darling with his smug, easy smile, and his face flushed;
Lovett with his dark eyes agleam and showing a crooked grin, so piratical-
looking that he might roar "Arrh!"; and Bury with a prim and grave expression.

"Here's to us, none like us, a band of bold British sea-rovers!" Lewrie intoned. He would have said English, but wasn't sure where his junior officers sprang from.

"To us!"

Lewrie saw them off into their respective boats, then took the night air on the quarterdeck.

"They sound an eager lot, sir," Westcott commented.

"And, hopefully, a young but ferocious and canny lot, Mister Westcott," Lewrie said with an easy smile; though he did cross the fingers of his right hand along the seam of his breeches.

CHAPTER SEVENTEEN

Once at sea on-passage towards the Old Bahama Channel, Lewrie put his small squadron to exercises. He placed *Reliant* at the rear of a column in-line-ahead, then signalled them to take stations in a column ahead and to windward or leeward of the frigate, close aboard with only two cables' separation, as if they were entering an inlet or back-of-the-island bay and expecting action, with the ships with shallower draughts making the attack, backed up by his heavier guns.

In the event that the squadron stumbled across a proper enemy warship, they practiced sheering off from that formation on a bow-and-quarter-line, the lighter ships altering course together while *Reliant* surged ahead to offer battle, and *Thorn*, *Firefly*, and *Lizard* could take the foe on from her un-engaged side.

He made them practice wearing about in order of succession and letting *Reliant* cover a withdrawal, if the need arose to flee from a much stronger enemy squadron.

A special signal not in the Popham Code book could shake them out into a Vee formation ahead of *Reliant*'s bows for general chase, and they practiced that. Half of each morning, besides the time for small-arms drill or exercising with the great guns, was spent on manoeuvring, before

Lewrie would allow yet another signal to be hoisted; which would free them to dash ahead and to either beam out toward the horizons, but still within decent signalling distance, on the hunt.

"I'm sure they're gettin' tired o' this," Lewrie told Westcott as the "Release" soared aloft, and he cocked his head back to watch as it was two-blocked—below his broad pendant.

Damme, but that bit o' bunting looks hellish-fine, he thought; *I could almost get used to it!* Until Spanish Florida was scoured free of privateering, or *Reliant* was ordered to other duties, he was his own man, "on his own bottom". His next orders from Admiralty might put him back under a *real* Commodore, or in some Rear-Admiral's squadron or fleet, and *Reliant* would be chained to a column of Third Rates to plod along like a dutiful elephant calf!

"I think not, sir," Westcott assured him, bestowing one of his savagely brief grins. "They're doing something useful, for once, and acting like real man o' war'smen. I'd imagine they're revelling in it. Getting a shot at serving under an officer with a reputation for fighting, made Knight and Baronet for courage?"

"Well . . . hmm," Lewrie grudgingly allowed. It was not the false modesty that he usually felt necessary, but real, for a rare once.

"Serving a man with a broad pendant . . . *other* than their former Commodore, too, hmm?" Westcott slyly added.

"Now now, Mister Westcott," Lewrie gently chid him. "We cannot disparage our seniors or fellow officers. Even if one of them is the laziest, most useless sod in all Creation, with the wits of a flea and the manners of a boar hog. It just ain't on!" he laughed, savouring the hour of sailing when he had at last hoisted his broad pendant, and had wondered what Francis Forrester was spluttering at the sight. Had he gone puce in the face? Cursed and stamped his feet in rage?

Lewrie certainly *hoped* that he had!

He strolled to the binnacle cabinet to fetch his own telescope and peered forward past the spread of the inner, outer, and flying jibs to watch his three small ships scuttling away, now free of manoeuvring exercises, and allowed free chase 'til sundown. No wonder the pirates of old had prized the Jamaican or Bermudan sloops, for they were fast and weatherly; *Thorn, Firefly,* and *Lizard* had spread more sail and were already more than a mile off in the short time since he had released them. By Noon Sights, they could be out on the horizon, with only top-sails showing!

"I'll be below for a bit, before Noon Sights, Mister Westcott," Lewrie told the First Officer.

He barely made it to the bottom of the windward ladderway when he heard a series of yips and barks, and spotted a shaggy tan-and-white dog dashing for him, its long-haired tail whipping.

"Where did that come from?" Lewrie snapped. "Mister Westcott?"

"Don't know, sir!" Lt. Westcott answered, looking down to the ship's waist from the quarterdeck nettings.

The dog whined and circled round Lewrie, tongue lolling, with what could be deemed a grin on its face, bounding up on its hind legs as if to encourage petting.

"Well, he wasn't aboard when we left England, nor Bermuda," Lewrie snapped. The dog was sniffing at his boots and knee buttons. It barked once more, then sat on its haunches for a brief moment before leaping once more. "Silly bastard," Lewrie growled; "where the Devil did you spring from, hey?"

He was answered with a whiny *"yah-yeow"* and another bound. He put out a hand to pat it on its head, and the next second, the hound had both paws on his chest, as high as it could reach, grinning fit to bust, and squirming with joy to be petted.

"Oh! Ah . . . !"

Lewrie looked forward to the hatchway to the gun-deck and saw Midshipmen Munsell and Rossyngton, looking extremely sheepish.

"Did you bring this dog aboard, young sirs?" Lewrie snapped.

"Sir, he's ahh . . . the mascot of our mess, sir," Rossyngton answered, after a gulp or two. "Get down, Bisquit! Here, boy!"

The dog looked up adoringly at Lewrie's face, gave him a look as if to say "see you later", and bounded off to the Midshipmen.

"You two snuck this dog aboard?" Lewrie asked, putting on his "stern" face. "Without permission? Found it starving on the streets of Nassau, did you; and took pity?"

"Oh no, sir!" Rossyngton corrected. "He came off the *Mersey*, sir. It was *her* Midshipmen that found him first, but their captain and officers ordered him gone. They've a pack of hunting dogs aboard, well . . . half a dozen or so . . . and didn't want a cur mounting their bitches when they came in heat."

"Put him back ashore *twice*, sir, but *Mersey*'s Mids always found a way to sneak him back aboard," Munsell breathlessly added. "Honest to God, sir, their captain was so angry they'd done so that he ordered Bisquit drowned in a sack, sir, and . . . it was take him as *our* mascot or see him killed!"

That sounds like Forrester! Lewrie thought in sudden anger; *He always was a cruel bastard!*

"He and his officers hunt on shore a lot, do they?" Lewrie asked.

"It would seem so, sir," Rossyngton told him, petting the dog which was pressing and nuzzling at his free hand for attention.

"We'll feed him from our rations, sir; he'll be no bother," Midshipman Munsell assured.

"That'll be the day!" Lewrie scoffed. "The Midshipmen's mess'd eat hay, and kindling wood, to get their fill! Even *double* rations are not enough for growing lads. That's why you purchase 'millers' from the Jack-In-The-Breadroom."

Nothin' more satisfyin' than roast rat that's fed on bisquit, oatmeal and flour! Lewrie recalled from his own younger days, and just how much meat there was on one, as good as squirrel any day, once the hide, dusted as white as a grist mill worker or baker, was removed.

"The Purser, nor the Cook, either, will issue you a mouthful more than your proper due," Lewrie warned them. "You couldn't keep body and soul together for yourselves, much less support . . . him."

"Bisquit, sir," Rossyngton reiterated.

"We were going to name him Bandit, for his mask and muzzle, sir, but . . ." Munsell stuck in.

Was it possible that the dog somehow knew that its fate was being decided? It came forward from the Mids to sit at Lewrie's feet and peer up, its stand-and-fall cocked ears perked. Lewrie could see why they'd almost named it Bandit, for its muzzle was much darker fur, approaching black, and there was a dark streak across its forehead and eyes, with the eyes themselves outlined in white fur. It whined and lifted one paw to touch Lewrie's knee.

"Male, is he? Not going to come in heat?" Lewrie asked.

"Aye, sir, a male," Munsell replied, sounding more hopeful.

"There's worse creatures carried aboard ships, I suppose. We had a mongoose the Marines had found aboard my old frigate, *Proteus*." Lewrie allowed. "Captain Speaks and his damned parrot. He'll need meat. He can't live on porridge, cheese, and wormed bisquit."

Lewrie looked about the deck in thought, noting that his crew seemed to be hanging on his decision, as well. He was the victim of a pacific mutiny! A friendly and playful dog would be the pet of the entire ship, not just the Midshipmen's mess, and they were all aware of its presence *days* before.

What's the harm? Lewrie asked himself.

"'Til we can obtain more, I've jerked meat and hard sausages for my cats, aft," Lewrie said at last. "I can contribute to feeding him, somewhat. As I'm sure the ship's people will be willing to hand over beef and pork bones, 'stead of casting them over the side."

"Thank you, sir!" Munsell exclaimed.

"God help ye, ye flea-ridden mutt, but I suppose you're ours," Lewrie decided, leaning down to pet the dog, which set off a frenzied and playful reaction. It even rolled over to have its belly rubbed!

"We'll take good care of him, sir, and he won't be in the way," Rossyngton vowed.

"Just keep him off the quarterdeck, and away from my cats," Lewrie cautioned.

"Aye aye, sir!"

Lewrie gave it one last patting, then went aft to the door to his great-cabins.

"No, Bisquit!" he heard Munsell say.

Lewrie turned back to see the dog squatting to take a shit in gratitude.

"And clean all that up!" Lewrie barked.

CHAPTER EIGHTEEN

Days later, *Reliant* and her little squadron struck the coast of Cuba, and the Old Bahama Channel, near Bahía de Nuevitas, and turned West-Nor'westerly to run up the deeps of the channel, skirting close ashore of Spanish Cuba, keeping an eye out for enemy shipping or privateers.

Lewrie regretted that he didn't have enough bottoms to maintain a close blockade of the Cuban coast, for, as Columbus had discovered long before, there were hundreds of places for privateers or warships to lurk behind the fringe cays, and in the many "pocket" harbours and bays that stretched from Nuevitas almost to Havana. There was Bahía de Jigüey, fronted and shielded from the sea by Cayo Guajaba, Cayo Cruz, and Cayo Romano. Bahía de Perros was also fronted by Cayo Coco to the West of Cayo Romano; even further West lay Bahía de Buena Vista and Cayo Santa Maria and Cayo Fragoso.

To satisfy his curiosity, and to assure that French and Spanish privateers were not using those havens, Lewrie took his squadron West up the Nicholas Channel, well South of Cay Sal Bank, along the long scattering of the Archipiélago de Sabana, which consisted of umpteen hundreds of cays, with so many channels and inlets between them that a foe could dash from one end to the next and pick any he wished to make an escape.

And, by the time that they had peeked into Bahía de Santa Clara, Bahía de Cárdenas, and Cayo Blanco, Lewrie was even further convinced that Cuba's North coast badly needed patrolling. He had not seen another British warship in all that time; not 'til they came level with the much larger and deeper Bahía de Matanzas, and the approaches to Havana did they come across a pair of sloops of war which stood off to form a weak blockading force!

Letters to Admiralty, soonest, Lewrie determined; *My Lords may I humbly submit . . . and all that blather. Hmm . . . fire one off to Forrester, too, and if he don't act on it, he just might end up appearin'* damned *idle, and dangerously remiss!*

His shallow-draught ships had cruised as close to the coast as they could go, and the biggest vessels they had reported had been two or three two-masted fishing boats, no bigger than fifty feet or so overall, and they had quickly scuttled through the nearest inlets to shelter behind the cays. Perhaps they were coastal traders from Havana or Matanzas that peddled needles and thread and such to the scattered and isolated coastal or island villages. Lewrie imagined that Spain had never put much money back into her colonies after extracting so much wealth; if there was one decent road the whole length of Cuba's north shore, he would be mightily surprised! Plus, it was a given that cartage by road in mule- or ox-drawn waggons was much slower than carriage by sea, and the tonnage of goods shipped was always greater aboard a merchantman.

What else had his sloops reported? Dozens and dozens of fishing boats, everything from small jolly boat–sized rowboats to one-masted launches, all of them scrofulous in the extreme but capable of panicky speed on their dashes to shelter behind the cays, some in so much fear that they had abandoned their buoyed nets! Though the squadron still was in need of more boats, they had not been able to capture any. The best they had done was to upset a few poor traders' schedules and ruin a great many fishermen's catches!

All in all, perhaps prowling the coast of Florida was the easier task, Lewrie concluded, after comparing charts of the coasts. While he was sure that someone would *have* to pay a closer watch on Cuba, Lewrie was a bit relieved that that someone would not be him. That would be a task worthy of Hercules . . . with eagle-eyed Argus thrown in for good measure!

⚓

"It isn't well surveyed at all, sir," Mr. Caldwell, the Sailing Master, glumly informed Lewrie as the squadron stood in close to scout Key West. "Once behind the cay, I doubt even *Firefly* could find sufficient depth of water."

"And the charts upon which we depend are copies made from Spanish charts, sir," Lt. Westcott added, "and God only knows how long ago the Dons drew them up, and what's changed in the meantime."

Even without his telescope, Lewrie could see the changes in the co-lours of the waters. There were steel-blue patches indicating deep water, surrounded by brighter aquamarine, with the aquamarine shading to bright green or milky jade-green nearer the shore of the key. The waves that broke upon it that early morning seemed as lazy as a wind-driven lake's waves; there was no real beach, unless one deemed rocks and pebbles and gravel a "beach". It was very pretty, though, which was about the best that could be said about it.

"Mast-head!" Lewrie yelled through a brass speaking-trumpet at the lookouts in the cross-trees. "Any settlements ashore?"

"*Shacks,* sir!" Midshipman Munsell yelled back. "Only a few shacks. There's no one about! No boats to be seen! Looks *abandoned,* sir!"

From the cross-trees high aloft, Lewrie expected that Munsell could almost see clear across the island to the far shore, for it was very low-lying, its mean elevation only a few feet above the high-tide mark. *God, 'tis only the* really *poor, and demented, who'd live here!* Lewrie thought.

"Hmm," Lt. Westcott said with his mouth screwed to one corner. "It's not even the first of April yet, sir. Perhaps the itinerants don't winter over, and they're not ready to start their fishing season, yet."

"Or, they've crossed back over to Cuba for Easter," Mr. Caldwell opined. "Papist Spaniards put a lot of stock in Easter. End of Lent, and all that? *Fiestas,* dancing, swilling, and stuffing their faces with whatever they gave up in penance?"

"Aye, cleansed, and free to sin all over again!" Lt. Westcott scoffed.

"Beyond the shallows back of the island chain, though," Lewrie spec-ulated, "the Florida Bay is deep enough to admit vessels with moderate draught. Right, Mister Caldwell?"

"Aye, sir," Caldwell cautiously agreed.

"It's broad enough here to allow privateers easy access to open seas, and stays broad right up to Key Largo," Lewrie pointed out. "If a priva-teer captain wished, he *might* be able to find a pass through these little isles to that deep water . . . either end of Key Largo, it seems," he went on, crossing to the chart pinned to the traverse board by the compass binnacle cabinet, forward of the helm. "Here, at the West end of Largo, or the North end near Isla Morada, or even take the pass into the bay that lies to the Nor'east of Isla Morada."

"A privateer of *very* moderate draught, sir," Caldwell warned.

"Perhaps, sir," Westcott suggested, "were we to take *Reliant* into the Florida Bay, and scout up the inside of the island chain, whilst our smaller ships each form a blocking force at the passes and inlets? If there's anyone lurking back there, we'd be the 'beaters', and *Thorn*, *Firefly*, and *Lizard* could form the firing line. Like going after grouse or pheasant?"

"And, do we flush a wild boar, *Reliant* gets the kill?" Lewrie asked with a brow up.

"Something like that, sir, aye," Westcott agreed most slyly.

Lewrie bent over to peer more closely at the chart. The Florida Bay began deep enough for *Reliant*, deep enough for even a Third Rate ship of the line, but it did turn shallow as one made way Easterly up the chain of islets. It was a tempting idea, but there seemed to be no exit if need arose, unless one put the ship about and returned to Key West and round it out into the Florida Straits once more, leaving the lighter ships on their own should they stumble over a well-armed threat. Lewrie shared a look with the Sailing Master, who gravely shook his head in an almost imperceptible "no".

"If we do spot someone hiding behind the islets, we'll find a way t'get at 'em, Mister Westcott," Lewrie decided, "but I'd not wish t'leave the rest of the squadron on their own for that long. Mister Rossyngton? Signal to the squadron to alter course to the Nor'east."

"Aye, sir!"

Am I goin' t'regret that decision? Lewrie asked himself; *But, I can't abandon the little ships.*

"Hands to the braces and sheets, Mister Westcott, and be ready to put about," Lewrie ordered as he paced forward to the full hammock stanchions and nets at the break of the quarterdeck.

"Aye, sir," Lt. Westcott replied, as crisply as if his suggestion had never been broached.

As the hands of the watch made ready to free the braces and the sheets to take the winds on a new point of sail, Lewrie caught sight of his cats making a beeline up the starboard ladderway to the quarterdeck. In rather a hurry, he noted, with their tails bottled up and their bellies low to the oak planks. For a brief second he reckoned that they were playing tail-chase, or were coming to see him, but . . . not a second later here came the damned dog, yelping merrily in close pursuit!

Spry Chalky, even slower and clumsier Toulon, gained the top of the hammock nettings' canvas covers in a flash, and dug their claws in so they could arch their backs, turn sideways in threat, and moan and hiss in anger. Bisquit loped up and began to bark, his bushy tail wagging.

"Damn my eyes, what'd I say about keepin' him off the quarterdeck, or scarin' the cats?" Lewrie snapped. "Down, you, down! And stop yer bloody gob!"

Bisquit stood on his hind legs, front paws on the nettings to reach them, safely just short of some tentative claw swipes.

"Down, I said!" Lewrie barked. "Down! And hush!"

The dog sat down, looking at Lewrie, then up at the cats, his tongue lolling, and damned if the silly thing didn't look like he was grinning! He uttered a few encouraging *woofs* at the cats, who would have none of it, of course, hissing, moaning, spitting, and hunkering.

"Hands are at stations, sir," Lt. Westcott reported.

"Very well, sir," Lewrie said, looking further afield. "Make the 'Execute', Mister Rossyngton."

In succession, *Thorn, Lizard,* and *Firefly* put about to the Nor'east to continue skirting up the Keys. Once they were all steady and their sails trimmed, Lewrie ordered *Reliant* put about as well, so that the three smaller ships formed a line ahead and to larboard, with the frigate standing further out to sea of them.

"Mister Rossyngton!" Lewrie snapped.

"Sir?" Right timid, that.

"Now there are no signals to be made for the moment, I wish you to see this . . . ," Lewrie began. The dog made a last playful leap at the hammock nettings, then turned to trot to Lewrie, nuzzling under a hand for attention. "Ahem! I wish you t'see this dog off the quarterdeck. Ask the Bosun for a length of line to make a leash or tether for him, so he can't romp up the ladderways again."

"Aye, sir!" Rossyngton replied.

The dog was licking his hand! Grinning upwards playfully and licking Lewrie's hand. Despite the sternness he'd intended, Lewrie found himself scratching him behind the ears, which elicited another goofy, tongue-lolling grin.

"Go on, now, ye daft thing," Lewrie growled. "Get below, and stay there. Hear me?"

Midshipman Rossyngton took the dog by the collar and led him to the top of the ladderway, then down to the ship's waist. A whine or two of complaint, and a longing look or two at the cats on top of the hammock nettings, perhaps at Lewrie, or the denied expanse of the quarterdeck, and Bisquit suffered to be led forward, his tail held low.

"It appears he likes you, sir," Lt. Westcott commented.

"Damn what he likes," Lewrie rejoined, going to the nettings to placate his cats. "There there, lads," he cooed. "Threat's over, and ye won't be eaten." He reached out to stroke them, but both Chalky and Toulon spat and hissed at *him*! They would not settle down and flatten their tail fur 'til they'd seen the dog securely tethered to the bottom of the boarding pikes stored upright round the main mast. Only then did they allow Lewrie to stroke them and pet them.

The cats seemed to gloat whilst the dog lay down with his head on his forepaws, looking up at them. One last hiss to get their message across, and the cats sat up and began to groom themselves.

"I'll uh . . . be below in my cabins for a bit Mister Westcott. You have the watch," Lewrie said, clearing his throat and hoping that his ears weren't turning red in embarassment.

"Aye aye, sir," Westcott answered, sounding as if there was a slight smirk deeply hidden.

As Lewrie reached the foot of the ladderway, the dog perked up in hopes, but Bosun Sprague was by his side, kneeling down to stroke and knead. "An' ain't ye a fine dog, now? Ain't ye, Bisquit?" the Bosun was cooing in a very un-characteristic voice, one which made sailors turn and gawp; Sprague was more used to bellowing at them than he was to speak softly.

Christ, now Sprague's *dotin' on the silly beast?* Lewrie thought; *This ship's turnin' into a schoolyard full o' boys!*

CHAPTER NINETEEN

A great many of the islets in the Keys were little more than hammocks of dry land a few feet above the sea, some as small as tennis courts, and covered so thickly with mangroves that it was hard to tell where the sand ended and the sea began, and birds were the only inhabitants. They were easy for the little squadron to pass by on their slow jog up the archipelago. The larger isles, though . . . despite the urge to rush on, Lewrie felt it necessary to land shore parties to inspect them if anything that resembled a settlement appeared; a clearing, the sight of farm crops, or the presence of domestic animals near the beaches. The landings pleased *Reliant*'s Marine Officer, Lt. Simcock, right down to his toes, since they gave him a splendid excuse to exercise his men away from the ship, and relieve the boredom of the daily routine. Frankly, the frigate's sailors, and the hands aboard the smaller ships, relished it, too, for it was a change of pace, with the prospect of discovering something useful, or edible, married with the hint of danger and action.

Strange fruits came back aboard the ships, now and then a small deer or wild hog, or some domestic chickens abandoned at a tumbledown collection of shacks.

And they did find settlements, of a sort. From the few who did not flee in fear, they found ragged remnants of the once-feared Calusa Indians, some Spaniards, Frenchmen, and Englishmen "gone native", along with runaway Black slaves, even some few Muskogee Indians with "itchy feet", driven from Georgia and Alabama by hordes of American settlers. The Muskogee had a name for those who would not stay in one place for long; they called them Seminoli—"wanderers".

They lived on fish, on squash and beans and maize corn, and had chickens and pigs. They had some muskets, but were always short of lead and powder, and depended on the bow and arrow. Their homes were little more than lean-tos or raised, roofed, sleeping platforms in the native style, and their boats were hollowed-out mahogany logs A few who could actually speak a little English said that they feared the Spaniards who came up from Cuba to fish, for they were not above slave-catching. Privateers? Big boats? None of them could say. Further up to the East, perhaps, there might be, closer to what was left of the old Mayami tribe? They might know.

"Any luck ashore, Mister Merriman?" Lewrie asked as the Third Officer stepped through the entry-port after a scramble up the boarding battens.

"Same song, a different verse, sir, sorry to say," Merriman reported, knuckling the brim of his hat in casual salute. "The few we saw are poor as church-mice. Their settlement's on the bay side, so it took a while to row round to it. Hello, Bisquit! Happy to see me back? Here, boy! I brought you a pig bone!"

The dog seemingly adored every Man Jack in the crew, whining in longing whenever the Marine parties and boat crews, some of the Mids or one of the officers, manned the boats and rowed off, then went into paroxyms of joy at their return.

"The settlement?" Lewrie prompted.

"A *bit* fancier than most, sir," Merriman replied, beaming at the sight of the dog trotting round the ship's waist to show his bone off to everybody. "About a dozen huts, but made from sawn planks for floors and walls . . . roofed with palmetto, though. The flats were so shallow that we had some trouble finding a way to the bay side, so by the time we arrived, they'd all scampered into the bush, but for a few of the oldest, and not one of them knew a word of English or French or my poor Spanish, sir. And the bay, as far as we could see, was empty."

"Good morning, sir!" Marine Lieutenant Simcock happily said as his boat came alongside, and he made the climb to the deck. Simcock was turned out in Sunday Divisions best, as if ready for inspection, right down to the highly polished silver gorget hung on a chain high on his chest; though his boots looked muddy and caked with sand.

"Good morning, sir," Lewrie said, answering his salute with a slight doff of his own hat. "Anything that caught your eye ashore?"

"Not all that much, sir," Simcock said with a cocky grimace of dismissal. "Unless you wished a new iron cook pot, or a painted clay one. Whoever the poor people are who live there, I pity them. Seems a shame, really . . . the natural beauty of these isles puts one in mind of the Greek tales about the land of the Lotus Eaters, yet . . . there's nothing there to live on."

"There's those little gardens," Merriman pointed out.

"Little bigger than Irish 'lazy beds', though, and the soil is too thin and sandy," Lt. Simcock countered. "Oh! One thing that I *did* notice, sir, is the lack of water wells. I can't recall seeing a one on any of the islands we've scouted."

"Aye, come to think on it, I can't say that I saw any wells at all, either," Lt. Merriman quickly agreed, brightening. "Sir," he said to Lewrie, "we've found barrels and large clay pots round the houses, with hollowed-out half-round sluices . . . to catch *rainwater*! Run-off from the planked rooves! There are no freshwater springs or wells!"

"Haven't seen any, yet, sir," Lt. Simcock added. "That's not to say that there aren't some on the larger isles closer to the mainland, but . . . ," he said, heaving off a large shrug. "Yes, hello, Bisquit! I'm back safely! Good fellow! Want a pig bone?"

Bisquit leaped, wagged his tail and his hindquarters in rapture, and pranced round the weather deck to show off his new one.

"No wells, no springs . . . no privateerin' lairs, then," Lewrie speculated. "A decent-sized ship could lurk round here for a time, with full water casks, but they'd have to go somewhere else to replenish. The only thing they could find here would be firewood and a hog or two."

"So searching the Keys would be a waste of time, sir?" Merriman asked, sounding a tad disappointed. Lt. Simcock looked downcast, too, as if the both of them had been having fun ashore and would hate to see their excursions end.

"From what I saw during the Revolution," Lewrie told them, "and what I've read of Florida, the mainland is rich with lakes, rivers, and streams. Privateers *could* base themselves on the *far* side of Florida Bay, but that's too far from the Straits for quick springs upon merchant ships."

And, did French or Spanish privateers base themselves on the mainland side of Florida Bay, they would have a long passage out round Key West and the Marquesas Keys to get to their cruising grounds, and a long passage back with prizes, Lewrie realised.

Damme, I might've been right the first time, he congratulated himself; *Florida Bay's a sack, a place where a privateer'd be trapped, if a force like ours came along! They're a greedy lot, but no one ever said privateers are stupid.*

"No, we'll be thorough," Lewrie said at last to his officers. "A few days more, and we'll reach the end of the Keys and strike the mainland. Damme, no springs or wells? Then, what does the wildlife do for water . . . the wild hogs, deer, birds, and such? Even *sea*-birds need to drink, now and again."

"Wait for a downpour, sir?" Lt. Merriman posed. "So far, we've seen goodly showers each afternoon, and there would be shallow puddles left behind them, for a while. As for the wild people who dwell here, I suppose they can *dance* for rain, like the Indians, and catch them a barrel or two of run-off. There are clouds gathering on the horizon even as we speak, sir."

"Seems a horrid waste, really," Lt. Simcock commented. "These wee isles *appear* idyllic, but one would have to be pretty desperate to live here for long. Alluring and all, but not worth a tuppenny shit for white men."

"Who knows, though, Arnold," Merriman said. "Did one dig a deep well and strike fresh water, one could go as native as a Tahitian in the Great South Seas!"

"Though it don't look promising for bare-breasted dancing girls in grass skirts," Simcock quipped, fanning himself with his hat.

"Invite Mister Westcott to go native with you," Merriman chirped, "and he'll turn them up in a Dog Watch. It comes to women, he's your boy!"

"Carry on, sirs," Lewrie said, hiding a smirk, and returning to the quarterdeck to fetch his telescope. He peered at *Lizard, Firefly,* and *Thorn* which lay to anchor close by. Their boats were also coming offshore, empty-handed it appeared. Well, Lt. Bury was studying something that might have been a horseshoe crab with a large magnifying glass. *No, he'd call it a trilobite,* Lewrie thought.

Lewrie lowered his telescope and turned to gaze out to sea. A bank of darker clouds was gathering as the heat of the day grew, threatening yet another afternoon shower or two. Four or five miles out from their anchorage, a slim glass-white waterspout was slowly snaking down to thrash the bright green waters to a froth; yet another nigh-daily occurrence since they had entered the Florida Straits and had begun their slow inspection of the Keys.

"Mister Grainger?" Lewrie called, after turning to note which lad was the Midshipman of the Watch on the quarterdeck. "Hoist 'Captains Repair On Board'."

Grand places t' lurk, but not to base, Lewrie thought; *unless ye fetch along all that's needful. Might as well be* at sea!

He went to the compass binnacle cabinet afore the helm to roll open one of the Sailing Master's dubious charts of the area, to look closely at the great bay at the North end of the Keys. Yes, it was as he remembered it from a first perusal . . . there were *rios* feeding into the bay, and rivers meant fresh water in abundance.

Time for a conference, Lewrie determined; *and time for a change of plans. Some midnight boat-work, to scout the bay out before we go barging' in.*

CHAPTER TWENTY

$\mathcal{F}$alse dawn had broadened the circle of visibility from the decks and the mast-heads, revealing low shorelands and forests, and the broad bay into which the squadron crept under reduced sail. The winds were light but steady, bringing the scents of sand flats and marsh, of woods and growing things, and the faintest hint of flowers ready to open to the first rays of the sun when the actual dawn came. The waters of the great bay at the end of the Keys were very calm, with no chop or white-caps, and slack-water waves no more than one or two feet high, so the bow waves and wakes of the four warships barely whitened to foam, and they all rode upright, with only a slight angle of heel to the winds.

The smaller three preceded *Reliant* by only half a mile, spread in line-abreast, with *Thorn* and her short-ranged carronades closest to the larboard shore, weaker 8-gunned *Firefly* in the centre, and *Lizard* on the starboard corner.

"Trust to the leadsmen in the chains," *Reliant*'s Sailing Master, Mr. Caldwell, said in a low voice as those sailors called back a depth of six fathoms, "If not completely in these ancient Spanish charts. I doubt the Dons ever contemplated a proper settlement *this* far South of Saint Augustine, sir, so how meticulous the first, perhaps the only, surveyors were . . . in such a malarial place, right on the edge of a great swamp, well . . ."

"Neither did British surveyors in the twenty-odd years we held Florida, Mister Caldwell," Lewrie pointed out.

The latest charts of the bay, and the shallow passage between a string of long barrier islands and the mainland, or the mouth of the river which fed into the bay, were an amalgam of old Spanish work and some sketchy surveys done between 1763 and 1783, though both doubted if much had been done to update them once the American Revolution had begun in 1775. Before, there had been no urgency, and once England was at war, there had been no need to correct maps done of such a minor, insignificant colony so far from the main scenes of action.

"Mayami . . . Tamiami?" Lt. Westcott posed with a brow up in puzzlement. "I suppose we should call it something, sir."

"Mayami, perhaps . . . for the local tribe," Lewrie speculated.

"Signal from *Lizard*, sir!" Midshipman Warburton called down to the deck from his perch at the top of the starboard main-mast shrouds, almost to the futtocks of the-main top. "Two vessels to starboard and ahead! *Anchored!*"

"And, there's the settlement, dead ahead, sir," Lt. Westcott pointed out, "the cook-fires we saw last night are still burning."

"Right where the river joins the bay, aye," Lewrie said. "Just heave a net, dip a bucket, and there's your breakfast and tea-water! Damme, do they look as asleep as I *think* they look? Two signals, Mister Eldridge!" he barked in rising excitement. "The first to *Thorn*. Make, her number, and engage shore. By the larboard halliards."

"Aye, sir!" Eldridge replied, turning to the ratings of the Afterguard who stood by the transom flag lockers, and fumbling with his illustrated lists of signals to call out the right numerals.

"Might be hard to read in this light, sir," Westcott warned.

"But streamin' to loo'rd in plain sight," Lewrie countered, "and if Darling kens the half of it, he may get my intent. For now, crack on a bit more sail, Mister Westcott, and let's close up within hailing distance, just in case. Let fall the fore course, and hoist the foretopmast stays'l and outer flying jib."

Lewrie turned to see Eldridge and the signalmen just then bending on the last code flag to the halliard. They were slow, or Eldridge was not yet familiar with the duty, but he could not goad him to haste . . . yet.

Eldridge seemed to blush, and sped his men to hoist away. Lewrie lifted his gaze to watch the signal soar aloft, then took a few steps aft to tell Eldridge, "Once *Thorn* shows the 'Affirmative,' or the 'Repeat,' strike that'un, and the second signal will be to *Firefly* and *Lizard*. Their numbers, 'General Chase,' and 'Engage The Enemy More Closely' . . . on the starboard halliards, if ye please."

"Aye aye, sir," Eldridge replied very formally, as if expecting criticism.

"Damme, we've finally something *t'shoot* at!" Lewrie chortled, putting Eldridge at ease, and raising a smile.

The light winds were just abaft of abeam, so the string of code flags to *Thorn* stood out a bit limply to larboard; legible, if the sky brightened a bit more. After a long moment's wait . . .

"From *Thorn*, sir!" Warburton shouted. "The 'Affirmative'!"

"Strike larboard for the 'Execute'," Eldridge ordered his signalmen. "New hoist ready to starboard . . . Ready? Hoist away, smartly!"

Lt. Bury in *Lizard*, and Lt. Lovett in *Firefly*, must have been expecting such an order, perhaps longing for one, for each rapidly put up the single flag for "Affirmative" and began to spread more sail, angling off to starboard to close the suspicious anchored ships almost before *Reliant*'s hoist had been two-blocked.

"We'll fall in trail position aft of *Firefly*, Mister Westcott," Lewrie snapped. "Mister Spendlove?" he called down to the waist.

"Aye, sir?"

"Open the starboard gun-ports and run out!" Lewrie gleefully told him. "And stand by to engage at close range!"

The gun crews gave out a loud, inarticulate growl of approval as the port lids were raised, and the gun-captains summoned the boy powder monkeys from amidships with the first charges of propellant.

A minute or two later, the sun burst above the Eastern horizon, and all that had been murky and ill-defined stood out starkly. Forests and beach-trimmed shores, the meagre clutch of shacks and large canvas tents ashore near the mouth of the river, and the anchored ships now could be seen in detail.

"No flags showing on the anchored ships, yet, sir," Lt. Westcott noted.

Both of them were two-masted, either topsail schooners or Bermudan or Jamaican sloops, neither much longer than *Lizard* or *Firefly*, with their jib-booms and bow-sprits steeved closer to the horizontal than was the usual fashion in merchant ships or purpose-built warships. Their hulls were so dark that they were almost black, with narrow hull stripes; on the nearest was a dark blue stripe, and on the furthest an odd blue-grey. Their masts were raked aft a bit more than usual, as if they followed the American shipbuilding fashion.

"Aha! Wakey-wakey!" Lewrie snickered after he lifted his telescope, and spotted men popping up on their decks, dashing about in confusion, as if ordered to man their guns, make sail, and cut their anchor cables, all at the same time. But they had no time.

Just bloody beautiful! Lewrie exulted; *Them, the bay, everything!* The bay was an artist's palette of dark greens, aquas, and jade, sparkling in the dawn light like a field of gems. And the trap he'd sprung . . . !

"Note in the log, Mister Caldwell," Lewrie called over to the Sailing Master, "that *Lizard* and *Firefly* opened upon the near vessel at . . . a quarter 'til six A.M.,"

Damme, that's *well done*, Lewrie appreciatively thought as *Lizard*, the slightly stronger ship in weight of metal, stood up to the nearest sloop and wheeled to lay abeam of her at a range of a single cable before she opened fire off the sloop's starboard bows, sails reduced and making a slow steerage way so Lt. Bury's gunners might be able to get off a second or third broadside in passing. *Firefly* followed in her wake, wheeling abeam in succession to add her four starboard 6-pounders a bit later.

At such close range, it was almost impossible to miss. Shot-splashes rose close-aboard the sloop's waterline, and roundshot punched holes below the sloop's row of gun-ports, and smashed chunks from her bulwarks, staggering her masts.

A few of the first sloop's gun-ports swung up, and stubby gun muzzles appeared as some were run out, but only two fired, aimlessly, before a scramble began to her un-engaged side as her crew abandoned the fight, leaping over the larboard rails for their boats, or a long swim to the beach.

"Carry on, Bury, carry on!" Lewrie yelled as if his voice would reach that far, hoping that the little two-ship column could engage the second sloop before she could prepare herself for battle.

"We're almost at a cable's range of the first, sir," Westcott judged aloud.

"My compliments to Mister Spendlove, and he's to open upon her the instant he deems it feasible, Mister Westcott," Lewrie ordered, quite looking forward to the thunder and clouds of powder smoke.

"Aye aye, sir!" Westcott replied. "Hoy, Mister Spendlove!"

The second sloop had managed to cut her single anchor cable and was paying off leeward as her crew got up a jib, and her main fore-and-aft gaff sail, very slowly sagging and swinging her bows towards the leading British ship, *Lizard*. Bad luck for her, for all that was doing was presenting her weak bow scantlings to a rake, and closing the range to her own mauling.

"*As* you *bear . . . by broadside . . . fire!*" Lt. Spendlove shouted, waiting for the decks to pause on the faint scend and the up-roll, when it was level and still.

The range was about a quarter-mile to the first sloop when the first of *Reliant*'s broadsides lit off, 12-pounder bow chase gun, all the starboard 18-pounders, the quarterdeck 9-pounders, even the 32-pounder carronades with their elevating screws fully down and their muzzles lifted to the fullest safe elevation.

The 6-pounders of the smaller ships had nipped and bitten the anchored sloop, but *Reliant*'s broadside was an iron avalanche. Just before the thick bank of spent powder smoke blotted out their view, Lewrie got a quick glimpse of bulwarks and upper planking shattering in dusty clouds of splinters and chunks, of large, irregular holes blossoming in her sides, and of both masts and tops'l yards coming apart in darting zig-zags of jagged ruin.

As the guns were swabbed, and the recoil and run-out tackle overhauled, the light winds wafted the reeking powder smoke alee to larboard, giving Lewrie a clearer view with his day-glass.

"I don't think she'll be needin' another broadside," Lewrie said, chuckling. The target was dis-masted, almost level with where the tops of her bulwarks had been, if they hadn't been blown to kindling. There were several holes in her upper and lower hull planking, and a large one just by her waterline. If anyone was still aboard her, they were out of sight.

Lizard and *Firefly* were engaging the further sloop, which by then was helplessly bows-on to their fire. Bury and Lovett had closed the range to the point that even their swivel guns were yapping like terriers. That sloop was being *sieved* with shot!

What's Thorn *doing?* Lewrie wondered, stepping over to the lee rails to get a better look. The smoke from his ship's guns, and the guns of the smaller ships, had mingled and accumulated rapidly, held together, perhaps, by the early-morning humidity, making a thick and drifting haze ahead and to larboard, but he could make out *Thorn* as she stood in close to the shore and the river mouth, and that encampment, beam onto *Reliant*. She was wreathed in smoke from her stubby but powerful carronades. Beyond her, trees and bushes writhed, the large tents and shelters were being whipped away, and *Thorn* must have hit something explosive, for there was a burst of flame and a thick cloud of dark smoke, and a shower of hot sparks that set even more of the camp afire.

"Ehm, captain, sir," Mr. Caldwell cautioned. "It's getting a tad shallow for us. Perhaps . . ."

"Aye, Mister Caldwell," Lewrie replied. "Mister Westcott, lay us two points alee, into the deeper water to loo'rd. Mister Spendlove? We're falling off alee. Serve that second sloop as best you can!"

"Quoins out a bit," Lt. Spendlove instructed his gun-captains. "And aim small, lads. Ready, the battery? On the up-roll by broadside . . . fire!"

The second sloop was almost bows-on to *Reliant*, with *Firefly* and *Lizard* standing well clear beyond her by then. The range would be closer to half a mile, and the target narrow, but the broadside roared out. Already damaged, that sloop shivered like a stand of saplings to the weight and fury of the frigate's hail of roundshot. Her jib-boom, bow-sprit, and foremast were scythed away, and misses frothed the waters close aboard her.

"Drop it, Mister Spendlove! Dead'un!" Lewrie shouted down to the waist, jeering in the vernacular of the rat-pit to urge a terrier to go kill another. "Cease fire, and secure!"

Beyond the shattered sloops there were several rowing boats, all pulling madly for the far shore or the long strip of barrier islands, like a gaggle of panicked ducks.

"Ye might have to spell this out, Mister Eldridge, but make to *Lizard* and *Firefly*, their numbers, and 'Take Prisoners'."

Oh, eager lads! he thought a moment later, even as the signal was being assembled, for Lt. Bury in *Lizard* was already leading her consort in pursuit, sailing much faster than the boats could be rowed, heading them off from escape.

"Belay, Mister Eldridge. It seems it's bein' done." Lewrie said, turning to share a grin with Lt. Westcott, then crossing over to the other side of the deck to see what *Thorn* was up to.

Lt. Darling had taken his ship past the encampment, almost to the mouth of the river before coming about to fire with her larboard battery, near the eyes of the wind for a bit, sails shivering or laid aback, before paying off Sutherly. When she was done, there was little sign that the camp had been there, but for the burning, smouldering ruin of the shacks and tents, and a new clearing littered with felled trees and up-rooted bushes.

"Mister Westcott, I'd admire did ye bring our head round into the wind and fetch-to, and have all the boats manned. Marines, too, to take possession of the prizes, and scout the camp."

"Aye aye, sir."

"Then, we'll find out just who, and what, we've captured," Lewrie said with a broad grin.

CHAPTER TWENTY-ONE

*T*he engagement had been great fun, but a short delight. After came a myriad of details and reports, questions, and tasks to be seen to, which took all the joy of it for Lewrie.

Lt. Simcock returned with half of his forty-man Marine complement from the encampment to report that he, his Marines, and sailors from *Thorn* had tallied up the dead, set fire to the last of the foodstuff and supplies ashore, then come away before suffering any casualties of their own. "It looked as if there might have been fifty or sixty or so ashore when we attacked, sir. We found about fifteen dead, but the rest ran off into the forests, and it appeared that they did so under arms . . . pistols and muskets and such. We scavenged what weapons left behind, but . . ." he ended with a shrug.

"There's nothing left of any worth to the survivors, sir," Lt. Darling proudly related. "I and my people saw to *that*. They'll not have a single drop of rum, wine, or beer, either. We, ah . . . appropriated a few kegs, and scuttled the rest, sir."

"You didn't find any American corn whisky, did you?" Lewrie took time to ask. "No? Pity."

Then it was Lt. Merriman, Midshipmen Entwhistle and Warburton, and the Bosun, Mr. Sprague, and his Mate, Mr. Wheeler, who came back aboard from the captured prizes with their reports.

"They are both Spanish, sir," Lt. Merriman told the assembled officers. "That'un yonder, is the *Escorpion*," he said, pointing to the first sloop, "and the second is named the *Santa Doratea*. Both are from Havana, each armed with ten guns. Most of the guns bear proof marks from Cuba, some from Cadiz, though there are some odds-and-sods . . . a few French, Dutch, or even one British."

"Tell me they're privateers," Lewrie urged with the fingers of his right hand crossed behind his thigh.

"Oh, privateers right enough, sir!" Lt. Merriman said with a beamish grin. "We found their registries, and their Letters of Marque and Reprisal, signed by the Captain-General of Cuba, along with their muster books. All told, there were nigh an hundred and eighty men and officers, though not all were aboard when we engaged them."

"I've their papers and muster books, sir," Lewrie's clerk, Mr. James Faulkes, interrupted. "Shall I stow them in your cabins, sir?"

"Aye, atop the desk, for now, thankee, Faulkes," Lewrie said. "Are they worth salvaging, Mister Sprague?" he asked the Bosun.

"Pish, sir!" Sprague scoffed, begging pardon long enough to go to the nearest spit-kid and hock up his worn-out bite of chew-tobacco. "They're both hulled clean through, aloft and alow, dis-masted, and what little spare spars and such the Dons had aboard are smashed, to boot. We got 'em re-anchored so they don't drift ashore, but sure as Fate, they'll both be on the bottom in a few hours, and fothering'd be a waste o' time, sir, and that'd be a cryin' pity, for one of 'em is made o' Cuban mahogany, and do ye maintain her proper, she'd last for ages."

"Kept nigh Bristol-fashion abovedecks, sir," Wheeler added, "but all Donnish below, all trash and filth. Damned idle Spaniards."

"Mister Mainwaring said to inform you, sir, that he counted four dead and two badly wounded aboard *Escorpion*, and six dead and five wounded aboard the *Santa Doratea*. He and the Surgeon's Mates are tending to them, but he suspects that three of the wounded will pass before dusk. He asks whether you wished the wounded be brought aboard *Reliant*, sir."

"Aye, before both ships sink out from under them," Lewrie decided. "You lads, row over to the prizes and help the Surgeon and his Mates fetch the wounded Spaniards off," he said to the Mids. "If they're not worth tuppence as prizes, we might as well scuttle them. Mister Sprague, I'd admire did ye see to speeding their destruction along. Pile up flammables, lay trains to their powder magazines, all that. How many hands will you need for that?"

"No more than the boat's crews t'take us over, sir," the Bosun reckoned. "We can start right away."

"Once their wounded are off the prizes, see to it," Lewrie told him, "and I'll let you know when to set them alight."

"Oh, well, sir," Lt. Darling of *Thorn* said with a resigned sigh. "It seems all we'll reap will be Head and Gun Money, with nought from their condemnations and sales."

"But that would have t'be done at the Admiralty Prize Court at Nassau, sir," Lewrie countered, grinning wryly, "where we'd most-like end up *owing* money to the Proctors, even if they were *scrupulously* honest, which I very much doubt. And besides . . . do ye *really* wish to be back at Nassau, for *any* reason?"

"A point well taken, Captain Lewrie, sir," Lt. Darling smirked.

"Hoy, the boat!" Midshipman Grainger hailed to a new arrival.

Now bloody what? Lewrie grumbled to himself, thinking that, did victory have an hundred parents, why was he the only one home to deal with the *minutiae,* and clean up the mess? He was missing breakfast!

"Permission to come aboard!" was the reply.

It was Lt. Bury from *Lizard.* Lewrie crossed to the starboard side to peer down at him, and waved him a welcome.

"Good Lord, Mister Bury, wherever did ye find that ugly barge?" Lewrie gawped. Bury was not in his usual smartly painted gig, but in a thirty-foot . . . something, which, by the fact that it floated, *could* be loosely construed to be a boat; slab-sided without the sweet curves of a proper boatwright, with a vertical stem post and bow, no sweep to its sheerline or gunn'ls, and appeared to be hard-chined aft and shallow-draught, perhaps even flat-bottomed. The stern was a vertical slab, and, all in all, put Lewrie in mind of a slice of "wooden" pie. Worst of all, someone had once painted it sky-blue, but that paint had peeled and blistered and chalked to the point that its colour was dingy grey.

"I shall not stand upon my dignity, sir," Bury called up from the bottom of the boarding battens as his bow man hooked onto the main channel. "Though, you might extend honours to my prisoner. He claims to be the captain of the *Escorpion.*"

All gilt and be-shit compliments to the loser, Lewrie thought.

"Side party, Mister Grainger," Lewrie ordered, as he stared at the stranger beside Bury, a fellow with long and lank black hair tied back into a loose queue, a swarthy complexion, and a neatly trimmed mustachio and beard.

"I do not claim . . . I *am*!" the fellow snapped.

Thank Christ he's some English, Lewrie thought; *I doubt we've no more than five Spanish speakers in the entire squadron.*

There was a snag to the welcome-aboard rite, though; both the Bosun and Bosun's Mate had already departed in the cutters, and only Marine Lt. Simcock was wearing a sword, and his boots were caked with sand and mud. Lewrie's Cox'n, Liam Desmond, who traditionally wore a silver call as his badge of office, hastily stepped in to pipe their prisoner aboard. That worthy ably scrambled up the battens to stand in the entry-port and brusquely doff his wide-brimmed straw hat with what seemed proud contempt.

"Welcome aboard His Britannic Majesty's Ship *Reliant*, sir, and my condolences upon your loss," Lewrie said, doffing his own hat with a *bit* more graciousness than the prisoner evinced.

"Sir, may I name to you Captain Alexandro Calderon, captain of the privateer sloop *Le Escorpion*," Lt. Bury gravely intoned, managing to make it "Alehandro", with an Iberian flourish to the ship's name. "Captain Calderon, the commanding officer of our squadron, Captain Sir Alan Lewrie, Baronet, and Captain of the *Reliant* frigate."

Black eyes flashed at him, and the Spaniard tossed his head to jerk up his chin, as if impatient with such honourable formalities.

"Eet ees my regret, *Señor Capitano* . . . Loo . . . Loo-ree, that I am weethout a sword to offer to j'ou een surrender. Eef j'ou do not mind? But, eef I was at sea, j'ou would never have catch me. None of j'our leetle sloops, certainly not j'our beeg *frigata*. *Le Escorpion* ees as fast as the wind."

"Then I suppose I should be grateful that we caught you and your consort at anchor, and asleep, *Señor* Calderon," Lewrie drolly replied, bestowing upon the Spaniard his best "shit-eating" grin.

Irksome bastard! he thought; *And can* any *bloody foreigner say my name right?*

"I see by your papers that your homeport is Havana, *señor*," Lewrie continued. "As was the *Santa Doratea*? The name of her captain escapes me."

"Don Juan Emilio Narvaez, *si,*" Calderon said, looking as if he wished to spit on the deck to cleanse his mouth of foulness.

"Then, may I assume that it was he who decided to anchor here in the bay?" Lewrie asked, "That this Narvaez was in charge?"

"*Si,*" Calderon snapped, scowling, "J'ou say j'ou have my papers? My Letters of Marque prove that we are legitimate *corsarios,* so j'ou must respect that, and treat us weeth the rules of war."

Insist, will ye? Lewrie griped to himself.

"*Corsarios?* Like corsairs? Is that not another word for pirates?" Lewrie posed with one brow up.

"No no, *señor*! *Corsario* ees not *pirata*!" Calderon countered, sounding more impatient with a hen-headed poor linguist than in fear of being hanged. "There are *many corsarios* who sail from Havana, from Cuba, but no *pirata.*"

"Despite our blockade," Lewrie said, sounding dubious.

"Blockade? Blockade ees joke! J'ou *ingleses* do not rule the seas, *señor*!" Calderon sneered. "No matter what j'ou do, merchants enter and leave Cuba, the West Indies, every day, by the hundreds, and j'our navy do not take one een ten! Blockade? Hah!

"So . . . j'ou weel now accept our parole and take us to Nassau." Calderon went on, in much calmer, but arrogant, takings. "And allow us to bury our dead?"

"Well, not right off, *señor,*" Lewrie told him. The very last thing he wanted was a return to Nassau, within reach of Francis Forrester. For that matter, he was also loath to delay the execution of the rest of his orders, even by a day. "Is Captain Narvaez one of our prisoners, Mister Bury?"

"If he is, sir, he has not announced his presence," Bury said.

"Narvaez was ashore wheen j'ou attack us," Calderon sullenly said. "Weeth hees *woman*!"

"Hey?" Lt. Westcott, who had been idling nearby, commented. "A woman, did he say?" Men of the Afterguard, some of the Midshipmen, and the other officers suppressed their snickers.

"Most-like a trull, Mister Westcott, not worth your trouble," Lewrie japed.

"No no, she ees *puta,* but *muy hermosa,*" Calderon insisted, all but lifting his fingers to his lips to kiss them in appreciation.

"My pardons, *Señor* Calderon, but you must be as dry as dust," Lewrie said; "how remiss of me not to offer you any refreshment."

"I've a . . . some champagne in my boat, sir," Lt. Darling piped up, a tad sheepishly, for such would have been looted from the encampment. "A whole case of bottles . . . French, to boot."

"Well, fetch one up, Mister Darling, and I'll send down to my cabins for glasses!" Lewrie enthused, clapping his hands in glee. "I expect the champagne will be *Señor* Narvaez's, but . . . In point of fact, Mister Darling, I'd admire a second bottle for a victory feast this evening."

"Ehm . . . I'll have the entire case fetched up, sir. There are *two* cases, really." Darling confessed, ready to wring his hands.

"Do so, sir! Do so!" Lewrie urged, then turned to his captive once more. "Had you been set up here in Mayami Bay for long, *Señor* Calderon? Much better for your purposes than the waterless islands in the Keys, hey? More game? Though, I would have thought that you might have preferred any of the inlets closer to Saint Augustine and its fort, and shore batteries. That's where I thought to find you."

"J'ou look for *me*, for Narvaez, *especialmente?*" It was his turn to gawp in astonishment, fearing betrayal by someone in Havana.

"No no, nothing like that," Lewrie cajoled. "My orders sent me to look for French or Spanish privateers in general."

The case of champagne in question arrived on deck, and Darling did the honours with the wire basket and cork. Pettus came up from the great-cabins with clean glasses, and Lewrie poured Calderon's full. It was warm, but Calderon tossed half of the glass back at once,

"*Gracias, señor*, I *was* thirsty," Calderon admitted.

"Ah! A very good French champagne," Lewrie commented, once he'd taken a deep sip himself. "Your compatriot has good taste, at least. A refill, sir? Here you go. I suppose, do so many of your merchant ships elude our blockade back in Europe, and here, that Cuba should be awash in champagne and fine French wines. Mean t'say, *señor*, you must get *something* in return for becoming a French ally."

"*Damn* the French!" Calderon snarled, well into his second glass. "And, damn all the *ateo traidores* back een Spain who take hands weeth France! So een love weeth a *república*, they turn their backs on king, on the Holy Church, on God! *Idiotas* who think they so smart, who geef part of our Navy to France, geef them *millions* in silver and gold, on the sly!

"Damn all j'ou *inglés* heretics, too!" Calderon ranted on, "for declaring war on Spain."

"Well, given the aid that Spain *was* handing over to our enemy, on the sly as you admit, England had no choice," Lewrie told him. "A great pity, but there it is. A refill, sir?"

Calderon was very agreeable to a third glass.

"The French are a rapacious race, *Señor* Calderon," Lewrie told him, striving for "chummy" and "sympathetic". "A greedy lot, indeed. Be the ruin of your home country, and of your colonies in the Indies, in the end, do your ministers like that Godoy fellow not come to their senses. And then, the French have the gall to send their privateers into *your* waters, *your* harbours, to compete with men such as you. Are there many French privateers working out of Cuba?"

"Are a few, *si*, but the Captain-General, the reech men of power, make things hard on them," Calderon admitted, offhandedly. "Such men, the dons, *hidalgos*, and grandees weeth money to make syndicates for our *corsarios* keep the shot, powder, and stores for themselves, so French *bastardos* have to beg in Havana. Florida . . . Florida ees, how j'ou say, 'out of sight, out of mind'?"

Damn my eyes! Has he gotten that drunk, this quickly? Lewrie wondered; *Or, did I just get hellish-lucky?*

"Ah, but how much support could a French privateer expect from Saint Augustine?" Lewrie hinted. "Hard to send supplies from Havana to there."

"Not from Havana," Calderon said with a sly, cock-eyed grin, as if he knew a secret. Warm champagne taken standing upright in the open on the quarterdeck, with the morning progressing, and the bay's heat rising, was doing wonders. Calderon jerked his chin Northwards in a silent hint, snickering.

"From the Americans, aye," Lewrie said, and Calderon's bitter laugh assured him that he, and Admiralty, were on the right track.

"A glass with you, sir!" Lewrie proposed, being liberal with the champagne. "To . . . His Majesty, the King of Spain!"

He wasn't quite sure who that was by name, but . . .

"*Viva la rey!*" Calderon cried, clinking glasses with him and tossing back a goodly gulp.

"I wish you better luck in future, Captain Calderon," Lewrie offered.

"Though, it might be best did you work out of the 'pocket' harbours on Cuba's North coast, or Havana, next time."

"J'ou advise me how to cor . . . privateer, *señor*?" Calderon said, finding that highly amusing.

Somebody should, *for ye've made a botch of this'un!* Lewrie told himself.

"Hoy, the ship!"

"You will excuse me for a moment, Captain Calderon? Something I must see to," Lewrie explained, then went to the starboard rails.

It was the Ship's Surgeon and his Mates, returning aboard with the Spanish wounded. "There's nought I can do for their dead, sir, but we've fetched their wounded, and I took the liberty of bringing the prizes' surgeons' chests. Ready to hoist aboard, sir," their burly Surgeon, Mr. Mainwaring, reported from his boat.

"Captain Calderon, could you come join me for a moment?" Lewrie asked.

"*Si, señor.*"

"There are ten dead Spanish sailors still aboard the prizes," Lewrie explained to him. "I was thinking that you might wish to bury them ashore, instead of me conducting a Protestant service. I'm told that three of your wounded are in a very bad way, as well, and won't be with us much longer. Do you give me your parole, so I may land them ashore, too?"

"J'ou have eet, *Señor Capitano*!" Calderon firmly declared.

"You have surgeons aboard your ships? Perhaps they could tend to the other wounded ashore, as well," Lewrie further offered.

"J'ou are the most gracious, *señor*!" Calderon said.

"Mister Bury," Lewrie said, turning to *Lizard*'s captain. "I'd be grateful did you use your boats to land *all* the prisoners ashore," Lewrie instructed, crooking a finger to draw him closer, and some distance from Calderon.

"Certainly, sir," Bury replied.

"Did any of them, get away?" Lewrie asked, in a mutter.

"Two boats did manage to escape us, sir, into the channel between the mainland and the long, narrow barrier island," Bury admitted, "They scampered off into the bushes, but we did fetch the abandoned boats off. We *did* plan to obtain bigger, better ship's boats, sir."

"Very good, Mister Bury, excellent work," Lewrie said with a grin. "I swear you read my mind. Now, I want you to take Lieutenant Simcock and a file of his Marines with you, for security, t'keep the Dons honest. After all the prisoners are ashore, though, fetch off *all* the boats . . . leave them nothing that will swim. We'll keep the useful ones, and scuttle the rest."

"Ehm . . . would we not be . . . *marooning* them, sir?" Bury asked as if he was being talked into a mortal sin.

"Not marooning, *exactly*," Lewrie pooh-poohed, slyy grinning. "The last I heard, that requires a barren, desert island, and they'll be on a mainland just teemin' with game and wild hogs, fish, birds, and oceans o' fresh water. Spaniards, ashore in a Spanish possession? What could be more humane?"

"Well . . ." Bury pondered.

"*Señor* Calderon and the rest can have a nice stroll to get to Saint Augustine, and there's sure t'be little Spanish settlements and farms along the way," Lewrie schemed on, "and all sorts of fruit and edible berries t'pluck. We leave 'em even one boat, Mister Bury, and sure as Fate, some of the damned fools'd try to sail for Havana, to arrange a rescue, and, what with waterspouts, sharks, currents, and the usual sea conditions in the Florida Straits, it just wouldn't be Christian. They'd be over-set, swamped, and drowned . . . or *eaten* . . .'fore they got halfway."

"Well, in that case, sir," Lt. Bury said, with the faintest hint of a smile on his face. "I, and Lieutenant Lovett, shall see to it, directly!"

"Capital!" Lewrie encouraged him, then went to the entry-port to inform Surgeon Mainwaring of the change in plans, then aft again to Calderon, who had been busy lowering the level of champagne in the bottle in his absence.

"J'ou land us ashore, *señor*?" Calderon asked, owl-eyed by then.

"All of you, sir," Lewrie told him, hoping that Calderon would take the gesture as magnanimous . . .'til the last moment. "I cannot find it in my heart to imprison such an affable fellow as yourself, or leave you on parole in such an expensive place as Nassau. Go with my very best wishes, sir! Here, take another bottle or two with you. Perhaps you can toast Captain Narvaez's brilliance with them, what?"

"That *idiota*!" Calderon gravelled. "Hees family was *hidalgo* een Spain, *conquistador* een Cuba. Family old and reech, weeth the many connexions, so the *sindicato* who back our voyage, they put *heem* in command. But, he ees the *marinero de agua dulce*! The . . . ah . . ."

"Complete and total 'lubber'?" Lewrie supplied.

"*Sí sí*, the . . . how j'ou say!" Calderon eagerly agreed.

They shook hands; Calderon even went so far as to embrace him and bestow a grateful kiss on Lewrie's cheek, to the amusement of the others on the quarterdeck, before stepping away.

"Uh, *señor*, j'ou geef back my papers? My Letters of Marque?"

"Sorry, *Señor* Calderon, but I must present them to the Prize Court at Nassau, as evidence that we took your ships, and lay claim to the Head and Gun Money for each man aboard at the time of capture, and for each cannon taken," Lewrie explained. "Like the Red Indians take scalps, hmm?"

"Ah. I see," Calderon said with a deep sigh, crestfallen. He would be un-employable as a privateering captain whenever he got back to Cuba, and was probably out a goodly sum of his own money as an investment in the venture, to boot.

He'll need a good, long vacation t'get over this, Lewrie told himself; *The long march to Saint Augustine ought to do it.*

Lewrie saw him over the side, doffing his hat in salute, and Cox'n Desmond made another effort at a departure call.

"Mister Westcott," Lewrie said, turning back in-board.

"Aye, sir?"

"Once all the Spanish are ashore, we're going to fetch off *all* their boats," Lewrie informed him. "Once that's done, and we've gotten all our people back aboard, we're going to sink the ones we can't use, and then . . . I wish you to see to the destruction of the prizes."

"Scuttle them as well, sir?" Lt. Westcott asked.

"No. Set fire to them and burn them to Hell."

"Cleverly done, sir," Lt. Darling dared comment. "Getting the information from the Spaniard . . . and gulling him."

Clever? Me? Lewrie scoffed to himself. *And all before breakfast? Mine arse on a band-box!*

CHAPTER TWENTY-TWO

*T*he urge to host a celebratory supper aboard *Reliant* was strong once the four-ship squadron gained the open sea, but there was still the coast above Mayami Bay to be scouted, the uncertainties of their charts to be dealt with, and sea-room out towards the Gulf Stream to be made. Lewrie sent round bottles of champagne from his newly won case—none necessary to the crafty Lt. Darling who had his own—and a bit of bad news for Lt. Lovett. *Someone* had to return to Nassau with the privateers' papers and Letters of Marque. Lewrie urged the energetic and piratical Lovett to make his stay at Nassau as brief as possible, then return to re-join *Thorn* and *Lizard* off Saint Augustine to form a scouting-blockading force; under no circumstances was he to be brow-beaten back into Captain Francis Forrester's clutches!

To Lt. Darling in *Thorn*, Lewrie sent formal written orders for him to take temporary command of the squadron 'til *Reliant* returned from her diplomatic mission and, once Lt. Lovett and HMS *Firefly* were back in the fold, to scout, harass, and engage any Spanish vessels they came across. Were there no merchantmen or light warships to fight, Lt. Darling was to make a nuisance along the coast, as long as he did not take on anything *too* rash.

"Boats away, Mister Westcott?" Lewrie asked as he mounted to the quarterdeck.

"Both away, and returning, sir," the First Officer replied, "orders, champagne, and all safely delivered. If the Mids in charge, or the oarsmen, didn't drink them right up."

"Something to be said for a late breakfast . . . or a very early dinner, combined," Lewrie commented, still savouring one of Yeovill's French-style *omelettes* with cheese, crumbled bacon, and onion, and a cup or three of strong coffee to slosh it down. He let go a discreet belch of appreciation, then turned to look aft and to larboard. The smoke from the burning ships and boats they had left in Mayami Bay still stained the horizon, even from ten miles offshore and twenty-odd miles astern. Lewrie smiled in satisfaction as he strolled to the hammock stanchions and nettings at the forward edge of the quarterdeck. "What's with the damned dog, Mister Westcott?" Lewrie asked. "I saw him huddled under the ladderway as I came up. Whining. Sick, is he?"

"It doesn't appear that the discharging of the guns agrees with him, sir," Westcott told him. "As soon as we went to Quarters, and the guns were run in for loading, he started cowering. I had one of the powder monkeys take him by the collar and lead him below to the orlop . . . with your cats, sir. Your steward, Pettus, will know more of what happened then."

"Well, cannon fire, or thunder, don't agree with the livestock up forrud, either," Lewrie said, "and don't get me started on what my eats do. Perhaps a warship isn't the right place for him. Might be, a farm'd suit him better. Then, he'd only have stormy weather t'deal with. Ye might mention that to the Mids, as to whether they think the poor thing'd suffer less ashore."

Midshipmen Munsell and Rossyngton, the youngest of the cockpit mess, at that moment strolled aft towards the base of the main mast, and, to their whistles and invitations, Bisquit darted out from his refuge and pranced about them, tail wagging madly.

"So much for being too fearful, sir," Westcott said with one brow up, and a quick, savage grin on his face. "Perhaps, like any 'pressed lubber, he'll learn to cope."

"He would . . . damn him," Lewrie muttered.

"He's good for the ship's morale, sir, you will have to admit," Lt. Westcott pointed out. "Everyone but your cats adores the beast."

"*Et tu,* sir? *Et tu?*" Lewrie said with a wry snicker.

Lt. Westcott's answer to that was a laugh.

"The last cast of the log, Mister Westcott?" Lewrie asked, turning to more practical matters.

"Eight knots and a bit, sir," Westcott said, more formally.

"Does this wind hold, then, we'll be off Saint Augustine about sundown tomorrow," Lewrie speculated. "We could leave the others then, or . . . we could stay long enough for the Dons to catch sight of us before breaking away. A Fifth Rate frigate will make a greater impression than three smaller sloops by themselves. After that . . . we will stand out to enter the Gulf Stream and rush on for Wilmington."

"Much of a place, is it, sir?" Westcott asked.

"Not as large a port as Charleston, but busy enough, so far as I remember from my times there in the Revolution," Lewrie told him. "Not that we'll see it, exactly, for the town proper's thirty miles up the Cape Fear River from the mouth. We'll have to come to anchor in the pratique ground, near old Brunswick Town . . . if it's still there. It was three-quarters abandoned and fallin' down in '81. I'll have to take one of the barges up-river. We'll send a Mid with the other for supplies."

"Firewood and water . . . a Purser's run . . . and sausages suitable for Bisquit and your cats, sir?" Westcott teased.

"If you, the Mids, and the other officers are so concerned with the dog's nourishment, one *does* hope a contribution will be gathered. Hmmm, Mister Westcott?" Lewrie japed.

"Well . . ." Westcott said, wincing. "So long as it's not too much. Mean t'say . . ."

"Got you, again, sir!" Lewrie snickered.

For a frigate like *Reliant,* which drew nigh-eighteen feet right aft, even approaching Wilmington and the mouth of the Cape Fear River was a nightmare. Entering the river through New Inlet to the East was out of the question; when the hurricane of 1761 had opened it, it was half a mile wide and eighteen feet deep at high tide, which could vary as much as six feet of ebb to low tide. Below the long sabre-shaped peninsula that lay on the East bank of the river, South of New Inlet, South of Smith Island, or Bald Head, depending upon which chart one used, lay Frying Pan Shoals that stretched out to sea for another eighteen miles, with shifting swash channels between used mostly by fishermen and small coastal trading vessels . . . so long as they could swim in six or seven feet of water!

Much safer, though by no means completely sure, was to approach well Westward of the shoals, under reduced sail, with leadsmen in the fore chains, and anchors ready to let go to haul the ship off quickly should she take the ground. A lot of the bottom was sand and shingle, but the charts showed several coral formations and rocks. From his time before at Wilmington, Lewrie recalled how quickly one could find good, deep water on one beam, and oyster banks and gin-clear water to the other, close enough to touch with an oar, and shallow enough for someone with a rake to stand knee-deep!

When the leadsmen called out that there were five fathoms off either bow, the Sailing Master coughed into his fist and vowed that it *might* be time to fetch-to and call for a pilot.

"Damned right, Mister Caldwell," Lewrie told him, letting out a whoosh of air. "We're temptin' Fate as it is. Mister Westcott? Fetch to. Hoist the 'Request Pilot' signal, and fire off a gun to wake 'em up."

It took some time before there was a cannon fired in reply, and a small two-masted vessel appeared near the Eastern tip of Oak Island bound out to them.

"Arnold Dubden, your servant, sir," the stout older pilot said once he'd gained the decks, doffing a wide-brimmed, nigh-shapeless hat. "You'd not be meaning to enter the river, now, would you?" he asked, looking incredulous.

"As I recall, Mister Dubden, that'd be asking too much," Lewrie replied, doffing his own cocked hat. "Captain Alan Lewrie, the *Reliant* frigate, and I am *your* servant, sir, in need of safe anchorage."

"That I can manage, Captain Lewrie," Dubden said with a laugh. "My word, but the biggest ship to even *try* to enter the river was the old *Hector*, back before the Revolution, and she was only two hundred thirty tons, and didn't draw twelve feet."

"Once anchored, I suppose I can find passage up-river to Wilmington at Brunswick Town?" Lewrie asked.

"Lord, sir . . . there aren't four buildings left o' Brunswick Town, and one o' them's the tavern," Dubden further related in amusement. "Smithville's the main settlement, now, mostly for the pilots, cross the sound from Oak Island, and there isn't what you'd call regular ferry service up-river. Catch as catch can, really."

"Purser's stores?" Lewrie asked. "Firewood and water?"

"You'll find some at Smithville, Captain, but the main chandlers are up-river. You could send for some, I suppose," Dubden told him.

"And the British Consul would also be up-river at Wilmington?" Lewrie pressed.

"'Fraid so, Captain, though he isn't British," Dubden related. "It's a parcel o' city lawyers who fill those posts. Well, there is a Frenchman who does for their consul duties, but the rest are local."

"Hmmm . . . sounds as if I should take one of my barges, then," Lewrie mused aloud. "Perhaps another for my Purser."

"No need to do all your carrying yourself, Captain," Dubden said. "Just send your needs up-river, and there's lighters aplenty that can fetch your purchases down. I see you fly a broad pendant, Captain. . . . There's not a squadron offshore, is there? Mean to say . . . we're not at war with you British again, are we?"

"Still completely at peace, and in total amity, sir!" Lewrie assured him. "My squadron at present is off Spanish Florida, looking for French and Spanish privateers."

"Well, then!" Dubden brightened, sounding somewhat relieved by that news. "If you will get your ship under way, there's deep water and good holding ground about half a mile further on, just off yonder."

When *Reliant* was safely anchored fore and aft, all the sails handed and gasketed, Dubden took his leave, announcing his fee for his services. "There's also one dollar due for the gunpowder, sir."

"Hey?" Lewrie asked.

"For the gunpowder we used to answer your shot, Captain," the fellow explained. "State regulations for pilotage."

"The rate of exchange would be, ah . . ." the Purser, Mr. Cadbury, reckoned, "about five shillings, sir."

Five shillings, for about ten pence of powder? Lewrie wondered; *These Yankee Doodles are nothing but a pack of skin-flints and "Captain Sharps"! When I get up-river, I'd better go with a satchel, or a keg o' coin!*

After consulting Dubden about the local tides and winds, Lewrie decided to sail up the river early the next morning in one of the thirty foot barges, taking the Purser along to negotiate for the goods that Mr. Cadbury could not purchase from the Smithville traders that afternoon.

Mr. Cooke, the ship's Black cook, was eager for Cadbury to buy Cape Fear Low Country rice, and corn meal, along with as many pecks of berry fruits as possible. Lewrie's own cook, Yeovill, popped up with a list of his own wants.

"Desmond?" Lewrie called down to the waist. "Come to the quarter-deck, if ye please."

"Aye, sor?" his Cox'n asked, once there.

"We'll take one of the barges up-river. Rig the best'un with two lugs'ls and a jib. I'll want you and Furfy, and only two more of my gig's crew . . . men you're sure won't take 'leg-bail' once we're at Wilmington," Lewrie directed. "It'll be me, the Purser, for passengers."

"Ye'll not be wishin' yer steward t'see to ye, sor?" Desmond asked, thinking it odd to not "show the flag" in proper style due the captain of a British frigate.

"We'll be among staunch republicans, almost as bad as the *sans-culottes* French, Desmond," Lewrie explained with a grin, "and the memories of the Revolution are still sharp. The less pomp and show, the better. Besides, there's an old friend of mine in Wilmington, one we may find welcoming. If the wind fails us, I'll take the tiller, and we'll have four oars t'make steerageway. Best turn-out, mind, and we will shove off round dawn."

"Aye, sor, the barge'll be ready," Desmond assured him, "even do I haveta bribe the Bosun for fresh paint!"

And let's hope Christopher Cashman's not turned into an American Jacobin, himself! Lewrie thought.

CHAPTER TWENTY-THREE

*I*t was a very pleasant day to be boating, even did it begin at "first spar-row fart" of a mid-April morning. Brown spotted gulls and white-headed gulls swirled round the mast-tops, and the black-headed laughing gulls flirted and mewed in taunting darts near the gunn'ls of the freshly-painted barge. Further off, dark cormorants hovered and gyred before twisting over to make their fish-killing dives, and clutches of pelicans winged along crank-necked further off. Flocks of white egrets and great blue herons could be seen, stalking on long legs on the nearest shoreline. Before the day warmed, the air was fresh and cool, redolent of marshes and fresh water, even as the barge breasted the surge of the making tide, leaving salt water for sweet. The boat heeled only slightly to a steady beam wind, churning a faint foamy-white bow wave and leaving only the faintest disturbance in the brown river in its wake. Looking up-river, or to either hand as it widened, the Cape Bear appeared a dark blue-green, but closer to, it was rich with leaf mould and the colour of aged tobacco leaves. All under the bluest morning sky, the whitest and least-threatening clouds, and the banks of the river lined with pine and oak brilliant with the fresh green leaves of Spring.

They passed a few landmarks that Lewrie remembered, like Orton

Pond and the magnificent house at Orton Plantation to larboard, the New Inlet and Federal Point to starboard, the other riverfront manses further up-river whose names he had never learned, or forgotten, and Desmond, Furfy, and the other hands marvelled and jested as they had a snack of fresh-baked and buttered corn dodgers and small beer.

"There's Wilmington, proper," Lewrie pointed out at last, "and that's the Dram Tree, that big cypress on the right bank. Sailors take a toast for a safe arrival, or at the beginning of an outward voyage, for good luck. Let's steer for the nearest docks, the ones in front of the Livesey, Seabright and Cashman Chandlery, Desmond."

"Take a dram, did ye say, Cap'm sor?" Patrick Furfy piped up. "An' an't it a foine tradition! Might be we . . . ?"

"For our departure, Furfy, sorry," Lewrie had to tell him. "But, if the chandlery has a keg of ale handy, we'll take a 'wet'."

"Hand the jib, Hartnett. Pat, your and Thomas see to lowerin' the lugs'ls," Desmond directed. They were far above the reach of the making tide, in fresh water, which made Wilmington a welcome harbour where saltwater marine growth would die whilst at anchor, but a goodly current was running. Lewrie tapped Mr. Cadbury on the shoulder, and they both fetched a pair of oars from the barge's sole, ready to be put into the tholes to maintain steerageway while the sailors saw to wrapping the lugs'ls round their gaff booms and lashing the sheets and halliards over the canvas. When it appeared that the barge would pay off and begin to be taken by the river current, Lewrie stood and took hold of the two stern-most oars in their tholes, and began to row, himself, just to keep them in place. It was not a task at which he could claim even modest expertise, but that stopped their drift.

"Ship oars!" Desmond ordered. "Take th' tiller, sor?"

"Bows-on between those two two-masters, if there's not room to land starboard side-to," Lewrie suggested, trading places.

Their arrival, with a British Union Jack slanted over the transom on a short gaff—a rare sight in an American port!—*and* the sight of a Royal Navy officer plying not one oar but two, seemed to have drawn a gap-jawed crowd on the piers of Dock and Water Streets!

Should've brought one or two more hands, Lewrie chid himself as he put the tiller over, once all four oarsmen were stroking hard; *This could look* damned *awkward and lubberly!*

"Toss oar, Hartnett," Desmond snapped, "an' be ready with th' bow line."

"Should I do something, sir?" Mr. Cadbury asked.

"Why, aye, Mister Cadbury," Lewrie exclaimed. "Stop sittin' on the starb'd dock line; and be ready t'toss it to the nearest helpful soul on the pier! Mind that the bitter end's still bound to the boat!"

Now, *there'd* been an embarassing mistake Lewrie had made, the first time he'd been given charge of a ship's boat, not a week into his naval career; he'd been sitting on the dock line, too, and had almost put the bow man arse-over-tit into Portsmouth harbour trying to come alongside a stone quay at the victuallers', claw the line from under his arse, and steer at the same time! The grizzled old wild-haired seaman's words came back to him: "*Thal't never make a sailorman!*"—making him blush anew.

"Toss oar, Pat," Desmond whispered to his long-time mate.

There were men on the pier who took their lines and whipped them expertly round bollards or posts, and they were safely at rest.

"Wahl, hoy th' boat, thar," a stout man on the pier drawled. "Has Adm'rl Nelson hisse'f come callin'?"

"Looking for an old friend with a pot of ale," Lewrie said, grinning back despite the man's derision.

"Will I do?" Christopher "Kit" Cashman interrupted, coming from the front doors of the establishment which partially bore his name. "Hallo, Alan, old son. Welcome to America!"

They went back a long way, to a failed expedition to carry, then escort, a diplomatic mission to woo the Muskogee, the Lower Creek Indians, to side with England and make war against Rebel settlers in 1782, when Lewrie was a Lieutenant, and Cashman a Captain of a Light Company of an un-distinguished regiment, the both of them expendable. A few years later, when British forces had invaded Haiti, then the French colony of Saint-Domingue, they had met on Jamaica, when Lewrie was Captain of the *Proteus* frigate, and Cashman had become a plantation owner, then the Lt. Colonel of an island-raised volunteer regiment, "hired on" in essence by the rich Beauman family, the bane of both Lewrie's, and Cashman's, existence. Lewrie had been Cashman's second in a duel with the unfortunate younger son, Ledyard Beauman, who had been the Colonel of the regiment, who had lost his nerve in battle in the hills outside Port-Au-Prince, shrilling for the regiment to retreat, then galloping off with his cronies in terror, and laying the entire blame for what could have been a rout and massacre on "Kit".

It had been Cashman who'd arranged Lewrie's "theft", or "liberation", of a dozen prime Black slaves from a neighboring Beauman plantation before he'd sold up and removed to the United States, and the one who'd sent a supporting (frankly lying!) affidavit to England which had gone a long way in getting Lewrie off at his trial years later for that theft, once the Beaumans had figured out who had done it.

Christopher Cashman had not changed much in the years since. His hair had thinned a bit, and civilian living and the accumulation of wealth had thickened his waist, but it only took a few minutes to remake their friendship, as cozy as an old pair of shoes.

"Now, what in the world brings you to Wilmington?" Cashman asked in amusement, over glass mugs of cool beer.

"Admiralty orders, to look for French and Spanish privateers fitting out in neutral ports," Lewrie told him. "Show the flag, consult with our consuls . . . be tactful and diplomatic."

"Tactful and diplomatic," Cashman gawped, "you? A bull in the china shop's more your style, as I recall."

"The Smithville pilot said our consul here is a local fellow?" Lewrie asked. "Who is he?"

"Mister Osgoode Moore, Junior," Cashman told him. "Esquire. An attorney, like his father, Osgoode Moore, Senior, who was a noted patriot during the Revolution . . . joined the Corresponding Society in the early days, the Sons of Liberty, got slung into the prison under the old Burgwyn house by the King's agents, Fanning and Cunningham, and got treated rather cruelly. Lucky to have survived it, unlike a few others. The father took arms when the local militia marched on Governor Tryon's house down at Brunswick to rebel against the Stamp Act. . . . He was said to have been one of the rebels who went aboard HMS *Viper*, seized the chests of stamps, and took back the papers of the ships held from trading for refusing to use them. Just like the Boston Tea Party, as they say, this side of the Atlantic, but *years* before Massachusetts revolted. He's a good-enough fellow, is young Moore, but . . . perhaps not all *that* enamoured of the post. It pays a tidy annual sum, without too much work to do, since Wilmington's not a major trader with England any more."

"Hmmm . . . just a *paid* agent," Lewrie gloomed. "His heart ain't in it . . . enough t'turn a blind eye?"

"Oh, he's a stickler, or would be, if anyone laid an information of some-one aiding the French or the Spanish," Cashman countered. "The interests of Britain, and the strict neutrality of the United States, are the same thing to him, I'm certain.

"Besides, Alan," Cashman continued, "I've my ears to the ground, and my own eyes on the chandleries, and the port. I can't give you a guarantee that the French or Spanish might put into one of the many in-lets for wood and water, but from Lockwood's Folly to Tops'l Island, I'm pretty sure that there's no collusion going on."

"The pilot told me there's a Frenchman here as their consul," Lewrie asked. "Could *he* be up to something?"

"*Monsieur* Jean-Marie Fleury?" Cashman scoffed, rising to go to the keg of beer at the back of his office for a refill. "I'm certain he'd *love* to . . . *anything* for *La Belle France*, and the Emperor Napoleon. Just so long as it doesn't drag him from his bed too early in the morning, involve a long, secretive horseback ride, or cost him a single dollar. I'm not sure why the French waste the money to keep a consul here, at all. There haven't been more than a dozen of their merchant ships calling here since the war began again two years ago."

"Though the Americans still think the French 'hung the moon'?" Lewrie posed. "Damned nice beer. I think I'll have a top-up, too."

"Oh, there's many who still adore them, no matter how bloody the French Revolution was, compared to theirs," Cashman scoffed as he re-filled Lewrie's mug, too. "Our good president Jefferson's in love with them, and so are all the newspapers. You came up-river with but four sailors, and nothing but your sword and their knives? Quite the risk for a bloody Brit, after dark, when the patriotic drunks spill out of the taverns on a hoo-raw."

"*You're* a bloody Brit!" Lewrie exclaimed in good humor. "You're not dead, yet."

"Ah, but I'm an *eccentric* Brit, and a harmless civilian trader, to boot. No threat to anyone these days," Cashman hooted with mirth as he came back to his desk. "I doubt I could stand for public office and win, but I care nothing for such, other than joining the local militia. My army back-ground is welcome, by most . . . even if I am once more back to the rank of Lieutenant, and the junior-most, at that. The militia's more social than professional," Cashman explained with a shrug. "When I bought into an old, established, pre-Revolutionary firm, founded by patriots, that went a long way towards acceptance. Hewing strictly to business, and avoiding politics, has gone a long way, too.

"Matthew Livesey . . . when it was Livesey and Son. The old man moved the family trade from Philadelphia long ago," Cashman expounded. "Dead and gone, now, but his grandson's still a partner. Old Livesey was part of the Corresponding Society with New Englanders, early on, and joined the Sons of Liberty. The Seabright part? Phillip Seabright was a Royal Artillery officer who came to survey old Fort Johnston, down near Brunswick Town . . . horrid folly, I've heard. Every time the guns were fired, it like to shook itself to pieces! Anyway, he ended up buying land and going into business with Livesey. When the Stamp Act was enacted, Wilmington, and North Carolina, almost seceded from Great Britain. Seabright and Livesey were part of the thousand men of the militia from New Hanover, Brunswick, and surrounding counties who rebelled. He married Livesey's daughter, Bess, before the war, and when it came, Seabright marched off with a couple of pop-guns to fight the Highlander Loyalists at Widow Moore's Creek Bridge, then served in the Continental Army against Cornwallis and Tarleton. Seabright's in his sixties, now, but his eldest son is with the firm.

"And . . . there's the fact that I married well," Cashman admitted, somewhat sheepishly.

"You married again, Kit? At last?" Lewrie hooted. "Mine arse on a band-box, that is capital! A good local family, I take it?"

"The Ramseurs," Cashman told him. "Before the Revolution, the old patriarch was 'Prince Dick'—Richard Ramseur—in comparison to 'King' Roger Moore, the grandest of the settlers who came up from Goose Creek, South Carolina, to found the borough. They're still not sure of me, I'll tell you. They're nowhere near as well-off as they were in the old days, but the Ramseurs still farm . . . rice, tobacco, cotton? They own nigh an hundred slaves, yet here I am kin to them, despite my vow against owning another slave as long as I live, after my experiences on Jamaica. Makes for testy suppers at their place, or mine. My wife, Sarah, well . . . we have house servants, as few as possible in bondage, and pay wages to the rest."

"Round here, you *are* eccentric," Lewrie said, shaking his head in wonder. "I doubt there aren't a round dozen gentlemen in the whole state of North Carolina of a mind with you. When you sent that affidavit about my theft of those dozen Beauman slaves that got me off . . . did that hurt you, hereabouts?"

"I swore it to Osgoode Moore, Junior . . . before he became the British Consul," Cashman told him, looking grave. "As my attorney, he is required to keep mum about the matter, and, as I said, Moore is a stickler, and as high-minded a gentleman as his father. No one knows of it, and, pray God, no one ever will."

"So, should I get in my cups whilst I'm in Wilmington, I'd best not mention all that?" Lewrie asked.

"Especially over supper tonight," Cashman replied, grinning. "I hope to dine you in at my house, and invite Osgoode Moore and his wife. You should also lodge with us for a few days. Much cleaner, and safer, than taking public lodgings. The other officer who came with you?"

"My Purser, Mister Cadbury," Lewrie said. "Only the one night, Kit. I expect he's with your clerks, purchasing fresh stores. I told him to use no other chandlery. . . ."

"My, and my partners', thanks, Alan!" Cashman laughed. "We'll have your Mister Cadbury to dine, as well. We've two spare rooms."

"He can eat with a knife and fork," Lewrie japed, "though, I don't know if he snores, or walks in his sleep!"

"Your sailors won't mind dossing down in the coach house and stables?" Cashman asked.

"So long as they've eat well, and had some rum, no," Lewrie replied, "though, they'd not make good supper conversation. I don't know if Cadbury's all that much a conversationalist, either, but . . ."

"One can never tell," Cashman mused aloud. "America is full of surprises. Planter grandees, tradesmen, and commoners . . . 'mud-sills' from the back country, as some say round here . . . one never knows where a good yarn can be had. Quite unlike British Society, hey? With industry, even a 'mud-sill' can become a grandee, and, do his sons and daughters get polished, there's no limit on how far they can go. I am continually amazed by the open egality and aspirations of Americans."

"Well . . . so long as one's White," Lewrie wryly countered.

"Well, there is that," Cashman ruefully admitted. "Now . . . let me get the invitations written, and send my wife a note that we'll have guests this evening. Moore will need a formal invitation. Anything to impress him? A medal or two, hey?" Cashman teased.

"Battles of Cape Saint Vincent and Camperdown," Lewrie smiled as he ticked his honours off. "Copenhagen, but they didn't hand out any 'tin' for that 'un. I command a very small squadron of very small sloops, but one can't see my broad pendant, all the way down-river to Smithville. Just say that Captain Sir Alan Lewrie, Baronet, will wish to discuss—"

"A knighthood? A baronetcy, to boot?" Cashman gawped, pen poised above the sheet of paper. "When did that happen?"

"Spring of 1804," Lewrie grinned. "Fought a Frog squadron off New Orleans and took all four of 'em so the French could not invest the city before Napoleon sold it to the United States."

"So your wife is now Dame Lewrie?" Cashman beamed, "Grand! I never met her, but—"

"She . . . passed away, three years ago," Lewrie sadly related, "in 1802."

"Lord, do forgive me, Alan, I had no idea!"

"I didn't write you of it, you didn't know, so there's nought to beg forgiveness for, Kit," Lewrie assured him. "I should've written, but . . . things happened in the meantime, and . . ."

Tell him how *it happened?* Lewrie wondered; *No, Americans adore the French. I say Napoleon killed her while trying t'have me killed, it wouldn't be . . . diplomatic. And diplomatic's what they sent me to be, ain't it?*

"Sarah will be delighted, even so, to dine in a Baronet, in his sash and star," Cashman breezily said, returning to his letter. "No matter America's distaste for aristocracy, you show them a lord, and they'll dearly love him."

"I left 'em aboard," Lewrie confessed. "I didn't know how all that might go down . . . how touchy peoples' feelings about England are even this long after the Revolution. Diplomacy, hey?" he added with a cynical shrug. "No mobs pantin' t'lynch a Tory."

"But you should've worn them, Alan!" Cashman exclaimed. "You're going about this 'show the flag' thing all wrong! You'll be calling along the coast to other port cities? Good. When you sail into Savannah or Charleston, be sure to wear them. A sash and star will make the Charlestonians gush over you, 'cause in their hearts, they'd wish to have one, too. You know what they say about South Carolinians . . . that they're the most Asiatic of all Americans? S'truth! For they eat a lot of rice, and worship their ancestors, haw haw!"

"And Savannah, and Georgia?" Lewrie asked.

"Of much the same mind, though nowhere near as polished, in the main," Cashman quipped again. "People in both the Carolinas are sure that 'all the rogues end up in Georgia'."

There was a knock at the office door, and at Cashman's bidding, *Reliant*'s Purser, Mr. Cadbury entered. "I believe we've found all our needs, sir, and on good terms, as well. Mister Cashman's clerks have been most helpful. Though, the bulk and weight of the stores exceed our boat."

"For a further modest fee, we'll see your purchases down-river in one of the 'corn-crackers' alongside the piers," Cashman suggested. "All our lighters are tied up at the moment, but I'm sure we can make an offer to one of the masters to make an extra run before he returns here to load his trade goods. Grains and such down the Northwest or the Northeast Branch of the Cape Fear, as far as Campbelltown or Cross Creek, and back again. Very fast and handy little vessels, even for the coasting trade from Beaufort and New Bern. Does one of them get underway by midday next, she could use the river current and the ebb of the tide and be off Smithville waiting for you."

"That'd be capital, Kit, thankee," Lewrie said. "Oh, by the by. You'd not have some dried meats in stock, would you? Sausages, strips of jerky? For the cats, d'ye see. And, the Midshipmen have adopted a stray mongrel dog, so . . ."

"You still keep eats aboard?" Cashman teased. "I've the very thing. Pemmican! The Lumbee tribe round Lake Waccamaw make it. It's God knows what sort of meat, flour, suet, molasses, and dried berries, pounded together. They bring it in by the bale, along with all the deer and alligator hides. Want some?"

"About an hundredweight will do, aye," Lewrie agreed.

Sounds toothsome enough; the beasts'll have t'fight me for it! he thought.

"Mister Cadbury, I've invited my old friend, Captain Lewrie, to lodge and dine with me, tonight," Cashman said as he quickly went over the tally his clerks had made, "and I trust that you will accept my invitation, as well."

"With pleasure, Mister Cashman!" Cadbury quickly replied.

"Once we've settled the reckoning, I'll see the both of you over to the house, then," Cashman further offered. "The pemmican on your own account, Alan? Call it ten dollars. That'd be . . . two pounds, at the current rate of exchange."

"Here you go," Lewrie said, digging into his coin purse.

"Your boat will be safe enough here at our pier for the night," Cashman said, once he had Cadbury's money, and Admiralty note-of-hand. "Bring your sailors along, and we'll get them settled in, as well."

With Liam Desmond, Patrick Furfy, and the other of the boat's crew in tow, Cashman led the party along Water Street, up Dock Street to round the uphill end of the actual dock cut into the river bank that gave the street its name, then over to Market Street, the main thoroughfare, and uphill again towards St. James Church and Fifth Street, which in Lewrie's brief time in the city had been the outer limit of Wilmington, with nothing but pine forests beyond to the sea to the East. But it had grown far beyond, since. Where most homes and businesses had been wood, plagued by almost annual fires, there were now impressive stone or brick buildings and houses, some as fine as anything in London. Where Lewrie remembered sandy dirt streets, and full of stray dogs, geese, chickens, and goats, there were now cobblestoned streets with sidewalks, iron lamp-posts, and very little livestock. There were many more fine carriages than he remembered, too, and a lot more people strolling about in finer clothing than that worn at the tail-end of a long war.

We've become a raree show? Lewrie asked himself, noticing how people stopped in their tracks to gawk and stare. He also noted that a parcel of gawkers, young boys mostly, had followed them from the chandlery, as if word had spread of a second British invasion, or bloody Tarleton or Lord Cornwallis had come back!

"Uh-oh," Cashman muttered under his breath.

"Uh-oh?" Lewrie parroted in query, expecting trouble.

"The French consul, *Monsieur* Fleury," Cashman explained, jutting his chin towards a foppish slim fellow at the corner by the church.

M. Jean-Marie Fleury was bristling with indignation at the very sight of a despicable *Anglais,* his exotic thin mustachios quivering in loathing, and his chin high. He was the epitome of a dandy, dressed in a long-tailed, waist-length, double-breasted green coat with lapels that ended near his shoulders, a short-brimmed thimble of a hat with a tricolour cockade, dazzling white trousers of almost painfully skin-tight cut, and brown-topped riding boots. Grey suede-gloved fingers flexed angrily on the gilt handle of his ebony walking stick, as if he would like nothing more than to dash forward and cudgel Lewrie to his knees.

"Faith, but ain't he a little terrier, ain't he?" Furfy said, snickering.

When they were within fifteen feet or so of that worthy, Fleury heaved a great sniff of disdain, stamped his walking stick on the pavement, and directed his gaze skyward and away, in the "Cut Sublime".

The derisive and insulting gesture made several people titter.

Lewrie came to a stop, staring directly at Fleury. He could not resist. He heaved off a loud "Harumph" of his own, stamped one booted foot, and turned his own head about so he could study the clouds, and the view North down Fifth Street, raising both hands to one eye like the tube of a telescope. That raised another titter from the crowd.

Then, Lewrie began to laugh, with a broad grin on his face. He looked back to Fleury, laughed some more, then walked on past the man, leaving the French consul stuck with his "Cut Sublime", and no chance of laughing it off, turning coral pink in frustration.

"Well played, Alan old son," Cashman muttered, restraining his own laughter. "By supper, that'll be the talk of the town, and every trick taken."

"D'ye think they'd call that *proper* diplomacy?" Lewrie asked.

CHAPTER TWENTY-FOUR

*T*hey had gotten a late start from the Wilmington docks the morning after supper with the Cashmans, but the barge was back alongside *Reliant,* and Lewrie and the Purser safely on deck, just before dusk. The Bosun and Bosun's Mate trilled the welcoming call, and the side-party saluted as Lewrie made it in-board of the entry port, doffing his own hat in salute, feeling much relieved to be back on his ship.

Bisquit the dog exuberantly pranced about the shins of the sailors and Marines, yipping, barking, and whining with joy, as if he had been cruelly separated from his master for over a year, and was in paroxysms of rapture to be re-united, which quite ruined the ceremony.

Lewrie gave the dog a pat on the head, reached into his pockets, and offered Bisquit a piece of pemmican, to shut him up. He sniffed, wagged his tail *and* his hindquarters, then chomped down and ran off with his heavenly new treat.

"Welcome back, sir," Lt. Westcott said.

"Thankee, Mister Westcott. Anything amiss occur while I was away?" Lewrie asked. "Anyone swim ashore and desert?"

"All's well, sir," Westcott assured him. "It seems that this little Smithville's not much of a temptation. I *did* allow the Mids to go ashore, along with Mister Spendlove and Merriman, for an hour or two, just to stretch their legs, but . . ."

"You did not, sir?" Lewrie asked.

"As I said, sir," Westcott said with a tight little grin, "it has no temptations, beyond a well-stocked tavern."

"No women, ah well," Lewrie teased.

"Might I ask how your trip to Wilmington fell out, sir?" the First Officer enquired as they fell into a side-by-side stroll towards the stern.

"Satisfyin', in part, un-satisfyin' in another," Lewrie said, "and damned frustratin' at the tail-end. Put a Mid and a work-party to heavin' up the stores we have in the barge, then join me in my cabins for a mug of ale, and I'll reveal all."

"Most grateful, sir," Westcott said, turning to whistle up men to assist Mr. Cadbury in unloading the barge.

By the time Westcott entered the great-cabins, Lewrie was down to shirt-sleeves, sitting on the starboard-side settee and having more fuss made of him by his cats, Toulon and Chalky, who found pemmican a tasty treat, as well.

"An ale for the First Officer, if ye please, Pettus," Lewrie ordered.

"Right away, sir!"

"Sit, Mister Westcott," Lewrie bade. "Here, try some of this pemmican. I fetched back an hundredweight of it for our creatures, but it's really too good for them. Ten Yankee dollars, in all. Two pounds sterling. You, the officers, and the Mids, make up one pound between you, and I'll call it quits."

"Damned decent price, sir . . . uhm, tasty, too!" Westcott said in appreciation.

"First off, our Consul in Wilmington, and the Lower Cape Fear, is a local attorney," Lewrie told him. "Don't pull such a long face, sir, for I found him honourable and decent, and quite diligent about representing England's interests . . . and America's strict neutrality, in equal measure. Between him and my old friend, Christopher Cashman, who knows the chandlery trade and the town's docks as well as any, I think we can write off Wilmington as a potential shelter for enemy privateers. We'll have to look elsewhere . . . to the South. Charleston, Georgetown, Beaufort, and Port Royal in South Carolina, for starters."

"More fun to be had in Charleston than little Smithville, aye sir," Lt. Westcott said with a hopeful grin. Chalky abandoned Lewrie's thigh, leapt down, and made his way to Westcott's lap stretching his neck and pawing for the remaining morsel of pemmican.

"Much more business bein' done, for certain," Lewrie agreed, in a way, "and a harbour much more accessible from the sea, with sufficient depth for fully-laden Indiamen. More temptations for local businessmen to dabble in privateerin', perhaps. Don't know about Georgetown, The Winyah Bay is rather shallow, with a narrow safe channel, and the town is mostly in the rice-exportin' trade. I don't even know if we have a consul there . . . and won't, 'til we speak to our consul in Charleston."

"Oh, here, you little pest," Westcott said, surrendering to the cat's manic intent to have the last bite. "You said the rest of your stay in Wilmington was less than satisfying, sir?"

"Well, Cashman's wife—lovely and gracious woman from one of the finest old Cape Fear families, by the way—laid on a splendid supper party for us," Lewrie said, making a wee wry grimace. "Took it a step too far, though. It was Cashman and his wife, our local consul, Mister Osgoode Moore, Junior, and his—"

"Junior, sir?" Westcott asked, looking askance.

"The American way of tellin' father from son, I gathered. So, that made six of us, countin' me and Mister Cadbury," Lewrie went on. "But, to dine in a Knight and Baronet, she also had in one of the old partners in Livesey, Seabright, and Cashman, Mister Phillip Seabright himself, and his wife Bess . . . both of whom took active parts in the Revolution in their younger days. That made eight guests, but, apparently Mistress Cashman thought the balance 'twixt gentlemen and ladies was off, so, she whistled up one of her neighbours, a widow, and her spinster daughter."

"And did you feel 'buttock-brokered', sir?" Westcott idly japed. "A knighted widower to be inspected?"

"No, none of that," Lewrie said, with a sardonic laugh. "The widow lady was in her late fifties if she was a day, though the daughter was fetchin' enough. Ah, thankee, Pettus," he said as his cabin servant/steward fetched him a fresh mug of ale. "No, the problem was they were Chiswicks."

"Ehm . . . ?" Lt. Westcott posed in query, not tumbling to it.

"My late wife's surname was Chiswick, and she, her parents, and her brothers were from the Cape Fear," Lewrie explained with a wince.

"Loyalist, Tory, supporters of King and Country during the Revolution, whereas *these* Chiswicks were the Rebel side of the family."

"Well . . . after all these years, sir, does it really matter any more?" Westcott asked

"It don't t'me, but it surely still matters to *them*!" Lewrie said, enlightening his First Lieutenant. "There I was, sponged off, clean-shaven, fangs polished, and my breath sweetened with a ginger *pastille*, just fit t'please. Even had my mind primed t'be tactful, witty, an' charmin', for God's sake, as we gathered in the parlour for sherry or Rhenish. The Moores arrived, and it's a fine beam reach and smooth sailin', couldn't *be* more congenial.

"The Seabrights arrive, and it comes out that I was once in Wilmington during the war, after Yorktown, for the evacuation of the British garrison and stores," Lewrie went on, "and, 'oh, hasn't their city grown since,' and 'were you truly a witness to Cornwallis's surrender at Yorktown?', and I got off my tale of escapin' the might before—tell ye that'un, someday— and 'isn't it wonderful t'be back at peace these many years?', and then I asked about the grand old house that used to stand at the top of the hill on Market Street, and Mistress Seabright says that that was the house her father, Matthew Livesey, had built once the firm was profitable, *before* the war came, and I made the mistake of sayin' that I'd known some people who lodged there just before the evacuation, and I felt the wind veer ahead to a close reach, and turn a tad nippy. The only people who lived there were *Tarleton's* officers, and refugeed Loyalists, so Mister Seabright launched into a scheme by the local lights t'dam up New Inlet to deepen the channels of Old Inlet t'let in bigger ships. The cat was still in the bag, then, and the change o' topic was welcome."

"This was *before* the angry mob with torches and pitchforks came to the door, I take it, sir?" Westcott asked, tongue-in-cheek, enjoying his captain's discomfort.

Lewrie gave him a scowl suitable to the occasion.

"In sailed the Chiswick ladies," Lewrie continued his tale of woe. "Fusses, ados, bows, and curtseys, and the introductions, first, and the servants fetched round more wine. Now, Widow Chiswick started out as a pleasant old chick-a-biddy, all grand manners and sweet as your white-haired granny. *Married* into the clan just after the Revolution, but she must've swotted up on Chiswick lore from her teens. The spinster daughter was about nineteen . . . blond, blue-eyed, pertly fetchin' . . ."

"I see, sir," Westcott said, rising to the description with an anticipatory grin . . . a rather feral one. Young ladies did that to him.

". . . as miss-ish and coy as any ye ever did see, just primed to thrill . . . perhaps too much so, 'cause I see no other reason she hasn't caught a beau, yet. Or, so I gathered," Lewrie described. "She even paid poor Mister Cadbury a fair share of attention."

"The lucky bastard, sir," Westcott commented with a brief scowl of envy to have not been there.

"At last, the major-domo, or butler, or whatever they call 'em in America, says that supper is ready, so off we trot, two columns in line-abreast, find our seats, and I found myself cross from the Seabrights, with the widow lady abeam, and the daughter two points off my starboard bows," Lewrie laid out, "and at first, things go swimmingly . . .'til Mistress Seabright asks do I have family back in England, and do I miss 'em sore, and here it came, cat's out o' the bag, at last, with the ends knotted. Wife passed away three years before? *Sugary* expressions o' sympathy. Daughter farmed out with my brother-in-law, two sons in the Navy . . . well, I had *t'name* 'em, didn't I, and there went the Chiswick nape hairs!

"My eldest is named Sewallis Lewrie, for my late father-in-law, d'ye see, Mister Westcott, and my daughter's named for my late mother-in-laws Charlotte Chiswick," Lewrie painfully elaborated, shifting uncomfortably on the thin settee cushions, "and she's stayin' with brother-in-law Governour. After that, I didn't have to say the name Chiswick, 'cause the family lore's just bung-full about 'em. My father-in-law, with some other prosperous planter gentlemen, raised a single-battalion Loyalist regiment and armed 'em with Ferguson rifles, and Governour and Burgess Chiswick were officers in that regiment. The old lady put it to me, 'and was your wife from the Cape Fear, Sir Alan?' and ye can't *lie* about such a thing . . . much as I wished! . . . so I says that Caroline *was*, aye, and ye'd've thought I'd said that she was the bastard git of the Devil himself! A full gale smacked me fine on the bow, leavin' me all a'back and 'in-irons'"

Lt. Westcott had himself a serious wince, in sympathy, saying, "Sounds rather . . . awkward, sir. Ouch! Your own kin . . . of a sort."

"Aye, one minute, it was all gushin', and makin' cow-eyes over me like I was the Prince of Wales, even if I *am* English. . . . Cashman was right when he said that even Jacobins'll go giddy over a 'lord'," Lewrie said with a mirthless laugh, "and the next minute, I'm a red-eyed Turk in a turban, Attila the Hun, and 'Bloody' Banastre Tarleton all rolled up in one! I got . . .

lectured, Mister Westcott, on the barbarities of the British during the Revolution, and the atrocities committed by those who sided with the King, and nothing that my host and hostess, or the Seabrights could do to dissuade 'em. I had t'sit and *take* it, totally dis-masted, and all guns out of action."

"Lord, how horrible, sir!" Lt. Westcott said, after a silence, and a sip or two of his ale. "Though . . . your predicament does have a certain bleak humour to it."

"I'm glad *somebody* thinks so," Lewrie gravelled. "Well, both the widow granny and the spiteful young mort gave me close broadsides for a goodly time, 'til they ran out of grievances . . . or air, one or the other," Lewrie said, shaking his head with a bleak humour of his own. "Christ, what a litany! Every burned haystack, stolen horse, looted house, butchered cow, coin-silver punch bowl, or broken teacup . . . every torched house and barn, every dead Chiswick or their neighbours, who was imprisoned, whipped . . . but when they did run out of wind, I got my own back. Didn't give a tinker's dam for 'tactful or diplomatic', by then."

"How so, sir?" Westcott asked, both rapt and darkly amused by the tale, by then.

"I told 'em that when I escaped Yorktown, got back aboard my own ship at New York, we sailed to Wilmington, and how I found the Chiswicks," Lewrie said, lifting his chin with stubborn pride of the doing, "of how my future father-in-law was broken in body and spirit, and how penniless they were, the three of 'em, and their one loyal old slave cook and maid-of-all-work, and what little they'd managed t'salvage, were living in one small room, damned near at the edge of starvation, and, had it not been for my pleas to my old captain, and his generosity and pity, they'd not have been able to buy passage to Charleston, and temporary refuge.

" 'Cause their own Chiswick kin, the ones who'd welcomed 'em with open arms t'settle in the Cape Fear country, and my mother-in-law's long-settled kinfolk, burned *them* out, murdered the youngest brother, George, when he tried to defend them, stole *their* livestock and looted *their* possessions, stole their lands, and drove off their slaves," Lewrie fumed in a dark taking. "And *damned* if they think to pretend that they were the ones with clean hands, or grievances!"

"Good, sir! Good!"

"Well, I didn't go *that* far," Lewrie confessed. "The recapitulation's harsher than the original, but . . . let's say that the supper party did *not* end with music, parlour games, or *écarté*."

The Chiswick ladies had departed in a huff, before the dessert, and the Seabrights soon after, Lewrie related. Poor Mister Cadbury had been relegated to an embarassed companion to Mrs. Cashman and Mrs. Moore for some *moody* three-handed cards, whilst Lewrie, Cashman, and Moore had remained at-table with port and tobacco, getting the King's Business settled anent French or Spanish privateers, and an agreement that Cashman and Moore would keep their eyes peeled for any merchants who might be aiding them. If discovered, Moore would lodge protests with the local courts, with the state government, and alert the British Ambassador in Washington City.

"Cashman and I sat up and downed a few," Lewrie said, sighing, and easing his position on the settee. "He had a crock o' Kentucky aged whisky, thank God, and I tottered up to bed quite late. Damme, but it's been a while since I slept in a soft feather bed . . . a bed that doesn't sway back and forth like a hanging bed-cot, and I don't think I got three hours' sleep. Cadbury snores, by the way.

"Then, to put the icing on the cake, who accosts me on my way back to the piers t'take our leave but a scurrilous little pest from the town *newspaper!*" Lewrie growled. He took a deep sip of his ale before going on. "*Demandin'*, mind, when Great Britain was going to stop inspectin' American ships for contraband, making prize of those bound for enemy ports . . . violations on free trade, and uppermost, when were we going to stop pressing American-born sailors to man our ships! Wished I could've strangled him on the spot. Wished I *had* strangled those two Chiswick bitches. Now there's *my* kind of tactful diplomacy!"

"Ever read Machiavelli, sir?" Lt. Westcott asked.

"Who the Hell's he when he's up and dressed?" Lewrie growled.

"An Italian writer of long ago, sir. Wrote a book of instructions for rulers, called *The Prince*," Westcott said, with a sly smile. "One of his pieces of advice was that a ruler should be more feared than loved. Since you obviously created little love in Wilmington, it might have been better for you to have spread a little fear."

"Hmm . . . doubt it'd do any good t'go back, with guns run out and matches lit," Lewrie said, sounding weary. "What's done is done."

Lewrie sat up and finished his ale.

"First thing in the morning, Mister Westcott, make Stations for

Weighing. Fire a gun, and make hoist for a pilot to see us safely out to sea. All purchased supplies loaded, I take it?"

"Aye, sir."

"Good," Lewrie replied, sounding and looking more alert. "Dine with me this evening, Mister Westcott. You, Mister Cadbury, who can contribute to the tale of my embarassment, and some others. I'll have Midshipman Eldridge in, as well. I haven't dined him in, yet."

"And, will you tell us the tale of how you escaped Yorktown, sir?" Westcott asked as he set his empty ale mug aside and stood.

"Well . . . if I must," Lewrie promised, grinning.

CHAPTER TWENTY-FIVE

*H*MS *Reliant* swanned a leisurely way from Wilmington to Charleston on a steady but light tops'l breeze, twelve or fifteen miles offshore, making no more than seven or eight knots, slow enough to trawl a large net astern to see what sort of fresh fish would turn up when hauled in. But for a brief rain squall in late afternoon, the jaunt was all blue skies and fine white clouds, over a steel-blue sea that glittered with white caps.

For the benefit of any fishermen or passing American merchantmen, Lewrie had the crew exercised on the great guns all through the Forenoon, with live firing, and ordered a fresh, large Union Jack to be flown aft, so that everyone who espied her, even from shore, would know that the Royal Navy was cruising American waters, and, perhaps not for any idle purpose, as Lt. Westcott had suggested, to inspire more fear than love.

By mid-morning of the next day, she was off Charleston Bar and calling for a pilot. There were several channels she could use through the Bar; the Sullivan's Island Channel to the North, which ran close under the guns of Fort Moultrie, the North Channel below Sullivan's, the Swash Channel which was only suitable for small vessels at high tide, and the Main Ship Channel, which lay closest to the lighthouse and beacon. Lewrie was taking no chances—he would use the Main Ship Channel. His old *Atlantic Neptune* still held true: Hold North-West, place the spire of St. Michael's Church square on the bows, and the lighthouse square off the stern once past it, into Five Fathom Hole, and there was deep water all the way to the Battery at the foot of the city, with good holding ground a bit west towards the mouth of the Ashley River.

"Like goin' to China, Mister Westcott," Lewrie said, rocking on the balls of his fresh-blacked boots as the pilot cutter approached. "South Carolinians eat a lot of rice, and worship their ancestors."

Hell, he *hasn't heard it yet, and it's true enough t'be funny,* Lewrie told himself.

"From that, one could construe that both the ship's cook, and yours, are South Carolinians, sir . . . when it comes to frequency with which rice accompanies our victuals," Westcott japed back, after he'd had a brief laugh at his captain's jest.

Three days a week, on Banyan Days, no meat was issued, and the rations were oatmeal, cheese, ship's bisquit, with nary a morsel of salt-meat, but with rice so cheap, the ex-slave cook, Mr. Cooke, and Yeovill boiled up enough to make the ship's people *feel* full. Even Lewrie's cats had gotten used to some rice with their sausages, pemmican, and jerky, or table scraps.

"Aye, and after Mister Cadbury makes a purchasing run ashore, there'll be even more of it," Lewrie told him. "Unless the officers of the wardroom wish to buy something else for their mess?"

"Potatoes, sir," Westcott idly said. "Mashed, baked, hashed with cheese, diced and fried . . . ah, an humble but regal dish in all its manifestations!"

"The pilot boat is coming alongside, sir," Midshipman Rossyngton warned.

"Very well . . . side-party, Mister Westcott," Lewrie ordered.

The harbour pilot turned out to be a cheery fellow in his mid-thirties, and, once the introductions were done, gaily announced "Welcome to Charleston, Captain Lewrie . . . the very place where the Ashley and the Cooper Rivers come together to form the Atlantic! I presume you wish a good anchorage, not *too* close to shore, to make it too hard for any of your sailors of a mind to run?"

"That'd be most welcome, sir, thankee," Lewrie replied.

The pilot pointed off the larboard bows to the open waters to the left of Charleston's Southernmost tip, the Battery, more towards the Ashley.

"There's good ground there, sir, well clear of any ship bound for the piers along the Cooper, well clear of the Middle Ground, and Shute's Folly. Bad for desertion, but a short row to town."

"There is a long tongue of shallows to starboard, from the city's tip to the deeper channel of the Cooper," Mr. Caldwell, their Sailing Master, said, pointing to his chart pinned to the traverse board of the compass binnacle cabinet.

"Sure is, and I'll conn you well West of it, sir," the pilot vowed. "With your permission, Captain Lewrie, I'll take charge of the deck?"

"Proceed, sir," Lewrie allowed with a smile.

The First Officer, Lt. Westcott, and Mr. Caldwell stood close by the pilot, as if ready, to second-guess the fellow, but not close enough to discomfort him.

"Topsl's, reefed spanker, and the inner and outer jibs will be enough, I think, on this breeze," the pilot said, peering about at his own set of harbour marks, the slant of the commissioning pendant high aloft, and the rippling of the sails. "Oh, one thing, sir. Hope you don't mind, but . . . would it kill your soul to be anchored within two or three cables of a French ship?"

That laid them all a'back, producing grimaces on the faces of the quarterdeck officers, some wide eyes on some, or slitted eyes on the others.

"What *manner* of French ship, sir?" Lewrie warily asked, after his initial surprise.

"Don't rightly know, sir," the pilot breezily admitted. "She's schooner rigged. Might have come up from the Antilles to trade?" he added with a shrug. "Ah . . . let's lay her head a point more to starboard, if you please, sirs. Steer direct for the tall church spire, helmsman."

"Did you pilot her in, sir?" Lewrie asked.

"Not me, no, Captain. She came in almost two days ago, when I was off," the pilot went on, pacing from one side of the front of the quarterdeck to the other, and peering close overside. When he returned to amidships, and the helm, he said, "I know the gentleman who did, though. He said she's fairly big, for a schooner. Might've been built in a New England yard, he reckoned, from her lines, and the rake of her masts."

"Did he comment on her being armed?" Lewrie further asked, his excitement rising.

"Lord, Captain Lewrie . . . who *ain't?*" the pilot cracked, cocking his head back for a good laugh. "What with the war and all, it's common sense to be armed. Never can tell when a warship, a privateer, or an out-right rogue pirate crosses your hawse, no matter which flag you're flying. War makes it parlous for merchant ships of any nation . . . the guilty *and* the innocent," he pointedly added, having a dig at the British practice of stopping and inspecting any ship that they encountered on the suspicion that they might be trading with the foe.

"Brace up, Bosun!" Lt. Westcott called out. "Mind the luff of the heads'ls and fore tops'l! Cast of the log, Mister Grainger?"

"Five knots and a bit, sir!"

They were past the lighthouse and the Beacon, now abreast of Fort Johnston on James Island, with the city beginning to spread out before their bows. Lewrie trusted that the pilot, and his officers, had the situation well-enough in hand to go forward to the break of the quarterdeck and lift his day-glass for a good look at the city . . . and spy out the French schooner.

If she's not *a privateer, I'm a Turk in a turban!* he thought, noting the rake of her masts that the pilot had mentioned, in Down East New England Yankee style, which would make her fly like a tern, and as weatherly as a witch. There was a large blue-white-red French Tricolour flag streaming over her stern, one more suitable to a frigate-sized warship, as if to proudly flaunt her nationality.

After a sniff of disgust, he swung his telescope to look over the city. The few times he'd put into Charleston during the Revolution, after General Clinton had conquered it, and given how short his shore excursions had been, he'd always been impressed by the beauty of the town, the impressive residences, and how wide were the streets; Broad Street, which ran across from the Ashley to the Cooper, was an hundred feet wide, and to a lad used to the close, meandering, and reeky lanes of London, the sense of open space had made quite an impression. Beyond that, Charleston was awash in palmettos, white oaks festooned by wreaths of Spanish Moss, in graceful weeping willows, and all manner of brilliant, flowering *flora*, as exotic as any isle in the Indies, but richer, grander, and more . . . civilised than even Kingston, Jamaica.

"Ever been here, Captain Lewrie?" the pilot took time to ask.

"Long, long ago," Lewrie told him, smiling in reverie, "when I was a Midshipman. Back when Saint Michael's spire was painted black."

"Some said that was for mourning, when the city surrendered to General Clinton," their pilot said.

Actually, the Rebels had painted it black so the British could not use it as a sea-mark or range-mark, but that had been fruitless, just as extinguishing the lighthouse and the Beacon had been.

"Always liked Charleston," Lewrie went on "though we never stayed long. Come in with despatches, sail out the next day, mostly. I ate well, when I was allowed ashore."

Rutted well, too, at that mansion-cum-brothel up the bank of the Cooper, Lewrie told himself with a smug grin, remembering how he and his fellow Mid, David Avery, had sought the place out to celebrate Avery's birthday . . . and how they'd been set upon by Rebel foot-pads on their way back to the docks. A quick peek with his telescope up the Cooper showed that the commercial piers and warehouses had grown past where that mansion had been. Another part of his past long gone, he realised, along with David Avery, who had fallen not a year later.

"I was always inpressed by how open and wide the town is laid out," Lewrie commented.

"That's to catch any cooling breeze in the summers, Captain," the pilot said with a wry snicker. "Nothing gets built too high, or too close together, if people don't want to melt like candle wax."

"Excuse me, sir," Lt. Westcott intruded. "Might you wish that we come in 'all-standing', and anchor 'man o' war fashion'? Just to thumb our noses at the Frogs?"

"Hmm . . . best not, Mister Westcott," Lewrie decided. "We're a bit out of practice at that evolution."

And, if we mucked it up, we'd never hear the end of it, Lewrie thought.

"When we come about into the wind, we'll let go the kedge, and stand on 'til we lose way, then let go the best bower," Lewrie said. "The depth there, sir?" he asked their pilot.

"Four fathom, and a bit, Captain. Unless we get a full gale, a rare thing this time of year, a three-to-one scope will suit," the pilot informed him.

HMS *Reliant* ghosted on another quarter-mile or so before their pilot suggested that she should be put about. That brought the ship within a cable of the anchored French schooner, whose decks were now full of spectators.

"Smartly, now, Mister Westcott," Lewrie snapped.

"Helm hard down, topmen aloft!" Westcott shouted.

Sailors scrambled up the shrouds to the tops'l yards to haul up and brail up in harbour gaskets, while hands on the gangways hauled at the clews to draw the tops'ls upwards, spilling wind from them. Other men tended the spanker over the quarterdeck, freed the stays'ls and jibs so they could fly over to the opposite tack and keep some drive going as the kedge was freed to splash into the harbour, and the thick hawse cable to run free. *Reliant* paid off the wind a bit, right on the edge of "stays" a while longer before the helm was put up, and the ship's bow faced the sea breeze directly, which slowly brought her to a full stop. At that moment, the bower anchor was let go.

After that, with the squares'ls gasketed, and the stays'ls and jibs and spanker handed, it was a matter of "tweaking" on the capstans to take in on the kedge cable, let out the bower cable, to place the frigate equidistant from her anchors, at equal strain.

"Nicely done, Mister West— What the Devil?" Lewrie began to say.

The crew of the French schooner had burst into song, shouting the words of "The Marseillaise" to taunt them. French sailors were in the shrouds, atop the bulwarks and lowered gaff booms, shaking their fists, slapping their arses in derision, and making insulting finger signs.

"Quite a lot of them," Lewrie pointed out, with a wry smile on his face. "Too many to be a merchantman."

"Do you wish to salute *them*, sir?" Lt. Westcott asked, looking as if he wished that they would. Some of Lewrie's officers and hands were scowling and cursing, already.

"Bosun Sprague!" Lewrie bellowed. "Hands to the larboard gangway!"

"Sir?" the Bosun asked, looking up at the quarterdeck, his face asquint.

"Two-fingered salute, Mister Sprague!" Lewrie ordered. "A two-fingered salute to those snail-eatin' sons of bitches!" By example he went to the larboard bulwarks and lifted his right hand, his fore and middle finger jutted upward into a Vee, a very British insult.

And fuck *diplomacy!* he angrily thought.

CHAPTER TWENTY-SIX

*A*ccording to the instructions from Admiralty, the British Consul at Charleston was one Mr. Edward Cotton, an Englishman, not a local man, who kept offices at the corner of East Bay Street and Queen Street, conveniently near the city wharves. Lewrie wished to go ashore at once to see him, but there was an host of things to see to, beforehand. The best he could do was to send Midshipman Entwhistle in a cutter with a quick, introductory note, and a request for an audience, though Lewrie halfway hoped that the rare appearance of a Royal Navy frigate would pique the fellow's curiosity and lure him to boarding *Reliant*, first.

There could be no shore liberty for any of his hands, for certain: It was a risk to send too many of the ship's boats ashore for firewood, water, and victuals, for the chance to desert would be quite a temptation, even to sailors who had been with the ship since she had been re-commissioned, and had pay and prize-money due. And, certainly, there would be many "patriotic" South Carolinians who would encourage *Reliant*'s people to flee "Limey despots" and become free Americans!

With a French schooner, most-likely an enemy privateer, present, he could not let his guard down by putting the ship "Out of Discipline" for a carouse, either. Marine Lt. Simcock already had fully uniformed men posted as sentries at the bow, stern, and on each gangway, fully armed with loaded and bayoneted muskets to prevent desertion, too.

Yet, some of his people *must* go ashore. Mr. Cadbury was eager, as were the officers, who busily invented excuses to set foot ashore for a few hours. Surprisingly, so did Yeovill and the Black ship's cook, Mr. Cooke, who accompanied Cadbury to the foot of the starboard ladderway to the quarterdeck. Both men were turned out in their best buckled shoes, canvas trousers, clean shirts with neckerchiefs, short blue sailors' jackets, and flat tarred hats, as scrubbed up and fresh-shaven as they would be at Sunday Divisions. Lewrie could not recall Cooke *ever* being turned out so well.

"Permission to go ashore with the Purser, sir," Yeovill said.

"Me too, sah," Cooke spoke up, looking puppy-dog eager.

"D'ye think that'd be . . . safe for you, Cooke?" Lewrie asked. "South Carolina's a slave state. If a gang o' bully-bucks decide to snatch you up for a quick profit, there's little we could do about it, but complain."

"Beg ya pahdon, sah, but I'd be with Mistah Cadbury an' Yeovill, heah," Cooke objected. "I'm in uniform, an' I don' sound like no po' field hand. Ain't no slavuh gonna mess with me, sah." Like all Navy hands, he wore a clasp knife in a leather sheath on his hip. And he was big and strong.

"Hmm . . . it'd be best did I write you out a certificate, just in case," Lewrie decided. "So you and Yeovill can protect the Purser, if some people try to mess with him. There may be some lingering resentment of anyone from England. Or Jamaica," Lewrie added with a wry expression. He didn't have to go to his great-cabins, for his clerk, Faulkes, was on deck, scrubbed up and dressed in clean clothes, hoping like all the others that he might get a few hours ashore, too. Once the certificate had been dictated, written out in Faulkes's excellent copper-plate hand, and given to Lewrie to sign, it was given to Cooke, who read it over, nodded, grinned, and carefully folded it to stick into an inside pocket of his short jacket.

"Thankee, Cap'm, sah," Cooke said, knuckling his hat brim.

"You can read and write, Cooke?" Lewrie had to ask, surprised.

"De ol' Sailin' Master in *Proteus*, Mistah Winwood, taught me, sah," Cooke said with a broader grin. "How else I follah de recipes evahbody give me fo' somethin' special, sah?"

"Very well, then, carry on, Mister Cadbury," Lewrie said.

"Anything special for you, sir?" Cadbury asked.

"Yeovill will see to my wants, but thankee for asking, sir," Lewrie told
him, with a quick grin. "Oh . . . just as there may be some hot-blooded
'Brother Johnathons' ashore who think the Revolution hasn't ended, keep
a weather eye for any French sailors. If that schooner's a privateer, as I'm
sure she is, it's good odds that her crew will be allowed more liberty than
a naval vessel."

"We will walk wary, sir," Cadbury promised him, daunted not one
whit and still eager to be off.

"Take what joy ye may," Lewrie said, a faint scowl appearing on his
face. "I will have to go below and change, to impress."

Best, and heaviest, broadcloth wool coat, Lewrie sourly thought; *silk shirt
and all, no matter how muggy it is. And that damned sash and star!*

Instead of his gig, Lewrie took the other cutter, with Midshipman
Grainger, and his usual boat crew, with Liam Desmond, his Cox'n, stroke-
oar Patrick Furfy, and seven other oarsman, all turned out in Sunday
Divisions best, too, with a boat jack flying from a short staff at the stern.
And, of course, his arrival at a landing stage a block or two short of Queen
Street drew a fair number of gawkers, making him feel as if he was the
star attraction in a raree-show. The arrival of a British frigate, Midshipman Entwhistle's jaunt to bear his note to the Consul, then Cadbury's
mission, with a uniformed Black sailor, had brought out the idlers of all
classes.

"Captain Lewrie, I presume?" a well-dressed gentleman at the top of
the landing stage called out to him, thankfully in an English accent.
"Edward Cotton, His Majesty's Consul to the port of Charleston, your
servant, sir."

"Good morning, Mister Cotton, and thank you very much for coming
down to meet me," Lewrie replied as the bow man hooked onto the stage
with his gaff, the oars were tossed and stood vertically, then boated
smartly at Desmond's commands. Lewrie stood, made his way amidships
of the cutter, then stepped from the gunn'l to the landing stage.

They doffed hats to each other, then shook hands.

"Your note did not inform me that you were a Knight of the Bath,
Captain Lewrie," Cotton said with a probing brow up.

"Baronet, t'boot," Lewrie said with a shrug, and a brief grimace. "Too recent t'sink in yet," he tried to explain.

"I see, sir," Cotton replied, seeming a tad disappointed that Lewrie didn't take his honours as seriously as he, and others of his social level, might have. "Reward for a gallant action, may I ask?"

"For a battle off the Chandeleur Islands, near New Orleans," Lewrie informed him. "We stopped the French from landing a regiment, and took four warships and a transport. September, two years ago. No one told *us* the French would sell Louisiana to the United States, a few months later!"

"The news of American purchase was an eight-day wonder to all here, too, Sir Alan," Cotton told him, with a laugh. "A pity that we could not dine you out with the leading citizens of Charleston, on the strength of that . . . how your actions guaranteed that Bonaparte abandoned hopes of a French lodgement in New Orleans, and France in charge of the vast territories west of the Mississippi. Everyone is simply thirsting for quick expansion of settlements in such a vast virgin land. But . . . your ship may only stay in Charleston for three days before you must sail."

"Hey?" Lewrie asked, confused.

"Well, Sir Alan, with a French vessel in harbour, the formalities must be strictly observed," Cotton said. "Admiralty Law, and the neutrality of the United States might have allowed you a longer stay, but for *her* presence," Cotton explained, jutting his chin seaward at the French schooner. "Just as your arrival will force Captain Mollien to sail. He could have kept his ship here for some time, yet, but for that."

"She's a privateer, isn't she?" Lewrie snapped, his suspicions confirmed, and his eyes going from blue-grey to a colder Arctic colour.

"I strongly suspect she is," Mr. Cotton agreed, "but . . . here, now. You will not make any moves against her, will you? Not right here in harbour, mean t'say . . . ?"

Lewrie's intensity, and those icy grey eyes made Mr. Cotton fear that Lewrie might be rash enough to attack the schooner outright!

"In a neutral harbour?" Lewrie scoffed. "Not likely, no sir."

Cotton was immediately and visibly relieved.

"Let us go to my offices, Sir Alan, out of the moring sun, so we may discover the reason for your port call," Mr. Cotton offered.

"Delighted, sir," Lewrie said, smiling again. "Mister Grainger, return to the ship. I'll be ashore some time, 'til supper at the . . ."

"Your pardons, Sir Alan," Cotton interrupted, "but I do hope you will allow me to offer you the hospitality of my house for the night, and a shore supper. Even at short notice, I could reserve a table at a public dining establishment and invite a *few* of Charleston's prominent citizens. Show the flag, all that, what?"

"In that case, I gladly accept your kind invitation, Mister Cotton," Lewrie said, thinking that a fresh-water bath would be more than welcome after sponge-bathing aboard ship with a meagre allotment of daily issue. "If it's possible, there is a Mister Douglas McGilliveray with whom I should very much like to make a re-acquaintance. I met him during the Quasi-War, when our Navy and the United States worked together against the French."

"A most excellent suggestion, Sir Alan!" Cotton enthused. "He, of one of the oldest families, and of a long-established trading firm to boot! I'll send him and his wife an invitation, at once."

"I'll sleep out of the ship for tonight, Mister Grainger," Lewrie told the Midshipman. "Return for me tomorrow, by Four Bells of the Forenoon. Warn Yeovill and Pettus."

"Aye aye, sir!"

"Shall we go, then, Sir Alan?" Cotton bade. "It is but a short stroll to my establishment."

"You are to fulfill your orders with but one ship, Sir Alan?" Mr. Cotton said, with a shake of his head, after he had read the directives from London that Lewrie had presented to him. "Such a task is quite Herculean."

"I scraped up three smaller sloops to help," Lewrie told him, between sips of hot tea. "They're prowling round Saint Augustine, at present. We've made a small beginning, putting a wee scare into Spanish privateers on the coast of Cuba, scouted the Florida Keys, and took on two schooners in Mayami Bay. Burned 'em. Spanish privateers I expect are as thick as fleas on a hound. . . . You haven't seen any o' *them* here at Charleston, have you, Mister Cotton?"

"No Spanish privateers, no, Sir Alan," Cotton informed him. "A rare Spanish merchantman, now and again, but none have put in in the last few months. American ships, with goods from Spanish colonies, dominate the trade, though there's little exported *to* the Dons. The Spanish crown demands a strict mercantilism. It must be imports from Spain, or another of their colonies, carried in Spanish bottoms, or nothing. There is a Spanish Consul here—*Don* Diego de Belem—twiddling his thumbs and attending parties, poor fellow, with nothing to do for his benighted country. Quite charming, actually."

"And the French?" Lewrie asked.

"Now and then," Cotton said with a sly nod. "Captain Mollien has put in several times, *ostensibly* on trade from the French West Indies isles, though there's never many goods landed, or cargo taken aboard for export. She's the *Otarie*, by the way, Sir Alan." Seeing Lewrie's brow go up in question, he added, "It means 'Sea Lion'."

"Are you able to determine what he does land, and what he buys in exchange?" Lewrie asked. "Goods looted from prizes? Powder and shot for his guns?"

"Thankfully, since my posting here three years ago, I have been able to cultivate good relations with the trading houses and the ship chandlers of Charleston, Sir Alan, so I am able to be made conversant of any violations of American neutrality. To aid on that head, there is a small United States naval presence in Charleston . . . one or two gunboats . . . and a cutter from the Revenue Service, to enforce the Customs House officials. I can assure you that no French vessel that puts into Charleston is able to purchase war-like *matériel*, or lands suspect goods."

"Well, good," Lewrie said, a tad relieved to hear that. That would be one more American port to scratch off his list.

"What happens in Stono Inlet or Edisto, however, is less sure," Cotton continued. "If an unscrupulous merchant could load up a small coasting vessel and meet a French privateer, well, I have no purview, and few ways of learning of such dealings. Though, as I said, the U.S. Navy and Revenue Service do keep an eye on the possibility, but not a constant watch."

"And Georgetown?" Lewrie asked, squirming in his chair.

"I look out for our interests in Georgetown, as well, sir," Cotton told him, "though I do not get up there more than once every two months or so."

"I *thought* to look in on our way South from Wilmington, but wasn't sure if I could get my ship into Winyah Bay," Lewrie said. "Are there any chandleries there that could handle the needs of privateers?"

"Wood, water, and perhaps some salt meats," Cotton said with a cock of his head, as if picturing the port and its waterfront in his mind, building by building. He then shook his head in the negative. "There is the rice trade, which draws middling-sized ships in the coasting business, river trade up the Waccamaw, Black River, the Pee Dee as far up as Buck's Port, and commercial fishing sufficient to the local market. Some coastal ships serve the slave trade . . . clothing, food, and such for the rice plantations, as well as slaves themselves, but most of that comes from Charleston, if it is not grown locally. At Buck's Port, there is a decent shipyard . . . boatyard, really . . . and there is some construction and repair at Georgetown itself, up the Sampit River. Is a vessel in need of cordage, sails, repair work, *or* powder and shot, they'd most-like call in Charleston . . . but, as I've said, a close watch is kept by the U.S. and South Carolina governments."

"Perhaps Savannah, Georgia, then," Lewrie said with a sigh as he finished his cup of tea, and wishing he could doff his coat and waist-coat and loosen his neck-stock. Though it was only ten of the morning, the Spring day was getting warm, and Mr. Cotton's offices were stifling.

"More tea, Sir Alan?" Cotton asked, inclining his head to summon a Black servant in a dark suit. "Perhaps in the side garden."

Mr. Cotton's establishment was a modest version of the grand mansions of Charleston, of only two storeys, not three or four, with his private study, library, dining room, and parlour, as well as his consular offices, on the first floor. The house was walled off from East Bay Street and Queen Street with brick walls topped with ornamental iron fences. Lewrie had noticed a small balcony above facing East Bay Street and the Cooper River, and the wharves, and a larger balcony projecting from the left of the house.

"Perhaps we could substitute a cooler beverage than tea, Sir Alan," Cotton further tempted. He rose from his chair and followed the Black house servant to a set of glazed double doors that led out to a side garden. Two or three steps down from the house and Lewrie found himself on a brick patio beneath that projecting balcony where there was a small, round table and four chairs, a pair of wood-slat benches, and several large terra-cotta planters awash in azaleas and roses; there were other flowering bushes and flower beds, though Lewrie could only be sure of the roses and the azaleas. There was a large patch of lawn before one got to the rear of the property where the kitchens were, to separate its heat from the house. Lewrie was amazed to feel a rush of coolness, even a mild, restoring breeze!

"We will have the citrus tea, Amos," Cotton ordered from his man-servant.

"Yassuh."

"Lemons and limes, wild oranges in season," Cotton explained, "with an admixture of *cool* tea. The physicians all say that drinking too much citrus juice in warm climates can ruin your health, but I've done it for years, here, and have yet to suffer."

"Long ago, I found that a pot of tea that had gone cold aboard ship was refreshing," Lewrie heartily agreed. "It was drink it, or throw it out, and, with some lemon juice and sugar . . . ! Except in very cold weather, I have a large pot brewed each day. Ashore, I allow myself a whole gallon!"

"Until the stored winter ice runs out, I prefer it with a sliver or two," Mr. Cotton continued. "Though, by high summer, ice is hard to come by in Charleston . . . anywhere in the Low Country. Sometimes I add a bit of sweet Rhenish wine . . . though that is also hard to come by . . . the war, do you see."

"Were you back in England, though, Mister Cotton, there'd be all the Rhenish ye'd wish," Lewrie said, sprawling at ease with his booted legs extended. "Our illustrious smugglers could even fetch you Arctic ice in August! French wines, brandies, Dutch gin? Napoleon Bonaparte can *claim* he's shut Europe off from Great Britain, but nobody told the smugglers!"

Mr. Cotton smiled and nodded in agreement, then turned soberer, looking off into the middle distance for a long moment before speaking again. "You know, of course, Sir Alan, that it took some time after the American Revolution before British goods were acceptable again in the United States. I doubt Charleston has seen a British warship in port since their Constitution was ratified. No . . . French goods were preferred, and still *are*, do you see."

"I saw that in Wilmington," Lewrie agreed as a large pitcher of the cool tea was brought out on a coin-silver tray, and two tall glasses were poured for them.

"Especially so here in the Low Country," Cotton went on after a pleasing sip. "Many of the settlers hereabouts were of French Protestant *émigré* stock, whose memories of being massacred by Catholic kings and cardinals dimmed considerably. France is elegance, style, and the epitome of gracious living to them, as it is with everyone in America who aspires to grandeur . . . and believe me, Sir Alan, no one aspires grander than South Carolinians. Now, when the Peace of Amiens was in force, Charleston was flooded with luxury French goods not seen since the first war with Republican France in 1793. The wines, the brandies, and exotic spirits you mentioned, as well as lace, satins, silks, furniture, chinawares, and womens' fashions from hats to slippers, came in regularly, and were snapped up practically the instant they were landed on the piers, the shop-keepers bedamned. Yet now, that trade is almost completely gone, again, the last two years entire. You mentioned smugglers?" Cotton coyly hinted.

"Meaning . . ." Lewrie slowly said, puzzling it out, "if there was a way to bring luxury goods in, people might turn a blind eye to the trade . . . and what's allowed in exchange, too? I gather that you *suspect* that this Captain Mollien is bringing in goods he doesn't declare to the Customs House . . . no," Lewrie said, dropping that thought as implausible. "His schooner's too small for a second, secret cargo, and if French luxuries are un-available t'honest traders, then where's *he* gettin' 'em? It don't make sense."

"It is only a suspicion, so far, Sir Alan," Mr. Cotton mused. "Perhaps from the cargoes of British ships he's taken, who knows?"

"Not from homeward-bound West Indies trades," Lewrie objected. "That's all rum, molasses, sugar, and dye wood. Trades headed *to* the West Indies don't feature French goods, either. Where *is* he . . . ?"

"Mistah Cotton, sah," the house servant said, returning to the side garden, "dey's a gennulmun come t'call on ya, sah. He says he has ta speak with ya."

"Tell the fellow I am busy, Amos," Cotton gruffly said. "Who is it, by the way?"

"It be Mistah Gambon, sah, the French Consul."

"Gambon? Damn!" Mr. Cotton testily snapped. "Of all the gall!"

"One thing the Frogs have in plenty, Mister Cotton, is gaul," Lewrie japed, "G-A-U-L, hey?" It didn't go down anywhere near how he wished it, though, for Mr. Cotton was too upset.

"Amos, tell *M'sieur* Gambon that I cannot receive him now, but if he wishes to—" Cotton began to say.

"*Bon matin,* Edward, good morning to you!" came a cheery, heavily accented voice from within the house as the fellow in question barged right out through the double doors to the side garden. "An' what a fine morning eet ees, *n'est-ce pas?* Oh my, *oui!* Such clear sky-es, such a cool breeze! 'Allo to all!"

Cotton and Lewrie shot to their feet, Mr. Cotton diplomatically struggling to hide his glower, and Lewrie with one brow up in wonder. He beheld a dapper, balding toad of a man not over five feet five in height, "gotch-gutted" and rotund with good living, and dressed in the latest fashion. *M'sieur* Gambon's shirt collar stood up in points to his double chins and splayed out as if to support his head which was as round as a melon, and his full-moon face. Gambon's sideburns were brushed forward, and what little hair remaining on his pate was slicked forward in a pomaded fringe. His fashionably snug trousers were strapped under elegant light shoes, yet they, and his short double-breasted waist-coat, bulged at the waist like a pregnant woman.

"You eentroduce me to your guest, Edward?" M. Gambon requested with a wide smile on his face as he handed his hat, gloves, and walking stick to the servant. "He, and hees terrifying warship are ze reason I 'ave come to call upon you, een such haste, after all, dear Edward. Een ze name of Emperor Napoleon Bonaparte and glorious France, I come to lodge ze strongest formal protest against the frigate's presence."

"The Devil you say, *M'sieur!*" Mr. Cotton spluttered, irked to the edge of "diplomacy" and beyond. "This is beyond the pale; it is simply not done in such fashion! And, might I remind you, *M'sieur* Gambon, that a British vessel is free to call at any neutral American port from Maine to—!"

"Edward! Edward, pray do not distress yourself," Gambon good-naturedly countered, as if enjoying his little game, "such distress ees bad for your liver. Ze choler . . . ze bile? You do not introduce me? Ah me, *pauvre* Gambon. *M'sieur Capitaine*, allow me to name myself . . . Albert-Louis Gambon, Hees Majesty, Emperor Napoleon Bonaparte's Consul een Charleston. My *carte de visite!*" he said with a bow before reaching into a slit-pocket of his strained waist-coat to draw forth a bit of pasteboard, and snapping it out within Lewrie's reach with the elegance and *panache* of a magician producing a coin.

"An' *oui, Capitaine, mon ami,*" Gambon added with a sly grin, "I *am* zee 'Frog' weeth a great *deal* of gall, hawn hawn!"

CHAPTER TWENTY-SEVEN

M'sieur Gambon, it is I who must protest your insistence upon entering my house in such an inapropriate manner," Mr. Cotton snapped.

"Tut tut, Edward, we are simply conducting ze beezeness of diplomacy," Gambon told him, most cherry-merry. "Weel you name yourself to me, eef Edward ees reluctant to do so, *M'sieur Capitaine?* An' ees that your delectable citrus tea, Edward? I do prefer eet best when ze peaches are een season, but . . . may I 'ave a glass?"

"I-I must . . . if only to get rid of you, you boorish pest," Mr. Cotton sourly gravelled. "*M'sieur,* I name to you Captain Sir Alan Lewrie, Baronet, commanding His Majesty's Frigate *Reliant.*"

For a gotch-gut, and a fellow who sounded so enthusiastic about the levelling glories of France, Gambon performed a very graceful and elegant bow, with one foot extended, *en pointe,* and one hand swept low across his body, like a life-long aristocrat.

Lewrie responded with a sketchier bow from the waist, and a nod of his head. "*M'sieur* Gambon," he brusquely said.

"Such suspicion!" Gambon replied, with a little laugh. "Such an aversion to the pleasantries . . . as eef I am ze Devil, heemself, ha!"

"No . . . you just work for him," Lewrie coolly said.

"Eet ees as I thought, z'en," Gambon replied, fazed not a whit, and still the "Merry Andrew". "Or, as I fear-ed, rather. Ze *Capitaine* ees implacable een hees hatred for everything French . . . so much so I fear he weel be unable to restrain heemself from making war upon innocent sailors, right here een Charleston 'arbour."

"Your *Otarie*, d'ye mean, sir?" Lewrie countered. "Your privateer schooner?"

"Ze 'onest merchant trader from ze French West Indies, who 'as come to trade," Gambon stated with another smile and a shrug.

"With such a large crew, and so well-armed, sir?" Lewrie scoffed. "Which island in the French West Indies?"

"Edward, I am certain *you* 'ave *amis* een ze Customs 'Ouse, een ze government, who tell you of *Otarie*'s registry, an' 'er manifests," Gambon breezed off, "wheech isle, I 'ave forgotten, but Edward knows. 'E can tell you, later, *oui*?' No tea for me?" he plaintively begged.

"Not for those who ignore the protocols," Mr. Cotton told him, "I'd much admire you state your business quickly . . . excuse though this call was to take Sir Alan's measure."

"*Très bien*," Gambon said with a put-upon sigh. "As you expect, Edward, *Capitaine* Loo—'ow you say eet?—I 'ave already lodged a formal protest weeth the American Navy officer present, weeth ze American government's senior representative 'ere and weeth ze Mayor an' ze council *de la cité*, denouncing ze presence of a British warship 'ere, expressing my fears that something untoward could occur eef eet stays one hour longer. I 'ave also express-ed z'at such presence ees ze insult to American neutrality, to ze United States, ze state of South Carolina, an' ze *cité* of Charleston . . . so much of an insult z'at ze local *citoyens* may take to ze streets een anger."

"Oh, please, Albert," Mr. Cotton spluttered in exasperation, making Lewrie feel that, in private, the two men got along a lot better than their Publick *personae* allowed. "And did you also tell them that *Reliant* is the vanguard of a British invasion? That she's going to open fire on the city, and land her Marines to rape their mothers?"

"I take my duty to Hees Majesty ze Emperor mos' seriously," Gambon bristled up like a hedgehog in a grand flounce, "an' I 'ave too much love and respect for ze people of America to see z'em 'arm-ed."

"And, how far did you get with *that* twaddle?" Cotton scoffed.

"Ze matter ees being looked eento mos' closely by ze officials to whom I spoke," Gambon assured them.

"Which is to say, they didn't even give you the time of day," Mr. Cotton said with a wry chuckle. "Is that all, *M'sieur* Gambon?"

"Eet ees not, *M'sieur* Cotton," Gambon replied, still on a formal "high horse" and in gravity. "I ask of ze distinguish-ed *Capitaine*, what was the time z'at your frigate came to anchor, *M'sieur*?"

"It's pronounced Loo-ree, accent on the first syllable, *M'sieur*," Lewrie told him in equal gravity, secretly amused by the posturing wee toadman, and his few streaks of pomaded hair. "We came to wind, and let go the bower at Three Bells of the Forenoon."

Gambon twitched his mouth, as if Lewrie was speaking Hindoo.

"That is to say, half-past nine this morning," Lewrie went on, grinning a bit.

"Z'en, I 'ardly 'ave to remind you, *Capitaine* Loo-ree, z'at ze Admiralty Law recognis-ed by all *civilised* nations require you to sail from Charleston before half pas' nine of ze morning, three days hence," Gambon slyly said. "Further, *Capitaine*, eet ees not permitted z'at you be allowed to *return* to Charleston . . . or any ozzer port een ze state of South Carolina weethout a *reasonable* time at sea . . . *beyond* ze limit of three miles so you do not violate American neutrality by remaining een coastal waters; *n'est-ce pas?*"

"Of a certainty, sir," Lewrie replied, beginning to get a sinking feeling in his innards that he was about to be "had".

"Een point of fact, *Capitaine* . . . an' Edward may bear me out on z'is," Gambon happily went on, "since ze United States ees by z'eir Constitution a Federalist *république,* not a confederation of sovereign and separate states weeth z'eir own maritime laws, it would be a gross violation of American sovereignty, and neutrality, eef you sail-ed into any *ozzer* American port until a reasonable time 'as pass-ed. I made z'is point weeth ze American government representative, and ze senior officer of ze American Navy. While 'e 'as but two small gunboats, an' cannot be expected to *enforce* hees nation's laws against such a powerful frigate, eet would be *mos'* regrettable should 'e fin' you loath to depart on time, or, 'ow you say? . . . break you passage . . . at Beaufort or Port Royal, perhaps even at Savannah, or Wilmington, *oui?*"

God rot the little shit! Lewrie silently fumed; *He's got me by the* 'nutmegs'*! Just look at him enjoyin' this!*

"I also mus' point out to your excellent *Capitaine*, Edward," Gambon continued, turning to Mr. Cotton, and almost purring in triumph, "z'at by Admiralty Law, to avoid ze effusion of blood, and ze introduction of *la guerre* mos' horrible in neutral waters, *Capitaine* Mollien of *Otarie* . . . an 'onest an' 'umble merchantman of ze mos' peaceful an' innocent intent . . . mus' be given ze grace period of at least twelve 'ours between ze time *'e* sails, an' ze time z'at *Capitaine* Loo-ree ees allow-ed to sail . . . hawn hawn. But of course," Gambon added, turning to Lewrie with the hugest "shit-eating" grin on his phyz, "so esteem-ed an officer een ze Royal Navy 'ardly 'as to be reminded of ze laws of nations, *non?*"

"Ehm, well, of course not, *M'sieur* Gambon," Cotton said with a scowl, and a darting glance at Lewrie, as if to wonder if he had known that beforehand.

Should've read up on 'em, first, Lewrie told himself, steaming.

"*En fin*, Edward, I present you weeth copies of my protests to ze authorities," Gambon said. "I take my leave, an' fin' my own way out, my duty to ze Emperor complete. *Au revoir, M'sieur* Cotton, *mon vieux! Au revoir, Capitaine* Loo-ree. I weesh you a *bon voyage* . . . but not *too* soon, hawn hawn?"

Gambon gave them both a sketchier bow from the waist and a dip of his head before turning to re-enter the house to gather up his hat, gloves, and walking stick.

"*Hmpf!*" Lewrie snorted, once he was sure that Gambon was out of earshot. "What an insufferable little . . . toad!"

"Insufferable at times, yes," Mr. Cotton agreed after wheezing out a deep sigh of relief from between puffed lips. "When not on official business, though, he can be quite witty and amusing. Plays a fine game of chess, and dances extremely well. The ladies of Charleston adore him, and invite him to many of their balls and cotillions."

"And Napoleon Bonaparte is kind to dogs and children!" Lewrie scoffed. "What was that nonsense about stayin' in port twelve hours after that Frog schooner sails?"

"Stuff and nonsense, indeed," Cotton said with a snort, sitting down to his tea once more. "My understanding of neutrality laws, as the Americans enforce them, allows you to sail the same time as he does . . . just so long as you do not engage him inside the Three Mile Limit. In international waters, you may do as you please.

"Though . . . it might not put our country in a good light, if you did,"

Mr. Cotton cautioned a second later. "Do, please sit, Sir Alan. Are you able to bring Mollien to action, it might be best did it happen fifteen or twenty miles offshore . . . out of sight, so that the patriotic citizens of Charleston have no reason to sour relations between our country and theirs, which are tetchy enough, as it is."

"And, when did that bastard come to anchor, sir?" Lewrie asked, beginning to suspect a very bad scenario, a pit-fall which he hadn't seen coming.

"About two days ago," Mr. Cotton told him, between sips of tea from his glass. "Strictly speaking, he must depart by tomorrow, but that hinges upon Captain Mollien's ship being deemed a National Ship of the French Navy, or a privateer, a naval auxiliary. If no one will declare the schooner a man o' war, a merchantman may stay as long as he likes."

"*I'll* have t'sail, while he can sit at anchor and wave his bare arse at me?" Lewrie gawped. "I could lurk five or six miles offshore and catch him when he comes out."

"Ehm . . . that *might* put a *strain* on things, Sir Alan," Cotton warned, slowly shaking his head in the negative.

He can stay a week or two longer, and I'd have t'stay, Lewrie angrily thought; *and there goes lookin' into Savannah, or re-joining the squadron off Saint Augustine!*

Lewrie sat, though nowhere near at ease, and took a sip or two of the cool tea. He screwed up his face in thought, realising that he was caught in a cleft stick. The only thing to do was to have a wee laugh.

"Sir Alan?" Mr. Cotton enquired, surprised by Lewrie's humour.

"I might as well have t'wait twelve hours, Mister Cotton," Lewrie told him, still with a sour grin on his face. "Were I Mollien, I'd wait 'til within an hour or so of the peak of high tide, and set sail for the Main Ship Channel, timing it so that I'm crossing the Charleston Bar at slack-water of that high tide. Imagine this, sir: As soon as I see him making up to a single bow anchor, I send ashore for a pilot. *Reliant* draws almost eighteen feet, whilst he draws much less, perhaps only twelve. Now, how quickly do ye think the French-lovin' local pilots' guild'd answer my request? At least one hour or maybe two hours later?"

"You would be forced to wait for the *next* day's high tide. I see," Mr. Cotton said with a grimace of sad understanding.

"He'll take *this* trick," Lewrie gloomed. "But, if he wants to keep his crew happy, he'll have to take prizes t'keep them in food and rum, and put money in their pockets. Privateers are like whalers: They sign on for a share, a 'lay', of the profits of a cruise. If he wants prizes from our big 'sugar trades', he'll have t'stay somewhere close to the Florida Straits, and the straits between the Bahamas and Spanish Florida. My contacts in Wilmington told me there's no privateers working out of North Carolina."

That Moore and Cashman know of, at any rate! Lewrie cautioned himself, with an urge to cross the fingers of one hand as he said it.

"They're mostly schooners or two-masted sloops, in the main," Lewrie continued, his head cocked over in thought. "They can't remain at sea much more than two months before they run short of everything, and, once our convoys come level with Charleston, they're catching a wind that'll carry them Nor'east, further out in the open sea, well to windward of Cape Hatteras, and harder to *find*, or chase after. This Mollien is most-like working out of Spanish Florida, or Cuba, where he can find shelter and sustenance with his allies, the Dons. Where he can sell his prizes in the open, 'stead of sneakin' 'em into an American port t'sell 'em on the sly."

"Why yes, Sir Alan!" Mr. Cotton energetically agreed. "Think of this aspect. Do enemy privateers' work from American ports, or inlets where unscrupulous traders sell them supplies and purchase their prizes, Mollien and his compatriots would be at the mercy of those traders . . . and the much-inflated prices they would charge, *and* the criminally low sums they'd pay to buy captured ships and their cargoes!"

"It'd take a fair parcel of money to cobble up false papers for a prize, aye," Lewrie said with a genuine laugh. "Perhaps the value of the cargoes, and the later sale of the ships somewhere else would pay for that, but the risk of atracting attention with the Customs or Revenue Services, well! Too much risk to engage upon?"

Then this whole jaunt down the American coast is a goose-chase, Lewrie thought; *dreamt up by pen-pushers at Admiralty, who've read too many bloody novels!*

"Where would a criminal trader get the captains and crews for the captured ships would be my question," Mr. Cotton said, topping up their glasses without summoning his Black house servant. "That's too many people in on the secret, and someone's sure to blab. Now, they *could* claim that they had sailed down to Havana with money and extra crew so they could pick up condemned vessels and bring them back to America to register them, along with Cuban export goods, which, in the main, are the same export goods one might find in the holds of a captured British ship—sugar, molasses, rum, and tobacco—but too many of such purchases would surely draw suspicions of the authorities. Register them in Savannah or Charleston, say, then hire on yet *another* captain and crew to sail them north to the Chesapeake, to Philadelphia, New York, or Boston? I hardly think so! It must all unravel, sooner or later," Mr. Cotton declared, quite sure of his logic.

"Hmm . . . in the cold light of day, it *does* seem rather implausible, doesn't it?" Lewrie admitted. "Perhaps the most risk that some criminal chandlers might run would be to supply privateers in one of the inlets you mentioned . . . in the dark of night and far out of sight of officials . . . to extend their time at sea without a long, unprofitabled voyage back to Cuba or Spanish Florida to re-victual."

"That would be much more feasible, Sir Alan," Cotton agreed.

"*Hmpf!*" Lewrie said, slouching in his chair, at more ease than a minute before. "I s'pose I still must peek into Savannah. Unless that twaddle about breaking my passage really *is* a violation of American neutrality."

"I think that would only apply were you being pursued by the enemy, in strength, and meant to avoid combat, Sir Alan," Mr. Cotton told him, then laughed out loud, "and I very much doubt that such an intrepid officer as yourself would ever do so, ha ha! It would be an act more suitable to an *enemy* warship trying to avoid the inevitable, yet unwilling to intern herself. In that case, the warship in question would be ordered out to sea within seventy-two hours or surrender herself to the care of the neutral country. You have orders to speak with the Consul in Savannah, Mister Hereford? Good. Go do so, and Gambon's screechy objections bedamned."

"Excellent," Lewrie said with a sigh of relief.

Mr. Cotton pulled a pocket watch from his waist-coat and opened the lid. "It is nigh Noon, Sir Alan," he announced, "and I must own to a peckish feeling. Might you wish to dine on the town, or will you trust that I have a very talented cook, who by this hour is usually ready to serve a toothsome dinner?"

"I would be grateful for more of your kind hospitality, Mister Cotton, and dining in would suit, admirably," Lewrie replied.

"Good, good! Another thing I must own to is a most lazy habit, Sir Alan . . . happily, one that is as prevalent in South Carolina's Low Country as it is in Spanish colonies," Cotton freely confessed. "I speak of *siesta*— the afternoon nap. Barring official duties, or a caller as upsetting as *M'sieur*

Gambon, I usually put my head down for an hour or two after dinner. Later in the summer in Charleston, the afternoon nap is a necessity, 'til late afternoon, and its coolness. You are welcome to a spare bed-chamber, one which, like my own, faces the prevailing breeze."

"I'll take you up on that, too, Mister Cotton, most gladly," Lewrie assured him, "and perhaps . . . a cool shore bath before supper."

"It shall be done, sir!"

Damn whether that Frog sails, Lewrie thought; *I'll have enough fresh water for a proper scrub-down, for a rare once!*

CHAPTER TWENTY-EIGHT

*B*y half past six that evening, Lewrie was much refreshed by a good nap in a sinfully soft bed, sprawled nude atop the coverlet and cooled by a gentle breeze. He was also much cleaner, after a brass tub full of cool water had been provided in the wash-house behind the house, with enough soap for a thorough scrubbing, behind his ears and between his toes. He'd sudsed his hair and used two whole buckets of water with which to rinse, too. He had shaved himself quite closely, but had submitted to the house servant's, Amos's, ministrations when it came to dressing in his best shore-going uniform that had been sponged and brushed free of cat-fur, completely so for a rare once, too. With his neck-stock tied just so, the sprig of hair at the nape of his neck bound with black ribbon, his gold-tasseled Hessian boots newly blacked and buffed, his sash and star over his chest, and his "hundred-guinea" dress sword on his hip, he could take time to stare at himself in the tall *cheval* mirror and deem himself one Hell of a natty fellow, and a man possessed of an athletic stature and slimness, despite being fourty-two years of age. He still had a full head of mid-brown hair, turned lighter by the sun below the brim of his cocked hat (thankfully closer to dark blond without a hint of grey!) that still showed no sign of receding. His face was bronzed by constant exposure, but it was not yet lined . . . though he thought that the "rac-coon eye" look of squint lines at each outer corner of his eyes, normal flesh colour against the ruddiness, did look a bit comical.

If people wished to laugh at those squint lines, though, there was the faint, vertical scar upon his left cheek, the mark of a long-ago duel on Antigua in his Midshipman days, to belie them.

He flashed his teeth, pleased that they looked whiter against his skin, then puffed his breath into a hand; one more of his ginger pastilles would not go amiss.

Witty and charming? Lewrie thought; *I think I'm ready t'please Charleston.*

Mr. Cotton laid on a two-wheeled, one-horse hack for the short trip from his house down to Broad Street, and a hotel which he assured Lewrie had a fine dining room. It would be a small dinner party, assembled at short notice, but Mr. and Mrs. McGilliveray would definitely attend, as well as the U.S. Navy officer commanding the two gunboats which guarded Charleston harbour, and a few others.

As they alit by the doors to the hotel, Lewrie took a moment to savour the early evening. Broad Street was awash in light from many large whale-oil lanthorns that bracketed the entrances of the shops, taverns, and houses, as well as regularly spaced tall street lanthorns, which were just being ignited. The skies and the thin clouds overhead were shading off to dusk after a spectacular sunset, and there was a welcome coolness to the breezes, though the air still felt humid.

"Red skies at night, sailors sleep tight, hey, Sir Alan?" Mr. Cotton japed. "Shall we go in and take a glass of Rhenish to prompt our appetite?"

"Certainly," Lewrie agreed.

"And, here are some of our guests, sir!" Mr. Cotton exclaimed, ready to make the introductions. Lewrie turned with a smile plastered on his phyz, recognizing Mr. Douglas McGilliveray, who had captained a con-verted merchantman, a U.S. Armed Ship, in the West Indies during the Quasi-War with France in 1798. There was a fellow in his thirties wear-ing the uniform of a navy officer, still the dark-blue coat with the red facings and lapels, the red waist-coat and dark-blue breeches that had been in style since the Revolution.

At least they got rid o' the tricorne hats and changed over to cocked hats. They looked like sea-goin' farmers, else!

Ever the good host, Mr. Cotton did the introductions, first to the Mc-Gilliverays, though Mr. Douglas McGilliveray eagerly offered his hand, and introduced his wife, himself.

"You're coming up in the world, Captain Lewrie," McGilliveray jovially said. "The last time we met, you wore but one epaulet, but now, ha ha! For bravery and success, surely."

"A squadron action off New Orleans, sir," Lewrie happily explained. "So good to see you, again, sir, and in such fine health. And, Mistress McGilliveray . . . your servant, ma'am," he said with a bow, and a doff of his hat.

"Sir Alan!" the older lady gushed as she dipped a brief curtsy. Evidently, even egalitarian Americans *did* "dearly love a lord"!

"*Hmpf* . . . what's *he* doing here?" Mr. McGilliveray muttered, making them all turn to take note of three men slouching against the side of a carriage further up the street.

"Sir Alan, allow me to also introduce to you Lieutenant Israel Gordon, the officer commanding U.S. naval forces in Charleston," Mr. Cotton soldiered on, after a nervous peek at the three men, "and his lady, Mistress Susannah Gordon. Lieutenant and Mistress Gordon, allow me to name to you Captain Sir Alan Lewrie, Baronet, of His Britannic Majesty's frigate, *Reliant.*"

"Delighted to make your acquaintance, Lieutenant Gordon, Mistress Gordon," Lewrie said, making another bow. "Your servant, sir . . . ma'am."

"And to make your acquaintance, Captain Lewrie," Lt. Gordon replied with equal gravity, in a jarring New Englander's accent; his wife sounded like a Down East Yankee lady, too, when she spoke. Mrs. Gordon found need to use a silk and lace fan, even after the day's heat had dissipated.

"But weel no one introduce *me* to such a grand *Anglais* sea-dog?" one of the men who had been slouching by the coach requested, forcing them all to turn to face him.

"And you are, sir?" Mr. Cotton archly demanded, screwing up his mouth over the man's impertinence.

"I name myself," the cheeky fellow said, smirking. "*Capitaine* Georges Mollien, of ze *Otarie* . . . *à votre service.*" He snatched off a rather small cocked hat, one whose ends had been pulled down nearly to his earlobes, and laid it on his breast as he performed a sweeping grand mock of a bow.

Bloody Frogs! Lewrie furiously thought; *Never more top-lofty and arrogant than when ye can't shoot 'em on the spot!*

This Captain Mollien was a short and wiry fellow, two inches shorter than Lewrie, with a pinched, foxy face. On his hip he wore a small-sword, and by the way his dark-blue coat sagged, there might be a brace of pistols in the side pockets. Behind him, grinning just as scornfully, stood two of his mates or crew, both "beef to the heel".

Lewrie had been the recipient of many a scornful look in his time, delivered by superior officers, gawping nobility, or St. James's Palace courtiers who'd caught him in "pusser's slops" or shirt sleeves, so he *knew* how to deliver one when given the chance. With one brow up in dis-belief, and a wee lift of a corner of his mouth for amusement, he slowly inspected Mollien from the top of his head of loose, lank, and long dark hair to his open shirt collar and neck-stock worn loose like a rag in the style of the *sans-culottes* revolutionaries, down an *écru* linen shirt front to a garish red waist sash, and scanned buff-coloured trousers crammed into a pair of top-boots indifferently buffed and blacked, to Mollien's scuffed boot toes, and back, again. At the end, he said "How marvellous for you," in a flat-toned drawl, and turned back to chat with his supper party guests.

"Well, shall we go in and take seats at our table?" Mr. Cotton quickly suggested.

"I weeshed to see ze man 'oo 'as come to mak' war on me," the Frenchman said, a little louder as if wishing to attract witnesses to his "bearding" of an enemy officer. "To tak' 'ees measure."

"You are impertinent, Captain Mollien," Lt. Gordon stiffly said.

"A dog in a doublet," Mr. McGilliveray harumphed.

"Make war upon you?" Lewrie purred, after fighting down an urge to swing about and punch the man in the face. "I certainly will, but not in Charleston Harbour. It'll come . . . all in good time, gunn'l to gunn'l," he promised with a bright smile. "Not in the middle of Broad Street, either . . . unless you *desire* a violation of the city's hospitality, and American neutrality. Is that what you came for, with your bully-bucks to protect you?"

"But I am ze peaceful *marchand* man, *M'sieur le Capitane*," Mollien said, wide eyed and with a hand upon his heart as if basely accused of wrongdoing, shrugging and smiling. "I do not fear one such as you. Ze soft-'anded *Anglais aristo*?" he added with another smirk.

"You should," Lewrie told him, stepping a bit closer, "Indeed, you should."

"'Ow much eet cos' you to *buy* your star an' sash?" Mollien asked him. "*Peut-être*, I can afford eet, too?" He was louder in his mocking, now that he had gathered a half-dozen or so strollers.

"Several . . . hundred . . . *dead* . . . Frenchmen," Lewrie gravelled back. "Think ye can afford *that*?"

Mollien pursed his lips to a slit, and he got a wary look on his face. His little bit of street theatre was not going the way he had thought; the idle fop *Anglais* he'd expected was turning out to be anything but, and . . . had the *Anglais*'s eyes gone as grey as a sword blade, from an inoffensive, merry blue?

"Oh, well said, Sir Alan!" Mr. Cotton crowed. "Well said, I *say*!"

"You've had your street raree show, Captain Mollien," McGilliveray gruffly said. "You delay our supper. If you're quite done . . ."

"*Un type l'aristo Anglais pédale*," one of Mollien's sychophant sailors muttered under his breath, elbowing his mate with a sneer.

He just call me a queer? Lewrie fumed to himself.

"Captain Mollien, the manners of your men, sir!" Lt. Gordon barked, one hand flexing on the hilt of his sword. "Such language in the presence of ladies! Are these the fine manners one usually expects from a French-man?"

"Fie!" his wife chimed in with an outraged hiss.

Mollien had rounded on his sailors to shush them, but it was too late to salvage the situation. When he turned back to face Lewrie, his face writhed between hang-dog apology and frustrated anger.

"Indeed, sir. Begone with you!" Mr. McGilliveray snapped, and shifted his grip on his heavy walking stick from elegant cane to hard cudgel.

"A t'ousan' pardons, *M'sieurs*, *Madames;* eet was unforgivable, and I weel be sure to puneesh 'eem as soon as . . ." Mollien tried to say.

"He can't help it, Mister McGilliveray . . . Lieutenant Gordon," Lew-rie drawled again, trying to recall the very words that that blood-thirsty old cut-throat and spy, Zachariah Twigg, had once said to that foul beast, Guillaume Choundas, to goad him at Canton, China, so many years ago. "Captain Mollien was born under a three-penny, ha'penny planet, never to be worth a groat . . . a swaggerin, 'gasconading' Frog who's but one step away from outright piracy!"

Mollien looked angry enough to draw his sword or one of his pocket pistols, rowed beyond all temperance by Lewrie's caustic slur. He also looked utterly cowed and defeated. Mollien had not put his wee cocked hat back on his head; he still held it in both hands as if deferring to his betters, gripping it so hard that he was wringing it out of shape . . . like a desperate beggar.

Can't find a way t'slink off? Lewrie gloated.

"You weel nevair catch me, *Capitaine*," Mollien said, chin up, though looking a tad shaky and unsure as he took a step or two away as if ready to depart.

"Yes, I will," Lewrie levelly promised him, "before the year is out. Run all ye wish; it don't signify. Leave port this instant, I and *Reliant* will find you, sooner or later. If not me, then it'll be another of our ships. The Royal Navy will be out there, looking for you and the rest of your privateersmen. We will *always* be there, just over the horizon. *Adieu,* Captain Mollien."

Mollien seemed so frustrated that he didn't even deny that his ship was a privateer. He performed a sketchy bow in *congé*, realising that his hat was still in his hand, and, pinch-faced with his cheeks aflame, stepped back and spun on his heels, bumping into his sailors. He shoved them back, hissing threats and curses at their unfortunate comment that had cost him his dignity, and had ruined his taunts.

"Ahem!" Lt. Gordon said. "Apologies, Captain Lewrie, for that fellow, but . . . *he* isn't an example of American manners, and I hope you don't think less of us for *his* low behaviour."

"Or, think less of our fair city of Charleston, Sir Alan," Mrs. McGilliveray said in a sweet Low Country accent. She had pulled her own fan out and was fluttering away at Mollien's effrontery.

"Short of a street brawl, Mistress McGilliveray, nothing ever could diminish my appreciation of such a lovely city," Lewrie gallantly responded. "Now that's over, does anyone feel as peckish as I do?"

"Indeed, let's go in!" Mr. McGilliveray seconded. "I'm fair famished!"

"Quite the street raree," Mr. Cotton commented, casting a last look down Broad Saint to assure himself that Mollien and his sailors were indeed gone. "One that redounded to Mollien's loss, ha ha!"

"At the end of a successful performance, one usually rewards the juggler or singer with tuppence, or five pence," Lewrie said, in good takings now that the fellow was gone. "Should I have tossed him something?"

"Oh, no more than a ha'penny, Sir Alan," Mr. Cotton snickered. "It wasn't all that good. Perhaps no more than . . . ha ha . . . a *groat*!"

As they were led to their table and took their seats, Lewrie did wonder
if Mollien was cleverer at sea than he was at mockery, or quick-witted
repartee. Had he goaded the man perhaps a tad too raw? And what would
a clever Frog do to get his own back?

CHAPTER TWENTY-NINE

*B*oat, ahoy!" was the shout from *Reliant*'s quarterdeck.

"Aye aye!" the cutter's bow man called back, showing four fingers in sign that a Post-Captain was aboard. It was absurd, really, for the boat was one of *Reliant*'s cutters, manned by Lewrie's usual boat's crew, and had left the frigate not half an hour before, and it would take a blind man not to see Lewrie seated aft by Cox'n Desmond in all his shore-going finery.

The bow man hooked onto the main chain platform with his gaff, and the oars were tossed vertically, then boated. Lewrie carefully made his way to amidships, stood on the gunn'l briefly, seized hold of the after most stays, and stepped aboard by the chain platform, then up the boarding battens. Bosun Sprague's silver call piped, the crew on watch faced the entry-port and removed their hats in deference, a side-party of seamen and Marines greeted him . . . and the ship's dog, Bisquit, went mad with joy, barking, yipping, and dancing about, daring to stand on his hind legs and put paws on Lewrie's midriff, his tail whipping like a flag in a full gale, and his tongue lolling.

"Welcome back aboard, sir," Lt. Westcott said, doffing his hat in salute, and trying not to laugh out loud.

"Thankee, Mister Westcott," Lewrie said, ruffling Bisquit on his head and neck with his left hand and doffing with his right. "I *would* stand upon my dignity, . . . if I could find it. Now, now! Get down, sir, and behave yourself."

"My apologies for cutting your time ashore short, sir, but, the French schooner began preparations to sail, and—" Westcott began to explain.

"And, you'd've preferred to go after her, instanter, but thought leavin' me behind'd look bad?" Lewrie interrupted, grinning.

"Something like that, sir," Westcott replied, shrugging. "She made up to a single bower, and hauled in to short stays, beginning about an hour ago. She's just taken a pilot aboard, and looks ready to weigh, sir."

"You sent for a pilot, sir?" Lewrie asked, removing a telescope from the compass binnacle cabinet, and going to the larboard side for a closer look at the French vessel.

"I did, sir, but so far—" Westcott said.

"But none have responded, so far, Mister Westcott?" Lewrie posed, sounding tongue-in-cheek and more idly amused than upset. "And, ain't that just uncanny!"

"Aye, sir."

"As I suspected," Lewrie told him over his shoulder, his attention focussed on the activity aboard Mollien's schooner. "Do we confer with the Sailing Master, I believe we'll find that she'll be crossin' the Charleston Bar just at the peak of high tide, right at slack-water, and, by the time a harbour pilot responds to our request, the tide'll be on the ebb. We *might* squeak over the bar . . . not that Mollien *needs* that much depth under his keel, but we *do*, more's the point. Captain Mollien will think himself a 'sly-boots' . . . but, he ain't."

"Mollien, sir? Is that the French captain's name?" Lt. Westcott asked.

"Aye," Lewrie told him, shutting the tubes of the telescope and turning in-board to face his First Officer. "Met him last night, him and a brace of his *larger* sailors. He almost ruined a most pleasant and congenial supper party," Lewrie said with a laugh, filling Lieutenant Westcott in on the confrontation, and on how Mollien had had to slink away with his tail between his legs, fuming. "Lieutenant Gordon of the United States Navy contingent, and his wife, accompanied Mister Cotton and me back to the Consul's residence afterwards, just in case Mollien felt pettish enough t'waylay me, but nothing happened. I had a good night's sleep, after that.

"Damme, what's the dog doin' on the quarterdeck, Mister Westcott?" Lewrie demanded of a sudden, noting that Bisquit had slunk from the sail-tending gangway to shelter by one of the 32-pounder carronade slides.

"Well . . . I expect he followed you, sir," Westcott replied. "He adores everybody, you included, . . . and has come to expect that anyone coming off-shore has a treat for him."

"Well, I do," Lewrie gruffly confessed, "but he'll get it on the weather deck, not up here. Mister Munsell, attend me, if you please."

"Aye, sir?" the Midshipman perkily replied.

"See that the dog gets this," Lewrie directed, digging into his shore-going duffel, "but not on the quarterdeck, hmm?"

"Aye, sir."

Too late! The aroma of fresh-fried ham on fresh-baked bisquits with gravy, carefully wrapped up in a packet of tarred sailcloth, got the dog to its feet. Instead of peeking longingly from the shelter of the carronade slide, Bisquit sprinted forward and began to prance and whine round Lewrie. Midshipman Munsell took him by the collar to tow him to the starboard ladderway and then to the main deck to feed him his treats.

"The rest of your time ashore went well, dare I ask, sir?" Lt. Westcott enquired.

"Main-well indeed," Lewrie told him with a pleased expression, further explaining that their Consul, Mr. Cotton, and his supper guest, Mr. Douglas McGilliveray, from one of the great trading houses in the state, and a man who had his finger on the pulse of Charleston commerce, did not suspect that any aid and comfort was being provided to French or Spanish privateers, and that vessels such as Captain Mollien's *Otarie* rarely called, at all. "No, I think we'll have to search further South of here, Mister Westcott—Hilton Head Inlet, Stono Inlet, Port Royal, or Savannah, Georgia."

"Beg pardon, sirs," Midshipman Rossyngton intruded, "but, the French vessel's anchor is free, and she's hoisting sail!"

"Calmly, Mister Rossyngton," Lewrie cautioned him. "There's not a thing we can do to stop her. I meant to ask, Mister Westcott," he went on, turning to the First Officer once more, "if there's anything out of the ordinary to report whilst I was ashore?"

"Everything went well, sir, with nothing out of the ordinary," Westcott told him. "Mister Cadbury did say that he and the working-party that went ashore with him *did* get some mild bother from some of the locals, and from a couple of seamen whom he suspected of being off the French schooner, sir, but, after getting a look at your Cox'n and Seaman Furfy, it came to nothing. Some foul looks and a comment or two about Mister Cooke, being Black and all, but Mister Cadbury said that there were many Free Blacks doing business who went about their trades un-molested."

"Free Black sailors off American ships are one thing, sir, but, a Free Black in Navy uniform, *British* uniform, is quite another, I do expect," Lewrie breezed off. "So! If we have to wait 'til the next high tide, what do ye suggest we do with the rest of this day, sir?"

"Uhm, there's some minor painting, sir . . . touch-ups, mostly," Westcott speculated. "Minor sail repair, some blocks aloft I'd desire to be greased, and one or two lines in the running rigging that need re-roving, that sort of thing."

"Mister Cadbury saw to it that we took extra fresh water aboard yesterday?" Lewrie asked, itching to get out of his finery, and back to his usual sea-going rig.

"Aye, sir," Westcott told him, "with more in the offing, if we desire."

"Paint and mend, the rest of the Forenoon, then let the ship's people do their laundry, and 'Make and Mend' 'til the end of the First Dog," Lewrie decided. "I'll be below."

Before he could quit the quarterdeck, though, there was Mister Cadbury, the Purser, with his ledger book, and a list of the victuals he had purchased ashore.

"Turnips, Mister Cadbury?" Lewrie enthused. "I'd suppose that it's too much to ask if ye found Swedes."

"No Swedes, sir, sorry to say," the Purser said with a moue of disappointment, "but your garden-variety 'neeps. *Garden*-variety, hah! Lashings of rice, of course, and I obtained field peas, in great quantity . . . odd ones called black-eyed peas for the black spots on them, along with sweet potatoes. Ehm . . ." Mr. Cadbury said more softly as he leaned forward, "Cooke tells me the reason they are in such quantity, and available at such low prices is that they, along with their rice, are considered *slave* food, sir. I'm not sure if the hands need to know that . . . might upset them that we feed them on such?"

"As they say in the Bahamas, though, Mister Cadbury, 'it eats good'," Lewrie said with a chuckle. "With fresh butter, baked sweet potatoes will be a treat, and with ham hocks or salt pork, the boiled peas will be hot and filling."

"Very good, sir," Mr. Cadbury agreed.

The French schooner's fore-and-aft sails were fully hoisted by then, and she was beginning to make a slow way, with some musicians aboard her skreaking or thumping out their revolutionary anthem once more, and her crew roaring the words, *hurling* the bellicose words, at HMS *Reliant*.

On-watch or off-watch, *Reliant*'s people would not stand for it, and began to jeer and hold up their fingers aloft in insult, shouting a cacophany of curses across the cable that separated their ships.

Lewrie would *not* dignify her departure with the use of a telescope, though he did stand and watch her go, with his hands clasped in the small of his back.

"*Au revoir, sangliants!*" came a shout from *Otarie*, amplified through a brass speaking-trumpet. Captain Mollien was having the last word.

"Oh, sir!" Midshipman Rossyngton gasped. "*Sangliant* refers to womens', ladies' . . . monthly . . . !"

"The French are crude, sir," Lewrie stiffly told him. "And I'm surprised ye know of such."

"*Au revoir, Capitaine, vous salaud!*" Mollien shouted. "*Pédale!*"

"Trumpet, Mister Rossyngton!" Lewrie snapped, and one was fetched from the binnacle cabinet.

Up forward, Lt. Spendlove and Lt. Merriman were beginning to lead the crew in a lusty, though not very musical, rendition of "Rule, Britannia". Lewrie hoped that Mollien could hear him over that din.

"Hoy, Mollien!" Lewrie shouted to the schooner, "*Vous absurde petit bouffon . . . vous ridicule petit merdeux! Va te faire foutre!*"

Midshipman Rossyngton burst into peals of laughter, though his cheeks and ears turned red from shock; it was not every day that one heard a dignified senior officer call someone "an absurd little clown" or "a ridiculous little shit", and certainly not telling another—even a Frenchman—to "Go fuck yourself!"

"Ye see, Mister Rossyngton," Lewrie said with a feral smile as he handed the speaking-trumpet back, "sometimes ye *have* t'match crude with crude."

Didn't know I could string that much French together, Lewrie congratulated himself. *And when we* do *run him down and take him, I'm going to ram those insults of his down his God-damned throat!*

"That's enough," Lewrie ordered as the French schooner sailed beyond easy earshot. "That'll do, Mister Westcott. Let's get people back to their duties."

"Very good, sir," Lt. Westcott crisply responded, though still grinning over the crew's response, and Lewrie's surprising outburst.

Lewrie went down the starboard ladderway to the main deck, and turned aft to enter his cabins, already tugging at the knot of his neckstock. Bisquit leaped to his feet, his feast done, looking for more, for Lewrie still had some sliced ham in his duffel for the cats. He planted himself in front of the door, tail thrashing, and Lewrie took time to pet his head and shoulders, and ruffle his neck fur, before reaching for the door. The Marine sentry presented his musket as Lewrie opened it, and the dog darted in in an eye blink.

"Oh no, dog, that's off-limits!" Lewrie snapped, pursuing him inside. "That's quite enough! Pettus, catch him and shoo him out!"

Bisquit did a quick trot round the forbidden cabins, sniffing at everything, as if he knew his time was limited; the carpets atop the chequered deck canvas, the canvas itself, the desk in the day-cabin, the hanging bedcot, the upholstery on the transom settee and the starboard-side settee and chairs, then into the dining-coach, where Lewrie's cats had dashed in panic to take shelter atop the side-board and hiss and spit. When the dog paused long enough to put his paws on the side-board and utter playful noises to entice the cats, Pettus caught him by the collar and led him, only a bit unwillingly, to the door. Damned if the silly beast wasn't *grinning*, tugging towards Lewrie and looking up at him with mischief, and gratitude perhaps, for his shore treat, before Pettus put him outside and shut the door.

"He likes you, sir," Pettus said with a lop-sided grin.

"He likes everybody," Lewrie growled, "the Bosun, the Master-at-Arms, the 'duck fucker' of the manger, even the Purser's Jack-In-The-Breadroom—anybody who'll give him the time o' day."

" 'E's right clever, sir," Jessop, the young cabin servant, shyly piped up. "Been teachin' 'im tricks, I has."

"Not in here, I trust," Lewrie said, peeling off his neck-stock and shucking his dress coat.

"Oh no, sir, never!" Jessop swore.

"Cool tea, sir?" Pettus asked.

"Coffee," Lewrie decided, removing his sash and un-buttoning his waist-coat. "Do stow all this away, and lay me out my comfortable old clothes, Pettus."

"Aye, sir," Pettus said, summoning Jessop to assist him, "Care for a bite of something, sir?"

"Our Consul sent me off with a solid breakfast, and his house servants washed and ironed most o' my things," Lewrie told him. "All I care for is coffee. I've a letter or two to write before dinner."

The supper party had gone past ten of the evening, and Lewrie and Mr. Cotton had sat up past eleven in discussions, over balloon snifters of brandy, before retiring. Lewrie had slept extremely well, but had risen early, had rewarded himself with one last shore bath, and had wolfed down fried ham, scrambled eggs, thick toast, and piping-hot hominy grits with cinnamon, sugar, and butter. If he didn't get started on his letters, he feared he might nod off over his pen.

There would have to be one letter to Admiralty to report upon what *Reliant* had done so far, and what he and their Consuls had discovered. A copy of that letter would have to be sent to the British Ambassador in Washington City. Once the official reports were done, there would be time to write his father, Sir Hugo, his sons Sewallis and Hugh—though if their respective ships were at sea it might be months before they received them—a letter to his daughter, Charlotte, who still lodged with his brother-in-law in Anglesgreen, and a fond one to Lydia Stangbourne. And one to his bastard son, Desmond McGilliveray.

It had been hard to find even a brief moment of privacy with Mr. Douglas McGilliveray to ask about Desmond, and unsure whether even a guarded enquiry might upset Mrs. McGilliveray, who might, or might not, know that Lewrie was young Desmond's true father, not her husband's late younger brother of the same name, who had been the family's agent to the Muskogees Indians, and guide to a fruitless expedition into the Florida Panhandle to bring the tribe into war against the Americans, an expedition of which Lewrie was a part. *That* Desmond had claimed both the baby, and his mother Soft Rabbit, a Cherokee slave to the White Clan, after Lewrie had sailed away, marrying her at the next Green Corn Ceremony the next Spring. The elder Desmond and Soft Rabbit had both died of a smallpox outbreak not long after, and the baby had been sent to Charleston to be with his White kin by the White Clan elders.

It was bad enough for young Desmond to be half-Indian in haughty Low Country Society; for him to have a *British* father might have made things worse for him, were it known! Hatred for England and all things

British were still alive, as Lewrie had already seen. Best all round for the lad was for the people of Charleston to believe that Desmond's sire had been a daring and resourceful, Oxford-educated, "far-trader" and frontiersman, one of their own kind and class, and the inconvenience of his late mother's race could be dismissed.

Thankfully, Mr. Douglas McGilliveray had provided an opportunity to speak, inviting Lewrie to join him in the tavern side of the establishment so he could savour a *cigarro* grown and cured Up State on the Piedmont and rolled in Charleston. Before Lewrie could declare himself a non-smoker, McGilliveray had tipped him a very broad wink.

"You wish to know how Desmond fares, I expect," McGilliveray had begun. "He's gotten your last two letters, but has been a tad busy to respond promptly. He's at the North in the Chesapeake."

Young Desmond was now a full-grown young man of twenty-two years of age, and had wangled a way to stay in the fledgling U.S. Navy after the short Quasi-War 'twixt America and France had ended, intending to make a career of it if he could. McGilliveray had proudly related how Desmond had already stood his oral examinations and had passed on the first try, making him a Passed Midshipman, eligible to be commissioned a Lieutenant in the future, should there be an opening.

"Promotion may come soon," Mr. McGilliveray had said, winking once more, and blowing a cloud of smoke at the ceiling of the tavern. "President 'Fool Thomas' Jefferson just *won't* see that we need a sea-going navy. Soon as he took office, he laid up all the good ships to rot away, and had all these damned coastal and river gunboats put into service. Lieutenant Gordon's poor pair are lucky to live, out past the bar, on a gusty day, and wouldn't be much of a deterrent to an enemy expedition. What little we still have in commission worth a thing are over in the Mediterranean, confronting the damned Barbary Corsairs. You know we lost the frigate *Philadelphia*. A shameful business! Stranded aground in Tripoli Harbour, and captured. Oh, we managed to board her and burn her, but it's pitiful how weak we are. The idea of sailing *gunboats* to Tripoli is laughable! Pressure is growing that we build newer, bigger, better-armed frigates, sloops of war, and brigs to scour the Barbary Coast and stop their foul business, once and for all! All the poor, murdered American sailors, all those captured and enslaved, forced to denounce Christianity and turn Muslim? Pah! They cry out for freedom, and vengeance!"

"So, Desmond could be posted to a new ship, as a Lieutenant?" Lewrie had asked.

"A very good possibility, Captain Lewrie," McGilliveray had imparted with a pleased smile. "Do you write him, send your letters to the brig o' war *Daring*. She's fitting out for the Mediterranean at Baltimore."

Lewrie suspected that Desmond wrote his Charleston family more often than he wrote him, and had pressed for more information on how he was truly doing . . . gingerly asking how the young man was being *accepted*, despite his antecedents. McGilliveray had turned sombre, leaning closer. Charleston Society would always look upon him as an exotic oddity, no matter the backing and full acceptance of his kin. His prospects of making a decent match, someday, would be bleak, *but* up North Desmond's Indian-dark hair and complexion could be mistaken for Huguenot French, for many of them had settled in Charleston and the South Carolina Low Country before the Revolution. And, having Lewrie's grey-blue eyes was a plus. His bastard son was strong and slim, and finely moulded, his manners impeccable, his seeming sense of place and his confident air of competent, gentlemanly leadership, and his proven courage and skill with weapons, actually made Desmond a welcome guest . . . in the states above Virginia, at any rate.

"He could come back to Charleston, someday, with a New England bride?" Lewrie had gawped. "What would the city think o' that?"

Mr. McGilliveray had at that juncture heaved a heavy sigh and had slowly shaken his head, before saying, "I fear that Desmond might never return to Charleston, at all, unless the Navy orders him here. He's become more a citizen of our whole country than he is of South Carolina, despite his family's desires that he stay a part of us."

Poor chub, Lewrie thought as he fetched out a fresh sheet of paper and dipped his pen in the ink-well; *though it may turn out for the best for him. And nothing that I could cure.*

III

BOOK III

PIRATE: A ſea-robber, or an armed ſhip that roams the ſeas without any legal commiſſion, and ſeizes or plunders every veſſel he meets, indiſcrimanatly, whether friends or enemies.

—*FALCONER'S MARINE DICTIONARY*
1780 EDITION

CHAPTER THIRTY

This whole expedition is just bloody impossible, Lewrie sourly told himself as he pondered the newest charts he had purchased ashore in Charleston. *Reliant's* Sailing Master, Mr. Caldwell, had been highly dubious of their usefulness, and would put no trust in them until he had compared them to his own sets, and then only begrudgingly told Lewrie that the Yankee Doodles had done a "passably accurate" job of surveying their own waters.

I've too big a damned ship for this work, Lewrie concluded.

To look into Stono Inlet, Hilton Head Inlet, Port Royal Sound, or Calibogue Sound, it had been necessary to fetch-to five miles off the coast and send both twenty-five-foot cutters and one of the thirty-two-foot barges inshore under sail, with a Lieutenant in each to keep order, on the pretense of fishing for sport, with the hope that the locals did not get too curious or upset to see British boats "poaching" upon their fishing grounds. There had been nothing in Stono Inlet larger than a ship's boat, but that proved little. Two nights later, and an *host* of raiders or privateers could have put in to victual under the cover of the night.

The boats had returned with a few fresh fish, and about one bushel basket of fresh-trawled shrimp purchased from locals to keep them mellow.

The only discovery of note was made by Lt. Merriman, who had peeked behind Hilton Head Island, and came back swearing that the channel between the island and the mainland looked to be the birthing grounds for half the sharks in the Atlantic, swarming as thickly as a creek full of eels!

He'd sent the Purser, with Midshipman Eldridge, and his boat crew in the second barge as far as the sleepy towns of Port Royal and Beaufort to see what their markets offered, and Mr. Cadbury had come back with very little to show for it, and with the depressing information that what little shipping was present was small and pacific. Mr. Cadbury had asked about, and if there was a British Consul there, a true Briton or a hired-on local attorney, no one on the docks or in the stores had ever heard of him.

"Have a nice afternoon, did you, Mister Westcott?" Lewrie asked once the First Officer had come through the entry-port in his rolled-up shirtsleeves, and doffing a wide-brimmed straw hat.

"A *lovely* day for boating, sir," Lt. Westcott said with delight, "though not a one for discovery, I'm afraid. The local fishermen we encountered were stand-offish, but once we bought some fish, and gave them a few shillings for them, they did turn chatty. Do you imagine that your cats savour fresh fish, sir?"

"I expect they do," Lewrie said, grinning back in like humour with Westcott, and looking at Toulon and Chalky, who were sunning all a'sprawl atop the cross-deck hammock nets. "Mad for it, they are."

Indeed they were, for Westcott had come aboard with a wet jute bag that positively reeked of fresh fish. As soon as they were aware of it, Toulon and Chalky sat up, their tails quivering and their whiskers stiffly pointed forward, craning their necks. Westcott reached into the bag and tossed two live shrimp to the planks of the quarterdeck. They sprang at once, chittering madly, and sat by the shrimp, lifting and patting them with one paw, sure that they were something good to eat, but unsure of how to go about it.

"Anything else of note, sir?" Lewrie prompted.

"Not really, sir," Westcott told him. "I enquired, as casually as I could, about French or Spanish vessels putting in here, and they said they couldn't recall any, in years. They hadn't seen any French *money*, either, though Spanish silver coins might as well be the legal tender in America. I don't know if the U.S. Government actually *has* a mint of their own. Our shillings and half-crowns were more than welcome. They spoke a lot of barter, sir."

Toulon and Chalky were making eager *mrrs*, slapping their shrimp in play-kill, and leaping in alarm when the shrimp limply thrashed in return. Chalky finally nipped one and ran off a few feet with it, but dropped it when its antennae wriggled.

"Just think of 'em as big cockroaches, lads," Lewrie told them. "Ye have no trouble with those."

"One thing in our favour, sir," Lt. Westcott pointed out, "the land round here is so marshy and flat, and the coastal forests so low, that any ship of decent size, with her masts standing, can be spotted quite easily."

"Unless they're of shallow-enough draught to make their way up the maze of rivers, and round a bend or two where the trees are tall enough to hide them," Lewrie rejoined with a glum look. "Back of the marshes, there's white oak and live oak forests, an hundred years old or better. *Hmpf!* Perhaps we ought to come back with barricoes of silver, and buy prime shipbuilding oak from America. We've scavenged our own forests, and half of Hamburg's exports, just t'keep the Navy in good repair . . . much less keep up with new construction. Come, sir . . . take a look at this chart of the Georgia coast round Savannah. It gives me a headache."

It wasn't that far South of where *Reliant* lay fetched-to, but it was rather daunting to contemplate how many inlets and sounds, how many rivers feeding into the ocean, into those sounds, lay before them, all of which could harbour enemy ships behind the myriad of fertile barrier islands, the Sea Islands.

Round the mouth of the Savannah River, there was Turtle Island and Jones Island on the North bank, with broad streams leading round and behind them. To the South bank, there was Big Tybee Island nearest the sea, with Cockspur Island and McQueen's Island between the mainland and Tybee Roads. Further South was Wassaw Sound below Big Tybee Island, with another snake's nest of tributaries, and the mouth of the Wilmington River which led deep inland. South of Wassaw Island, lay Ossabow Sound, another deep gash, with Racoon Key at its upper reach, fed by the Vernon River, and the Little and the Big Ogeechee Rivers.

"It gets worse," Lewrie said, running a finger down the chart to St. Catherine's Sound, Sapelo Sound, Doboy Sound, and Altamaha Sound at the mouth of yet another long, inland river. The charts showed a small port, Brunswick, near Kings Bay and St. Simons Sound, further South of there, then Jekyll Sound, St. Andrews Sound, and Cumberland Sound (past islands of the same names), where the St. Mary's River fed into Cumberland Sound, and that river was the border between the state of Georgia and Spanish Florida.

"Good Lord, but this could take 'til mid-century, sir," Lieutenant Westcott commented with his head cocked over in awe.

"Once we've recovered all our boats, I wish us to get under way and come to anchor in Tybee Roads, if there's enough daylight to see what we're doing when we get there," Lewrie said, stepping off the short distance with a brass divider, and measuring the span against the mileage legend on the side of the chart. "Come morning, we will signal for a pilot . . . assumin' we can get up-river with our depth of keel. That failing, I'll take one of the barges up-river to confer with our Consul in Savannah. God, *another* couple of days in flummery!"

"Whilst I and the other officers can look forward to even more fishing and 'yachting', sir?" Lt. Westcott said with a snicker.

"Round the mouth of the river, perhaps," Lewrie said, tossing the brass dividers into the binnacle cabinet. "To probe all of these sounds, you'd need the rest of our wee squadron, and all *their* boats. We've been away too long as it is, and God knows what they've gotten into."

"Aye, sir," Westcott replied. "I shall get way on the ship directly."

"Lord, lord, a whole bushel o' shrimps!" Mr. Cooke marvelled once he'd clapped eyes upon them. "Lookee heah, Mistah Yeovill! Dey be enough fo' de Cap'm's table *and* de whole wardroom!"

"They look like *bugs*!" Midshipman Entwhistle disparaged.

"Dey eat good, sah," Cooke assured him, "oncet ya boil 'em up an' peel 'em. Folks up in Charleston ain't high on 'em, but back on Jamaica, we know how t'do 'em right."

"Nothing for the cockpit?" Midshipman Grainger asked, sounding plaintive. "Not even a morsel for our mess?"

"Beg pahdon fo' askin', Mistah Grainger, sah, but . . . what'd *you* bring back?" Cooke asked. The ship's cook, was a big and burly fellow with a rumbling and loud bass voice, and could seem quite daunting to those who did not know his pleasant nature.

"Well, a drum fish, a sheepshead, and some mullet," Grainger tallied up.

"Yah messman kin bake 'em for yah," Cooke told him.

"I bought a decent lot of blue crab at Port Royal," the Purser piped up. "For a nominal sum, I could provide a few to the cockpit's mess."

"Shrimps, *and* crab!" Cooke barked in glee. "Mistah Yeovill, I do b'lieve we could do up a boil fo' de cockpit, de wardroom, *and* de Cap'm."

"I'll add mine to that," Lt. Westcott eagerly offered, waving his sack of shrimp. He tossed it to Cooke, who emptied it into the bushel basket, along with the rest of the shrimp.

"Beg pardon, Mister Westcott, but all our boats are secured," Bosun Sprague reported, squinting dubiously at the basket's contents. "People eat those things?" he muttered.

"Very well, Mister Sprague," Westcott said after looking over to Lewrie. At his nod, he further said, "Pipe 'Stations' for getting under way, if you please."

Just a bit before a spectacular sundown, HMS *Reliant* rounded up into wind, took in sail, and dropped her best bower to come to anchor in Tybee Roads. Once the hands of the Afterguard had brailed up the spanker and mizen tops'l and had coiled up and stowed away all of the running rigging lines, Lewrie could take a slow stroll round the quarterdeck and look outward to see what he could see, and to savour the sunset. The heat of the day was going, and the light winds blowing from the Sou'east were pleasantly, almost tropically, warm and comforting. *Reliant* had not yet lit her taffrail lanthorns, belfry lamp, or deck lanthorns for the night, though the other ships anchored in Tybee Roads already had. He thought of fetching a telescope, but the daylight was fading too quickly for close study. Even without one he could determine that most of the anchored ships were brigs or brigantines, most moored further up the mouth of the river nearer Turtle Island, and the few larger three-masted, full-rigged ships were anchored below Cockspur Island in deeper water. One of them had barge-like hoys and sailing lighters nestled alongside her, as if her master was loath to sail all the way up-river to Savannah's docks, and was lading or discharging his cargo here; perhaps Savannah's exports and imports were handled in that way, for ships which couldn't find enough depth?

As light as the sundown wind was, it was sufficient to stream *Reliant*'s large Union flag to advert her nationality to one and all. All the other anchored ships, both big and small, displayed the blue-and-starry canton, and the red and white horizontal stripes, of America.

Lewrie heaved a small, wary snort. He had used the ruse of flying a false flag in the past to stride up within pistol-shot of an enemy ship, before whipping it down and hoisting true colours at the last instant. What he, or any other nation, could do, anyone else could do, be they a merchantman *or* a privateer. Might one of the brigs or brigantines be a Frenchman in disguise, this very moment?

Two Bells were struck on the ship's bell; it was half past six, and one half-hour into the short Second Dog Watch. Marine Lieutenant Simcock was mustering and inspecting his sentries in the waist before posting them at the forecastle, on the gangways, and the taffrails to guard against hostile raiders or deserters willing to try a long swim to freedom.

Time for a drink, Lewrie told himself; *for it's been a long and depressin' day.*

"I will be aft and below," Lewrie told the Midshipman of the harbour watch, Mr. Warburton. On his way to the starboard ladderway, he stepped on something both squishy and crunchy. He picked it up; it was one of the shrimp that his cats had slapped about, then abandoned un-eaten. *Toulon's, most-like,* Lewrie thought as he heaved it over the side; *I'm sure Chalky managed his.*

He looked round for the pestiferous ship's dog, but there was no sign of it. Bisquit was likely below on the mess deck or in the Mid's cockpit, begging affection . . . or in the warm galley with Mr. Cooke, awaiting his evening tucker. It was safe for Lewrie to open the door to his cabins!

"Evening, sir," Pettus greeted him, looking up from the dining table where he was laying a place for one. "Care for a glass of something before supper, sir?"

"A nice, cool white wine, Pettus, thankee," Lewrie said, going to the starboard-side settee to fling himself down on it and prop his booted legs atop the round brass Hindoo tray table. "It's seafood, tonight, so a white'll do main-well. Here, lads! Here, cats!"

"Right away, sir," Pettus replied, going to the wine-cabinet to rummage round 'til he found the right bottle. "Yeovill said he was preparing something new for your sweets, sir . . . a pie that he and Mister Cooke discovered at Charleston. Sold on the streets by Black ladies, he said, and it took quite a lot to worm the receipt from them on how to prepare it, he said. What Yeovill called pecan pie, sir."

"Oh, I *had* a slice o' that when I dined ashore, aye!" Lewrie enthused.

"*Sinful*-good, it was, and so sweet and gooey, it could make your teeth hurt. I'm lookin' forward t'that."

Pettus brought him a glass of Rhenish, though it was hard to take a sip once he got it, for Toulon and Chalky had swarmed his lap, stomach, and chest, purring and shoving their heads under his hands for long-delayed affection.

A hellish task I've been set, t'peek into all these damned inlets and sounds, Lewrie told himself; *but, at the end of the day, at last, there's pleasant rewards.*

CHAPTER THIRTY-ONE

*L*ewrie had heard of the beauty and elegance of Savannah, but at first impression, the moment that his barge ghosted up to the teeming commercial docks, it looked as dowdy as any seaport. And, so many miles inland from Tybee Roads and the reach of a fresh sea-wind, the place had a reek about it. Add to that the fact that it was by then late May and the climate was warm, humid, and almost steamy, and Captain Alan Lewrie would have gladly avoided the place, if he could.

He had brought along the Ship's Purser, Mr. Cadbury, of course, to purchase fresh victuals, though there was little the ship needed at present, after their previous stops, and in the course of that, to spy out the commercial trade to see if any war *matériel* might be stocked for sale to privateers . . . on the sly, if Cadbury could manage it.

He had also brought along Mr. Midshipman, the Honourable Albert Entwhistle, who was by then a seasoned, and most presentable, twenty-year-old. His barge was manned by his Cox'n, Liam Desmond, with stroke oar Patrick Furfy, and the same hands who'd accompanied him up the Cape Fear River to Wilmington. Lewrie, Cadbury, and Entwhistle could possibly be lodged with their consul's residence, and the hands in his coach house; if not, Lewrie had come prepared with a full coin purse for food and lodging.

Their consul, though . . .

There had been no time to send an introductory letter up-river after anchoring the evening before, so Lewrie and his party arrived as a surprise. Once the boat was secured at a riverfront chandlery, he and his men set out to find the consul's residence, or his offices. A clerk at the chandlery assured them where Mr. Hereford could be found, in an office behind the sprawling docks and warehouses, not two blocks off . . . though the clerk did not sound all that respectful.

Lewrie discovered the reason for that dis-respect when he got to the given address, and found that Mr. Hereford kept a small office in a brick building full of lawyers, a pre-Revolution mansion that had seen better days, and had been sub-divided into a nasty warren of tiny suites. An upper-storey door to one suite bore a painted wood plaque announcing "Mr. R. L. E. Hereford, Esq., H.M. Consul", and Lewrie rapped on it several times, with no response. He tried the door knob and it opened easily, so he swung the door fully open and stepped in.

"Excuse me. Anyone in?" he called out as he entered a small anteroom filled with bookcases, a desk, chair, and a sitting area off to one side. There was a settee there, and from it sprang a liveried Black servant, his white periwig askew, and his eyes as wide as saucers. He emitted an "*Eep!*", gulped twice, and looked as if he would run, given the chance.

"Captain Alan Lewrie," he told that quaking worthy. "I'm come to speak with the British Consul. Is he in?"

"*Eep!*" the servant reiterated, twitching his clothing back to good order, and fussing with his wig. "Mistah . . . Mistah Hereford, he's in, sah . . . Cap'm sah . . . but . . . !"

"Announce me if you will, there's a good fellow," Lewrie said.

"Yassuh, yassuh, right away," the servant said, going to the other door at the back of the anteroom and slipping inside, closing it behind him.

"Damn' odd way to maintain offices, sir," Midshipman Warburton said in a sidelong mutter. "Must not do much business here."

Lewrie thought much the same, for the book cases were crammed with piles of loose correspondence angled any-old-how, legal books in piles on the floor, on the small outer-office desk, and all filmed with a noticeable coating of dust, as if nothing of import had taken place in a month of

Sundays. From behind that second door, Lewrie could hear water being splashed, some impatient mutters, and then the sound of *gargling* and spitting. The door was opened again, and the liveried Black servant stepped through to the anteroom, shutting it at once, softly. "His Excellency, Mistuh Hereford, will be with ya sho'tly, Cap'm." He then stood by the doorway, waiting, eyes half-shut.

His "Excellency", mine arse. Lewrie scoffed to himself.

After a long wait, the door to the inner office opened, and a gentleman stepped through it. Mr. Hereford's reaction to the sight of a Royal Navy officer was most unlike his servant's; the fellow scowled and squinted as if Lewrie's presence was a bother.

"Richard Hereford, your servant, sir," the fellow announced as he performed a slight bow from the waist. "My man said you are Captain . . . uhm?" he prompted, with a brow up and hand waved in the air.

"Alan Lewrie, captain of the *Reliant* frigate, Mister Hereford," Lewrie told him, performing a deeper bow. "My pardons for not sending word of my arrival in Tybee Roads last evening, sir, but the lateness of the hour would not admit rapid delivery. Allow me to name to you one of my senior Midshipman, Mister Entwhistle. I am come—"

"Welcome to Savannah, Captain Lewrie, Mister Entwhistle," the Consul said. "God help you," he added with a sneer. "One supposes that your errand is of an official nature, hmm? If you will follow me to my office, we may discover the nature of your visit. Will you take wine, sir, or might you prefer tea? Tea, it is, then." He sounded a tad disappointed. "Ulysses, fetch the captain a pot of tea."

"Yassuh, Massa," the servant said, scuttling out into the hallway.

"A servant, or a slave, Mister Hereford?" Lewrie asked once he was seated in front of Hereford's desk with his hat in his lap.

"Bought him," Hereford answered, "the idle fool. One can't do a thing in the American South without slaves. Even the poorest Whites, begging in the streets, reject the notion of house service, or body service. Gad, to recall how close I came to a posting at the North! Philadelphia, New York, or Boston, which are at least *civilised*, and cooler. Yet, here I find myself, croaking like a frog in a Georgia marsh, in a place as dis-agreeable as 'Sweaty-pore' in India.

"Now, Captain Lewrie . . . Sir Alan, one would suppose, hey? . . . what has brought you to Savannah?" Hereford asked. As Lewrie laid out his mission, where he had been so far, and upon whom he had called, Hereford made the proper "ahems" and "ahas" and "I sees" at the right places, and even dragged out a sheet of paper and a lead pencil with which to make notes. In the middle of all that, the pot of tea arrived, and the servant, "Ulysses", poured cups for all, and offered cream and sugar. Mr. Hereford reached behind him to a sideboard and book case hutch for a decanter which he waved to them in invitation, filling the office with the tang of rum as he pulled the stopper. He shrugged at Lewrie's and Entwhistle's refusal, then openly poured himself a dollop into his tea, and damned what they thought.

Lewrie looked round Mr. Hereford's inner office. It was bigger than the anteroom, and featured a set of glass-paned double doors leading out to a wide, railed balcony, as if the entire suite had at one time been a spacious bed-chamber, music room, or upper parlour. It was just as dusty, as crammed, and dis-organised as the anteroom office, though, and featured a suspiciously deep settee in one of the dark corners, furthest from the glazed doors. The cushions, and the pillows, still bore the impressions of its owner's head and body. It appeared that Mr. R. L. E. Hereford, Esq., rarely saw visitors, and took long naps through his idle mornings.

"Privateers, do you say, Sir Alan?" Hereford mused aloud after a sip or two of his tea, leaning far back in his leather-padded chair to rest his cup and saucer on his upper chest. "I can't say when the last time was that a French or Spanish vessel of any description put into Savannah, or even anchored at the mouth of the river. I arrived at this posting during the Peace of Amiens, and there *were* some ships from France, Spain, and Holland who came to trade, but . . . since the renewal of the war, the trade has shrivelled up to nothing, more's the pity. One cannot *imagine* how dear a case of good wine, or a simple bottle of champagne, has become! At least our American 'cousins' do still trade with the Spanish West Indies, and tobacco is available in quantity. Why, were it not for the rare British ship, it would be impossible to obtain decent *clothing* or fabrics to entrust to clumsy local tailors, haw!"

Much good that does you! Lewrie sneeringly thought, for "His Excellency" Mr. Hereford's suitings, expensive as they looked, were ill-fitted, rumpled from his naps, and in need of a good sponging to remove some stains. He wore a snuff-brown coat of broadcloth wool, a pearlescent waist-coat of a light gold colour, and a pair of buff trousers, all worn so long that every joint in his body had creased them into permanent wrinkles. His neck-stock was pale blue, badly, indifferently bound, too. To top it off, Hereford was possessed of one of those clench-jawed and "plummy" Oxonian accents natural to those born to the upper aristocracy, or those who affected it, that had always set Lewrie's teeth on edge.

I'll wager he drives Savannahans mad, too, he told himself, and imagined that was the reason the clerk at the chandlery had spoken so derisively of the British Consul. *I don't think I like him very much.*

"I see that there's only the one wee port South of here, the town of Brunswick, before the border with Spanish Florida, sir," Lewrie posed. "Do you happen to get down that way very often?"

"Brunswick?" Hereford scoffed, pouring himself another dottle of rum into his tea. "A sleepy little place, a bare cut above a hamlet. Is there any trade conducted there, it is of little import, and strictly a local affair, conducted by vessels little larger than fishing smacks, mostly to serve the Sea Island plantations. Would that His Majesty's Government see their way to providing me a *decent* subsidy, I would establish myself on Tybee Island for a summer residence.

"The planters, do you see, Sir Alan," Hereford imparted with a smile, "the immensely wealthy ones, and many with the *pretensions*, maintain inland plantations, and *summer* plantations on the Sea Islands, which are so much healthier. Can they not get away from their active lands, they will at least send their women and children to Saint Simons, Jekyll, and Cumberland Islands to survive the heat and the humidity, if not the sicknesses, of the mainland. If a plantation out there will not do, they will at least have summer houses and truck gardens."

"So, you don't get down to Brunswick often, sir?" Lewrie asked once more, striving to *not* sound impatient with the fellow.

"Hardly ever a reason to do so, Sir Alan," Hereford idly waved off, and took a deep sip of his "tea" with a welcome sigh.

"Might it be possible, then, Mister Hereford," Lewrie went on, shifting in his chair, "for foreign vessels to put in there for a day or two . . . put into Wassaw or Ossabow Sounds, or one of the sounds below Brunswick, to take on firewood and water, and perhaps meet with a local chandler or trader, and re-victual without your knowledge, or the knowledge of American authorities?"

Hereford seemed stumped by the question, laying his head over to one side to ponder his answer for a long moment. "I would imagine that anything is possible, Sir Alan . . . though hardly *plausible*, d'ye see. Just how, for instance, could a foreign trader—most likely a smuggler wishing to avoid American import duties than a privateer—inform a nefarious trader from Savannah of his date of arrival, or which sound or inlet he will use for that particular cargo? On the other hand, how might the aforesaid nefarious trader communicate his wishes to the smuggler, what?

"In any case, such smuggling . . . if such *is* being conducted . . . would be of more concern to the United States Revenue Service than to Great Britain," Mr. Hereford jovially dismissed. "We of the Consular branch do not interfere with the sovereign rights of our host nations. Neither do we presume to enmesh ourselves in the manner in which host nations enforce their customs fees or their laws, except when those laws, fees, and regulations involve British ships calling at American seaports. Anything else beyond that limited brief is *ultra vires* . . . a legal term for 'actions beyond one's legal authority or power'."

Hereford gave them a little concluding smile and simper, then took another sip of his rum-laced tea, as if it was all settled.

"So, you would only look into rumours of smuggling, or supplying privateers, if they involved British merchantmen, or privateers, sir?" Lewrie summed up, feeling a very strong urge to leap across the desk and seize the arrogant fool's neck and squeeze . . . hard!

"Well . . ." Hereford flummoxed, taken aback by the question. "If evidence—evidence, mind, not mere rumours—was brought to my attention that Crown subjects were engaged in smuggling, I would give the American authorities, both local and Federal, my most strenuous support. But such activities are *most* implausible, I assure you, Sir Alan. Upon *what* enemy trade might British privateers prey, sir, hey? There may be some crumbs to be gleaned in the West Indies, and in European waters, but not this side of the Atlantic, heh heh. Our merchant vessels calling at Savannah come from the West Indies in convoy, where your own Navy bonds them, and their cargoes are mostly salt, molasses, rum, dye wood, and tobacco, perhaps the most valuable commodity being refined sugar . . . as well you might know, had you ever served in the West Indies yourself, Sir Alan," Hereford simpered again, condescendingly. Lewrie put a brow up and a scowl on at that remark, but that didn't signify to Mr. Hereford; he would make his little jabs for the idle fun of them.

"Last Spring, I was part of an escorting squadron to a 'sugar trade', Mister Hereford," Lewrie replied. "We lost three ships when level with Georgia and South Carolina, to French privateers who took us from the landward side, and hared off with their prizes to the West and Sou'west.

That makes me think that they based themselves somewhere along the American coast, or had arrangements with Americans to sell off their stolen cargoes and ships without going all the way to Cuba or the Spanish Main. D'ye see what I'm drivin' at?"

Hereford might not have; he sat perfectly content with his cup on his chest and stomach, blinking beatifically.

"If stolen ships were brought into Savannah under pretense of false registries, or sold here to un-suspecting buyers in need of new bottoms, would you have any way of knowing, Mister Hereford?" Lewrie asked.

"Unless someone familiar with such a vessel saw her at anchor in the river under a new flag, and brought that to my attention, no, Sir Alan," Hereford easily admitted. "Only if a British-flagged ship were contracted to be sold to an American buyer would I become involved, merely to note the transfer of ownership, flag, and registry, and assist the Crown subject selling her with my best advice as to the particular details of such a sale . . . and perhaps suggest ways that he not be gulled by a low offer, hmm?"

"You are on good terms with the chandlers, the import-export trading firms here at Savannah, sir?" Lewrie went on, wondering just what Hereford *did* do to earn his salt at Crown expense.

"Reasonably so, Sir Alan," Hereford told him as he snapped his fingers at Ulysses to pour him a fresh cup of hot tea. "Though, they are in *trade*, and for the most part are an avaricious and common lot, the epitome of the fabled sharp-practiced Yankee trader, even though one could expect that the heat and humidity of Savannah's clime would engender a torpor which slows their frenetic *greed*, haw haw! A batch of 'chaw-bacons' . . . or 'chaw-*baccies*', more to the point! I do not associate with them on a daily basis."

For which they surely thank the Lord! Lewrie thought.

"But, have any of them struck you as more sharp-practiced than most, sir?" Lewrie pressed, wondering if he could extract a positive and informative answer from the top-lofty idler before sundown. "Do you keep your ear to the ground, so to speak, as to which *might* be engaged in smuggling, or supplying enemy privateers on the sly, should the opportunity fall in his lap? Keep tabs on them?"

"As I said earlier, Sir Alan, and must point out again, criminal behaviour by American traders and chandlers is a matter for the *American* authorities," Hereford told him, getting a bit testy as he shifted in his chair. "That would be beyond my purview, and to probe into their doings, well!

That would smack of *spying* on them, sir! An activity that no *gentleman* would conduct in one's host nation! The very idea!" Hereford harumphed, and openly glowered, as if Lewrie had touched upon his honour, and was impatiently waiting for an apology for making such a suggestion.

You ain't worth a tuppenny shit! Lewrie fumed to himself, trying to keep a level expression on his face.

"I see," Lewrie said after a long blink and a sigh. "Well, I was ordered to come and make your acquaintance, Mister Hereford, and to discover to you Admiralty's suspicions, and that, I believe, I have done. All Foreign Office can ask of you is that you keep your eyes open, and advert to the American authorities, and our Ambassador at Washington City, any suspicious activities. That ain't spyin', 'cause you'd be helping Brother Johnathon enforce his touchy sense of neutrality, and I trust ye won't think it so. As soon as the tide in the river turns, it might be best did I set off to re-join my ship . . . unless you think that a shore supper with some of the prominent citizens of Savannah could be arranged on short notice? In that case, I would take lodgings for the night *somewhere,* and set off tomorrow morning."

That's a hint, ye thick turd! Lewrie thought.

"I fear that the suddenness of your un-anticipated arrival may not admit of such a supper gathering, Sir Alan," Mr. Hereford quickly said, sounding relieved that Lewrie would toddle off and leave him to his rest once more. "Now, had you given me two or three days notice, I could have accommodated you, and shown the 'country-put' locals what an English gentleman looks like, ha ha! They will raise cheers for the so-called Common Man, but would dearly love knighthoods and titles of their own. Show them what they gave up with their damn-fool rebellion, and what little dignities they got from their independence, what?"

Hereford gulped the last of his tea and stood, beaming at one and all, sure that the interview was over, quite jolly once more.

"Any suggestions as to lodgings, sir?" Lewrie asked as he stood as well. There was no way he could stomach the thought of sharing the Consul's residence, even for one night, sure that they'd come to blows before midnight if he did, but Hereford should make the offer.

"There are some few lodging houses, though none that rise to the level of amenities that a gentleman such as yourself could abide, Sir Alan," Hereford was quick to warn. "Even the lone inn with aspirations to quality, I found, before obtaining a wee residence in town, offers hard, thin beds, perfectly tawdry and squalid furnishings, and your choice of lice, fleas, or bed bugs. The food is insufferably bad, to boot."

"Surely not that bad, sir," Lewrie said, as if bandying jovial words.

"I would offer you and your Midshipman the hospitality of my residence, but for the fact that I am in the process of re-plastering and re-painting at the moment," Hereford told him, almost but not quite looking sorrowful that he could not dine them in and offer beds.

"I came up-river with my Purser and a party of five hands from my boat crew, so . . ." Lewrie said as they made their way to the outer office.

"There would have been no room for them, in any event," Mister Hereford said with a shake of his head. "If you lodged them at one of the sailors' inns, well . . ." It seemed that Mr. Cadbury, a man engaged in "business" aboard a warship, and lived and died on the slim profits earned 'twixt buying and selling, was one of these abysmal people in "trade", too, to Hereford's lofty lights.

"No matter, then," Lewrie said as they reached the door to the hall-way, which the slave Ulysses held open for their departure, and seemed as eager to see the back of them as his master; perhaps he needed a longer nap before dinner, as well. "Never been to Savannah," Lewrie lied. He had been up-river with despatches, once, from Tybee Roads when British forces still held it. "Perhaps Mister Entwhistle and I could hire a carriage for a brief tour before dinner. I am told that the city's layout by Governor Oglethorpe is most impressive."

"A most inventive and creative gentleman, he was," Mr. Hereford agreed. "His plans for Savannah were quite inspired . . . though, one does wish that he created his Eden anywhere else but *here*, hey?"

"Good day to you, Mister Hereford, and thank you for receiving me on such short notice," Lewrie said in parting, "You have been most helpful."

"Sorry that I could not be more so in aid of your quest, Sir Alan," Hereford said. "Good day to you, and may you have a safe and successful passage."

They bowed themselves away, the door closed, and Lewrie could imagine long, deep sighs of relief from both Hereford and his slave, before he and Midshipman Entwhistle trotted down the stairs and to the street.

"Might I ask, sir," Entwhistle hesitantly said, "if you found him as useless as I did?"

"That I despise him for a pus-gutted, slovenly, arrogant, *idle* waste of the Crown's money as ever I clapped eyes on, sir?" Lewrie hooted. "Aye, I do find him useless. So useless and un-informative, in point of fact, that I could easily suspect him of bein' hand-in-glove with criminal traders and enemy privateers, if anyone gave me a strong hint in that direction. What a goose-berry bastard he is!

"Not that we should speak ill of our compatriots in Foreign Office, Mister Entwhistle, God forfend!" Lewrie added with mock solemnity, with a hand on his heart. Entwhistle was all but cackling out loud.

"Hold my coat for a bit, Mister Entwhistle," Lewrie bade as he peeled it off, and slipped the bright blue satin sash clear of his body, then plucked the enamelled silver star from the coat, stowing them in the side-pockets before donning his coat once more. "Bloody silliness . . . wasted on *his* sort. Most-like wasted on the people of Savannah, too. Makes me feel like a monkey on a leash!"

Entwhistle looked a bit scandalised that his captain put little stock in the hard-won marks of distinction that every young officer-to-be desired, but said nothing.

"There're more picturesque public squares in Savannah than you and I have had hot dinners, Mister Entwhistle," Lewrie told him with a grin, "and all of 'em, and the broad streets between, lined with mansions as grand as Grosvenor Street in London. Let's go find the Purser and our hands, and have us a carriage tour!"

CHAPTER THIRTY-TWO

*W*elcome back aboard, sir," Lt. Westcott said once Lewrie had taken the salute from the side-party and the hands on deck. "And how was Savannah?"

"Just *ever* so jolly, Mister Westcott, and thankee for askin'," Lewrie drawled in broad sarcasm. "In point of fact, it was just too infuriatin' by half. Didn't learn a blessed thing, and our Consul in Savannah is as useless as teats on a bull. Oh, Mister Cadbury found a few things on your and the Bosun's list, and there'll be a barge to come alongside tomorrow, just after Noon, if tide and current will serve. I need an ale . . . badly. I'll be aft and below."

"Very good, sir," Westcott said, looking a bit mystified.

"I'll fill you and the other officers in later, sir, after I get comfortable," Lewrie promised. "An informal conference in my cabins, after supper?"

"I will inform them, sir."

Pettus and Jessop were caught unawares by Lewrie's quick return to the ship, so there was no pitcher of cool tea brewed for him. His cook,

Yeovill, had to scramble to whip up a supper, too, expecting that Lewrie would spend the night in Savannah; he popped into the cabins just long enough to enquire if an omelet with hashed potatoes, toast, and a slice off a cured ham would suit, then loped off for the galleys.

Pettus drew him a tall mug of pale ale from a five-gallon barricoe stowed aft under the transom settee, as Lewrie shed his shoregoing uniform and flopped on the settee to accept his cats' welcome.

"Ah, that's good," Lewrie said after a deep quaff. "Had some in the boat on the way back down-river, and that made me thirsty for beer."

After gathering Mr. Cadbury, Desmond, and Furfy, and the boat crew from their prowl through the chandleries, Lewrie had hired two open carriages for that promised tour, which had put everyone in jolly takings. The tall houses with their ornamental iron-railed gardens in their fronts, the raised foundation homes with their high stoops, and the lushness of the gardens that were railed in, had struck them all as simply grand, as grand as anything in the West End of London, indeed . . . but, that was nothing to the many squares. Each was a miniature park, overshadowed by tall, twisting, twining live oaks draped with Spanish Moss, planted flowering bushes in every colour, palmettos rustling spiky leaves to the light wind to add a touch of the exotic set against the brick walks and well-tended lawns. There were even fountains in the middle of some, and their sprays, along with the shade provided by the oaks, obliterated the heat of the day each time they reached one.

Following that, they had returned to the docks and loaded their barge with what goods that Mr. Cadbury deemed essential, then visited the street vendors for a mid-day meal, getting hard-boiled eggs, fried chicken, cheese, bisquits, and small, sweet fruit turnovers to eat once they were under way down-river. Since the boat crew would miss their usual mid-day rum issue, a disaster to Navy sailors, Lewrie had to sport everyone to a small two-gallon barricoe of beer, and purchase enough wooden mugs for all. Once tapped, it had been pronounced good beer, stronger than the weak small beer served aboard ship, which was little more than beer-flavoured water, which kept much longer in cask than water.

They shoved off and rowed out far enough from the docks until they could hoist both lugs'ls and a jib. Once all sheets were belayed, Desmond and Furfy led the hands in the ancient game of "who shall have this'un, then?" to share out legs, thighs, and wings. Lewrie, Cadbury, and Midshipman Entwhistle had had to settle for the dryer, less desirable white meat breasts. All in all, even counting the rent of the carriages, it cost Lewrie less than board and lodging overnight.

With their boat under sail, and the river current wafting them on, there was little for the crew to do but admire the sights of the journey, over the foreign-ness of the birds, the salt marshes that seemed to stretch to the horizon in every direction, rarely broken by small groves of trees on the islands, or on higher, dryer, hammocks, and the other river traffic. If a barge or lighter coming up-river neared them and it had a woman aboard, the sailors shouted greetings and cat-calls, no matter how old or ugly.

All was as calm and easy and pleasant as a slow drift on the upper Thames in mid-summer, as a punt among the swans at Henley. That early in the season, the vast, wind-ruffled seas of reeds and marsh grasses were new-shoot green and pleasing to the eyes, not the cured-tobacco-leaf or old-parchment brown of late Autumn. Two or three of the sailors had begun a soft crooning song. The return journey was so close as any of them would get to the royal leisure of "yachting" that they could conjure that they were sailing to the legendary sailors' Eden, Fiddler's Green, where the beer and rum never ran out, all the doxies were beautiful, and the publicans never called on them for the reckoning, and the landing to that Paradise was just round the next bend in the river.

Except for Lewrie.

After eating, a mug of beer, and a dip of his hands into the river to wipe them and his mouth of grease, he had turned quiet and sombre, pondering upon all that he still did not know of enemy privateers' activities, or American involvement in support . . . and upon how short a time he had remaining to "smoak" them out.

Once *Reliant* weighed anchor and set sail from Tybee Roads, he could not linger off the coast of Georgia to look into the sounds, or put in to tiny Brunswick, without exciting the American authorities and provoking a diplomatic incident upon suspicion that he was "blockading" a neutral nation! He could not play the innocent "we're just fishing" ploy again, so soon after employing that ruse off Port Royal, or lying at anchor for two days in Tybee Roads, which was just a hop, skip, and jump from the Sea Islands and their sounds! From the mouth of the Savannah River, it was but half a day's *slow* sail to Cumberland Sound, and the mouth of the St. Mary's River, where Spanish Florida began.

The only thing he could do would be to admit failure and join *Lizard*,

Firefly, and *Thorn* off St. Augustine. He had grimaced, nigh-winced, as he'd thought of how he'd word a fresh report to Admiralty. The only slightly cheering idea that had come to him was his estimation of Consul Hereford, which he would also send to the British Ambassador in Washington. If he needed a good excuse, "His Excellency" R. L. E. Hereford would do quite nicely!

Idly stroking the cats, now they had calmed down from frantic welcome, and lifting his mug now and again for a sip of beer, Lewrie tallied up what little he *did* know, so far.

Firstly, he could safely rule out any privateering activity from North Carolina. Their hired Consul, Mr. Osgoode Moore, and his old friend, "Kit" Cashman, had an eye on things, from Topsail Island to Lockwood Folly Inlet. What might transpire North of Topsail Island from Beaufort, or the Albemarle or Pamlico Sounds, was beyond their ken, but . . . most British convoys made sure that they were well out to sea, and clear of any risk of being driven onto the Hatteras Banks, the Graveyard of the Atlantic, and his orders from Admiralty had not mentioned any losses from those convoys that far up the American coast.

Secondly, Mr. Cotton at Charleston had established good relations with the trading firms and chandleries in South Carolina waters, and was *fairly* sure that Georgetown and Winyah Bay, where so many rivers joined, dealt mostly in rice exports.

Charleston had the Ashley and the Cooper Rivers, but the only traffic on them was barges and small boats, and Charleston was not so far up-river from the sea. It was the most important seaport in the American South, but it was open, garrisoned by American troops, with Revenue cutters and Navy gunboats, and even if there were major shipyards, and many chandleries and trading firms that *could* be in collusion with enemy privateers, Cotton had left Lewrie with the impression that, but for the presence of Mollien's privateer schooner, the problem lay elsewere. If there was indeed a problem!

Lewrie felt that he could have been hunting leprechaun's gold, for all the good of it, so far, yet . . . Mollien *had* been there, sure sign that he was hunting British ships somewhat close to Spanish Florida. He might have put into Charleston to flaunt his country's flag, or to call upon a decent tailor.

Stono Inlet had been a bust, as had Edisto, too. Port Royal, and the other Beaufort (in North Carolina it was "Bo"; in South Carolina is was "Bew") had seemed intriguing, but had little in the way of ship chandlers or trading houses, little shipbuilding beyond large fishing boats, and no one they had encountered could recall French or Spanish vessels of any description entering the sound in ages, so Lewrie *might* be able to rule them out.

"Top-lofty bastard," Lewrie muttered to himself, thinking about Hereford.

"Sir?" Pettus asked, from the bed-space, where he was sponging Lewrie's best-dress coat.

"Just maunderin', Pettus," Lewrie assured him. "Thinkin' of a man I met in Savannah."

"Oh, sir," Pettus replied, "before Lights Out, sir, I think we need a pot of water boiled in the tea-pot. Your sash got all crumpled up in your coat pocket, and it needs a good steaming before it goes back into its box."

"Aye, boil away," Lewrie allowed. "Have Cooke heat up an iron in the galley, if ye think it's needful."

"Brr, sir!" Pettus commented with his mouth pursed. "Got to be careful with silk or satin, sir. A too-hot iron will scorch them something horrid."

"Whichever ye think best," Lewrie said, bringing the mug to his mouth. There was only a swallow left, and he thought of ordering Pettus to tap a second, but forbore.

Georgia . . . bloody Georgia, he silently mused; *the worst maze o' creeks, inlets, sounds, and channels back o' the islands of all I've seen, so far. Worse than the bayous in Louisiana! If ever a place was made for pirates, smugglers, and privateers, that'd be it. I wish t'God I could linger long enough, I'd be sure t'find something.*

Lewrie wondered if his suspicious feeling had more to do with his anger over Hereford's sloth-like reaction to his suggestion, and his haughty rejection of looking into even the most overt violations of American neutrality, standing on his lofty and too-fine sense of personal honour. If Hereford wouldn't look into things, and Lewrie couldn't stay long enough to do it himself, then that left the coast of Georgia, and the port of Savannah, the last area that had *not* been absolved.

What'd they say? That all the rogues went to Georgia? Lewrie thought with a mirthless grin; *Or gets sent there, an Crown expense, to do nothing!*

On their carriage tour, their coachee, a Free Black fellow, had pointed out several of the sights, naming each square, and indicating the stately homes by their owners' names, assuring them that they were all prominent Savannah residents of long standing. He had seemed delighted to mention who the significant patriots of the Revolution were, and what roles they had played. Some homes had temporarily been used by British "occupiers" for headquarters, officers' residences, barracks, or stables, the churches and their pew-boxes being grand horse stalls. "And o' course, gennelmuns, dat house on de right, dar, be yo' Consul's home, dat Mistah Hereford."

Dammit, it had been grand; not as large and imposing as its neighbours, the other manses that lined the streets or fronted upon the green public-squares, but it had been impressive enough.

And it didn't look as if there were any plasterers or painters workin' on it, either, Lewrie fumed; *It was a lot finer than Mister Cotton's at Charleston. And, just how much* does *a consul get paid on a foreign station?*

Britain's public services, and government offices, were rife with jobbery, graft, and "interest". There was good reason for families to wheedle a minor clerk's job for their sons, for aspiring men to spend as much as £5,000 to gain a government post that paid no more than £300 or £500 a year. Once in place, and assured a life-long living, the sky was the limit on how much they could earn on the sly in bribes. Christ, they even knighted some of the bastards at the end of a long career!

Lewrie wondered if Hereford's eagerness to see him off quickly was due to catching him asleep in his offices, and most remiss in his duties overall, or did Hereford fear that he might learn something criminal about his dealings if he stayed a night or two?

Hereford could be a haughty, useless fool with a private income from his family in England, or have umpteen thousands in the Three Percents and a slew of annual interest, Lewrie considered. The British pound sterling was worth a lot more than any unit of currency that the United States could ever issue, so an hundred pounds could go a very long way towards purchasing, or running up, a house. A private income, plus his annual pay and expenses for a residence and offices, could be a more-than-tidy sum.

Or, he could be a shifty criminal in league with his country's enemies! At the very least, making money on the side by looking away, not looking at all, from the dealings of a Savannah businessman.

Damme! Lewrie chid himself of a sudden; *If I hadn't been so angry, I should've looked up . . . what were their names?*

During the Quasi-War 'twixt France and the United States over high-handed French boarding and seizure of American merchants who were *not* trading with France, there had been a "hostilities only" bought-in ship, the U.S. Armed Brig *Oglethorpe*, fitted out and armed by eager public subscription in Savannah, and crewed by merchant masters, mates, and sailors, for the most part, with a sprinkling of U.S. Navy officers who had no ships in which to serve. She, Captain McGilliveray's *Thomas Sumter*, and the U.S. Frigate *Hancock*, had formed a squadron in the West Indies to protect their country's shipping, and seek out any French merchantmen they could find, and, most honourably, fight and take any French warship or privateer they encountered, too.

And *Oglethorpe*'s captain had been a Savannahan gentleman seafarer named . . . ? *Randolph!* Lewrie recalled; *If I didn't have my nose outta joint, I could've looked him up and asked* him *a few questions! Too damned late, now!*

Lewrie also glumly considered that Randolph might have stayed in the sea trade, and might have been halfway to Canton, China, or he might have passed away of something; a lot of people whom Lewrie had known from his time round Jamaica, and at Nassau, as he'd learned from his recent call there, had joined The Great Majority.

Toulon and Chalky had abandoned his lap and thighs and gone to the middle of the settee to groom themselves before supper, so Lewrie could get to his feet and stroll aft to the larboard side to step into his quarter-gallery toilet to relieve himself of beer. The upper sash-windows were open for the sundown breeze, and *Reliant* had swung on her single anchor to face her stern up-river, so he could savour another fine sunset as he piddled.

I have t're-join the squadron off Saint Augustine, he thought; *I've already been away too long. But, if Darling, Lovett, and Bury say that blockadin' the place ain't worth a candle, what's t'stop me from bringin' 'em back up here t'prowl the Georgia coast for a bit? Maybe poke into the St. John's River in Spanish Florida on the way? And, do we use some o' those boats we captured at Mayami Bay, and keep well to the Spanish side o' the Saint Mary's . . . ? Hmm.*

As he did his breeches' buttons up, he stepped to the aft windows for a last peek at the sunset, and a deep, appreciative breath of cooler evening air. The larger merchant ships that had been anchored off Cockspur Island the night before, on the Southern side of Tybee Roads, were reduced in number. There had been four, but now there were only two, surrounded as before with lighters nuzzled alongside like a pack of nursing piglets. Up-river, nearer Turtle Island and Jones Island, the night lanthorns had already been lit on the clutch of smaller brigs and snows, also attended by lighters. Some of the lighters sat lower in the water than others, evidently still full of exports or chandlers' goods, to be laded in the morning.

And, coming down-river was a pair of those stout and dowdy cargo barges under two masted lugs'l rigs with single jibs. With the sun low on the Western horizon, almost lost in the trees, the sails glowed amber against the red band of sunset, and tiny, glim-like lanthorns at their binnacles and sterns winked a cheery yellow. Quite pretty, Lewrie thought, in all.

Lewrie left the quarter-gallery and shut the door behind him, and took seat upon the upholstered transom settee to continue watching the sunset through the transom sash-windows. The lower halves of the windows were kept closed at all times, so one, or both, of his cats on a romp or gambol in the night, did not fall out and be lost at sea; they needed a cleaning of salt-air rime on the outside, and smudges of paw prints on the inside. He had to stand again to watch through the open upper halves.

The sailing barges stood on, bound for the larger ships which lay off Cockspur Island, almost passing out of view as they neared the starboard quarter. But, they weren't reducing sail.

What the Devil? Lewrie wondered, going over to the starboard side of his cabins to open the door to the other quarter-gallery, which was used for storage, so he could follow the barges' progress.

They weren't stopping at the large ships' anchorage; they were bound out to sea!

Where the bloody Hell are they *goin'?* Lewrie asked himself; *At this time o' night?* Pettus and Jessop hadn't bothered to clean the window panes in the starboard quarter-gallery, since it was not used as a lavatory, so Lewrie had to pull out his long shirt-tail to scrub himself a clear patch, but all he accomplished was a worse smear. His curiosity piqued, he dashed for the door to the waist and ran up the ladderway to the quarterdeck in his shirt sleeves.

"Captain's on deck," Midshipman Warburton cautioned the idling quarterdeck watch, and the officers who had come up before their own supper for a smoke, or a breath of air.

"Glass, Mister Warburton!" Lewrie snapped.

"Something amiss, sir?" Lt. Westcott asked, coming to the starboard bulwarks a step behind his captain.

"Those two sailin' barges yonder, sir," Lewrie said over his shoulder. "They're not closin' with those anchored ships; they're on their way to sea. Lading's done for the day, so where are they goin', I wonder. Why are they bound out just at sundown, not . . . ? Thankee, Mister Warburton," he said as the requested telescope was fetched.

He couldn't see all *that* much, even if the barges were only a mile or so off. The telescope was a day-glass, with little light-gathering strength. A night glass would have shown more detail, but its assortment of internal lenses resulted in an image that was upside-down and backwards.

"They look t'be about fourty or fifty feet, or so, two-masted, and . . ." Lewrie muttered. "Do they look like the run-of-the-mill barges you've seen, Mister Westcott?"

"I *suppose* so, sir," the First Lieutenant admitted sheepishly, "I fear I've not given any of them more than a passing glance. Just work-boats," he said with a shrug.

"Have any of you seen any o' them goin' to sea, or entering the Roads from seaward?" Lewrie asked.

His sudden appearance on the quarterdeck had drawn the other two Lieutenants, and the Marine Officer, from the idle gathering, and to stand near him by the starboard bulwarks in a befuddled pack.

"I cannot say that we have, sir," Lt. Spendlove, the most earnest of them, confessed.

"As Mister Westcott said, sir . . . just work-boats," Lieutenant Merriman seconded. "Strings of them come down-river each morning, and return to Savannah in the afternoons, mostly."

"Or, they spend the night alongside the merchant ships, then sail the next morning, sir," Lt. Spendlove added.

"Is their going to sea suspicious, though, sir?" Lt. Westcott asked. "There are plantations on almost every island along the coast, I heard, so . . . they must get goods from Savannah somehow."

"After *dark*, though?" Lewrie pointed out. "It'd make more sense to sail from the Savannah docks at dawn, and get to Saint Simon's, or Jekyll Island, or Brunswick port, in late afternoon, in safety, and not risk the barges to the shoals and such in the dark."

"Even goods required instanter, sir?" Marine Lt. Simoock asked.

"Instanter, my foot!" Lt. Merriman scoffed with a laugh. "It would take a whole day to send an order by boat from Brunswick, and a day to fill it, then a third day, weather permitting, to ship it down to them."

"Instanter's what you have at hand, and snatch up quickly," Lt. Spendlove added.

"Well, I'm no mariner, I will admit," Simcock replied, "so I will trust to your seasoned judgement."

"There *is* the possibility that those two barges are from one of the Sea Islands further South, sir, or belong to a Brunswick merchant, returning home," Westcott slowly speculated. "If their masters know the waters well enough, and stand far enough offshore during the night, they may not think a night passage all *that* much of a risk."

"An everyday or weekly occurrence, then, sir?" Lewrie asked, lowering his telescope, and wondering if he was grasping at straws in the need to discover *something* criminal to justify the days that he had so far wasted chasing after Will-O'-The-Wisps. "Possibly," he allowed . . . grudgingly.

Wish I could send a cutter in chase of 'em, Lewrie thought; *or shadow 'em and see what they're up to.*

He closed the tubes of the telescope with a thump and heaved a deep sigh, partly in disappointment, and partly to calm his excitement and appear "captainly" to his officers and men. He turned and handed it back to Midshipman Warburton with a polite "Thankee."

I send a cutter t'board 'em in the dark, or lurk so bald-faced in American waters, I could halfway start a war! he told himself.

"Good evening, gentlemen," Lewrie said to one and all, on his way to the head of the starboard ladderway, then paused at the top. "There will be some of those lighters alongside with the Purser's goods tomorrow. Without appearin' *too* curious, let's take her measure, and ask about the barge trade. And, keep a closer eye on the traffic in the Roads, hey? *Bon appetit!*" he bade them on his way to his supper.

CHAPTER THIRTY-THREE

*T*he sailing barge from Savannah came alongside *Reliant* in the middle of the Forenoon, and Lewrie made sure that he was on deck for her arrival, as were his off-watch officers, Bosun Sprague, and his Mate, Wheeler. Lines from her bow and stern were taken aboard to be bound to the frigate's mizen and foremast chains, and the barge crew heaved over great hairy mats of ravelled rope to cushion the contact between the hulls.

There were light articles of cargo on the barge's deck, containing live chickens and layer hens, some squealing piglets, and sides of fresh-slaughtered beef in jute sacks, sacks of flour and cornmeal, and casks of spirits, along with wooden cases of goods for the officers' wardroom, the Mids' cockpit, and the captain's cabins.

Lewrie stood idle by the mizen mast shrouds to look down into her. The barge was closer to fifty feet on the range of the deck than his earlier estimate of fourty, very wide-beamed, and flush-decked with a single cargo hatch between her masts, and smaller crew hatches at bow and stern. Her master was White, as was her helmsman, though the rest of the small crew were Black, most likely slaves.

"We'll have the light goods, first," Bosun Sprague bellowed to the barge crew. "Lines comin' down, and we'll drag them up the loading skids."

"Is she about the same size as the barges you saw at Savannah, Mister Cadbury?" Lewrie asked the Purser as he stood on the quarterdeck with a ledger book and a pencil, to cheek off each bought item as it came aboard.

"About average, sir," Cadbury told him. "There are some smaller, thirty or thirty-five feet or so," Cadbury told him. "I would say that this one is representative of the bulk of the barge trade. Many of them serve plantations and hamlets up the river, as well. As for the barges you noted leaving port last evening, sir, they *may* have been bound for the Sea Island plantations landings, for the channels behind the islands."

"Out to sea just long enough to enter Wassaw or Ossabaw Sounds, then go up the other rivers?" Lewrie asked, leaning most "lubberly" on the bulwarks where the quarterdeck ended and the larboard sail-tending gangway began, with his arms crossed.

"Very likely, sir," Mr. Cadbury agreed with a primly happy expression, glad to be of assistance. "While I am not a 'scaly fish' of experienced seamanship, this barge does strike me that its upper rails are tall enough to weather a stiff beat to weather, well heeled over, long enough at least for a short sea journey from one sound to the next."

"As beamy as a Dutch lugger, aye," Lewrie judged, "so she'd be quick to make leeway. And, from here, it doesn't look as if her hold is all *that* deep. She might not draw much more than seven or eight feet. Mister Rossyngton? Are you ready, sir?"

"Aye, sir," their slyest and cheekiest Midshipman eagerly said.

"Then pray do go on and be all boyish curiosity," Lewrie told him. Rossyngton dodged a crate of chickens and several sacks of meal to the open larboard entry-port and did a quick scramble down the man-ropes and battens to hop aboard the barge, ostensibly to oversee the ship's working-party who would strap up the heavier items of cargo and prepare them to be hoisted aboard with the main course yard as a crane.

"And when you were on the docks, Mister Cadbury, did you see or hear anything odd?" Lewrie further asked, turning to face the Purser once more.

"Well, not really, sir," Cadbury replied, half his attention on the goods coming up in a cargo net, and eager to go down to the waist to check items off. "I saw no war-like goods, beyond a few kegs of gunpowder in the chandleries, a brass swivel gun or two, but nothing in sufficient bulk to draw any suspicions. Of course, even in peacetime, merchant ships of any worth carry *some* armament for their protection."

"How very true," Lewrie replied, though thinking that it was a rare ship's master who would put up much of a fight if he found that he could not out-run or out-sail a pirate or privateer.

"Compared to the reception we got in Charleston, sir," Cadbury happily burbled on after checking off two more crates, "I found that Savannah's merchants were much more agreeable."

"No French ships anchored in port, most-likely," Lewrie said. "No one to show off to."

"I gather that it has been a month of Sundays since any Royal Navy ship has called here, so I and my party were looked upon as something of a raree, sir," Cadbury told him. "The gentleman with whom I arranged these goods, sir, a fellow named Treadwell, when he heard that a British Navy shore party was in his establishment, came out to speak with me, personally, and was hospitality itself, even treating me to a glass of Rhenish, and when he heard that you had requested me to find you a crock of aged corn whisky, he was that eager to turn up five gallons of what he assured me was the very *best* Kentucky!"

"Not too dear, I trust," Lewrie said.

"A most equitable price, sir," Cadbury replied, naming a sum that didn't make Lewrie wince or suck his teeth. "A very striking man, is Mister Treadwell. Most fashionably dressed in the latest new London style, much as we saw back home before sailing, and . . . he's no older than you, sir, but has the most remarkable head of silver-white hair. I took it at first for a wig, but, upon closer inspection, it proved to be his own . . . very full and curly. All the more striking, given his deep tan. Well set-up, of a lean but muscular build, almost six feet in height."

"White hair?" Lewrie asked with a puzzled frown. "Did he get scared out of his wits once, d'ye imagine, Mister Cadbury?"

"When he noticed me looking, Mister Treadwell explained that he had once been pale blond, but, spending so much time at sea or upon the rivers hereabouts, bare-headed in the sun, when he was making his fortune, it gradually turned silvery-white, and there's no one that could explain it for him."

"Uhmm, how many o' these barges does he own, d'ye expect, Mister Cadbury?" Lewrie asked, thinking that the only youngish people whose hair had turned white so early were pink-eyed albinos, and most of those in the circuses.

"A fair parcel, I would expect, sir," Cadbury answered. "For I think there were at least half a dozen lading or un-lading at his wharf whilst I was there, and, on our way down-river, I spotted several others. All fly a white burgee with a blue star, like a company house flag . . . just as this one does, sir."

"The barging trade 'twixt Tybee Roads and the city," Lewrie mused aloud, "up-river to the inland towns. Perhaps out to sea for the island plantations?"

"Very possibly, sir," Cadbury agreed. "Excuse me, sir, but if you will spare me, I must see to the kegs as they come aboard."

"Very well, Mister Cadbury, carry on," Lewrie allowed, pushing off the bulwarks and pacing down the gangway to look more closely into the barge's hold, which looked to be a tad deeper than his first estimation, suitable for bulk cargoes such as rice or cotton or tobacco in loads large enough to make each barge able to carry several tons at a time . . . so it would not take dozens of them to service one vessel. And, he surmised, that to own too many barges to do the work would be too expensive to maintain, with too many masters and crewmen to hire, or slaves to clothe and feed, to make the trade pay.

A working-party of *Reliant*'s sailors were grouped round the entry-port and the stout loading skids forward of that, crowding the gangway impassable, so Lewrie stepped back out of their way and slowly paced to amidships of the quarterdeck, where Mr. Caldwell, the Sailing Master, was taking the air and using a wee pocket-knife to sharpen a set of lead pencils.

"Seen their like, Mister Caldwell . . . the barges?" Lewrie asked him.

"In almost every port in the world, sir," Caldwell jovially replied. "Or, something akin. Boats the size of the one alongside could fit into the coasting trade back home quite easily, even serve as water or supply hoys to the Channel Fleet ships on the French blockade. Stout, slow, and clumsy, but sea-kindly even in a good blow."

"So, one like this 'un could make a passage from here to the sounds, or Brunswick, with no trouble?" Lewrie posed.

"I wouldn't think so, unless they were caught on a lee shore in a full gale, sir, or a hurricane, which are known to strike these shores," Caldwell said, sure of his conviction, and, since the question had nothing to do with *Reliant*'s work on the open sea or guiding her up the Savannah River, did not draw upon his chief duties. Then, he would be much more cautious in his conclusions. The prospect of a whole day more at anchor was just gravy to Mr. Caldwell, with nothing to do, and lots of idle time to catch up on his sleep. "I gather you suspect that Savannah is the likeliest port you've seen so far, sir?"

"It is," Lewrie said, clasping his hands in the small of his back. "It has the most extensive barge traffic, a lot more than Wilmington. Charleston's wharves are so handy to the sea that there's no need for them, and 'twixt here and Charleston, there's not enough big ships puttin' in that need 'em, either. All the sounds, inlets, and rivers South of here, though . . . so many islands and back channels . . . all the way to the Saint Mary's and the Saint John's rivers in Spanish Florida, that, if someone didn't mind takin' French or Spanish gold, he could keep 'em supplied, on the sly, very easily."

"Well, there's still the matter of what the privateers do with their prizes, sir," Caldwell mused with his head cocked over in puzzlement. "Slipping the Frogs and Dons supplies might pay well, but the real money's won at a Prize Court. Perhaps forged American registry papers would be safer to sell than taking them into Savannah for sale as legitimately owned ships, but . . ."

"Which wouldn't be accepted by a Prize Court like Havana, and wouldn't fetch much from Spaniards lookin' t'buy a ship or two," Lewrie huffed, fed up with the whole business. He didn't know a blessed thing, and it looked most unlikely that he'd learn a whit more.

Admiralty should've sent someone else, he glumly thought; *in a handier ship for inshore work, and a lot more wits and guile! Did I suit 'em 'cause I could flash my bloody star and sash and* awe *the Yankee Doodles into confessin'?*

"Well, it all seems beyond me, Mister Caldwell," Lewrie said as he shook his head wearily. "I think I'll take myself below for a long ponder . . . or a sulk, whichever comes first!"

"We'll get to the bottom of it, eventually, sir, no error," the Sailing Master said with a hopeful note to his voice.

Pettus and Jessop were cleaning the sash-windows in the transom and both quarter-galleries when Lewrie entered his cabins, with young Jessop perched on a sill, and the upper half of one window down onto his lap, with his arse hanging over the stern.

Lewrie thought to find some peace and quiet, but with supplies coming aboard, *Reliant* was echoing to various thuds, booms, screaks, and rumbles as the heavier items of cargo were swung up out of the barge and over the gangways and thumped to the deck in the waist, and then lowered down to be stowed on the orlop deck, some items lowered down steep ladderways, a deck at a time, with much stamping of feet and groans from sailors.

After about an hour of brooding over his desk with a sheet of blank paper, an open inkwell, and a steel-nib pen in hand with nought to show for it, the din finally ceased, and the Marine sentry banged his musket butt on the deck, calling "Midshipman Rossyngton, SAH!"

"Enter," Lewrie gloomily answered.

"Beg to report, sir!" Rossyngton said with a happy grin.

"Go on, sir," Lewrie bade him.

"I struck up a conversation with the master of the barge and his mate, sir, the mate being a fellow not much older than me. He was curious about our ship, and what sailing round the world is like, so I struck up a good conversation. They work for a rich merchant in Savannah by name of Treadwell. He does a lot of the barge traffic, and owns more than a dozen or so, all sizes, as well as some small brigs in the coasting trade, and a brace of bigger ones that sail as far as Baltimore and Philadelphia, in season, to garner a fair portion of Northern imports to Georgia. The mate my age is looking forward to sailing in one of those someday, sir.

"I asked if he ever got out to sea, even for a bit, or was he limited to the river trade, and he said that he'd been down South as far as Cumberland Sound, a time or two, sir," Rossyngton went on, nigh breathlessly. "He's put into Brunswick and most of the Sea Islands. When I asked if he'd had trouble with shoals and such, he told me that most barges, like the one alongside, only draw seven or eight feet if fully burthened, and they're built with very stout bottoms and 'quick-work' so if they do touch a shoal, they can usually work off, without much damage.

"But, when I got round to asking about Cumberland Sound and the Saint Mary's River, the master rounded on us and ordered him to get back to work, and went 'cutty-eyed' on me, sir," Rossyngton exclaimed. "Glared daggers at me, he did, and asked me flat-out what my interest was in where they went!"

"And how did you finesse that, Mister Rossyngton?" Lewrie said, feeling a rising excitement, but crossing the fingers of his right hand under the desk, in hopes that young Rossyngton had a deal more cleverness than he had.

"Well, sir," Midshipman Rossyngton replied with a sly grin, "I told him that I'd heard some of the older hands speak of seeing alligators as big as cutters, white dolphins and sea cows that can walk out on land at night when they were on this coast, and how I wanted to go and have a look round, and meet the blue-eyed Red Indians said to live in the woods . . . and how their young women . . . welcome sailors."

Rossyngton had the good grace to blush a bit.

Lewrie cocked his head to one side and chuckled.

"He told me I was a damn-fool 'younker', sir, and should not be listening to old sailors' yarns, or put any stock in them. After that, he wasn't talkative, but I don't *think* he took my questions as prying, but, who knows, sir?" Rossyngton concluded with a hapless shrug.

"Loath to let on whether he's been in Cumberland Sound, or up the Saint Mary's, was he?" Lewrie responded with a hopeful smile. "On his employer's secret business? Perhaps because he *has,* and that business is to *stay* a guarded secret. Damn my eyes, Mister Rossyngton, but, unless that master *did* tumble to your ploy, that was well done on your part! Well done, indeed!" Lewrie thumped a fist on his desk.

"Thank you, sir!"

"We might not yet know just *what* is goin' on South of here, but, it sounds suspicious enough to warrant further inspection. Now we have a name, this Treadwell, one shipping company to suspect, and we *might've* narrowed our area to search to something manageable," he told Rossyngton, who was all but polishing his fingernails on his uniform coat's lapels in self-congratulation.

"Most happy to have been of service, sir," Rossyngton said.

"Thank you, sir, and you may go," Lewrie said, rising. "I have some scheming to do."

He went to the sideboard in the dining coach and poured himself a tall glass of cool tea, then entered the wee chart space to peruse the American-made chart that spanned from Savannah to the St. John's River in Spanish Florida, looking for "hidey-holes" off the channels into the sounds, and places with sufficient depth where a privateer that drew ten-to-fourteen feet could find shelter, either a schooner or a small brig. A raider, *and* a prize or two that she'd taken? Any merchant ship cut out of one of the big trade convoys might draw as much water as his own frigate, fully laden, so he had to widen his search, and reject the shallow channels behind the many islands.

Thank God for cheeky, "sauce-pot" Midshipmen! Lewrie thought, humming to himself; *I can bring the squadron back here and stop that Treadwell's business. Is he the guilty one? Must be! In league with that arse Hereford? Damme, but I wish! This could be wrapped up and done by mid-Summer.*

Lewrie felt a sudden daunting moment, though, wryly recalling that whenever he'd thought he had all the answers in the past, Dame Fortune had always found a way to kick him in the fundament.

But, what can go wrong with this'un, this time? he asked the aether; *Or, is that askin' too damned much?*

CHAPTER THIRTY-FOUR

$\mathcal{H}$is dreaded come-down, that "kick in the fundament" came not a day later as HMS *Reliant* butted her way South against the currents of the Gulf Stream to meet with the small consorts of the squadron. It came from the First Officer, Lt. Westcott.

"Seems to me, though, sir, that strongly suspecting where the privateers are being victualled by this Treadwell fellow, if indeed it is he who is in collusion with them, and nabbing them in the act, are two different things entirely, sorry to say," Lt. Westcott mused as he and Lewrie strolled the quarterdeck from the taffrails to the nettings at the fore end, and back again, with Lewrie next to the windward rail and Westcott in-board.

"There is that," Lewrie gloomily agreed as they halted and turned to face each other before headed aft once more. "If we keep close watch on the area, they won't ever show up, like watchin' a boilin' pot, which never does 'til ye leave it be. And a close watch is sure t'raise the ire of our American 'cousins'."

"Well, it may be worse than that, sir," Westcott went on. "We haven't a single clue as to which barge, or barges, that leave Savannah are sailing on innocent passages, and which are engaged in dealing with privateers. We can't be certain if the ones that put into Cumberland Sound or either of the river mouths *are* aiding enemy raiders, or just making a tidy profit by selling neutral American goods to the Dons in Spanish Florida, which is perfectly legal. Bothersome to us, but still legal, since the United States and Spain are not at war."

"Good God, d'ye mean that this Treadwell is makin' money on the sly by landin' goods with the Dons, who can sell it or give it later to privateers, and there's nothing we could do about it?" Lewrie exclaimed. "Mine arse on a band-box!"

He hadn't thought of that, and it irked to hear of it.

"It would be a clever dodge, sir," Westcott said with a brief, sour grin, "with no real risk to his purse, his hide, or his repute in Savannah Society. Even if caught at it, he could thumb his nose at us and just sail away."

I'm an idiot, Lewrie chid himself; *a cack-hand, droolin'* . . . !

"Then, there is the problem of how often, and when, the barges are to meet with a privateer, sir," Lt. Westcott added. "A schooner or small brig with a crew large enough to man her and fight her, and carry extra hands and mates for prize-parties, might be able to keep the sea for two or three months, whether they take any prizes or not. Is that the arrangement, since communications 'twixt their source of supply and their ship are impossible? Every two or three months for a 'rondy', sir, or do the barges cache supplies for them on shore and sail away?"

"Fairy stuff," Lewrie said with a sniff. "Leave bisquits and milk on the stoop at night, and find a purse of gold coins come daybreak? Like hell! Who knows *who* could pilfer the goods in the meantime, or make off with the payment before the barges could return to pick it up?"

"Just a thought, sir," Westcott said, with a shrug and a laugh. "No, it would make more sense if they had arrangements for face-to-face meetings, but when, or where, and how often are the mysteries. And, do they vary, I wonder."

I could learn to loathe him, Lewrie quietly fumed.

"One could be in the Saint John's River, safe as houses even if caught in Spanish territory," Westcott relentlessly schemed on, "and the next set for the Saint Mary's, the third behind Cumberland Island, then back to the Saint John's and *etcetera* and *etcetera*."

"Might be a tad too complicated," Lewrie countered.

"True, sir," Westcott allowed, nodding his head toward Lewrie. "Though, were I in the looting trade, I would make such arrangements, to keep anyone hunting me in the dark for as long as I could. I fear, though, sir, that catching our privateers and their abettors red-handed is almost impossible. As you say, we can't lurk off Savannah, and chase after any barges heading South of Jekyll or Cumberland Islands, not with a frigate . . . not with any of the ships in our squadron, either. They could spot us a dozen miles off on a good day, and put into Brunswick and lay up 'til we have to sail on, playing innocently dumb, then finish their voyage, laughing at our haplessness."

"And, we can't leave a picket line of ship's boats as watchers, either," Lewrie fumed. "They'd be able to shadow them, perhaps, but they'd have to signal us that the game's afoot, and that puts *Reliant* or the others within sight from the barges. Well, shit."

"Finally, sir . . . ," Lt. Westcott said with a mournful, sigh.

Dammit, just hammer it home, do! Lewrie thought.

". . . even if we could stand into the sounds and the rivers as if they were all enemy waters," Westcott pointed out, "the odds are that we would do it at the wrong time, and there would be nothing there, even if we *did* know the exact spot where they meet, every time."

Lewrie came to a halt near the larboard taffrail and the flag lockers, his mouth wryly pursed, with his hands in the small of his back. He spent a long time studying the toes of his boots, then the seaward horizon. At last he hitched a deep breath and let it out in a long sigh, sourly wondering if one's body could deflate as completely as one's high-flown hopes and schemes!

"I might've over-thought this whole problem, Mister Westcott," he told his patient First Officer. "The straight-forward thing for us to do is to trail our colours up and down the Florida coast, from just below Saint Augustine to the Cumberland Sound. *Thorn*, *Lizard*, or *Firefly* can stand in much closer than *Reliant*, and, when we *do* reach the Northern end of our patrolling, we can send one or two of 'em in within three miles before we put about."

"Aye, sir," Westcott said, nodding.

"Nice, and slow under reduced sail, so we linger for a while off the entrance to the Saint Mary's River," Lewrie said on, "perhaps fetch-to for an hour or so, without violating anyone's neutrality. Whather it's that Treadwell fellow, a Sea Island planter with a ship of his own, or a trader in Brunswick supplyin' the privateers, we'll put the wind up him, and make him think twice about doing anything as long as we're there often enough.

"You recall that damned convoy we escorted last Spring, sir?" Lewrie asked with more energy.

"Unfortunately, I do, sir," Westcott said with a wince.

"Once the privateers, at least two of 'em, maybe three, caught their prizes, they hared off Sou'west, which would've put 'em off the coast of Georgia, if they held course." Lewrie sketched out. "There was no place for them to sell their prizes but Saint Augustine, or at Havana, and the shortest way home *was* to the Sou'west, *against* the Gulf Stream current, which don't make for a fast getaway unless they had shelter, and sure replenishment, somewhere round the border with Florida and Georgia . . . a place to lay up for a spell and victual for a voyage *to* the nearest Prize-Court! Back yonder is still the right place!" he said, gesturing at their wake, to where they had been.

"So, if we haunt the area below Savannah as often as possible, sir, sooner or later we'll snare something?" Westcott said, looking hungry and eager to be at it.

"*Fairly* sure, Mister Westcott," Lewrie assured him. "And even if we don't, our continual presence will deny any privateers the hope of using their hiding places. Sooner or later, they'll see that the game is up and look for another source of shelter and re-supply, and whoever it is that aids 'em will have t'give up the business, too."

"Simple and straight-forward it will be, then, sir," Westcott said with a laugh, baring his teeth in one of his quick and savage grins, "and a chore that doesn't keep me up nights in a perpetual fret over who, what, where, and when."

"Mind, now, I still would dearly like to nab whichever Yankee Doodle is in on it," Lewrie admitted with a laugh of his own, "wrap the whole business up in ribbon, and toss it into their President Jefferson's soup, and force him to pay more attention to maintaining neutrality. Maybe even see the bastard hung, or ruined."

"Deck there!" the main-mast lookout on the cross-trees cried. "Sail *ho*! Strange sail, *two* points off the *starboard* bows!"

"Shall we beat to Quarters, sir?" Westcott eagerly asked.

"Not just yet," Lewrie decided. "She's still on the horizon, and most-like, she's one of ours blockadin' Saint Augustine. We have time to determine her identity. Mister Caldwell assures me that we are at least six miles off Florida at present, and the strange sail is inshore of us. For now, I'd admire did you make a slight alteration of course towards her. Carry on, Mister Westcott."

"Aye aye, sir!" Westcott replied, briefly doffing his hat and turning to go to the middle of the quarterdeck.

Simple and straight-forward, is it? Lewrie scoffed to himself; *So simple that even a fool like* me *can perform it? So much for me to try and be clever, Logic and reason really* are *bastards!*

"Just a simple *sailor,* me," Lewrie sang under his breath, then did a few dance steps. "Simple's all I'll *ever* be . . . rovin' round a *dilberry* tree," he extemporised on the spot, "Sailin' all *year* for one *pen*-ney . . . *arrh!*"

I could play that on my penny-whistle, he told himself with a laugh; *come up with a whole tune, and sell it all over England!*

Within half an hour *Reliant* had fetched the strange sail hull-up over the horizon. Even though miles still separated them, lookouts aloft could espy British colours, then, just to be certain, a reply of flag hoists in that month's private signals. She was little HMS *Lizard* and Lt. Tristam Bury's command.

"I wonder if he's found a new sort of fish," Lewrie said with a laugh as *Lizard* jogged up to join, about two cables off the frigate's starboard side.

"Darling, Bury Lovett," Lt. Westcott japed; "there's a good fellow. Or, you'll Bury Darling? I'd Lovett."

That made Lewrie turn his head to peer at his First Officer.

"We're not boring you that badly, are we, Mister Westcott?" he asked with an eyebrow up.

"Well, sir, since fetching Bermuda, it has been 'all claret and cruising'," Westcott said with a shrug, and a rare sheepish grin, "We had one brief morning's action at Mayami Bay, and I must admit that I *am* desirous of something . . . definitive concerning privateers."

"Or pleasureable?" Lewrie hinted.

Westcott's answer was a smile and a nod.

"Ye never can tell what'll fall out before the year's out, sir," Lewrie told him. "If nothing else, we might be able to cross hawses with that bastard Frenchman, Mollien, and put paid to *him*."

"You would take him and his ship to Nassau, and not burn her, sir?" Westcott asked. "Hang what the Prize-Court costs us in the long run in Proctor's fees. Some brief time ashore would be nice."

Lewrie knew exactly what was ailing the First Lieutenant, and it was not the lack of combat. *He's gone so long without a chance to "top" a woman, the Crack o' Dawn ain't safe!* he thought.

"I'll see what I can do, sir," Lewrie promised. "But . . . your little play on names'd be best kept to yourself. There's no need for the 'younkers' t'hear 'em."

"Of course, sir," Westcott vowed with a wee bow of his head.

Lizard was rounding up, pointing her bows at *Reliant* as she performed a wide arc to lay herself within hailing distance alongside the frigate's starboard side, Once she was within musket-shot, and her sheets had been belayed, *Lizard*'s crew began cheering and waving their hats as if the frigate had just come to her rescue, or they had won a victory.

"Hallo, Captain Lewrie!" Lt. Bury shouted over the short distance between them, with a brass speaking-trumpet to his mouth. "It is good to have you back with us!"

"Glad to be back, sir!" Lewrie responded in kind. "What have you been up to in my absence?"

"We have been making a grand nuisance of ourselves, along the coast, as you desired, sir!" Lt. Bury hailed back. "It has been the most delightful *fun!*"

By God, it must've *been, for* Bury *t'sound enthusiastic,* Lewrie thought, recalling how sombre and grave the fellow had struck him at their first meeting.

"We have taken and burned five fishing boats, sir!" Lt. Bury happily went on, with an actual smile on his lean and scholarly face, "and captured two more we thought useful! We made prize of one small Spanish vessel attempting to land military goods at Saint Augustine—she is under *Thorn*'s lee at present, South of here—and we took and burned a Spanish privateer that took shelter from us in Mosquito Inlet"

"Well done!" Lewrie cheered him.

"Oh, buggery," was Lt. Westcott's glum, muttered assessment.

"We have made amphibious raids ashore, too, sir!" Bury boasted. "*Near* Saint Augustine! Would you care for a fat boar or two, sir? We brought off what livestock we could find!"

Lt. Bury looked as if he would burst from pride of their accomplishments, spin in a circle and snap his fingers, or shoot out his arms and spin some St. Catherine's Wheels in delight!

"Where away are *Thorn* and *Firefly*?" Lewrie asked, feeling a bit jealous that he had missed out on all that excitement, himself.

"They are South of Saint Augustine, at present, sir, *prowling* in concert, sir!" Bury informed him.

"Very well, Mister Bury!" Lewrie shouted over. "Take station ahead of me and lead me to them . . . within, three miles of Saint Augustine on the way!"

"Gladly, sir!" Bury shouted back and waved his speaking-trumpet over his head in glee.

Lizard cracked on sail while *Reliant* had to take in her tops'ls to the first reef and brail up her main course to match the speed of the smaller sloop.

"Lucky fellows," Lt. Westcott growled, once done with the reduction of sail aloft.

"Enterprising fellows," Lewrie amended, looking past the bowsprit and jib-boom, and the feet of the heads'ls, to appreciate the sight of *Lizard* heeling over slightly to starboard and slowly hobby-horsing along, spreading a clean, white wake astern. "For which enterprise, I will dine them aboard this evening, t'hear their tales and celebrate. You will join me, sir?"

"Aye, sir . . . even do I grind my teeth in envy," Lt. Westcott said.

"That promised fat boar's better exercise for your teeth," Lewrie said with a laugh as he looked aloft to the commissioning pendant. "Let's give the Dons at Saint Augustine something to think on, Mister Westcott. Hoist my broad pendant, and let 'em know that we are back, and ready to bedevil 'em even worse!"

CHAPTER THIRTY-FIVE

*W*e decided to emulate your example at Mayami Bay, sir," Lieutenant Darling of *Thorn* jovially said as he paused in slicing himself a bite of roast pork, "and set the crew of the privateer ashore on their own soil . . . minus their sea-going kits, of course, even closer to Saint Augustine than the crews of the two privateers we took earlier. They should have no trouble finding shelter. Of course, we kept all of her papers, her muster book, and Letters of Marque."

"And, it was Bury's turn to carry them to Nassau," Lt. Lovett of *Firefly* was happy to add. "There and back again, weren't you, Tristam? In record time, too!"

"Well, I didn't want to miss anything," Lt. Bury shyly agreed.

"And how was Nassau?" Lewrie asked, smirking.

"The port did strike me as much busier than Saint George's, on Bermuda, sir," Bury answered rather sombrely and cautiously.

"And Captain Forrester?" Lewrie pressed.

"Ehm . . . I got the impression that he was impatient over something, sir," Bury said, ducking his head as if loath to speak ill of a senior officer, or speculate aloud. "When I reported aboard *Mersey*, sir, he *did* ask of you and your doings, and when he may expect you to return to the Bahamas."

"It was all I could do to wrest myself and my sloop free to rejoin," Lt. Lovett griped. "Since your *Lizard* is larger, I'm sure that he wished to keep you for his squadron, too."

"Just so long as you don't send *me* with the proof of our next successes, sir," Darling pled with a laugh. "*Thorn* is the largest, *and* the best-armed. Damme if I do not sense lust from here!"

"You haven't told me how you nabbed the privateer. Pray do," Lewrie bade as Pettus refilled his wine glass.

"Oh, it was priceless, sir!" Darling hooted in glee. "Just at sunset, we were off Mosquito Inlet and about to put-about Northerly and gain some sea-room for the night, when out she darted from shoreward. Tried to take Lovett on."

"I was leading, do you see, sir, and Bury and his *Lizard* was astern of me by about seven or eight miles," Lt. Lovett said, taking up his part of the tale. "She flew no flag, and seemed to come on most aggressively, so we lowered our own, tacked about in a panic, and hared out to sea, to lure her on. Bury evidently saw what was taking place, and stood on, closer inshore."

"I signalled *Thorn*, sir, got shoreward a bit of her, then went about in chase," Lt. Bury contributed. Lewrie expected him to elaborate, but Bury lifted his wine and took a sip, as if done.

"She strode up to us and called for us to strike, sir," Lovett went on, "so we hoisted colours and served her a broadside at about a half a cable. When *Señor* saw that, they broke off, but there was the *Lizard* 'twixt her and her lair, so she was caught between us. And not a quarter-hour later, just at sunset, Lieutenant Darling and *Thorn* hove up and she struck without firing a return shot!"

"She was the *Torbellino*—the "Whirlwind"—out of Havana, sir," Lt. Darling gleefully said. "Fifty men, eight six-pounders, and a pair of six-pounder carronades. A two-masted lateener, like an Ottoman xebec, of all things, sir, of about an hundred tons!"

"Handy on a beat to weather, though," Lt. Lovett opined. "The Spanish found them useful back in European waters, so it's no wonder that they'd employ them out here."

"Carronades?" Lewrie asked, shifting in his chair in un-ease. "I'm not aware that anyone but Great Britain mounts carronades on their warships. God help us do the French copy 'em."

"Well sir, they *are* British," Lt. Darling told him, "from the Carron

Iron Works, with proof marks to match. The Dons were using them for chase guns."

"But, where in Hell did the Spanish get 'em?" Lewrie pondered, twiddling with the stem of his wine glass. "Could an American chandler or merchant *order* the bloody things, and pass 'em on to just anyone with enough 'tin'?"

"Perhaps to a Spanish . . . or a French . . . privateer that shows up at one of the 'rondys' which you suspect take place somewhere along the lower Georgia coast, sir?" Lt. Bury gravely suggested, after dabbing grease and sauce from his thin lips. "If, as you already suspect, French privateers are being supported and aided, who is to say if the Spanish do not avail themselves of the same aid? That would save them a long voyage back to Havana to re-victual, and their solid coin is just as good as French *specie*, sir."

"Matanzas Inlet, Saint Augustine, and the Saint Mary's and the Saint John's Rivers, would be close enough to Savannah for scheduled meetings," Lt. Lovett added. "It is a crying shame that we allowed the Dons to land ashore before we could put the question to them, sir . . . but we did not know at that time of your suspicions anent Savannah."

"Just as we let the Spanish go free at Mayami Bay without any questions, either," Lewrie gloomed, drumming fingers on the tablecloth, "for lack of suspicions at the time. Damn! That is a shame, sirs. What of the Spanish merchantman, then? Have any of you asked her master and crew if they know anything about privateers being based upon this coast? Perhaps *she* was bringing them supplies."

"It doesn't appear that she was, sir, from her cargo manifest," Lt. Darling said. "She carried rice, flour, and cornmeal, on order to the commanding officer of Castillo de San Marcos, to feed his garrison, and powder and *heavy* shot for the fortress's guns, sir, along with over one thousand flannel cartridge bags for twenty-four- and thirty-two-pounder cannon. But nothing small enough to mount on a privateer."

"Well, at least we have a prize that won't end up costing us," Lewrie said with a sigh. He noted that Lt. Darling was looking a tad cutty-eyed. "Don't we?" he further asked.

"I sent her master and crew ashore, too, sir," Darling admitted. "With a load of gunpowder aboard, I didn't wish to risk any of them remaining aboard and creating mischief. I also had it in mind that fifty or more penniless mouths to feed would cause the Spaniards more trouble than it be worth to keep them ourselves. In your absence, sir, you left me in temporary command, so . . ."

"Quite so, Mister Darling," Lewrie had to say after a moment to stifle his frustration; those Spaniards *might* have known something! "I see the sense of your reasoning. No use cryin' over spilt milk, hey? She must be sent in to Nassau to be adjudged. I can't send *you*. . . ."

More's the pity! Lewrie thought.

"Thank God, sir!" Darling exclaimed with a *whoosh* of relief.

"She might not need escort, either, for such a short voyage," Lewrie mused aloud. "One of your Mids, and enough hands to man her?"

"So long as I may expect to get them *back*, sir," Lt. Darling said, a bit worried. "I am already two hands short of full complement, and my senior Mid, Mister Bracegirdle, is rated Passed Midshipman, and quite valuable to my ship."

"For a day or so, he may style himself *Sub*-Lieutenant, then," Lovett said with a laugh.

There were so many small vessels in the Royal Navy like those in Lewrie's little squadron that were Lieutenants' commands, that they had, since 1804, been allowed a second Sailing Master to serve as an additional watch-standing officer, and one seasoned Passed Midshipman who would hold the temporary rating of Sub-Lieutenant for as long as he was aboard that particular ship, returning to his Midshipman's rank when re-assigned. Most of the Navy thought that the term sounded a trifle silly and pretentious.

"You want him back, sir, he'd best not claim *bein'* one,'" Lewrie hooted, "else Forrester'd poach him off you, quick as a wink! Why, with enough hands, *and* a Sub-Lieutenant, he might be tempted to arm and fit out a jolly boat to protect New Providence from the Dons! That'd be a fine addition to his squadron!"

"That is, indeed, what I most fear, sir!" Darling said with a mock shiver.

The rest of their doings along the Florida coast had been just as eventful, and Lewrie's young officers were more than happy to tell him all. With the use of the larger boats they had seized at Mayami Bay—scrofulous enough to appear civilian, and harmless—they'd sailed or rowed into every inlet they could find, into every river's mouth, in search of trouble. The few small clusters of huts they had encountered—far too small to even be called hamlets—they had raided and burned to the ground, rounding up what livestock they could catch and sailing off with

it. Settlements were few, and the number of settlers even fewer, an amalgam of dirt-poor Spaniards, half-breed survivors of the original Indian
tribes, and runaway Black slaves from plantations in Georgia, and the results of inter-breeding of all these who'd come to eke out a living in Spanish Florida. Only twice had they met any resistance to one of their
pre-dawn landings; they had raided Matanzas Inlet, cutting out a large
thirty-two-foot fishing boat, and had landed armed sailors near the mouth
of the shallow Matanzas River, where they had found a ruined earthen
fort, a small settlement, and little else. The inhabitants had run off, there
was little to loot, and they were just about to return to their boats when a
small troop of Spanish cavalry had shown up from St. Augustine, about
twenty or so, who had charged them. With a low berm to raise them
above the ground, and the remains of the fort's wall, even sailors could
face the terrors of a cavalry charge, and they had skirmished with them,
killing two of the soldiers, wounding a few others who had reeled in their
saddles, and had run the rest off back to the town.

"A hellish-scruffy lot, sir, even for soldiers!" Lt. Darling boasted. "Being Spanish, though, what could one expect? The Indians were better
at it."

During another pre-dawn landing, at Amelia Island, North of St. Augustine, and the burning of what few buildings were there, they had been
hailed by an Indian in deer-hide breechclout and vest, his head swathed in
what looked like a Hindoo turban with feathers . . . hailed and cursed out
in good *English,* and told to bugger off if they knew what was good for
them! Lt. Lovett had led the shore party, and had laughed him off . . .'til
the arrows had started flying and several muskets had been fired in their
direction.

"I think their first volleys were more dire warnings than any real attempt to kill us, sir," the piratical Lovett imparted. "He just popped out
of the brush, about a long musket-shot off, said that he and his people
were Seminoli, and that we were scaring off the deer, and we should go
away, for there was nothing of value to loot, sir. We never got a clean
shot at any of them, the way they only stayed in sight long enough to
shoot at us, then disappear again. I considered that discretion the better
part of valour, and ordered the men to make their way back to the boats,
in parties of ten. When they saw that we *were* going to leave, they stopped
shooting, and it was only once we were headed out to the ships that they
stood up and showed themselves."

"*Met* some Seminoli, long ago," Lewrie was happy to reminisce. "During the Revolution, when we went up the Apalachicola River in West Florida to treat with the Muskogee. The Seminoli *are* Muskogee, and the new tribe's name means 'Wanderers'. With the original tribes wiped out by the Spanish long ago, I s'pose this land's empty enough t'suit 'em. They let you off easy, Lovett. I once saw a Muskogee bowman take down half a dozen Spanish soldiers and their local Indian allies in half a minute. Notch an arrow, draw, aim, shout '*Yuuu!*' and down they went! *Flick, flick, flick!*"

"Bows and arrows seem so . . . crude and ancient, though, sir," Lovett pooh-poohed, raising a laugh among the other supper guests. "Damned near in-elegant!"

"You'd think so, 'til skewered by one," Lewrie drolly rejoined.

"There hangs a grand tale, I should think, sir," Lt. Westcott, who had been listening to the derring-do of the others, and, most-like grinding his teeth in envy, spoke up at last. "What you were doing in Florida regarding Indian tribes. . . . I believe that you made brief mention at Charleston that you had first made the acquaintance of that gentleman, Mister McGilliveray, with whom you dined ashore, during the Revolution? Something to do with the what-ye-call-'ems, the Muskogee?"

"A kinsman of his, a younger fellow, was the family firm's agent to the Muskogee . . . half-Indian, himself, though educated at Oxford," Lewrie told them all. "He and a Foreign Office fellow went with us to get them to agree to raiding Rebel lands, with the weapons and powder we brought along. It didn't turn out well. And, it may be a better tale for another night. Don't wish to turn into one of those maundering old bores who talk yer legs off over brandy; bad as a soused uncle, hey? What I wonder about, sirs, is what sort of boats did you decide to keep? And, what did you do with those captured carronades?"

"Well, I got a better, sir," Lt. Bury said with a shy smile.

"A hollowed-out log canoe would have been better than that old ark you took, Bury!" Lovett declared with a laugh. "Never saw a worse excuse of a boat, or such a sorry splotch of paint! Bury gave it the 'deep six', soon as he snatched up a proper cutter, sir!"

"It was a tad sick-making, to look upon," Lt. Bury agreed.

"Hammered together by a poorly-skilled *house* carpenter, with not a clue beyond right angles!" Lt. Darling further teased.

"It was 'an ill-favored thing, sir, but mine own'," Bury quoted the Bard, showing a faint hint of amusement at their camaraderie and japing.

"To Bury's sadly departed boat!" Lovett cried, raising his wine glass in toast. "Long may it frighten bottom-feeding fish!"

"Seriously, though," Lewrie said after they had toasted that ugly old scow, "we did keep the carronades? And two larger boats?"

"One is a thirty-two-footer, about the size of an eight-oared barge, sir, fitted with but one mast," Lt. Darling told him. "T'other is a about twenty-eight feet, rigged the same. Both are very beamy and of shoal draught. Quite roomy. Before we burned the privateer, we took off her guns and parcelled them out between us as ballast in our holds. We still do have the carronades, and their swivel mounts, along with all her two-pounder swivel guns and iron stanchions."

"Hmm . . . sounds to me as if they might make passable gunboats for future shore landings," Lewrie decided. He sopped the last bite of his fresh-baked cornbread through the spicy juices of roast pork, popped it into his mouth, and chewed as he mulled things over. "They were usin' the carronades as swivel guns as well as bow chasers?"

"The wooden slide mounts were mounted on swivelling platforms to either bow, sir," Darling said. "That might have made the privateer a *tad* bow-heavy, but all in all, it was a rather neat arrangement."

"We could mount one in each bow of the captured boats," Lewrie sketched out. "Mount the captured two-pounder swivels on either beam, perhaps put ten Marines in each as well, and we'd have decent-sized gun-boats that could go up the rivers further than our sloops. Do we find a reason, we could put together a whole flotilla of armed boats, and get at any privateers, or supply vessels, no matter haw far up-river they're an-chored. Sail 'em as far as we can, fire the carronades just a few degrees either side of the forestays, then lower the masts and row 'em like they did galleys in the Mediterranean in the old days."

"When we do, sir, I *implore* you, allow me command of one!" Lt. West-cott exclaimed in some heat. "These fellows have been having too much fun. Surely, they could share it round!"

" 'Who shall have this'un, then?' " Lt. Lovett bellowed, imitating the ritual of the lower deck. "Give it ol' Westcott; *'e's* deservin'!"

"Gentlemen, I give you Mister Geoffrey Westcott," Lt. Darling quickly proposed, making Pettus and Jessop scramble to top up their glasses, "a fire-eater of the first order, ha ha!"

" 'For he's a jolly good fellow, for he's a jolly good fellow!' " Lovett sang out, and they tossed their fresh wines back to "heel-taps".

"'Deed he is," Lewrie said once the song was done, "And the very fellow to whip up some drawings of how the carronades are to be mounted on swivelling platforms. A dab-hand artist, I have found."

"You draw, sir?" Lt. Bury asked, blinking in surprise. "You must show me your work."

"Aye, I'm told by Captain Lewrie that he found your artwork a wonder, as well, Bury," Westcott replied, "though I must own that it is rare that I attempt sketches in colour. More black-and-white are mine, with *passable* use of *chiaroscuro*." he said with a modest shrug.

"I should be delighted," Bury responded quickly, glad to find a fellow who shared his artistic bent. The others at table shared a few secret amused looks, for they had already heard of Bury's fishes, and the lengths he went to for accuracy in form and colouring.

"Beg pardon, sir," Pettus asked at Lewrie's shoulder. "Should I clear, and set out the port and bisquit?"

"Aye, Pettus, so long as ye don't include the dog," Lewrie told him with a snicker.

"Once the new gunboats are made suitable, sir, *might* we essay further raids ashore . . . even *closer* to Saint Augustine?" Lt. Lovett asked with a sly and hungry loot.

"Yes, now you're back with us, sir, we could use *Reliant*'s Marines," Lt. Darling enthused. "Let's see any scruffy Spanish cavalry charge us, then!"

"Gentlemen, I am delighted with all you've accomplished in my absence," Lewrie told them. "*Damme*, but you're all possessed of such bottom, daring, and cleverly applied energy that I'm fair-amazed by you. Now I'm back, I fully intend to keep the Dons on the hop, just as you did. We shall poke round further North, to see if any French privateers lurk along the lower Georgia coast, as I strongly suspect. Catch one, and frighten the rest off, perhaps? Or, nab a criminal Yankee Doodle who has truck with them, into the bargain, as I hope. It may be that our continued presence up yonder will scare the privateers off to safer hideaways. Blockade them in, and save our commerce? Drivin' 'em off might have to suit, if we can't bring 'em to action. But, in the meantime, bedevillin' the Dons will suit, too!"

"Confusion to the Spanish!" Lt. Westcott proposed.

"Confusion to the King's enemies!" Lovett proposed, next.

"Really, sir . . . you spent time among Red Indians?" Darling asked once the din had subsided from their vociferous shouts of agreement with the toasts' sentiments. "Do the . . . Muskogee really practice cannibalism, as I heard?"

"Not cannibalism, no," Lewrie said with a chuckle; "I saw no sign of that. No heaps of skulls, either, though there was the odd scalp hung up here and there, but even their principal war chief, a fellow by name of Man-Killer—truly!—of the White Clan, and one of the fearsomest fellows ever I did see . . . said that it was Whites who started scalping, so they could have proof of payment from the old royal governors. He was *tàstànàigi*, a senior war chief, though they didn't make war all that often. After we got back to the coast and had our set-to with the Dons and their Indian allies, after I got accepted as *anhissi*, 'of their fire', they named me *imata làbotskàlgi*, or 'Little Warrior' . . . though I don't know if it was said in jest or not."

"Ehm . . . my word," Lt. Bury said with a gulp.

"Man-Killer thought it a grand jape t'marry me to a Cherokee girl they'd captured on one of their raids, too," Lewrie added, chuckling. "I had to pay him a good pistol for the privilege!"

"You *married* her, sir?" Lt. Westcott marvelled.

"Had to," Lewrie told him, grinning. "She was 'ankled', and it was my doing. Think of a 'sword-point' wedding, with tomahawks." He had not intended to, but, since there were no impressionable and innocent Midshipman at-table this evening, he elaborated on the story.

"Her name was Soft Rabbit. I don't know t'this day if that was her Cherokee name, or one the Muskogee gave her, but it suited her," he told them. "First time I saw her was at sundown, when we were bathing at the shore of a lake. Wore nothing but a breechclout, she did, the wee-est, loveliest young woman ever I clipped eyes on, with hair as black as a raven's wing, and the biggest deer-doe eyes. . . ."

Lt. Geoffrey Westcott, ever the ship's Casanova, shifted about on his chair, making it squeak as if to ease himself, too taken by the image to top up his glass of port or pass the bottle larboardly to the next officer.

Lewrie had no fear that he would be deemed a maundering old bore, for once he began, everyone sat rapt.

CHAPTER THIRTY-SIX

$\mathcal{N}$o matter Lewrie's vow for further amphibious landings, he had to take the little squadron South, again, to peek round Cape Florida into Mayami Bay once more to assure himself that that grand anchorage was not being used. They probed round Cape Canaveral and into the Banana River, then each inlet they found on their way back North to re-commence the loose blockade of St. Augustine. In the main, they found nothing of value to loot or burn, and no sign of privateers from any nation.

Reliant and *Thorn* lay at anchor a mile offshore of the Matanzas Inlet once more, whilst *Lizard* and *Firefly* were anchored in shallower waters closer in. The two new gunboats, along with a gaggle of ship's boats, had staged another raid, strong enough to go deeper inland. If they found no enemy, they could forage.

After the first hour, with no sounds of combat coming from shore, and no tell-tale plumes of smoke from gunpowder discharges or burning huts, Lewrie gave up pacing the shore-side of the quarterdeck, and had his collapsible wood-and-canvas deck chair fetched up, along with his pennywhistle, for a good sit-down and a tootle or two. For a bit, he considered having the quarterdeck awnings rigged, for it was a hot day with light sea winds and a blistering mid-June sun.

Toulon and Chalky were spraddled out atop the cross-deck hammock nettings like sleeping leopards, and did not even open one slitted eye as he began to work his way through "The Rakes of Mallow." He was into a second rendition when Bisquit began to howl from beneath the starboard ladderway. Lewrie stopped and the dog stopped. He started again, and Bisquit bayed and yipped like a lonely wolf's keening. The watch-standers and the hands on deck found it highly amusing.

"We've a singing dog!" Midshipman Grainger hooted to his mates.

As many nights as possible during the Second Dog Watch, there was music and singing on deck, even some dancing of hornpipe competitions, to mellow the ship's crew. That was what the posted notices had promised back in Portsmouth when *Reliant* was recruiting: "music and dancing nightly!" Lewrie would now and then lounge on the quarterdeck to listen or to watch—but he couldn't recall a time when sailors' music had set the dog to howling.

Lewrie got to his feet and looked down into the ship's waist to eye the dog. Bisquit was out of his wee cobbled-together shelter, or dog-house, and was on his feet, tail wagging, with his head cocked over as if waiting for more. Lewrie *fweeped* a few random notes, and damned if the dog didn't throw his head back and bay once more!

"Ehm, Bisquit does the same, when the Marine fifer plays the rum keg up on deck, sir," Grainger helpfully offered. "And when the Bosun pipes a salute at the entry-port, he howls then, as well. It must be something about fifes and whistles that excites him, like the horn will stir up the fox hounds."

"Have ye noticed if he bays when I play when I'm aft?" Lewrie asked, skeptical.

"No, sir, not then," Grainger told him with a grin. "I imagine the sound doesn't carry far enough, even though his dog-house is right up against the bulkhead to your great-cabins."

"D'ye mean t'say, I can only play my bloody whistle when I'm out of ear-shot, Mister Grainger?" Lewrie harrumphed.

"Ehm, it would appear so, sir," Midshipman Grainger said, with his eyes alight with mischief, about to break out in titters. Lewrie had never mastered even the penny-whistle, much less proper musical instruments, and his attempts had become a running joke after a while aboard every ship he had commanded.

"Mine arse on a band-box," Lewrie said with a put-upon sigh. "Very well! I can take a hint." He stuck his head over the hammock nettings to look at the dog. "And thankee for the compliment!"

"Deck, there!" the mast-head lookout called down. "Our boats is comin' off shore!"

Lewrie traded his penny-whistle for a telescope and went back to the bulwarks to look them over for clues, counting them for losses, despite the complete lack of battle sounds. Once out of the shallow inlet, the boats broke off to return to their respective ships; all were there, and rowing in good order. The two new gunboats were closing on *Reliant,* with red-painted tompions in the muzzles of the commandeered carronades, and a file of red-coated and white cross-belted Marines seated in-board of the oarsmen. He could see Lieutenant Merriman and Midshipman Eldridge in one, with Marine Officer Simcock, and Lt. Westcott and Midshipman Warburton in the other. God knows where he'd found it, but Westcott had a wide-brimmed straw hat on his head, which he took off and waved once the gunboat met the first sea waves and began to hobby-horse.

"The dog and I are glad to see you back aboard, Mister Westcott," Lewrie japed once the First Lieutenant had come through the entry-port and had gained the quarterdeck. True to Grainger's statement, the dog *had* "sung along" with Bosun Sprague's calls to welcome the officers aboard. "Accomplish anything?"

"Not a blessed thing, sir, sorry to say," Westcott said with a scowl on his face. He took off his straw hat and mopped his brow with a handkerchief. "After our last raid into the inlet, the Dons learned their lesson. The civilians hereabout seemed to have moved away and abandoned what settlements they had. Into the safety of Saint Augustine, most likely. We *did* spot a few Spanish infantry lurking in the woods, far off, but as soon as Simcock sent a file of Marines in their direction, they scampered, and gave us no problems. Arnold is piqued, I must warn you, sir. His Marines got their boots muddy and their kits soiled for nothing. He'll be in the 'Blue Devils' for two days."

"At least you got yourself a new hat," Lewrie pointed out.

"There was an abandoned cornfield, sir, with a scarecrow stood up in it," Westcott told him, displaying his hat. "The hat is almost new. So was the maize . . . too green to pick, so that was a bust, too."

Westcott appeared crest-fallen and weary. After his initial excitement of arming and fitting the gunboats—and sharing his drawings with Lt. Bury during the process—he had been *panting* for the opportunity to use them against the Spanish, and Lewrie had sent him off on almost every landing . . . with little to show for it, and not a single chance of action, since.

"Sorry you found no fun," Lewrie said, more sincerely.

"Well, sir, there was *some* excitement," Westcott said. "One of *Lizard*'s sailors almost got bitten by a snake, a coral snake, Lieutenant Bury said it was. Pretty as anything, but deadly. It took a good dozen *very* scared sailors to club it to death with their musket butts, and after that, everyone was skittish of where they stepped."

"Let me guess," Lewrie japed. "Bury claimed it, and is even how painting a picture of it."

"If not this instant, he will be soon, sir," Westcott said, with a brief show of good humour. "Some of our sailors thought to tangle with an alligator . . . a young one, no more than six feet long," the First Officer went on. "That wasn't a fair fight, either, and the alligator won. No one got hurt," he quietly assured Lewrie, "just some feelings. Oh, Lovett's men found a dead cow that the locals had left behind, but it was gone over in the heat. So much for hung beef, too."

"I always said that Florida isn't worth a tuppenny shit," Lewrie said, "and I can't imagine how desperate ye have t'be t'live here."

"Aye, sir . . . all biting flies, gnats, sand fleas, and mosquitoes and such," Westcott firmly agreed. "Once one is in off the beach, it is hellish-warm without a whiff of wind, too. The Spanish are welcome to the place!"

"Fetch anything offshore for the dog, Mister Westcott?" Lewrie asked. "Ye noted how *fond* was his greeting to ye, second fiddle with the Bosun?"

"Not a single thing, this time, no," Westcott said. "He *does* sound fond of me, Simcock, and Merriman, doesn't he?"

You'll tumble to it, sooner or later, Lewrie thought.

"Let's give the shore party a quarter-hour to get settled, and time at the scuttle-butts for water, then we'll hoist signal for all ships to weigh," Lewrie decided. "Time enough to sponge yourself off?"

"Thank you, sir," Westcott said with a brief grin. "I do allow that after a morning in that stifling heat, I am a bit 'high'. Shall we sail as far as the rivers, or Cumberland Sound, sir?"

"I think a loaf off Saint Augustine is in order, first," Lewrie told him. "The soldiers you saw in the woods surely have reported our presence, and it's time to drive the point home."

By mid-afternoon, the wee squadron was two miles off St. Augustine, temptingly trailing their coats within Range-To-Random Shot of the heavy guns of the Castillo de San Marcos, and daring the Spanish to waste powder and shot. They had worked together long enough by then to be able to tack or jibe about in line-ahead whenever *Reliant* hoisted a flag signal for "Tack In Succession" or the riskier "Tack, Reversing The Order Of Sailing In Column". It was their way of showing off to the Dons, or "cocking a snook", whilst honing their ship-handling.

"Sail Ho!" a lookout shouted down after their third parade down the coast. "Off the larboard beam!"

Westcott and Merriman had been below, napping through the day's warmth in the wardroom, but came boiling up in curiosity to join the officer of the watch, Lt. Spendlove, and Lewrie, at the bulwarks with their telescopes to their eyes.

"Aloft, there!" Spendlove bawled. "How many sail?"

"Just the one, sir!" the lookout wailed back.

"Looks t'be a large jib . . . no, two jibs, and a large mains'l," Lewrie speculated aloud. "She's bows-on to us, so . . . her mains'l's winged out, on a 'soldier's wind'."

He glanced up at the commissioning pendant to determine that the winds were from the East-Sou'east, so if the strange sail was on a winged-out run, she was coming from the Bahamas.

"I think she's almost hull-up," Lt. Spendlove commented. "And I think I can *almost* make out a speck of colour at her mast-head."

"Red and orange?" Lt. Merriman asked, wondering if the colours of Spain were in the offing.

"All I can make out is red," Spendlove told his compatriot.

"She might be one of ours," Lewrie said, catching the tiniest flash of colour in his ocular, too. With the wind directly astern of the strange sail, any flag aloft would stream directly at *Reliant*, and only a slight fluke of wind could display it properly. "It does look red."

"Odds are, sir, no Spaniard would be coming from the Bahamas," Lt.

Westcott announced. "Any of their ships, naval or merchant, would approach Saint Augustine from the South."

Oh, Christ! Lewrie thought with a sinking feeling; *Forrester's got the collywobbles that the Dons're about to invade his patch, and wants my frigate t'back him up! When Bury came back from Nassau, he* said *the bastard was anxious about something! The fubsy toad!*

"Whoever she is, she's coming right for us, sir," Spendlove said, closing the tubes of his telescope and returning to the middle of the quarter-deck to resume his attentive watch-standing duties.

"Deck, there!" the lookout shouted down. "She's hull-up from the cross-trees! Sail is a one-masted cutter!"

"An *aviso* from Nassau, with orders, most-like," Lt. Merriman concluded, his telescope still glued to his eye. "Aye, sir! I can definitely make out a Red Ensign at her mast-head, now. She is one of ours."

Lewrie shut the tubes of his day-glass, too, his mouth screwed up in mild disgust. Forrester *was* ordering him back to Nassau, with his prime mission incomplete. *He'd better have a* damned *good reason!* Lewrie fumed.

CHAPTER THIRTY-SEVEN

*T*he single-masted cutter, which proved to be HMS *Squirrel,* came close-aboard *Reliant,* within easy speaking distance as the squadron jogged slowly North up the coast a bit beyond St. Augustine, and her commanding officer, bellowed, "I have despatches and mail and some men of your squadron!"

"I will receive them all!" Lewrie shouted back, then turned to Midshipman Warburton. "Hoist signals to the other ships, sir. Make 'Send Boats' and 'Have Mail'."

"Aye, sir!" Warburton eagerly said. *Reliant* had not received any word from home since departing Portsmouth nigh six months before, and word of mail, or newspapers, set everyone to rubbing their hands in expectation.

The seas were running light, the winds were soft, and the space between the frigate and the cutter was not an hundred yards, with no rushing, foaming wakes to conjoin, so *Squirrel*'s boat made a quick and easy transit to hook onto *Reliant*'s main chains and send a Midshipman and ten of *Thorn*'s long-lost sailors aboard.

"Allow me to name myself, sir—John Bracegirdle," the new-come Midshipman said, doffing his hat and bowing from the waist.

"Lieutenant Darling will be very glad to have you and your men back, Mister Bracegirdle," Lewrie told him, saluting him back. "You have the squadron's mail in that bag, do you?"

"Aye, sir," Bracegirdle replied, unslinging it from round his neck and shoulder. "And I have a despatch addressed to you, sir."

That wax-sealed letter was brought from Bracegirdle's pocket and handed over. It *was* from Captain Francis Forrester. Lewrie took a breath, held it, then let it out through pumped-out lips before he turned away to rip it open and read it, dreading the worst.

I thought I told the toad my squadron had Admiralty *orders, and I ain't his junior, but . . . what the* Devil? Lewrie thought, stunned by the letter's contents.

Forrester would *not* hook him or net him. He had bigger fish to fry . . . ; so did every Royal Navy warship in the West Indies! The note was more by way of a warning that the French were on the prowl!

Since early May, rumours of the presence of a squadron of Third Rate 74s, some frigates, and troop ships, had come up the island chains of the Windwards, from Trinidad, Barbados, and Grenada. Was it eight or ten warships? Or, was it only four or five? Were they come to stiffen the garrisons of the French colonies of Guadeloupe and Martinique, or would they come to invade British islands, or reclaim the islands taken from the French after the war had re-begun in 1803? No one knew.

Captain Francis Forrester's brief letter said that he was summoning the few brig-sloops under his command, and would lead them South as far as Antigua to re-enforce any Royal Navy squadron he encountered.

> *Since you made it so evidently plain that you are not under my Command, I must trust that you possess enough Sense to see your Duty clearly, and, if you will not join me out of Patriotism, then in my Absence you will abandon your insignificant Quest after spurious Privateers and take upon yourself the temporary Protection of the Bahamas until my return.*

"Mine arse on a band-box!" Lewrie said with a snort. "Put the onus on me, and dash off for glory, will you?" He was torn, though, by the temptation to dash off South and participate in a real battle, whether he had to place himself under Forrester's haughty and vindictive command or not, for doing so beat his fruitless patrolling and the uncertainties of American collusion all hollow. Except for their few shore raids, he'd been doing the dullest sort of blockade duty with not a blessed thing to show for it, nothing of consequence, anyway.

It's impossible to protect the whole Bahamas with one frigate and a handful of sloops, he furiously thought; *any more than Forrester could with a pair o' brig-sloops and his own ship . . . and her damned near aground at Nassau for months on end!*

But, he quickly realised, if he *did* dash off to Antigua or St. Kitts, that would leave the Bahamas with nothing but sloops like his and a parcel of cutters like *Squirrel* to challenge an French invasion, not the Spanish invasion that Forrester had dreaded when he'd spoken to him in the early Spring!

And just why the Devil would *the French even* care *to take the Bahamas?* he further asked himself. If they had sent a small squadron to the West Indies, re-enforcing the islands they still held made a lot more sense. So did invading one or more of the British Windward Isles.

The big sugar trades! Lewrie thought, getting a leap of his stomach in his chest, and a touch of cold chill. If the French took Nassau and New Providence, Bimini and the Berry Islands, perhaps even Grand Bahama and the Abacos, they could dominate the Florida Straits! No convoy, no matter how well-escorted, would survive, and it would not be the odd privateer preying on them, but frigates, too! There would go a large portion of British trade.

"*Guerre de course,*" Lewrie muttered, recalling the French concept of commerce raiding to disperse the strength of the Royal Navy, which would give their fleet an even chance to sail out and fight on more-equal terms, even weaken Channel Fleet to the point that their Emperor Napoleon Bonaparte's vast invasion armada could succeed in landing that two-hundred-thousand-man army of his in England and destroying the last opponent between Napoleon and world domination!

If I were "Bony", that's what I'd do, Lewrie told himself; *but, Christ, we've at least twenty ships in the West Indies, and the Frogs are still over one thousand miles from here. It's no use borrowin' trouble. Or, jumpin' at shadows.*

"Mister Warburton?" Lewrie said, shaking himself free of his fretting, and returning to the here-and-now. "Pass the word for my clerk, Mister Faulkes, to attend me in my cabins, instanter."

"Aye, sir."

He dashed below and sat down at his desk in the day-cabin with no mind for the cats, who were glad to see him, but disappointed by his inattention. He opened the ink-well, dipped a pen, and began to write the gist of Forrester's note for each of his subordinate captains.

"You sent for me, sir?" Faulkes said a few moments later.

"Aye, Faulkes. Will you make three copies of this at once," Lewrie said, "and they are to go to *Lizard*, *Thorn*, and *Firefly* with the Mids who come to collect the mail. There's already one of *Thorn*'s Mids on deck. Make sure that Mister Bracegirdle gets her copy."

Faulkes blew on the hastily written note to dry the ink, reading it as he did so, and hitched an audible breath at its contents.

"A French squadron on the loose, sir?" Faulkes asked wide-eyed. "Might they come here, do you imagine?"

"Not all that likely," Lewrie told him after a moment more to mull it over. He got back to his feet and headed for the deck again, leaving a puzzled Faulkes and two frustrated cats in his wake.

He got back to the quarterdeck just as HMS *Thorn*'s temporary "Sub-Lieutenant" was regaling the watch officers with his tale of woe at Nassau.

". . . thought we would be slung into irons and kept as replacements 'til next Epiphany," Bracegirdle was chortling, "As for my part, I was allowed liberty on the town, but our poor hands were sent aboard *Mersey*, in lieu of a proper receiving ship. It was only when Commodore Forrester announced that he would be sailing that her First Officer said that *Mersey* was at full complement, and released them as supernumary, and it was only the kindness of Lieutenant Richmond of *Squirrel* who thought to fetch us back to the squadron, ha ha! We would have *stayed* at Nassau, kicking our heels, else!"

"Ah, Captain sir!" Lt. Merriman said, noting Lewrie's arrival on deck. "It appears that *Squirrel*'s captain, Lieutenant Richmond, did us good service in delivering Mister Bracegirdle back, and further good service by sorting out the despatches and mail into packets for each ship, beforehand."

"Capital!" Lewrie said. "We will distribute ours, at once, at the start of the First Dog. *Mersey* has sailed, Mister Bracegirdle?" he asked the Midshipman, who appeared to be a cheerful and competent fellow in his early twenties.

"Aye, sir," Bracegirdle replied, "though I thought I'd never see the day," he added with a hint of amusement.

"Ripped herself free of the coral under her keel?" Lewrie asked, tongue-in-cheek. "Or was it a reef o' salt-meat bones?"

"A bit of both I would expect, sir," Bracegirdle said, grinning.

"The French squadron," Lewrie posed, "is it rumour or were there definite sightings?"

"Rumours at first, sir," Bracegirdle informed him, "then it was mentioned in the latest newspapers from home. It is certain that they sent a *small* squadron under an Admiral Missiessy to the Windwards back in the *winter,* and there's quite a stir that an Admiral Villeneuve has escaped Toulon with a larger squadron. The London Exchange suffered a huge fall in the price of consols at the news, and that the blame was put on Admiral *Nelson* for not blockading Toulon as closely as demanded, if you can imagine, sir!"

For anyone in government, the newspapers, or English Society to cast any aspersions on Horatio Nelson by then was un-thinkable, especially in the closer society of the Navy, after his many crushing victories, and everyone on the quarterdeck growled objections.

"But the papers also say that Nelson has gone after them with the entire Mediterranean Fleet, so God help the French when he catches up with them!" Bracegirdle confidently declared. "Even if Villeneuve comes to the West Indies to join the other fellow, Nelson will settle their business!" That was greeted by agreeing growls and cheers.

That's *a diff'rent kettle o' fish!* Lewrie thought; *If Nelson's on his way, he will* lash *into 'em . . . if only to shut his detractors up, and win himself more glory and praise! The preenin' wee coxcomb! No worries, then. Forrester's off on a goose-chase.*

"My quick note to Lieutenant Darling did not contain that information. Pray do deliver it verbally to your captain once aboard *Thorn,* Mister Bracegirdle," Lewrie bade him.

"Hoy the boat!" Warburton shouted to the first approaching boat.

"From *Firefly,* as ordered!" her lone Midshipman shouted back.

Faulkes came on deck at that moment with his freshly penned notes and Lewrie handed Bracegirdle one. "More scribblin', Mister Faulkes. Sorry," he said to his clerk. "Something I just learned. Oh, Hell, it is faster t'just tell it to the other ships' Mids. Never mind."

I'm babblin', Lewrie chid himself; *Stop* that!

As each sloop's boat came alongside, Lewrie handed over their packets of mail and newspapers, and had a word with the Midshipmen from *Firefly* and *Lizard*, stressing that there might be upwards of ten or more French ships far down in the Windwards, but that Nelson would be chasing after them with a powerful fleet of his own, and that for the moment, the squadron would continue its patrolling off Spanish Florida.

Once that was done, and the boat from *Thorn* had arrived and departed with her lost seamen, he turned to look seaward, and there little *Squirrel* still was, loafing along one hundred yards off his frigate's starboard beam.

S'pose I should invite him aboard for a drink, at the least, Lewrie thought; *I might even dine him in.*

He went to the binnacle cabinet, took up a speaking-trumpet, and went to the rails to shout an invitation over. Lt. Richmond was happy to accept a supper.

"We will be standing out to deeper waters at the start of the First Dog, Richmond!" Lewrie called over. "If you will take station astern of me, that will save you a long row in the dark!"

"Most welcome, Captain Lewrie!" Richmond replied. "At any rate, I hoped to remain in company 'til dawn before returning to Nassau. We are being plagued by reports of a French privateer in our waters, and I do not relish making my little ship an appetiser!"

"A French privateer?" Lewrie bellowed back, "Have any ships been lost?"

"No way to know, sir!" Richmond responded. "Settlers on Grand Bahama and the Abacos have sent word to Nassau that they saw her, and one of our local merchantmen came in and said that she'd been pursued, and only made her escape by reaching shoal waters!"

Richmond was right; there was no way to know if any ships had been taken. Once a merchant ship dropped below the horizon from New Providence, out-bound, it was just *assumed* that she would complete her voyage. If a merchantman left England, Boston, or Charleston for the Bahamas, no one there could know she was coming, or when she was expected to make port . . . or if she had ever existed! It would only be the owners and investors, the "ship's husbands", who would mourn her inexplicable loss, months or *years* later.

Lewrie suggested that Richmond come aboard at the beginning of the Second Dog, at 6 P.M., gave him a cheery wave, then returned to the binnacle cabinet to stow the speaking-trumpet, then peer into the compass bowl, up at the commissioning pendant and the sails to judge the strength and direction of the wind, and ponder.

Forrester had word that a privateer or two might be loose in his "patch", but he sailed off, anyway? Lewrie thought with admitted wry amusement over the failings of a long-ago, none-too-loved shipmate; *He always* was *a damned fool! With* Mersey *and the brig-sloops gone with him, there's nothing of worth left t'guard Nassau and adjacent waters. He's off for glory, his name in the newspapers, and a pat on the back from Admiralty for his boldness.*

Lewrie reached into a side pocket of his uniform coat to draw out Forrester's note to re-read it. Once he'd done so, he began to grin in delight, seeing the possibilities. Forrester had snidely asked him to take his place while he was gone, a request that Lewrie was sure was already a complaint in Forrester's report to London that would be a black mark against him. But two could play that game, Lewrie thought with a rising excitement.

There was a French privateer prowling the Bahamas. Could it be Mollien and his *Otarie?* Catching him would be sweet! From Charleston, where he had first seen that schooner, to the Bahamas was close to the suspected aid and comfort of the lower Georgia coast.

Lewrie looked cross the quarterdeck to the shore. The coast of Spanish Florida was a thin green streak, and of late, not a very productive one. He contemplated leaving Bury in *Lizard,* and Lovett in *Firefly,* to continue the patrolling and partial blockading of St. Augustine, but . . . if he *did* run across a privateer in Bahamian waters, he would need them and their shoal draughts to chase the foe where his frigate could not dare go. Besides, if he did manage to find a real enemy, it would be unfair to deprive them of the excitement!

Long ago, he in *Alacrity* and his old friend Benjamin Rodgers in Sloop of War *Whippet* had raided on Walker's Cay to suppress piracy, and it was *Alacrity* that had to strike from the West at dawn. "Lewrie, I dasn't risk the Banks," Rodgers had said of the treacherously shoal Bahama Banks. There was shelter for a privateer up yonder, and only a sloop of shoal draught, and the new gunboats, would be able to get at it.

Might he leave HMS *Thorn?* No, he rejected that, too, for there might be need of her heavier firepower closer to the shoals that ever *Reliant* could get. *Hang it, I'll take 'em all!* Lewrie thought.

"Mister Warburton," Lewrie said of a sudden, "pass word for my cook, Yeoviil, and hoist a signal to all ships. 'Captains To Supper,' at the start of the Second Dog Watch. Then, 'Alter Course' to Seaward."

"Aye, sir."

This was the sort of thing that he would have to impart to all of them, face-to-face, this change of their area of operations, and a new mission.

Now in much surer takings, Lewrie began to pace from the head of the starboard gangway to the taffrails and back again, working up his appetite for supper, and pondering just what he should serve, and what Yeoviil could come up with on short notice.

"Look at that!" Midshipman Warburton whispered to Midshipman Munsell, who shared the watch with him. Both slyly grinned, and then caught Lt. Merriman's attention, jerking their heads in Lewrie's direction, bringing a grin to Merriman's face, too. "I wager he doesn't even notice!"

The ship's dog, Bisquit, had slunk up the ladderway to the quarterdeck, that tempting forbidden territory, had hidden by the binnacle cabinet 'til Lewrie's back was turned, and had then begun to pace along a few steps behind Lewrie's shins, mouth wide open in what could be construed as a grin as he looked up with his ears perked, and darting ahead of him whenever Lewrie turned about to continue his slow pacing, then "take station" off his quarter once more, and with Lewrie so lost in his thoughts that he was all un-knowing.

CHAPTER THIRTY-EIGHT

*R*eliant's little squadron, augmented for a while by Lt. Richmond and *Squirrel*, quartered the seas as they beat their way Eastwards into the Northwest Providence Channel, with the smaller ships ranging back and forth to peek in at Bimini and the Isaacs, into Cross Bay on Grand Bahama and the hurricane hole that Lewrie had used 'tween the wars, as if the frigate was the Master of The Hunt and the sloops were the fox hounds. They stopped and inspected a few schooners and small brigs in case they were French or Spanish privateers flying false colours, and "spoke" to many local fishing boats which might have seen any sign of an aggressive strange sail, or seen any British vessel being pursued by one. They poked into the Berry Islands, then dropped *Squirrel* off to make her way to Nassau with Lewrie's latest reports and replies to the newly received mail, and steered for the Northeast Providence Channel and the Abacos.

The mail, well! After sorting through and filing the important letters, and sending the least important to the quarter gallery for use as toilet paper, Lewrie had had time to savour personal news from home before his captains had come aboard for supper.

There were several from Lydia, all warmly fond, chatty, and informative. Beyond all sense, her brother Percy was going to wed this mid-Summer,

though people in Society thought him daft for taking a circus rider like
Eudoxia Durschenko for wife! Eudoxia's evil-looking father, Arslan Ar-
timovich, was already looking yearningly at their vast stables of saddle
horses and the racing thoroughbred, and was then at their principal estate, installing himself as Master of Horse!

There were letters from Sir Malcolm Shockley, an old ally in Parliament; his father, Sir Hugo; brother-in-law Burgess Chiswick; and reports
from dour Governour Chiswick and his wife Millicent on his daughter,
Charlotte's, progess.

And, one from his youngest son, Hugh, now a Midshipman aboard
HMS *Aeneas* under another old friend, Captain Thomas Charlton. That
one was most informative, and news that Lewrie could pass along to all
of his captains over that supper. *Aeneas* was in the Mediterranean, and a
part of Admiral Lord Nelson's fleet!

That French Admiral Villeneuve had slipped out of Toulon early in the
year in a storm, whilst Nelson's fleet had been loading supplies at Mad-
dalena Bay on Sardinia. They had sailed as far East as Alexandria in
Egypt in search of Villeneuve, fearing a second attempt at building a
French empire in the Middle East and the Holy Lands, but Villeneuve had
slipped *back* into Toulon. By mid-March, they had learned that the French
had sailed again, and they had gone as far as Sicily in search of them before hearing that the French had slipped past Gibraltar and were bound for
the West Indies.

> . . . *fears that Villeneuve's ultimate Ambition is the Conquest of
> Jamaica, so we are off, all of us, in hot, pursuit, and Huzzah! I know
> not if Sewallis in Pegasus is still on the Brest Blockade, but if so, will
> he feel Envious! We pray earnestly that we catch up the foe and bring
> him to action!*

"One can only hope that Captain Forrester and his brig-sloops do not
cross hawses with this Villeneuve on his own, sir," Richmond had said at
supper.

"If he and the first French squadron unite, who knows how many ships
of the line that will be," Lt. Westcott had commented, looking a tad grim-
mer than was his usual wont.

"The entire French Toulon fleet? What'd that be, I wonder?" Lt. Darling had speculated. "And did he pick up any Spanish ships of the line with

him? Twenty, twenty-five sail of the line, and at least half a dozen frigates?"

"If Jamaica's their intent, the Bahamas will be safe," Lewrie had told them. "And when Nelson lays into them, so will the rest of the West Indies, perhaps the Med, too, once the French have nothing left."

"Hear hear!" Lt. Lovett had exclaimed, raising his wine glass on high. "Gentlemen, allow me to give you Nelson, and a bloody battle!"

"Nelson, and victory!" Lt. Bury had soberly amended.

All in all, it had been a cheering supper, but for the dessert, for neither Yeovill nor Cooke had been able to master the receipt for pecan pie, despite their experimentations.

Once *Squirrel* had departed them, the squadron had sailed on out the Northeast Providence Channel, past the lower-most tip of Great Abaco, the Hole-in-the-Wall, then up the Eastern coast past Cherokee Sound, Little Harbour, Hope Town, and Marsh Harbour, the main settlement, and seaward of the chain of cays; Man O' War, Great Guana, Green Turtle, and Powell Cay, bound for the Northern-most end of the Bahamas where the Little Bahama Bank continued beyond Little Abaco and Fox Town and Walker's Cay, where lay the East entrance to the inner Bank, Walker's Cay Channel.

This should *be good lurkin' grounds,* Lewrie told himself as the seventh day of their search went on with nothing to show for it.

Ships bound in or out of Nassau had to use either of the Providence Channels, and if one did not have enough ships to watch each of the channels simultaneously, the best bet would be to cruise north of the Little Bahama Bank, making long transits to the East-Sou'east to watch one channel, and to the West-Sou'west to watch the other, with a "hidey-hole" round Walker's Cay should a warship turn up. It was the very place Lewrie would have chosen, had he been a privateer in search of prey, but . . . perhaps the French didn't think like him, he was beginning to doubt.

They had seen several American ships bound for New Providence, or returning to home ports from the island, and had stopped and taken a look at them to ask if they had seen any privateers. Despite his cautions to treat the Yankee Doodles and "Brother Johnathans" with respect, and to eschew the urge to check the *bona fides* of their crewmen to determine if any of them were British, none of them had departed from those encounters happily, even if none of their sailors had been press-ganged. Stopping them for what seemed no cause was irritating enough! Some of the boarding parties reported that they had been accosted with shouts for "Free Trade, and Seamen's Rights!" no matter how politely they had been handled.

Should he give up this search and head South? he speculated. The pickings for a privateer further down the island chain would be leaner, the prizes almost too small to be worth the effort, if the Prize Courts which served the enemy were as parsimonious as the ones he'd dealt with. Or, by late afternoon, they might put about and go Nor'east round the top of the Little Bahama Bank to do it all over again.

Reliant was at the North end of a line-abreast patrol line with only four or five miles between ships, with little *Firefly* the closest to the pale green waters of the Bank. The weather was clear and the winds a touch lively, strong enough to mellow the heat. The seas were sparkling, glittering in medium-length waves not over three or four feet in height. All in all, it was a pretty morning, but it didn't appear as if it would be an eventful one. Lewrie was just about to decide to send down for his deck chair when a lookout shouted down to the deck.

"Signal from *Thorn*, sir!" Midshipman Grainger added from his perch halfway up the larboard shrouds of the main mast.

Lewrie fetched his telescope and peered outward, trying to read it for himself. There was *Thorn* four miles off the larboard beam with a hint of *Lizard* four miles further off, almost hull-down and perched off *Thorn*'s stern, almost masked. She, too, flew the same signal. The *Firefly* was only a tops'l over the horizon, completely masked by HMS *Thorn*, the originator of the alert relayed up the patrol line.

"The hoist is 'Enemy In Sight', sir!" Grainger shouted.

Lieutenant Lovett was not the skittish sort; if he said that he could see an enemy ship, then an enemy there was in the offing.

"Mister Spendlove," Lewrie ordered the officer of the watch, "Beat to Quarters"

"Another signal, sir!" Grainger shouted once more. "Enemy Is A Brig', and 'Enemy Is Flying . . . South'!"

"Mister Eldridge?" Lewrie said, turning to the older Midshipman aft by the taffrail signal-flag lockers. "You're fluent and fast by now, I trust?"

"I will try, sir," Eldridge replied.

"This is going t'be complicated," Lewrie told him, taking one quick look at the chart on the traverse board. "First, a hoist for *Firefly* and *Lizard*, their numbers, for 'General Chase', adding 'Inshore'." He wished his smaller ships to pursue, slanting toward the Little Bahama Bank to deny that brig a chance to get into shoal water. He hoped that "Inshore", would convey that desire, and had to trust to Lovett and Bury to want to cut her off.

"Second hoist will be to *Thorn*," Lewrie explained, waiting impatiently as Eldridge scribbled it down on a scrap of paper. "Her number, and 'General Chase', adding 'Seaward'."

"I relieve you, sir," Lt. Westcott told Lt. Spendlove as he gained the quarterdeck in a rush, still fumbling with his coat, sword belt, and hat. He knuckled the brim of his hat in salute, Spendlove replying as casually, before dashing to the waist where the gunners were assembling by their pieces. "We've found something, sir?"

"It appears we have, Mister Westcott," Lewrie told him. "Do you wait 'til the hoists are completed, then shape course Due South to pursue. The Chase is a brig that Lovett deems a foe."

Lewrie looked aft as the signal halliard blocks squealed. The first signal was soaring aloft to be two-blocked. While Lewrie was waiting for it to be repeated, Pettus came up with the keys to the arms lockers, which Lewrie passed on to Lt. Merriman, and his sword belt, and his pair of double-barreled Manton pistols.

"I'll see your cats to the orlop, sir," Pettus promised.

"Have Jessop see to the damned dog, too," Lewrie ordered.

Thorn hoisted a repeat of the first signal, and then there was a long wait 'til the mast-head lookouts could report that *Lizard* had made the hoist to *Firefly*, and an even longer wait 'til *Lizard* made a single-flag hoist for "Affirmative" back to *Thorn* and then to the frigate.

This is one hellish-poor way t'speak with each other, Lewrie thought, regretting that he had spaced his patrol line so far apart; *This command of a squadron, and sendin' orders and hopin' for the best, is enough t'tear my hair out! But, if Firefly hadn't been down South so far, we might've missed the Chase altogether.*

The blocks were squealing again as the first signal was lowered and the second was hurriedly bent on to the halliards. With commendable despatch, Eldridge got the second one to *Thorn* two-blocked not a minute later. With only four miles between them, Lt. Darling's ship was quicker to respond with the "Repeat," and no "Query" or "Submit" to delay the process.

"Strike it, Mister Eldridge," Lewrie ordered, which was the order for *Thorn* to execute. As soon as *Thorn* whisked her Repeat down, her helm was put over and she wheeled Sutherly, hardening up her gaff sails and bracing round her tops'l and wee royal for drive.

"Alter course, Mister Westcott," Lewrie snapped.

"Aye aye, sir!"

Reliant spread more sail aloft, too, braced her square sails and yards for more speed, and hoisted the outer flying jib and both the fore and main topmast stays'ls. She leaned her starboard shoulder to the sea and began to lope South, her forefoot smashing and parting the sea, her hull and masts humming and trembling in haste.

"We might be up level with *Thorn* in an hour," Lt. Westcott speculated aloud, "though I doubt either of us will be of much help to Lovett and Bury'."

"The important thing is for us to be *seen*, West of the Banks, so the Chase can't hope to hare off that way," Lewrie said, feeling a need to cross his fingers; what he *hoped* to occur could still turn to shambles. "The wee sloops can deny the Chase an escape *into* the Banks, and *Thorn* can loom up in a stern-chase. So long as she's a brig of average size, *Lizard* and *Firefly*, can catch her up and take her. We'll be 'In Sight' of her taking. Think there's a penny or two per hand in that, Mister Westcott?" he said with a grin.

"Only if she's full of solid coin, sir," Westcott disparaged.

The enemy brig loomed up over the horizon after an hour or two of pursuit, with *Lizard* and *Firefly* visible to the East of her, and closing fast. Lt. Darling was getting a good turn of speed from his brigantine, too, and was several miles ahead of *Reliant*, standing out to the brig's West, and within what looked to be two miles of her.

"Deck there!" all the mast-head lookouts cried, almost in chorus. "Gunfire! *Lizard* and *Firefly* are engaged!"

Lewrie was so fretful that he slung his telescope over his shoulder and scaled the shrouds of the mizen mast to see what he could see, which wasn't all that revealing. By then, the enemy and his two smaller sloops were almost hull-up to him, merged together and almost impossible to demarcate one from the other. The sounds of their engagement could not reach his ears, but there was a growing pall of spent gunpowder smoke down yonder. He swung the lens to the West and there was *Thorn*, rapidly closing aslant, still with an eye towards closing the door to any escape towards open water and the inlets of far-off Florida. She had yet to commence fire.

"Deck, there!" the main-mast lookout shouted down. "Chase is bein' doubled! Bound Sou'west!"

She was trying to get away, trying to get out to deep water, but *Lizard* and *Firefly* were now engaging her on either quarter, maybe on either beam, denying the brig a chance to flee. And, if she did turn away by then, she would lay her vulnerable stern open to a rake from one of the sloops, and a broadside from the other!

"Deck, there!" the lookouts whooped. "Chase has *struck*!"

"Ease helm a bit, Mister Westcott, and lay us about a mile to their lee, and once level with 'em, we'll fetch to," Lewrie ordered.

"'Twixt the Devil and the Deep Blue Sea,' she was, by then," Lt. Westtott cheered with a feral flash of his teeth.

Before the next hour was out, all of *Reliant*'s squadron, and their prize, were fetched-to within rowing distance of each other. The frigate had been stood down from Quarters, the gun tools stowed below in the racks over the mess-tables, tompions re-inserted into the guns' muzzles, and the arms lockers locked, and the keys returned to Lewrie's care. Boats were coming to the frigate from *Lizard* and *Firefly* bearing the triumphant Lieutenants Lovett and Bury . . . with a few strangers, Lewrie noted with his telescope.

It ain't Mollien and his schooner, more's the pity, Lewrie told himself; *So who did we bag?*

BOOK IV

"We'll roll him high and we'll roll him low
'Way down in Florida,
We'll heave him up and away we'll go,
And we'll roll the woodpile down!
Rolling, rolling rolling the whole world round
That brown gal o' mine's down the
Georgia Line
And we'll roll the woodpile down!"

–Sea Chantey Anonymous

CHAPTER THIRTY-NINE

*O*nce Lt. Lovett and Lt. Bury had been piped aboard, and congratulations had been bestowed, Bury motioned for one of the strangers to come forward.

"Allow me to name to you, sir, the master of the prize," Bury formally intoned, "Captain Charles Chaptal, of the *Insolent*."

They ain't makin' Frogs like they used to, Lewrie thought as he eyed the short, slim, and almost reedy fellow who stood before him with his hat raised in salute over his carroty, frizzled hair. He looked no older than *Reliant*'s junior lieutenants!

"*M'sieur Capitaine*, allow me to name to you Captain Sir Alan Lewrie, Baronet, of the *Reliant* frigate," Lt. Bury went on. At that point, Chaptal performed a very graceful "leg" with a sweep of his hat across his breast. Lewrie touched the brim of his cocked hat. "He offers you his sword, sir, in light of his defeat."

"Put up a decent fight, did he, Mister Bury?" Lewrie asked.

"A mos' *spirited* resistance, M'sieur!" Chaptal boasted, "agains' four-to-one odds. I regret, z'ough, z'at you 'ave ze best of me at ze end."

They may come weedier, these days, but just as boastful, Lewrie thought with a sigh; *Exasperatin' bastards!*

"In light of your honourable resistance, you may keep possession of your sword, Captain Chaptal," Lewrie allowed. "Though, you were at only two-to-one odds, since my ship, and our brig did not engage. Your home port, sir?"

"Basse-Terre, on Guadeloupe, *M'sieur*," Chaptal freely admitted with a very Gallic shrug and *moue*, "z'ough, we do not spend much time z'ere. We find better prizes 'ere, of late," he smugly hinted.

Lewrie took note that Chaptal might have put up a good fight, after all, and was more nervous than his mien might admit. The fellow was smudged with gunpowder smoke, and his waist-coat and trousers were splattered with blood drops. And, despite his bold attitude, his hands were shaking.

"That is a long way to go to find a Prize Court, sir," Lewrie pointed out. "Perhaps your allies at Havana are more convenient?"

Captain Chaptal opened his lips as if to reply, but then thought better of it and put an innocent smile on his face, licking his lips and saying "*Je regret, M'sieur*" with another shrug.

"No matter, sir," Lewrie told Chaptal with a grin, "for I do believe we have your ship's papers, right, Mister Bury?"

"Aye, sir," Bury said with a cryptic ghost of a grin, "Letters of Marque, muster book, captain's logs *and* accounts ledgers."

"Profit and loss, where and when he victualled," Lewrie said, happily smirking, which took Chaptal's mood down another peg. "You are fluent in written French, Mister Bury? Good. Pray do go through them quickly, and let me know what you discover of Captain Chaptal's doings.

"*M'sieur*," he said to the Frenchman, "while I will allow you to keep your sword, I regret that I cannot allow you to *wear* it or hold it sheathed in your hand. No worries, it will be returned to you when you have given your parole at Nassau, where you, your men, and your vessel will be taken tomorrow morning. In the meantime . . ."

Lewrie looked out toward HMS *Thorn,* thinking that Lt. Darling's brigantine had a crew large enough to spare a prize crew for Chaptal's brig, and could spare hands to guard the prisoners aboard his ship and the prize. *Besides, it's Darling's turn,* Lewrie thought; *howl about it though he may. And let* him *dine the Frog in for the night!*

"If you would be so good as to surrender it temporarily to my senior Midshipman, Mister Entwhistle, who will convey you to the care of the *Thorn,* which ship will carry your back to Nassau, hmm? Mister Entwhistle? Pass word for a boat crew to see Captain Chaptal over."

"Er, aye, sir," the surprised Mid replied,

"Upon arrival, inform Lieutenant Darling that he is to escort the prize and the prisoners to Nassau with all despatch, see them into the Prize Court, then rejoin the squadron which will be awaiting him Nor'west of Bimini."

"Aye aye, sir," Entwhistle said. "If I may have your sword for a brief time, sir? And if you will follow me?"

"Full departure honours, Mister Westcott," Lewrie added.

"Aye, sir," Westcott replied, then in a more casual way, said, "Darling will make bad weather of it, though."

"Captain Forrester won't be there t'plague him, so it'll be an easy duty, with a shot at a run ashore," Lewrie reminded him.

"In that, case, send *me*, sir!" Westcott exclaimed.

"What sort o' fight was it, Mister Lovett?" Lewrie said to the other victor who was looking anxious to boast of his deeds.

"Sharp enough, sir, for a privateer," Lt. Lovett glady related. "When she saw that there was no escape, Westward, she opened fire upon me, to which I replied. She had ten six-pounders, and they were well-manned and well-drilled, but not all that accurate, thank the Lord. I opened at about a cable's range and scored some hits, then Bury and *Lizard* came up off her larboard quarter and served her a broadside."

At the mention of his name, Lt. Bury looked up from the captured books he was rapidly scanning, and gave a little smile.

"This Chaptal fellow couldn't out-foot me, though he did try to put helm up and come down on me," Lovett went on, "at which point Bury fell off the wind and gave her a stern-rake, the same time as I hardened up to keep aloof of him and gave him another broadside, which forced him to haul his wind, else Bury would rake him again. I hauled wind, and we ended up on either beam, blazing away like mad, and that was enough for them! With her sails in rags, she struck."

"Before the action began, sir," Lt. Bury absently said, his attention still glued to the books and ledgers, "the *Insolent* bore sixty-eight hands, in all, and lost nine dead and fourteen wounded to some degree." Bury looked up long enough to reward them with another of his shy grins, then returned to his delving. "We shot very well."

"Our Surgeon's Mates are seeing to them, sir," Lt. Lovett said. "Three or four are in a bad way, so, perhaps your Surgeon, Mister Mainwaring, might assist them?"

"Pass word for my Cox'n and boat crew, and for the Surgeon," Lewrie ordered. "He's needed on the prize, tell him."

"There's another matter, sir," Lt. Lovett said, turning grim. "These two sailors were captured. They *claim* to be American, but one of them is as Irish as Paddy's Pig, and the other might as well have been hauled up from a Welsh coal-mine."

"On a French privateer?" Lewrie said with a frown, rounding to look at the two men whom Lovett indicated.

"Could be deemed treasonous, sir," Lt. Lovett gravelled.

"Indeed it could," Lewrie said, pacing over toward them where they stood by the entry-port, tarred straw hats in their hands being nervously turned round and round, and trying to look inconspicuous, as if they took up little space, perhaps no one would notice them. Both were dressed in typical sailors' garb of loose shirts, one in gingham check, the other in tar- and smoke-stained plain linen, tucked into the usual canvas slop-trousers which almost hid the toes of their buckled shoes.

"And who are you, my lads?" Lewrie gravely demanded.

"Michael Innis, so please ye, sor," the taller and fairer of the pair nervously replied, "cutty-eyed" and unable to look Lewrie in the eyes. His accent was straight out of a peat bog.

"And you?" Lewrie asked the other, who was shorter, wirier, and black haired, with almost a Cornish beak for a nose.

"Dyfid Evans, sir," the young fellow said, "David, t'at is, but some call me Dewey. T'is t'patron saint, d'ye see, and . . ." He withered under Lewrie's stern glare, and shut his mouth.

"Two British subjects, serving aboard an enemy privateer in time of war," Lewrie accused. "That's a foul business, my lads."

"But Oi'm *not* British, sor, arrah!" Innis protested in a sputter. "Nor Oirish neither! Swear by Christ, sor! Oi've me citizenship papers in me sea-chest t'prove it! Moy fam'ly an' me, settled in Darien, South o' Savannah, a whole ten *year* ago, sor!"

"And I'm from Savannah, sir," Evans insisted. "I've been American t'ree years, now! I got my certificate, too, sir, if you'd let us fetch 'em and show t'em to ya!"

"American consuls hand 'em out by the thousands to whoever wants 'em," Lewrie scoffed. "They print 'em up and *sell* them, and hand lots over to jobbers to sell for a cut! They aren't worth the price of the ink!"

"No, sir! No, sir!" Evans frantically rejoined, "Beggin! your *pardon,* sir, but mine isn't from a *consul*, sir, but t' Mayor o' Savannah! When I first shipped aboard tradin' ships, knowin' t'at t'e war was on and all, me Da wouldn't let me go 'less I had solid proof, so I wouldn't be pressed!"

"We come t'America ten year ago, sor, when I was but a wee lad," Innis stuck in. "Oi been a Georgian *since*! Loik Davey here says, sor, when Oi thought t'leave the bargin' trade and go t'sea, Oi went to a local magistrate at Sunbury for a certificate, for the same reason!"

"Mister Caldwell," Lewrie called over his shoulder to the Sailing Master. "Do you know of any places named Darien or Sunbury?"

"Ehm, sir," the ever-cautious Caldwell said, referring to one of his American-drawn charts. "I do see the names, which refer to river settlements of little importance. There is a notation that the region is referred to as the Midway settlements."

"Aye, sor, Midway's closer t'Savannah, an' Sunbury oncest was a rival t'Savannah," Innis exclaimed with a hopeful note to his voice, as if proof of his town's existence was proof of his innocence.

"But, why the Devil would ye sign aboard a French privateer in time of war?" Lewrie pressed, shaking his head at the lunatick nature of such service. "Surely, ye'd know did you get taken, there'd be a good chance of hangin'."

"Well, sir," Evans said with a sheepish, grin, "t'ere's a power more money t'be earned t'an aboard a merchantman, and a chance t'see more o' t'e world t'an Havana or Basse-Terre."

"Beats th' bargin' trade all hollow, too, sor," Innis added.

"*Only* Havana or Basse-Terre?" Lewrie asked, perking up. "There and back again was all you did?"

"Well, sir, we did see Fort-de-France on Martinique, once," Evans offered, shrugging and almost smiling in remembrance of a good time, despite his circumstances.

"Do either of you speak French?" Lewrie asked them, curious as to how the pair of them had fit in aboard a French raider.

"We learned enough o' their words for sail-tendin' an' such, sor," Innis told him, "and, seein' as how short they were o' sailors, they made sure we picked up their palaver roight quick, but . . . they rated us Landsmen, sor, and niver paid us no mind off-watch."

"Butt o' t'eir japes, more-like, sir," Evans added. "I spent a year and a half a merchant mariner and got rated Ordinary, but not on t'e *Insolent*. She's a poor 'feeder', t'boot."

"The merchant trade," Lewrie slowly said, hands in the small of his back and his gaze averted to the horizon. "Out of Savannah, to French or Spanish ports . . . nowhere else? What *sort* o' merchant work?"

Innis and Evans shared a look, nigh-shrugged at the same time as if resigned, then announced, "T'e Prize-Court trade, d'ye see, sir? Seein' what prizes t'at *Insolent* and t'e others took t'sell at Basse-Terre or Havana," Evans told him.

"Then ship aboard another bound back t'Savannah, sor," Innis chimed in, "t'do it all over again. Got roight boresome, it did."

Lewrie whirled to gawp at them with as much delight as if the Christmas holidays had come early, just for him!

"The others, you say?" Lewrie asked them. "*What* others?"

"Well, there's the *Otarie*, what means t'e 'Sea Lion', for one," Evans confessed. "T'en t'ere's t'*Furieux*, but her captain's a real Tartar. *Sea Lion*'s captain . . ."

"Mollien," Lewrie stuck in.

"Aye, sir," Evans said. "He's good at it, but can't hold a patch t'Captain Chaptal. T'at's why we signed aboard her, sir, for he's t'e most successful, young t'ough he be."

"There was a Spaniard, too, now and again, the *Torbellino*," Innis told Lewrie. "Moighta been a Catholic-run ship, but there's no way Oi'd *ever* take articles with a *Don*, sor!"

"We nabbed her," Lewrie boasted. "Here now, lads . . . how would you two like *not* to hang?"

"Well, o' *course*, sor!" Innis exclaimed.

"Do anything, sir!" Evans swore. "A Bible-oath I would!"

"Lieutenant Lovett?" Lewrie said. "I'd admire did you take these two prisoners back to the prize, so they can fetch their sea-chests and determine if they possess worthless Consular certificates, or genuine papers."

"Very good, sir," Lovett replied, sounding as if he would have relished a hanging instead.

"Then bring them right back here," Lewrie went on, turning to face the pair once more. "I want you to tell me everything you know about your so-called 'Prize-Court' trade, who arranges it, and where, and how it's conducted. If your certificates are genuine, you *could* be imprisoned at Nassau like the rest of your crew.

"But," he insisted, raising a finger in warning, "if you tell me all, I'd be of a mind t'let you two volunteer into the brigantine yonder. Lieutenant Darling, her commander, told me he's two hands short. Not *pressed*, but allowed the Joining Bounty. Think upon it. You've no hopes of even *tuppence* of what pay, or shares in captured ships, you were due. You have your kits and sea-chests already, so *Thorn*'s Purser can't charge you much if you volunteer."

That beats prison hulks, or a 'Newgate Horn-pipe', Lewrie told himself; *but not by much*, recalling what Dr. Samuel Johnson had said of sea-service—that it was like a prison, in which one has the chance to drown!

"Why, t'at'd be more t'an fair, sir!" Evans exulted, whooshing with relief. "I'll do it, and tell you all you wish!"

"If Oi kin have some'un wroite me fam'ly an' tell 'em where Oi be, sor," Innis quickly agreed.

"Off ye go with Lieutenant Lovett, here, then," Lewrie said. "And when you return, we'll have a good, long talk, hey?"

Good God above, they're in in up to their necks! Lewrie thought in joy; *They've seen the whole scheme from the* inside! *By sunset, we may be able to "smoak out" the entire enterprise, and put an end to it!*

He did feel a moment of trepidation, though. Those two might not really know all that much. Or, could he really get that lucky?

He could almost hear Dame Fortune laughing in the wings.

CHAPTER FORTY

I find them most convincing, sir," Lt. Bury said after he and Lewrie had looked the certificates over in *Reliant*'s great-cabins, as the two sailors in question, Innis and Evans, stood before the desk in the day-cabin portion, nigh-shivering as their fate was determined.

"Good bond writing paper, not 'flimsy'," Lt. Westcott agreed as he held them up to the light of the overhead lanthorns to squint over them, "and the letterheads are embossed. If they *are* sham, they are the best I've seen. Aye, like Bury says, they seem genuine."

"Let's accept them at face value, then," Lewrie decided. "Lads, I believe you when you say you're American citizens of Georgia. You'll not hang, not this year, at least. Now I'll ask ye to fufill your part of the bargain."

In vino veritas, Lewrie thought; *or, in* beer *veritas. Get 'em 'wet' and loose-tongued. Where . . . ?*

"Mister Westcott, let's you and I take the chairs; Lieutenant Bury, do you drag one from the dining-coach, and you two have a seat on the settee yonder," Lewrie bade them as genially as he could. "Pettus, please draw us five mugs of beer. Innis . . . you said you worked on the barges out of Savannah, first?"

"Aye, sor, Oi did," the fellow said, grinning in relief, but a bit hesitant in his response. It might have had something to do with being seated like an equal with officers. Even in a looser, more easy-going Society like America, there were still lessers and betters, and enough who would insist on deference from one like him. "First off, Oi was bargin' timber from the mills to Savannah, and goods back, but that was low-payin' and bore-some, and . . . like Davey told ye . . . Oi wanted t'see a bit more o' the world. Went t'work for the Tybee Roads Tradin' Comp'ny for more pay, but that was just river-work from Savannah down t'the Roads and back."

Lewrie looked over at Bury, who had been scouring the captured privateer's ledgers during the time it took to take Innis and Evans to the prize and return; Bury gave him a sage nod. The name of that company featured prominently on the meticulously recorded receipts.

"Did that for about a year, afore," Innis went on, pausing as a foaming pint mug was offered him, and he took a deep swig, wiped his mouth with the back of his hand, sighed, and said "Ah, that's toppin', thankee, sor! The barge master, he took me aside one ev'nin' and asks me, would Oi care t'make five or six dollar more a week, and o' *course* Oi said I would, but that'd depend on if Oi could keep me mouth shut, and not go blabbin' did I get a skin full in the taverns. Then, Oi got on the coastin' barges . . . down t'the Cumberland Sound and up the Saint Mary's or the Saint John's. Not all the time, maybe one trip or two ev'ry two, three months."

"And what was secret about those trips?" Lewrie casually asked, not wanting to press him too sharply, but mightily intrigued.

"We'd meet the privateers, sor," Innis almost happily admitted. "They'd've fetched their prizes into the rivers, and needed supplies . . . vittles, mostly. We'd break-bulk the prizes' holds o' what they carried and put it aboard the barges t'run up t'the warehouses in Savannah, leave the most o' the captured goods aboard, and bury 'em in lumber, rice, cotton, tobacco, whatever'd be welcome in Havana or the French islands."

"T'at'd be so, did one of our ships be stopped, boarded, and inspected by a ship like yours, Cap'm sir," Evans contributed. He had been silent up to that point, but had downed half his mug of beer and was almost youthfully eager to relate their doings. "There'd be false manifests, like the whole cargo was export goods, not loot."

"So . . . when the prizes made port, the valuable British exports from the West Indies . . . or British goods sent *to* the West Indies . . . would earn more money from the French or Spanish Prize Courts?" Lewrie hesitantly summed up, "more than if the prizes were full of Georgian produce?"

"Aye, sor, that's the way of it," Innis agreed, grinning like a loon. "And the stuff from England, aye! Sterling and plate, crystal and china, bales o' ready-made stuff, bolts and bolts o' foine cloth, pianers and furniture? Kegs and crates o' wine and brandy?"

"A grand market for a share of that in Savannah, too, if snuck past t'e Customs House," Evans added, "or, put aboard one o' the company ships bound for t'e Chesapeake, Philadelphee, Boston, nor even New York! T'at's what I was doing, workin' the ships t'Charleston, Port Royal, and ports North and back. We'd be lyin' in t'e Roads awaitin' a wind with local goods aboard, when the barges'd come alongside in t'e nighttime and load t'e good stuff, and no matter how innocent we were told t'play it, we knew *somet'in'* was queer!"

"That's what Oi wished t'do, aboard the ships loik Davey was workin'," Innis told them. At Lewrie's wave, Pettus brought round a fresh pair of mugs for their "testifiers". "And, after a while, when the bossmans thought Oi was trustworthy, that's what Oi got. Or, Oi *thought* Oi did."

"Bossmans?" Lt. Bury asked with a quizzical *moue*. "What does that mean?" He had been taking notes in a ledger of his own.

"T'at's what all t'e Cuffies say do ya ask 'em somet'in, sir," Evans easily breezed off. "T'ey say 'yas, massah' or 'yas, bossmam'," he mimicked in slave *patois*.

"So, eventually, the both of you ended up crewing the prizes to French or Spanish Prize-Court ports. On the same ship every time?" Lewrie asked "Where you became mates?"

"Not all that many the bosses'd trust, sor," Innis said with a shrug. "Not all that many who could keep their stories straight, too!"

"Stories?" Lt. Westcott asked in a skeptical tone.

"Well sir, afore we could set sail for Cuba, or t'e French islands, a clerk'd come down from Savannah and give t'e captain his new papers," Evans took up the tale. "Oncet a prize come in, she'd need a new name, so we'd rip the quarterboards or transom boards off or paint out t'e old and paint in a new . . . get rid of a figurehead was it too fine or somone might recognise her by it? Some'd say t'ey were owned by t'e Tybee Roads Comp'ny, some by others."

"Altamaha Comp'ny, the Ogeechee Comp'ny," Innis recited as if by rote, "or named after the squares in Savannah. Some o' the ships were s'posed t'be Charleston ships, Boston ships, God knows where-all, sor. Faith, ye'd o' thought they'd *flog* ye half t'death did ye not be able t'keep your wits about ye, if we got stopped and inspected."

"And did that happen often?" Lt. Bury enquired.

"Not all that often, no sir," Evans assured him, "and when we were, except for fear o' bein' pressed, we were let go right easy, comin' and goin'!"

"With supposedly innocent cargoes each way?" Lewrie mused.

"Innocent as all get-out on t'e way back, for sure, sir!" Evans said with a laugh. Lewrie summoned Pettus for more beer, all-round. Listening was dry work!

"And, what about the profits from the sale of the prizes?" Lt. Bury softly queried, looking up, at them with solemn eyes. "How were they handled, or concealed? In French or Spanish coin, or by draughts from one bank to another?"

"Niver saw any o' that, sors," Innis said with a puzzled shrug after a moment or two of thought. "Us *sailors* got paid at the end of a voyage, at Havana, say, or after we got back to Savannah. *Good* pay, it was, for as long as it lasted."

"And all gone by t'e time we shipped aboard a comp'ny ship for t'e return voyage, sirs," Evans said with a sad shake of his head over the quickness with which it went. "French or Spanish inn-keepers were more t'an glad t'see us, and t'e ladies, too, for certain. But, by t'e time come t'sail, we were mostly 'skint'."

"Savannah publicans'd leave us 'on the bones o' our backs' as good as the Frogs and Dons, too, sor," Innis ruefully told them.

"That's every sailor's complaint," Lewrie commiserated.

"I'd like to ask a question," Lt. Westcott said, still looking grim and distrustful. "It sounds like you could play the innocents on either leg of your journeys with the prizes, but . . . how were the crew and mates of the prizes concealed on the way to Havana or other ports?"

Innis and Evans looked at each other as if where those people had gone had never come to mind. Both cocked their heads in wonder, then turned to look at the officers, and shrugged.

"I can't recall any of t'em bein' aboard when we took charge o' t'e prizes, sir," Evans said. "T'ey might've been slung below in irons aboard t'e privateers. Weren't t'ere when we were, sirs."

"Mayhap they'd a'ready been sent down, t'Saint Augustine," Innis supposed. "When we put into the Saint John's River t'take charge of a prize, Oi just assumed they'd been marched off t'Saint Augustine. We niver saw hide nor hair of 'em, nor their sea-chests, neither, roight, Davey?"

"All t'eir beddin' and' kits were cleared out like t'ey never were t'ere," Evans agreed. "By t'e time we went aboard a prize, she was painted up new and re-named like she was fresh from t'e builder's yards, 'cept she was loaded and ready t'sail."

Lewrie shared a suspicious look with Westcott and Bury.

"One wonders, Captain Lewrie, if their prisoners were landed at *all*," Lt. Bury icily accused, peering hard at the two sailors. "Might I enquire if, during your time aboard the *Insolent*, you brought the master, mates, and sailors in with a prize . . . or, were they murdered and put over the side?"

"Jaysus, Mary, and Joseph!" Innis erupted in shock. "Nary a hair on their heads was touched once they'd struck! Swear that on me sainted mither, sor!"

"Hardly anybody was ever killed, nor even *hurt* when we took 'em, sir!" Evans hotly protested. "T'is t'e rare master'd put up any kind o' fight when we overhauled 'em wit' t'e guns run out, guns o' t'eir own aboard or no! Cheese-parin' masters never sign on hands enough for a fight, 'less t'ey're an Indiaman!"

"Cap'm Chaptal niver messed with the prisoners, sor, other than pennin' 'em up below oncest they was taken, and soon as we put in, we sent 'em off with all their kits," Innis bubbled out in a rush to show his innocence. "He wouldn't let no man mess with any wimmen, neither."

"Women?" Lewrie barked.

"Wives o' t'e masters, sometimes, passengers now and again and t'eir maids and such," Evans told them. "Some real fine ladies."

"But, what happened to them once landed?" Lt. Bury demanded. "Who took charge of them?"

"Well sors, did we land 'em in the Saint John's River, there was dry land handy, and there'd be Spanish-lookin' fellers, some Free Cuffies with guns, or Indian-lookin' men'd show up with horses and a cart'r two, and they'd march 'em off South. There's a good road down t'Saint Augustine. Did we put into the Saint Mary's, we'd put 'em in Comp'ny barges and sail or row the prisoners sev'ral miles up-river t'where there's solid land, and there'd be armed guards waitin'. Don' know if *they* was Comp'ny men or not, but we'd land 'em and that's the last we saw of 'em, honest. Ain't that right, Davey?"

"T'ey'd put any wounded, t'e women, and t'eir sea-chests on t'e carts, kind and gentle as anyt'ing, sir!" Evans assured them.

Lewrie sat back in his chair and gazed levelly at them.

I hope to God they ain't *lyin'*, he thought; *Maybe they believe what they've been told, and are too simple t'question it. Or they're too in-curious to bloody care! I* still *don't like the smell of it.*

"You never heard any talk, or wondering, about their fate?" Lt. Bury pressed. "No sidelong glances, or warnings to hush?"

"They wasn't any o' our bus'ness after we landed 'em," Innis replied with a shrug, and another deep swig of beer.

"Right, then," Lewrie said as he sat his empty beer mug down on the brass Hindoo tray-table with a click of metal on metal. "Whenever your Captain Chaptal brought in a prize, and the prisoners were taken away . . . *wherever* . . . how did he send word that he was back, in need of supplies and such?"

"Well, sor," Innia croaked, still shaken by new-found, dread suspicions, "most o' the time, the barges was already *there*, waitin'. There was only the oncest we came in off-schedule and had t'send one o' the mates up the Darien Road t'Savannah by fast horse."

"And why would they be waiting so long between the arrivals of the privateers?" Lewrie further queried.

"Every two or three month, sor," Innis told him. "At the dark o' the moon, ev'ry second or third month, when I was working barges. Reg'lar shipments o' vittles and such, exports'd be sent down ev'ry new moon, and if they had any special orders t'be filled, a barge'd go back t'Savannah t'fetch the goods afore *Insolent*'d sail, or one o' the prizes'd sail when we were workin' that side o' the trade."

"And does the place change with the timing of the new moons?" Lt. Bury asked. "Every second month the Saint Mary's River, and then the Saint John's River on the third, say?"

"In t'e beginnin'," Evans confessed, "but t'e Saint Mary's is handier, closer t'Savannah, and if anyone ever stumbled over us when we were there, we'd just shove off, hug the Spanish side, and sail or row up far enough t'strand anyone chasin' us on shoals."

"If it was an American Revenue cutter, aye," Innis added, "but if someone like you, your honour, sor, caught us, we'd hug the *other* bank, Georgia bein' neutral and all, and if we had to, we could slip over the side and swim or row to American soil and be safe as babbies."

Lewrie lowered his head and rested his upper lip on the forefinger of his right hand, mulling all that he'd been told. At last he lowered his arm and looked to either side at Westcott and Bury.

"Do any of you gentlemen have any other questions for these men which might further enlighten us?" he asked. "Any part of their tale that needs further explanation?"

"How long had your privateer been at sea?" Lt. Bury thought to ask. "Were you due in the river soon, or would your Captain Chaptal wait 'til he had a prize?"

"We was in two month ago, sor, with our last prize," Innis said, looking as if he would care for a fresh mug of beer. "In any case, we can't stay out much more'n three 'til the rum, whisky and beer runs out. We'd just started prowlin' the Bahamas for pickin's, coz your Navy's convoy escorts is gettin' too strong."

The last thing that a privateer ever wanted was a hard scrap with a warship, or even a well-armed merchantman with a master determined enough to put up a fight, which might cripple the raider and cost her captain, owners, and investors a steep repair bill. Against a warship, the only thing a privateer could do would be to flee, and pray for a clean pair of heels. Even a well-armed privateer's guns were more for show to daunt the desperate, not for a slugging match.

"So, the next new moon would be the next 'rondy'?" Lt. Westcott asked, shifting in his chair hard enough to make it squeak, sounding canny and eager. "For you, or another privateer?"

"Well, aye, sor," Innis said, looking surprised, that anyone *had* to ask; it was plain as day to *him*!

Westcott sat back with a smile on his face, quite satisfied.

"Anything else?" Lewrie asked, smiling contentedly. "No? Then I suppose we've kept these men long enough. Mister Westcott, would ye kindly pass word for a Midshipman of the duty watch, and arrange for a boat to carry Innis and Evans over to *Thorn*?"

"Of course, sir," Westcott agreed, rising to go to the door to the weather deck. Lewrie stood, too, as did Bury.

"You two are gettin' off by the skin of your teeth, ye know that," Lewrie told the sailors. "Ye've been up to your necks in an evil trade. I'm still not satisfied that the crews off the prizes are safe . . . or even alive. Understand me? Aye, you think upon that, and thank God I can't link you to their fates. Volunteeering for the Navy's your second chance. I strongly advise the both of you to make the most of it, obey orders chearly, and sing small. It may not pay as good as merchant service, *or* 'lays' in a successful privateer, but pay it is. Don't make me, or Lieutenant Darling, regret givin' you the benefit of the doubt!"

"We won't, sor, cross me heart an' hope t'die!" Innis swore.

"A fine gentleman ye are, sir, and a merciful one!" Evans said.

"Off with you, now," Lewrie gruffly ordered, shooing them to the forward door. Once they were gone, Lewrie cast his eyes on the overhead and let out a long, weary sigh.

"Lieutenant Darling will not thank you for them, sir," Lt. Bury softly said. "They're 'King's Bad Bargains', if ever I saw any."

"I expect you're right, Bury," Lewrie grudgingly agreed, "but I made a bad bargain of my own, to get them to talk so freely, and I have to keep to it, no matter my personal feelings.

"You suspect that the people off the prizes are dead, the same as I do?" Lewrie asked as he turned to look at him.

"I hope not, sir, but it does not sound promising," Bury said most gravely. "But for the most scrupulous Prize-Court officials, the muster books listing crew members suffice, so for a privateer captain, the temptation to save rations and money by eliminating them is quite strong, and saves him the trouble of guarding and sheltering them, yet . . . I cannot imagine that being done by even the most cold-blooded and piratical. There *are* rules of war, after all, a code of gentlemanly conduct, of *honour*! Those two, Innis and Evans, saw the prisoners being marched away, so they *were* brought in. If they were to die, why not kill them far out at sea?"

"I hope you're right," Lewrie moodily replied, "but, this insidious scheme hangs on secrecy. If the prisoners were kept in some holding pen out in the wilds, even in a warehouse at Saint Augustine, there's always the chance that a few might escape and make their way to American authorities, and the entire enterprise falls apart, with arrests and trials all round. Even held *incommunicado* 'til the end of the war, whenever that'll be, they'd have to be released *then*, and if evidence of what they witnessed comes to light, a lot of people would be ruined."

"But perhaps it is not the French privateers who would stand to lose the most, sir," Bury sagely pointed out. "To men like Chaptal, what matters most is *operational* secrecy, and a way to dispose of his prisoners and prizes quickly, and remain on his 'hunting grounds' without a long and risky voyage to do so, or putting them all aboard a neutral ship for a *cartel* to land them in a neutral port or return them to a British port."

"And, thumb his nose at us," Lewrie sourly added.

"That, too, sir, but . . . who runs the greatest risk of having his activities in support of a belligerent exposed?" Bury asked. "Who is more liable to be ruined and imprisoned?"

"Whichever bloody American is running this arrangement for 'em?" Lewrie realised.

"And, sir . . . if the American behind it wishes even more profit from it, why waste funds on marching the prisoners all the way to the Spanish authorities?" Bury continued. "It costs to build holding pens for prisoners, to feed them, and guard them. Captain Chaptal and the other privateer captains might not know the fate of their captives once landed, and might not much care. Despite our long-held distrust and loathing for the French, for the most part they fight a gentlemanly war, whereas an unscrupulous American man of *business* . . . might *not*."

Someone not *a soldier, or Sea Officer,* Lewrie thought, sneering; *just a bloody* "tradesman", *with his soul bound in double-entry account books! No,* no one *could be that cold-blooded!*

"Marching 'em to the Dons'd be a cost of doin' business," Lewrie said with a grimace. "Once at Saint Augustine, they're no longer his concern, either, and he'd let *them* feed and guard 'em."

"If he could run the risk of exposure, sir," Bury said.

Bury had risen at the dismissal of the two captured sailors and still had his beer mug in hand. He looked down and seemed surprised to see it. He took a sip and set it down on the brass tray-table and exchanged it for the captured stack of Captain Chaptal's books, sorting through them to find a journal.

"Despite the haste required to look through Chaptal's accounts, sir, I noted that he was meticulous about listing his prisoners, by name and numbers, and how many were turned over," Bury said, flipping through the pages. "He was also most secretive, referring to where he landed them as either 'Loire' or 'Saône', instead of the Saint John's or the Saint Mary's Rivers, with no way to know which is the correct river, or rendezvous. He noted how '*mon vieux*' met him with proceeds from previous sales. . . ."

Bury fumbled to pick up a second ledger, eager to impart what he had learned.

"Sit, Bury, so you don't spill 'em," Lewrie kindly offered as he sat himself back down on the settee.

"Thank you, sir," Bury replied, his attention rivetted on finding the right references. "Ah. *'Mon vieux'* is his code for the man behind it all on the American side, and the firm in question he calls just *'la compagnie'*! But *here*, sir . . . !" Bury excitedly said, picking up that second book and flipping through it, "are his meticulously-kept accounts for the owners and investors in his ship, to prove how successful he's been, and how much he's earned them, less demurrage in Prize-Court harbours, in Proctors' fees, less operating costs and repairs, and those are *not* in a personal code."

"So, you think you have an idea of who's guilty, Bury?" Lewrie asked, sitting up straighter and scooting to the edge of the settee.

"I do, sir," Bury said with a sly smile. "All his payments are to one firm, the Tybee Roads Trading Company, of Savannah. I also . . . here," Bury went on, laying aside the accounts ledger and picking up a thicker book, nigh the size of a thick dictionary. But when Bury opened the cover, it was revealed to be a box. "To prove to his investors and owners that each purchase and outlay was legitimate, Captain Chaptal kept signed receipts. While some are signed by various factotums of the Tybee Roads Trading Company, a great many, as well as receipts from Prize Courts at Havana, Fort-de-France and Basse-Terre, are signed by a Mister Edward Treadwell, who styles himself as President of the firm. This Treadwell and his firm appear to make over ten percent of each prize, plus Chaptal's ship's needs. There are stacks and stacks of them, seemingly filed in this box in neat, chronological order. Though . . ."

"We know the firm, we know the company, and we know the bastard behind it!" Lewrie crowed in glee. "Do we take these books to the authorities in Savannah, they'll hang him!"

"Though, sir, there may be a second unidentified man," Bury said, frowning in puzzlement. "For the most part of Chaptal's journal he refers to *'mon vieux'* as his principal dealer, but in the last two references to prizes brought in, he mentions someone he calls *'coton'*, so there may be another company, and without corroborating account books, I cannot—" Bury was cut off by Lewrie's peel of laughter, by his rocking back onto the settee's back and slapping his knee.

" 'My old', and 'Cotton', and Treadwell, are one and the same, Bury!"

Lewrie hooted, loud enough to make his cats start. "Chaptal calls him 'mon vieux' not in the 'old friend' sense, but because this Treadwell *looks* old, no matter he's no older than me. He calls him *coton* because he has a very full and curly head of white *hair*, as white as carded and washed *cotton*! My Purser, Mister Cadbury, met him at Savannah, and remarked on his appearance. Now!"

Lewrie sprang from the settee and went a bit forward to the starboard-side chart space, fetching a book off the fiddled shelf to bring back into better light. He sat down and opened it, running a finger down the tightly spaced entries, squinting over the wee type.

Damme, do I need spectacles? Lewrie thought, vexed; *I ain't that old, surely!*

"According to the ephemeris, Lieutenant Bury, the next dark of the moon is in eleven days," Lewrie said, looking up from the book at last. "Eleven days from now, once *Thorn* rejoins us, I intend that the squadron be off the Cumberland Sound and up the Saint Mary's River t'see what we can catch. Pen 'em in and row up to destroy 'em, or catch 'em as they try to run. Either way, we put paid to this fiendish business!"

CHAPTER FORTY-ONE

$\mathcal{W}$e will not get far up the Saint Mary's, I fear to say, sir," Mr. Caldwell, the Sailing Master, cautioned as he, Lewrie, and Lieutenant Westcott huddled over the dining table two days later, where one of the purchased American-made charts was spread out.

"Not with *Reliant*, no," Lewrie said, lifting Chalky off to set him back on the deck, "and not with a cat in the way. At the best, we might ascend the river as far as the narrows 'twixt Cumberland Island and Amelia Island, then come to anchor athwart the channel with springs on the cables to block any escape with our guns. If these soundings are right, there seems to be about thirty to fourty feet of depth for her. From there, it'll be up to the sloops and gunboats."

Actually, the American-drawn chart, told them little. The river entrance was called the Saint Mary's, the bay to seaward was named the Cumberland Sound, but once in the entrance, the river itself was named Cumberland Sound, no matter its narrowness.

There was sufficient depth in the entrance narrows between Cumberland Island and Amelia Island on the South bank, with a width of half a mile. Once past the narrows, the Cumberland widened to about two-thirds of a mile and swung Nor'west to make a fairly large bay before trending more Northerly and narrowing once more to less than a half mile. If one followed the main course of the Cumberland Sound far enough, the chart finally referred to it as the Cumberland River, and fed into the much larger St. Andrew Sound below Jekyll Island.

Spooked privateers, pirates, or smugglers could flee up that way and make the sea, or scuttle up one of the minor rivers or creeks and run for miles before they turned narrow and too shallow.

Making pursuit worse, barely half a mile past the entrance to the Cumberland, the Amelia River fed in from the South behind the island of the same name, and snaked round before being joined by the Bells River and Lanceford Creek.

And just where the Cumberland veered North lay yet another of those joinings; the *real* St. Mary's came in from the West, but not an hundred yards off the river's mouth there was the Jolly River, which ox-bowed through swamps and marshes from the Sou'west!

"There's more waterways than a dog has fleas, it appears, sir," Lt. Westcott glumly said. "The privateers could flee up any one of them as soon as they spot us. We will have to block this Amelia River as soon as we enter . . . unless that's where *they're* anchored. Then we'll have to be quick about it to reach this second fork, where the Jolly River and the Saint Mary's enter. We might need double the number of boats." Westcott was impatient, bored, and he *would* pick nits.

"I see no notes indicating the rate of the currents," Lewrie complained, scanning the margins of the chart, "nor are there any tide measurements. I wonder if our privateers and smugglers lay out only one anchor, or two, depending on how strong the currents are, or if the tide flow is stronger. Depending on how high up past the entrance they moor, of course. If by one, they might be stern-on to us, and slowed by the currents when they try to cut and run."

"But we would be slowed at the same rate in our pursuit, sir," the sailing Master just had to point out.

"Our best bet is to catch them sleeping," Lt. Westcott suggested, "before they realise we're among them. We will be under sail, or under sweeps and oars, and we could catch them before they wake, cut their cables, and hoist sail."

"Or man their guns," Lewrie added.

"And manning their guns at the same time, aye sir," Westcott agreed. "Just where, though . . ." He trailed off, making a humming noise through his nose and drumming the point of his pencil on the chart. "How high up must we go before we meet up with them, that is the question. How far would they go to feel safe from prying eyes?"

This lower-most part of the Georgia coast was much like the marshes to either side of the Savannah River; it was as flat as the top of a dining table, and most of the shoreline maritime forests were wind-gnarled and did not grow very high, though they were dense, a mix of hardwoods and slender pines. Perhaps a mile or so inland along one of the minor rivers or creeks, in still-water sloughs behind the Sea Islands, there might be cypresses and live oaks which would screen the top-masts of ships from observation from the sea, but . . . where?

"Recall what those two sailors told us," Lewrie called to mind. "They boasted that if caught by an American Revenue cutter, they'd hug the South bank of the Saint Mary's and be in Spanish territory. And, if someone like us came along, they'd row over to the North bank and be 'safe as babbies in their mither's arms?' " he said with a chuckle as he mimicked an Irish lilt. "The entrance to the Cumberland Sound, and the wide part of the river to the mouth of the Saint Mary's, is divided down the middle 'twixt Spain and the United States, as is the Saint Mary's itself. They get behind Cumberland Island and they're out of sight from seaward. They get into the mouth of the Saint Mary's, and go up about half a mile, and they would be all but invisible. There," he said tapping a finger on the chart, "or here, a bit up the Amelia River, are the likeliest places, I should think."

Mr. Caldwell pulled a brass divider from his pocket, laid its spread points along the half-mile scale on the chart and stepped off the distance from the entrance narrows to the mouth of the St. Mary's River proper, then grunted. "We shall either come upon them almost at once in the Amelia River, or have to go about two miles further on to the mouth of the Saint Mary's, and perhaps another half mile up-river. You will wish to strike just at dawn, I would assume, sir?"

"At murky, sleepy *pre-dawn*, if we can pull that off, depending on the river current and the tide," Lewrie eagerly told him. "Are your books sufficient, Mister Caldwell, or should we gut a few chickens to read the auguries?"

Caldwell raised a brow and harumphed, in good humour over his captain's jape. He turned to his tide table book. "That may be asking a lot, sir. Eight or nine days from now? Hmm."

While Caldwell hummed, hawed, and pondered, Chalky hopped back atop the table and sprawled on his back, belly exposed and his forepaws waving for attention. Westcott reached out to teasingly touch him on the back legs and belly, making Chalky squirm, writhe, and lash his tail madly, trying to seize the finger for a nip and gnaw.

"Too quick for you today, hey?" Westcott gloated. "Ow!"

"Twine or a length of wool's safer," Lewrie cautioned too late.

"Ahem," Caldwell announced at last, clearing his throat in preface of his "ruling" on the matter. "This part of the American coast had never been adequately surveyed, sir, and any estimates of local tides are mathematical extrapolations from better-surveyed ports up the coast, such as Savannah or Port Royal. Loose 'lick and a promise' extrapolations, mind. It would appear that the most desirable *high* tides occur two or three hours after midnight, and the rise *might* be between three and a half to five feet. This chart describes only the sketchiest attempts at measuring it. The *low* tides occur mid-morning."

"Damn," Lewrie groused.

"The ebb below *mean* low-tide depths marked on the chart, though, are reckoned to be only three-quarters to one and a half feet," the Sailing Master went on with a happy uplift of one corner of his mouth. "Given the indicated depths in the entrance channel where you wish to anchor our ship, sir, which range from thirty-three feet to fourty or more, *Reliant* should be quite safe, even at the greatest variation of a new moon low tide. Of course, such does not signify for the rest of the squadron, which only draw ten to twelve feet. Barring the presence of unforseen silt and sediment shoals, even *Thorn* will swim most ably into the Cumberland, and up the tributaries . . . the Saint Mary's most especially."

"Very well, then!" Lewrie declared, rubbing his hands together in relief. "There's where *Reliant* will come to anchor nine days from now," he said, using a pencil to make an X on the chart just outside the entrance channel, "say, around midnight, giving us bags of time to man the gunboats and the smaller boats, sort them out into order, and . . . Get out of the way, Chalky!"

"With less chance that any watchers posted near the channel might see us," Westcott agreed, "or warn them before we're on our way to their lair . . . whichever river it will be."

"The Saint Mary's," Lewrie assured him. "It's the likeliest."

Settled upon that destination, Lewrie leaned down to peer at the chart more closely, tracing the course of the St. Mary's West to the first bend which sharply turned South, about two miles along, and ran South for another mile before yet another ox-bow that led to the Nor'west. There was a good, deep channel all the way, deep enough for any of their ships if they kept to the Spanish side 'til they reached the Southern bend. There was a patch that showed only thirteen feet, before hitting a deep pool at the ox-bow bend with nigh-fourty feet of water on the American side, then averaged twenty to twenty-four feet on the Spanish side of the river to the next bend. The chart did not cover enough territory; it was more concerned with the immediately accessible waters near the sea.

Far as I know, the bloody river snakes its way to the Gulf of Mexico! Lewrie thought; *Surely, we won't have t'chase 'em that far! If it is navigable that far, shouldn't there be a town of some kind up there, far inland, where they can dash ashore and get lost in the population? Damn, and double-damn!*

"Well, thank you, Mister Caldwell, you are most re-assuring," Lewrie said, returning to the here-and-now. "Thankee, indeed."

"My pleasure, sir, and my duty," Caldwell preened, bowing his head. "If I may be excused now, sir, I told the youngest Mids that I would test them on their knowledge of the principal stars."

"Of course, Mister Caldwell," Lewrie gladly told him.

Just so long as ye don't think t'test me! Lewrie thought; *What got lashed into me, I've mostly forgotten!*

Lewrie rolled up the chart to stow it away, spilling Chalky onto his feet most-nettled that "play" was over. Toulon had finally gotten from the deck to a chair seat, thence atop the table, and sat on his haunches, looking about to see what fun he might have missed. He and Chalky got sufficient "wubbies" to mollify them.

"Care for some fresh air on deck, Mister Westcott?" Lewrie invited. "It's hot and stuffy in here."

"Delighted, sir," Westcott agreed.

They spent some time strolling the quarterdeck to savour the wind and the clear sunshine. Far to the Sou'west the isle of Bimini was just above the horizon, a wee speck set in the heaving and short-chopped seas near the Northwest Providence Channel. They paced side-by-side for several minutes without speaking, 'til Lt. Westcott spoke up.

"Have you given any thought to the allocation of the gunboats, sir?" Westcott asked in a low voice, "And which of us will stay with the ship?"

"I'm torn between whether the armed ships' boats will lead, or whether the gunboats should," Lewrie mused. "It could turn out to be a cutting-out, if all goes accordingly, and we might let some of the sloops' crew manage that, with some of our Marines parcelled out with them. With the gunboats very close astern, with our hands and more Marines in them. Perhaps all at once, ships' boats and gunboats working in concert."

"Hmm . . . depending on whether we achieve complete surprise or not, sir," Westcott seemed to agree. "Though, once we anchor, there is the very real possibility that it will take longer than planned to get everyone ready to go. It always does, sir, or *seems* to."

"Aye," Lewrie said. "There's many a slip 'twixt the crouch and the leap."

"Our cutters and barges, sir," Westcott went on, "that's four. Two boats of decent size each from the other ships, that makes a total of ten."

"Lovett's *Firefly* has no Lieutenant, and only one Midshipman," Lewrie pointed out. "Perhaps only eight boats, divided into two divisions, or flotillas, or what-you-call-'ems. It'd be best did Lovett keep his small crew together. That will require an aggressive officer to command one division, on the water and closer to the action."

"Aye sir, it would," Westcott said through taut lips.

"I think you're best for that, Mister Westcott," Lewrie told him. "You'll take one of the gunboats. I assume that's what you're drivin' at?"

"It is, sir, and thank you!" Westcott exclaimed in relief that he would not remain aboard the frigate and miss out on the action.

"Merriman's junior. He'll command *Reliant*," Lewrie decided. "Spendlove can take the other gunboat, and we'll put our oldest Mids in charge or our boats, leaving Munsell and Rossyngton behind, to aid Merriman. *Thorn* can spare Lieutenant Child and one of her Mids, and Bury can place Rainey and a Mid in her boats. We'll speak with Simcock as to how many Marines he can spare for it."

"Ehm . . . Merriman will command our ship, sir?" Westcott asked. "Where will you be?"

"I think I'll go in aboard one of the gunboats," Lewrie said, "either yours, or Spendlove's."

"You will, sir?" Westcott gawped.

"Spendlove's," Lewrie announced. "I'd not wish t'crimp your style, Mister Westcott."

"Ehm, well . . . thank you, sir," Westcott said, grinning.

"I've been bored shitless, I've been insulted, demeaned, and I've been rebuffed and dismissed at every port we've called at," Lewrie went on. "Not to mention discumbobulated and mystified, and, now that there is a good chance the privateers, their prizes, and this blood-thirsty Treadwell bastard might be there with some of his damned barges, damme if I'll miss a shot at settlin' their business for good and all!"

He paused a moment to look up at the commissioning pendant and the top-masts, rocking on the balls of his booted feet.

"Besides, Mister Westcott, even if they *ain't* there, and we hit an empty bag, at least we'll be *doin'* something!"

CHAPTER FORTY-TWO

*A*nchored by best bower and kedge, sir, with springs on the cables, and the guns will be manned and loaded once all our boats are clear," Lt. Merriman reported. The night was so dark without a moon, and the usual lights at forecastle belfry, binnacle cabinet, and the taffrail lanthorns extinguished, that Lewrie could not see that officer's glum expression, though he could hear the disappointment in his voice.

"Very well, Mister Merriman, you have charge of the ship until our return," Lewrie told him. "Mister Spendlove, Mister Westcott, are the gunboats alongside?"

"One to either beam, sir," Spendlove reported, "and the barges and cutters waiting astern of them for boarding."

"Let's get on with it, then," Lewrie ordered, resisting an urge to pull out his pocket watch. It was so dark that that would be bootless, for the night's gloom did not allow even the faintest hint of starlight by which to read it; there had been a warm and steady rain offshore that afternoon, and the skies were solidly overcast after its ending.

Sailors and gunners descended the man-ropes and battens to the gunboats, followed by files of Marines with muskets. Lewrie waited 'til the last had left the ship before clumsily descending, himself, burdened with both his double-barrelled pistols and a cartridge pouch and brass priming flask, his rifled breech-loading Ferguson musket and a second cartridge pouch and priming flask for that, as well, along with his hanger on his left hip.

"There is a hooded lanthorn under a scrap of canvas aft, sir," Spendlove offered, "do you wish to determine the time."

"Good. You have your copy of the river chart?" Lewrie asked.

"Right here, sir," Spendlove assured him, patting his chest coat pocket, "though it may be some time before we may refer to it,"

Before *Thorn* had returned from Nassau to rejoin the squadron, Lt. Westcott with his draughting skills, and Bury with his artistic talents, and Lewrie's clerk, Faulkes, had made free-hand copies of the chart for all officers and Mids in charge of the boats, distributed to all captains at a planning conference aboard *Reliant* the day before they departed the Northwest Providence Channel for the Georgia coast. Once the slightly brighter pre-dawn greyness came, they might prove useful.

"Shove off, there, bow man," Spendlove ordered in a theatrical loud whisper. "Ship oars . . . and give way."

The converted fishing boat moved off only a long musket shot before the hands rested on their oars, and let her lie rocking on the tide and current, making room at the entry-ports for the cutters and barges to be manned and rowed off to join her.

As Lewrie waited, he peered out to either beam, searching for *Lizard* and *Firefly* to see how they were coping with disembarkation. Clear of the ship, he could barely make out the faintest ruffles of slightly whiter water breaking along their waterlines, and further off, the hint of lazy lake-like waves breaking on the shores of Cumberland Island and Amelia Island. Ahead of his gunboat, the river was as black as his boots!

He sat himself down on a damp thwart near the tiller, fighting the urge to duck under the canvas to check his watch by the light of that hooded lanthorn. The less of that, the better, but . . . this sort of complicated operation could not be done in *complete* darkness.

The final plan that they had threshed out at the conference in *Reliant*'s great-cabins made allowance for *some* signal lights during the darkest part of the night and the wee hours of the morning. Once all the various boats were manned and on the water, bobbing about like so many sleeping ducks, Lewrie would order two flashes from that lanthorn to the rowing boats to head up the entrance channel. A second series of *three* flashes to Lt. Westcott's gunboat and he would begin to row after the boats in his division. Four flashes would be directed to *Lizard*, *Firefly*, and *Thorn* to begin to make way in their rear, with the two smaller sloops employing their rarely used sweep oars, and *Thorn* doing her best against the current and ebbing tide under sail.

What sort of shambles, what sort of pot-mess that several hours could produce almost could not be contemplated! If *Thorn* could not breast the current, she and her heavy guns might end up too far back when dawn broke, and might end up using her original ship's boats and more of her reduced crew to *towing* her into action!

The longer that Lewrie sat and pondered, fretting and squirming, the dafter his plan became, and he began to feel sure that when dawn did come, he began to feel torn as to which would make him look even more foolish—how badly it had fallen apart, or that they had stumbled in to find no sign of privateer, prize, or criminals!

"I'll take a peek at the time," he whispered to Spendlove, at last, ducking under the canvas, opening the shutter of the lanthorn, and discovering that it was almost 4 A.M.

If Caldwell's right about the tides, he thought, dredging up one lean scrap of hope, *slack-water's over, and it's beginning to make.*

"I think that I can make out two of our boats astern, sir," Spendlove said, his whisper muffled by the canvas, "and there are two more off the starboard beam. *Lizard*'s, I think."

"Are they sparking?" Lewrie asked, emerging from the cover of the suffocating canvas, glad for the sudden rush of cool night air.

"They are, sir!" Spendlove said, sounding not only relieved, but amazed that the boats from *Lizard* assigned to his division would be able to find them in the dark and link up. He drew out an un-loaded Sea Pattern pistol—a heavy and clumsy weapon of such poor accuracy that it was best when fired against a foe's chest or belly—blew on the pan just to make sure that there was no priming powder, and drew it to full cock. Holding it aloft he pulled the trigger, and the flint created a brief but bright shower of sparks as it scraped down the raspy face of the frisson. That was another necessary violation of complete black-out, but a useful one suggested by Lt. Lovett. "All our boats answer, sir!"

Lewrie stood, resting a steadying hand on Spendlove's shoulder, and peered far out into the North, looking for a matching set of sparks between Lt. Westcott's gunboat and his assigned rowing boats.

"Yes, I think I see them!" Lewrie eagerly hissed. "Three . . . four. They're all assembled, too. Show two flashes from the lanthorn, Mister Spendlove, and let's get this procession under way."

The plan laid out was for assorted rowing boats to lead, with a gunboat close astern of each group. Once past the entrance channel Westcott's group would take the centre of the river, whilst the boats under Spendlove would press towards the shore of Amelia Island, and the mouth of that river, in case any privateers or prizes were moored there, closest to a quick exit from Cumberland Sound.

Astern of the two boat groups, *Lizard* and *Firefly* would try to row in abreast using their longer, greater sweep-oars, with Lovett's *Firefly* stationed near the North Bank, and Bury's *Lizard*, with more 6-pounders, would provide support for Spendlove's group should they run into awake and well-armed resistance.

At least it looked good on paper, Lewrie miserably thought as he recalled the last briefing to his officers, his over-sized sketch of the entrance channel, the rivers, and their bends, with pecan shells to represent the major vessels, all moving along in parallel columns abreast, with *Thorn* trailing closely. What it looked like now in the dark, what it would look like when false dawn greyed the sky, would be a sloppy other matter.

Silence was essential, yet the oars still creaked as they were hauled despite the rags over the thole-pins to muffle the *skreak!* of wood-on-wood. Oarsmen had to breathe hard, and sometimes cough. The Marines had to fidget and rattle their weapons and accoutrements, and the gun crew of the 6-pounder carronade now and then created wee rumbling noises as they swivelled the slide platform about. The rush of the river seemed a loud rush-gurgle as the boat ploughed through it, the bow lifting at each rhythmic stroke of the oars.

"I think I can make out our boats, sir," Lt. Spendlove whispered close to Lewrie's ear, almost making him jump out of his skin.

It was true. Ahead, Lewrie could barely see the white-painted transoms of the two boats from *Reliant*, and the four others off the sloops! He looked astern and *thought* he made out the foresails and fore gaff sail of *Lizard*, too. A quick duck under the canvas, again, and a furtive slit opening of the hooded, lanthorn showed him that it was almost five in the morning; false dawn would come a quarter-hour later. He closed the lanthorn and came back to the cooler air, looking North to see if he could spot Westcott's division, but they were still invisible; he didn't even try to hunt for *Thorn*. To the South, there was nothing to be seen in the mouth of the Amelia River. There were no ship's riding lights one might expect to see aboard a ship at safe anchorage.

"We'll have to steer larboard, Mister Spendlove, just to make sure there's no one in there," Lewrie said.

"Ehm . . . how do we tell the other boats to do that, sir?" Lt, Spendlove asked.

It was still thankfully dark enough to hide the stupefied look on Lewrie's face. He had planned for them to be off the river mouth with just enough light to see up it, and had made no contingency plan for supplemental signals!

"Let the other boats proceed," Lewrie snapped. "We'll go a few hundred yards or so up the Amelia on our own, and catch up later."

"Aye, sir," Spendlove said with nary a dubious note, and whispered to the helmsman to put the tiller over. The boats ahead rapidly melted back into the gloom, and they were alone, steering South into the river mouth. Lewrie stumbled forward to the boat's single mast to cling to it and peer ahead.

"Easy all," Lewrie ordered. "Rest on yer oars for a bit."

He got the sense that they were further West than the middle channel. There was a strong hint of the bulk of Amelia Island to his left, and a smell of marsh to his right, as if they were nearer to the West bank. What he *could* see was a faint mist beginning to rise and cling to the surface of the water. There were no ships in sight.

"Let's put about, Mister Spendlove, and catch up our boats," he ordered after making his way back to the stern.

The larboard oarsmen backed water, the starboard oarsmen pulled, and the gunboat slowly swung about to row Nor'west. As they did so, a spark loomed up off the starboard bows. A moment later there came a second shower of sparks.

"Best answer that, Mister Spendlove," Lewrie said.

"Hoy, there!" a voice called. "Who are you?"

"Spendlove!" Lewrie replied as loud as he dared.

"*Lizard*, here!" Lt. Bury called back. "For a minute, we almost fired into you! Did you get lost, Spendlove?"

Sure enough, the sloop loomed up in the dark, her sails rustling and her sweep oars groaning.

"We detatched, to look into the river," Lewrie told him. "My idea. If you swear not t'run us over, we'll be catching up our boats."

"I will veer off Nor'west, sir, to avoid that!" Bury promised.

"Let's get a goodly way on," Lewrie told Spendlove.

He pulled out his pocket watch once more to duck under the canvas, but found that he could almost make out its white face, and barely identify the hour marks! Turning about, he saw Spendlove referring to his boat-compass without the use of the lanthorn! It was false dawn at last! Without straining he could spot the gaggle of rowing boats that had gone on without him, far off, see the splashes of each oar as they bit the water, and the low, swirling mist they passed through. To the North, he could finally see Lt. Westcott's division, and *Firefly* astern of them! They looked to be in good order, for a wonder!

The gunboats stroke-oar set a hot pace, and the oarsmen gasped and grunted as they rowed, but they began to close the distance to the other boats, which had swung Nor'-Nor'west for the mouth of the Saint Mary's River. The Midshipmen in charge of the largest boats from the frigate spotted them, and slowed their stroke to allow them to rejoin.

But, when the gunboat was slightly less than a cable off, there came spark signals from Entwhistle and Grainger, and all of the boats laid on their oars, slowly coasting to a stop.

Mr. Entwhistle was standing and waving his arms over his head to get their attention, then pointing towards the river's mouth. Two minutes longer on, and the gunboat was within hailing distance.

"Lights, sir!" Entwhistle called out with his hands cupped by his mouth. "Riding lights in the river!"

"By God, they *are* there!" Lewrie crowed, immensely relieved to know that they had not punched an empty bag, that *this* new moon was a rendezvous for a privateer and his supplier. "We're about to catch *somebody*, Mister Spendlove. Lay on yer oars for a bit, lads. Sorry about the long row. Load your weapons. Load and prime the carronade!"

CHAPTER FORTY-THREE

*O*nce all weapons were loaded, and the oarsmen took up the stroke again, a slower and more cautious one this time, the confluence of the Jolly and the St. Mary's Rivers spread wide before them, revealing not just one or two ships, but half a dozen anchored up the St. Mary's. A schooner lay closest to the South bank, stem-on to them as it streamed to the river current. A French Tricolour lazily flew over her transom!

"That's Mollien's schooner, by God!" Lewrie said with a laugh. "That snail-eatin' bastard we saw at Charleston!"

Beyond her lay a larger brig with no flag flying. Up-river on the American side lay yet another brig, with several masted barges at her larboard side. Even further up-river yet another vessel could be seen, this one a full-rigged ship with a few more barges alongside her. And beyond Mollien's schooner lay a brig that flew a French flag, and another brig with a French flag strung above a British merchant ensign in sign that she was a prize!

"It's as crowded as the Pool of London!" Lt, Spendlove rejoiced. "Which do we take on, first, sir?"

"The *Otarie* . . . the schooner!" Lewrie quickly decided. "She's the strongest opposition." He looked round his gaggle of boats, sorting out the best for the task. He would need the Marines, and most of them were in his gunboat and *Reliant*'s two boats. "Mister Rainey?" he called to *Lizard*'s Lieutenant. "We're taking that'un yonder! Once we do, I wish you and your men to guard any prisoners and take charge of her. Work her out to the middle of the Cumberland if you can. Once that's done, I'll take the gunboat and my two boats from *Reliant* and press on to the prize anchored above her. Sergeant Trickett, you and your Marines fix bayonets and be ready to board!"

Please stay sleepin', just a bit longer! Lewrie prayed as the boats crept into the St. Mary's. The men aboard the privateer would be sleeping, snugly anchored. They weren't Navy men, so they might not keep a strict watch if they weren't at sea. They might have been carousing the night before, contemplating the value of their prize and might already have money in their pockets from previous captures, and lashings of celebratory drink. If only . . . !

No lights glowed behind the sash-windows in the schooner's transom, so her captain might still be abed. Lewrie could not see any men walking her decks. They were only one hundred yards off from her when a hesitant and reedy voice called out *"Qui vive?"* A sailor, no more than a ship's boy, stood by the schooner's taffrails in a wool stocking cap over thick blond hair, peering at them wide-eyed with a gaping mouth. The next instant, the lad ran forward with a wordless, shrill or of alarm. The next instant, the schooner's watch-bell was being rung! *"Garde à vous! Aux armes! Les Anglais, mon Dieu!"*

"Well, shit!" Lewrie spat. So much for stealth. "Gun-captain, d'ye have a clear shot? Then put one right through her transom! Wake her captain up! Go, go, go!" Lewrie shouted to the rest of the boats.

The carronade was swivelled to the proper angle and the round platform was pegged in place. The gun-captain drew the trigger line taut, bent to assure his aim one last time, then leaned away and gave the line a hard jerk, and the carronade squealed back on its slide carriage as it went off with a very loud bang. Sleeping shore birds, sea birds, and a flock of white egrets and blue herons cried in alarm and rose from the marshes and woods in swirling clouds.

The privateer's graceful wide transom was punched clean through, leaving a star-shaped hole of shattered planking and a cascade of glittery glass shards!

If that don't wake 'em all up, the damned birds did! Lewrie told himself as both of *Reliant*'s boats went alongside the schooner, grapnelled to her, and Midshipmen Entwhistle and Grainger led their boat crews and Marines up to her low bulwarks, cheering like mad!

"Come on, come on!" Lewrie exhorted, going to the gunboat's lone mast once more to take hold of the larboard stays, ready to board her himself. "Lay her alongside her quarterdeck, Spendlove!" Pistols were popping aboard the schooner, and British cutlasses were clashing tinnily with French ones. Feet were thundering as *Otarie*'s sleeping crew came boiling up from below, ready to fight for their lives.

There! There was the schooner's main-mast chain platform, and hand-holds by which to scramble up. Three of the gunboat's sailors and two bellowing Marines preceded him before he could reach out and grab hold. He got his feet on the platform, and a Marine reached back to hoist him up and over. He was greeted by a shot, and the bumblebee drone of a musket ball singing past his ear!

Lewrie spotted the shooter, drew one of his pistols, and cocked both locks, raised it, and fired. One of Mollien's escorts ashore at Charleston, a large "side of beef", dropped his musket from nerveless hands and clutched his chest before thudding to the deck on his back!

There were three French sailors who had just emerged from the fore hatchway to their belowdecks quarters. One was shot, one was spitted on a Marine's bayonet, and the third took a cutlass swing on the side of his neck that halfway decapitated him, raising a fountain of blood and a hopeless scream before he tumbled back down below to block others trying to rush to the deck.

"*Vous!*" Captain Mollien cried, coming to his quarterdeck from an after hatchway, sword in his hand and ready to fight, rushing at Lewrie at once with his small-sword levelled for a thrust.

"You!" Lewrie shouted back, shooting him in the middle of his chest with the second charge in his pistol. Mollien's charge veered off to Lewrie's right as the Frenchman stumbled, tripped over his own feet, and fell to his knees by the helm, the hilt of his sword held in limp, twitching fingers. Lewrie stowed his first pistol in a pocket of his coat and drew the second, cocking the right-hand barrel.

"I *told* you we'd nab you 'fore the year's out, ye little turd," Lewrie gloated as he stood nearby. "Clumsy try, that."

Mollien keeled over to lay on his side, mouth gulping for air like a landed fish, his teeth stained red with his own gore. "*Vous. . . . Anglais . . .*

pédale, you cannot . . ." More blood from a punctured lung gushed, and his eyes glazed over, unseeing.

Damme, *but that felt* hellish *good!* Lewrie thought, turning to face the schooner's bows in search of a new threat, but it appeared that their boarding action had been successful. There were over one dozen bodies on the deck, un-moving, and several more propped up on gun-carriages or mast trunks, badly wounded. Even more stood crouched with their arms over their head and their hands empty of weapons.

"There's more of them below, still under arms, sir," Midshipman Grainger reported, pointing at the hatchway with a bloodied dirk.

"Sergeant Trickett?" Lewrie called for the senior Marine. "I'd admire did you and your men go down the aft hatchway and work your way for-rud. Root 'em out. Mister Grainger, how's your French?"

"Passably good, sir," Grainger replied.

"Shout down to the hold-outs that we'll be setting this ship afire in fifteen minutes," Lewrie instructed him to say, "and if they don't wish t'burn, they'll come on deck, un-armed, and quickly."

There was a great cheer coming from somewhere, and Lewrie turned to find that *Lizard* was passing the privateer schooner close-aboard, her long sweep-oars now stowed away and ghosting along on a very faint breeze. Her crew stood by the bulwarks and rails, waving their hats.

"We will be taking the brig beyond, sir, if you do not object!" Lt. Bury shouted over, waving his own hat on high.

"Aye, Bury, take her and, welcome to her!" Lewrie shouted back, laughing and doffing his own hat. "Go get her, Lizards!"

As *Lizard* wafted by, Lewrie could look across the river and see Lt. Westcott's boats approaching the prize brig that was surrounded by sailing barges. There were French sailors aboard the brig, a harbour watch; it was a bit too far for him to see if they were armed or not. He was already so laden with weapons that he had not brought his telescope. There were some American sailors aboard her, too, possibly the crew that would have taken her to Havana or other Prize-Court ports. *They* were not waiting around to be captured. They were scrambling to board their barges, cut loose, and make sail up-river, out of reach of the British raid. Others were going over the brig's starboard side to some rowboats to make a quick dash to neutral ground.

Below his feet, boots were thundering on the schooner's lower deck, doors were being smashed open, men were shouting, and there was a sharp volley of musketry, and a scream or two, as Trickett and his Marines made their way forward through the mates' wardroom and into a series of storerooms, bound for the foc's'le. Lewrie took time to re-load his first pistol and re-prime the pans. By the time that he was through, Lt. Lovett's *Firefly* was almost up to the prize brig on the American side of the river, and Westcott's men were swarming the brig and the remaining barges. There were only a few shots fired, and the deck and gangways of the brig looked to be populated only with British tars.

With nothing better to do, Lewrie descended the steep ladder to Mollien's small cabins. The smell of spent gunpowder was strong, but could not overpower the stench of sweat and soiled and mildewing clothing and bedding.

"Man lived like a pig," Lewrie muttered. "Did he *ever* bathe?"

He poked around in the wee desk, into a sea-chest, and under the transom settee to the storage lockers. He found the ship's muster book, Mollien's accounts ledgers, logs, and a heap of letters, along with the precious Letter of Marque issued by the senior officer commanding at Basse-Terre on Guadeloupe; proof positive that the schooner *Otarie* was "Good Prize" for the Court at Nassau.

All that he stuffed into a pillow case. Lastly, there was one of those boxes that looked like a thick book; when opened, he found heaps of receipts, all from the Tybee Roads Trading Company!

"That Treadwell shit'd better hope he's powerful friends, or he's a goner," Lewrie muttered again, quite pleased with himself as he made his way back to the deck. Even if Treadwell was not here, there was solid proof that he had aided at least two French privateers over a year or more, and when the evidence was presented at Savannah, there was a good chance he would pay for it.

His own hands were cheering and jeering as the last French hold-outs came up from below, tossing aside their muskets, pistols, swords, and cutlasses, even personal knives, onto a loose pile of weaponry. A lone Marine emerged from the forward hatchway, his uniform and his kit still in Sunday Divisions best, with his musket slung over his shoulder and a bundle of abandoned weapons in his arms to add to the pile.

Lewrie went forward as Sgt. Trickett appeared from the hatch.

"Beg t'report, Cap'm sir," Trickett said, stamping and stiffening in parade-ground fashion, "all the lower decks're clear o' enemies. No weapons remainin', no spirits looted, and guards on their run and such. The

Frogs did put up a wee fight, up forrud, but we ended that right quick. There's two dead and five wounded still below. None o' our lads, though, sir!"

"Very well, Sergeant Trickett," Lewrie replied, looking over to his Mids, Entwhistle and Grainger. "Any of our people hurt, sirs?"

"Some nicks, cuts, and bruises, sir, that's all," Mr. Entwhistle reported.

"Well done, lads!" Lewrie congratulated them all, "Damned well, and briskly, carried! Do you be free with the French's scuttle-butts and drink some water. There's more work up-river. Fun's not over!"

"Sir! Sir!" Lt. Rainey from *Lizard* cried, once he and his men had boarded and secured their boats to take charge of the prize. "The other privateer is cutting her cable and making sail! She and her prize! I do believe they're trying to escape us, further up-river!"

"Right, then! Drink up, lads, and we'll get back in our boats. Mister Rainey?" Lewrie said. "The prize is yours. I will leave you five of my Marines to help guard the prisoners. Be sure that no one gets into the rum, and all those weapons get moved aft of the helm."

"Aye, sir, I have charge of the prize," Rainery agreed.

Reliant's cutter and barge refilled with men and shoved off as Lewrie waited by the entry-port. The gunboat was brought alongside, and sailors and Marines tumbled down into her, Lewrie going last.

"Shove off, and get a way on!" Lewrie snapped to Spendlove once seated aft by the tiller on a thwart. "Take us close-aboard *Lizard*, if ye please, sir. I wish t'speak to Bury as we pass."

"Aye, sir," Spendlove said.

Lizard had gone alongside the prize brig up-river of Mollien's schooner, and British sailors were swarming her bulwarks and the sail-tending gangways. Bury stood aft, evidently waiting for Lewrie. He leaned far out to shout his news.

"The French guards took a boat and rowed to the Spanish side, sir!" Lt. Bury told him. "But the prize's master, mates, and crew are here on board. We've freed them!"

"Let *them* work her out to mid-river short of the entrance channel, Mister Bury, and anchor!" Lewrie directed, standing in the boat. "We'll need their testimony before we let 'em sail off! I have need of your ship up-river!"

"I *see*, sir, and I shall follow you, directly!" Bury promised, pointing up the St. Mary's to the fleeing privateer and prize brig, and the gaggle of

barges that were trying to escape. Two of them had men at the rails tossing goods overboard to lighten them to reduce their draughts, and im-
prove their speed. "We will have *those* soon!"

"There's enough wind, it seems, sir," Lt. Spendlove told him. "Should
we hoist sail?"

"Aye, let's give it a try," Lewrie agreed. "It's a lovely morning for a
race." The oarsmen aboard heartily agreed with that as well, and raised a
brief cheer as the jib and gaff lugs'l were hauled aloft, the halliards
cleated, and the sheets drawn in. It was not a good wind they found, but
the gunboat did begin to move forward, breasting the river current and
heeling over a few degrees.

It's a river, so it must be fresh, Lewrie thought. He hadn't taken his own
advice to drink from the freshwater scuttle-butts aboard the privateer.
He dipped a hand over-side, took a tentative taste of the river, then
scooped up several handfulls to slake his thirst. It was fresh, with a silty,
leaf-mouldy taste.

"*Hmph,*" Lt. Spendlove commented, looking off the gunboat's starboard quarter. "That's expedient."

"What?" Lewrie asked, turning to see what he was talking about.

"Mister Westcott's cut the last barges free, and is letting the river current take them out into the Cumberland Sound, sir. I think he's getting the
brig under way . . . but I don't see many hands aboard." Spendlove pointed
out.

"If the harbour watch and guards have abandoned her, she'd not need
many t'work her out," Lewrie speculated. "Some of *Thorn*'s hands, perhaps."

"None of her own still aboard her, then, sir?" Spendlove asked with a
worried frown. "Already marched, off, or . . . slain?"

"God knows, Mister Spendlove," Lewrie said with a sigh.

All of Westcott's Marines and most of his sailors were getting back
into their boats, leaving not over a dozen on board. Lovett's sloop, *Firefly*, had not waited for them to complete their work and had continued
sailing on, her sails limply filling and flagging as she left the North side of
the river for mid-channel and began to slant nearer to Lewrie's gunboat.

"Hoy, Captain Lewrie!" Lovett bellowed through a speaking-trumpet.
"Do you wish me to pursue, or should I board the three-master to see if
she can be worked out of the river?"

Lewrie looked at the three-masted ship that was slowly looming up on the Spanish side. He could not see anyone aboard her above her bul-warks, or on her gangways or quarterdeck. No one was working on her forecastle to cut her anchor cable, and no one had laid aloft to free any sail. She might have already been abandoned by the French sailors who formed her harbour watch.

If Lovett fetches alongside her, it'll take him half an hour t'work back to the speed he's already got, Lewrie thought, scheming an answer as quickly as he could; *He's best left to pursue.*

"View, halloo, Lovett! Go after them!" Lewrie shouted to him, and even from two hundred yards away, Lewrie could see how much that order pleased the fellow. "Tally ho!"

What about *the three-master?* Lewrie asked himself.

"Mister Entwhistle!" he called forward to *Reliant's* barge. "I fear that you and Mister Grainger must go aboard this prize, here. Spendlove and I will continue on with the gunboat!"

"Aye aye, sir!" Entwhistle replied, looking crestfallen.

"Once the river's clear astern of you, you may try to get her anchor up and work her out, and anchor short of the entrance," Lewrie added, more as a sop to their disappointment than anything else. The excitement of the day was over for those lads.

Lewrie looked round again. There was *Firefly*, slowly stepping away ahead by about an hundred yards. *Lizard* was astern of his boat by about two hundred yards, standing away from the freed brig. Lt. Westcott and his gunboat, cutter, and barge formed a short column on the American side of the river, astern of them all but making sail.

"Still have that chart with you, Mister Spendlove?" Lewrie asked.

"Aye, sir." Spendlove said, pulling it from the breast pocket of his coat and handing it over. Lewrie spread it out on his knees. They were past a possible escape route, the very shallow Point Peter Creek on the Ameri-can side, and there was marsh on either hand for at least a mile on the Spanish side and the North, so . . .

There came a series of distant bangs from astern. Lewrie saw puffs of powder smoke rising from the marshes on the North bank, and return fire from Westcott's boats.

"Some of these that ran off must have poled their boats into the marshes, and are firing from cover of the reeds," Spendlove guessed aloud.

"Yes, well it won't do 'em—" Lewrie began to say, when the hum of a musket ball sang past, and some shots were fired at them by someone hiding in the marshes on the South bank! Puffs of smoke rose as if by magic, and a ball caromed off the gunboat's gunn'l, taking a divot of painted wood.

"Warnt us t'shoot back, sir?" a nervous Marine private asked.

"Waste o' shot and powder," Lewrie told him. "We can't see 'em 'til they pop up just long enough t'fire. They're wastin' powder, too, if that's any comfort."

Lt. Lovett obviously was not quite as sanguine. *Firefly*'s larboard 6-pounders erupted one at a time, each evidently loaded with a charge of grape, musket balls, or langridge, for the marshes twitched and shivered in wide swathes. Lovett had turned those four cannon into shotguns. A minute or so later, there were two musket shots from the marshes, another broadside from *Firefly* that must have been carefully aimed at roughly the same point, another great parting of reeds and marsh grasses like a full gale, and after, that . . . nothing.

There was still some sniping going on against Westcott's boats. The boat carronade at his gunboat's bows erupted, and his Marines and sailors let off a volley of musketry.

It was Lt. Darling's *Thorn* that settled the matter. She had slowly worked her way past where the first privateer and the prizes had been anchored and turned her much heavier guns, the six 18-pounder carronades of her starboard battery, loose on the sharpshooters with much the same results that Lovett had. There were no more shots fired at Westcott's boats!

"They're almost at the narrows, the bend of the river, sir," Lt. Spendlove pointed out, holding up a length of spun-wool to judge the wind's strength and direction, and tautening the main sheet just a bit snugger.

The prize brig was showing her larboard side as she made the turn that led South, with her captor, the other privateer brig, in her wake. As the privateer began her turn, her sails shivering, she let loose with a stern chase gun and the after-most of her larboard battery. The round shot passed so close to the few fleeing barges that two of them shied away off course for a moment, and one sheered North to run for the marshes. Lewrie did a quick estimate of where it might run aground and found that there was a spit of dry land behind all the marsh, perhaps only a tenth of a mile for her small crew to scramble before reaching some woods. Ahead, *Firefly* was running out her starboard battery in hopes of smashing her to kindling once level with the grounded barge!

Firefly was beginning to make good progress in her chase, closing the distance on the remaining sailing barges and the bend in the river. Astern, Lewrie could see that *Lizard* had a wee mustachio of foam under her forefoot as well; the wind was freshening just a bit. All of Westcott's boats were now under sail, the thirty-two-foot barge with two lugs'ls footing away from the single-masted cutter and the gunboat. As Lewrie watched, Westcott put his oarsmen to work once more for just a bit more speed!

The two fleeing brigs might have gotten round the bend, but were still in plain sight above the grasses of the marshes, showing themselves in profile. The privateer opened fire with her larboard guns and roundshot howled overhead, mostly aimed at *Firefly*, which had little in the way of bow-chasers with which to reply. The wind was on their beams, whilst the pursuing vessels had the winds astern in a sudden shift. The sun was not *quite* risen, but the East horizon showed a lighter blue-grey streak of clearing behind the darker gloom of the night's overcast.

"Try a shot with the carronade, sir?" Spendlove asked, eager to be doing something other than tending the sheets.

"Still too far for a light carronade," Lewrie decided as Lovett opened fire on the barge which had indeed grounded on the North bank, near that long narrow spit of dryer land. *Firefly*'s four 6-pounders on her starboard side raised great splashes all round the barge, scoring at least one hit that tore her transom open; the range was not one hundred yards from mid-channel to the marshes. Two or three sailors on the barge had been going over her bows to wade through the clinging mud and silt, but two of them whirled and fell, likely splintered by the shards from the shattered transom. The barge began to sink.

A minute later and *Firefly* was at the bend of the river, with *Lizard* striding up to join her, passing both gunboats, much to the frustration of Lewrie, Spendlove, and, obviously Westcott, who held up a fist and shook it at the sloops, shouting something best not heard by gentlemen.

Firefly quickly went about, her sails luffing and re-filling on a new course, with *Lizard* nipping at her heels.

"Should we continue, sir?" Spendlove asked, sounding weary.

"As long as we can, sir," Lewrie told him. "I want t'see how it ends. Be in at the kill, even if we can't contribute much to it."

Two minutes more and their gunboat was at the bend, too, and going about. Lewrie consulted the hand-drawn chart once more, noting how short this leg was to the South, just over half a mile, with the best channel nearest the Spanish bank, and a long, narrow, and shallow shoal in

mid-channel that widened and shoaled further where the river made a
turn to the Nor'west for a bit, then bent again to the West. Lewrie saw
what they might be driving for; on the North bank there was dry and
neutral ground on the American side of the St. Mary's, right down to the
river, with over twenty feet of depth! They hoped to ground there!

"Whoa, that's a close'un!" One of the gunboat's sailors cried, snapping Lewrie's attention ahead once more.

The privateer was nearest to them, still firing, slowly overlapping her
prize brig, stealing her wind. It looked as if the two of them were abreast,
and close enough to scrape hull paint!

"She's run t'other'un aground!" the sailor exclaimed a moment later.

"There's no room for both in the channel!" Lewrie crowed. "It's not
an hundred feet wide! We've got the prize, at least!"

"We will board her, sir?" Spendlove asked.

"No, she's a dead'un. Leave it," Lewrie laughed aloud. "We're after the
privateer."

Lovett and Bury were ahead of their gunboat, by then, and when they
came level with the prize, they veered East of her. Lovett could not resist
the urge to hear loud bangs, it appeared, for he fired his starboard battery
into her to make sure that she would not be worked off the shoal. The
range was almost hull-to-hull, and the brig flung parts of herself into the
air when struck. A minute later and damned if the phlegmatic Lt. Bury
didn't do the same thing!

First *Firefly*, then *Lizard*, reached the deep channel that led round to
the Nor'west in pursuit of the privateer, slewing far to the South to follow the deep channel, then wearing to take the wind on the other quarter
and hardening up a bit to claw over to the North shore to follow the channel to the American side. As each wore, they fired a full broadside at the
privateer, which was stern-on to them.

"Got 'er, they did! They 'it 'er 'twixt wind an' warter!" the garrulous
sailor cheered. "Huzzah, *Firefly*, huzzah *Lizard*, ha ha!"

The privateer's main tops'l's yard was shattered, and her top-mast
swung a full 180 degrees to hang inverted. Across the marshes all could
see her stern chewed up, with gouts of old paint, dirt, and shattered planking flung out in clouds.

"I don't think she's turning," Lewrie said, quickly looking at the chart
on his lap, excitement rising. "There's over fourty feet o' water yonder,
then one foot or less, right by the bank of the—"

"She's aground!" Spendlove shouted, waving his hat in joy.

"We've *got* her," Lewrie said in delight. "A clean sweep!"

"Do you think we could put up a broom at the main top, like the Dutch did ages ago, sir?" Spendlove chortled.

"Hoy, there's boats puttin' out from the grounded brig," the gun-captain of the carronade pointed out. "Can I try my eye on 'em, Cap'm?"

"Blaze away," Lewrie was happy to allow. The boats had been towed astern of the brig before she grounded, and people had tumbled into them on her larboard side as soon as they were hauled up by the towing lines.

"Damme, is it him?" Lewrie muttered as he saw a tall man with white hair making his way down the battens to the second boat with a musket slung over his shoulder and a red-leather pouch on his hip.

Their gunboat was less than a quarter-mile off the brig's stern. It was possible that both rowboats might get away. The first got away from the brig's side and headed for the deep channel. The gun-captain swivelled his carronade round trying to aim at it, but the jib was in the way, its foot less than a foot from the carronade's muzzle. If he fired, he might set it afire.

"Hand the jib for a while!" Spendlove ordered. "Give the gun a clear shot!"

The second rowboat was now clear of the brig, hands aboard it hastily hoisting a lugs'l and jib. Others were aiming their muskets astern. Some of them fired, and rounds sang past, one *thunk*ing into the gunboat's hull. Far beyond the range of a musket, that!

Lewrie saw two of them standing up to re-load, placing a ball in the muzzles and shoving them down with their ramrods . . . shoving hard!

"They have rifles, not muskets," Lewrie warned the boat's crew. He reached for his Ferguson rifle, stowed aft near Spendlove and the tiller. The morning had been so damp and muggy that he had not loaded it, depending on his pistols and sword for fighting.

He turned the long, sweeping trigger guard around one full turn, lowering the thick vertical screw behind the breech. From his rifle pouch he drew out a paper cartridge and shoved it up into the breech. A turn of the screw in the opposite direction sealed the breech once more and ripped the paper cartridge end to expose the propellant charge. Drawing the lock to half-cock, he opened the pan and sprinkled fine-mealed powder in, then closed the pan and pulled the lock to full cock, then turned to sit across the thwart and take aim. *Thunk!* came another rifle ball from the rowboat which was now under full sail. "Ow, God 'elp me!" an idle oarsman cried as a second shot hit him in his upper arm.

Bang! went the carronade as the gunner finally got a clear bead on the first boat which was still under oars. Lewrie waited for the smoke from the carronade to clear, wondering why he had not practiced with his rifled musket more often, thinking that if there had only been something worth hunting at Bermuda, in the Bahamas . . .

There! The white-haired man was standing to re-load, placing a thin leather patch and a ball atop the muzzle of his Pennsylvania rifle. He began to push down as Lewrie took careful aim, holding a bit above the man's head so the drop of the round would strike somewhere in mid-chest. He took a deep breath, let it out, and gently stroked the trigger with the tip of his forefinger.

The powder in the pan flashed off in a cloud of sparks, then an eye-blink later the powder in the barrel took light and the rifle shoved him in the shoulder. He blinked, waited for the smoke from the muzzle to clear.

"Praise th' Lord, Cap'm, ye got him!" a Marine whooshed in dis-belief. "At nigh-on a hundred an' fifty yards, is it a foot!"

Held too low, or my aim shifted, Lewrie thought, but all in all he could be quite pleased with his marksmanship. The white-haired fellow wore a shiny white satin waist-coat and a pair of buff trousers. There was a splotch of blood between the bottom of his waist-coat and his groin. Right into the guts, and a death wound for sure! Not right away, of course. That might take several agonising days. The fellow collapsed into the arms of his compatriots, who showed no more interest in shooting back.

Bang! went the carronade once more, and the boat's crew whooped in joy to see the first boat shot clean through and begin to take on water at once. The men aboard went over the side, a rare few of them swimming to the shallows of the American side, and safety. Most of them, though, were like British sailors, who could not swim a lick. They floundered, kicked, and wailed to keep their heads above water, but the St. Mary's had them, and by the time the gunboat reached the spot where only the up-turned bow of the rowboat remained afloat on a pocket of trapped air, there was only one survivor to pluck from death.

The other boat from the brig, the one that had been under sail, made the turn to the Nor'west at the end of that stretch of river, wore, and rounded the last of the shoal on the North bank. When in the shallows where it grounded, and its survivors could splash madly into the marshes, it was abandoned.

"Let's close that'un, Mister Spendlove," Lewrie ordered. "I want t'see if that fellow's the white-haired bastard behind all of this . . . that Treadwell."

"Aye, sir."

The current had lifted the boat from the mud and silt, and the loose grip of the first of the marsh grass reeds. Like Moses' baby cradle set afloat on the Nile, it rocked gently as the gunboat came alongside it.

The gunboat sidled up to the rowing boat, and sailors took hold of its gunn'l 'til a couple of short lines could be lashed between some thole-pins, and Lewrie could step over from his boat to the other, and kneel on a thwart to look down at the man sprawled in the inch or so of water in the boat's sole. He was a well-dressed gentleman in a satiny waist-coat, a ruffled shirt and white neck-stock, in buff trousers and top-boots. But, he was groaning and gasping in pain, those trousers dark-stained almost from his waist to mid-thigh with blood, with a visible bullet-hole seeping almost in a flood.

"Do you think that is he, sir?" Lt. Spendlove asked.

"Treadwell. Edward Treadwell of the Tybee Roads Trading Company?" Lewrie asked in a loud voice as if trying to rouse the dead.

"Ye-yes," the fellow weakly admitted. "He-help me for . . . for the . . ." He had to stop to stifle a loud cry.

"I fear, sir, that with a wound like that, there's nothing to be done," Lewrie told him with a shake of his head, not even trying to be sympathetic; it had been a fine shot after all! "You're slain . . . and bound t'meet your Maker before the hour's out. All your friends and partners are run off without a care for you, too. We've stopped your business with the privateers. You're through!

"Now, think of this as a death-bed confession, sir," Lewrie continued, leaning closer, looming over Treadwell, filling his sight, and softening his tone. "Don't face Eternity with a lie. What did you do with the people off the prizes when they were brought in?"

"Su-surgeon," Treadwell gasped, instead, writhing about and trying to both claw at, and staunch, his wound.

"No help, there, I told you," Lewrie snapped. "What . . . did . . . you . . . do . . . with . . . the . . . *prisoners?*"

"Aah!" Treadwell cried, whimpering. Tears rolled from his eyes; of pain, or fear of death . . . or for the ruin of everything he'd built? There was no telling.

"The prisoners!" Lewrie roared.

"Sa-safe. Saint Aug-Augustine," Treadwell whimpered so faintly that Lewrie had to bend to hear him. "Spanish have . . ."

"Good," Lewrie said, leaning back. "Thank you for that. Well, I'll leave you to it," Lewrie cheerfully added. "Give my regards to the Devil."

Lewrie stood up to return to his boat, but took a moment for looting, instead.

"Would you care for a Pennsylvania rifle, Mister Spendlove?" he said, lifting Treadwell's piece, its powder horn, priming flasks and leather pouch. "It's a rather fine one, custom-made, I'd expect."

"Ehm . . . thank you, sir," Spendlove hesitantly said, stunned by his captain's revelation of a very ruthless nature. "We will simply *leave* him, sir?" he asked once Lewrie was back aboard.

"Like the Vikings saw off their kings," Lewrie told him with a grin. "Set his boat adrift to get snagged in the marshes, or waft out to sea. It was his river . . . ; let it have him. Let's go see if Bury and Lovett are done with the privateer. She should've struck by now."

"Aye aye, sir," Spendlove replied, much subdued.

Lewrie sat down on the after thwart once more and dug into his cartridge pouch for a worn-out toothbrush, an oily rag, and a length of twine with a small weight on one end and a brass slot for a cleaning patch on the other, opened the breech of his Ferguson rifle-musket, and began to clean the bore, the pan, and touch-hole.

He looked up, distracted by the cries of marsh birds. The sun was fully up, at last, and the sounds of combat had silenced, allowing the myriad flocks of gulls, terns, sandpipers, herons, ibises, egrets, and skimmers to soar up from hiding. The clearing sky was teeming with them in their swirling thousands. Beyond round the bend of the river, *Firefly*, *Lizard*, and the privateer were close together, the smoke from the last broadsides still risen above them, as if from eye-level from his boat a naval battle was occurring on a vast green lawn, with the last of the river mist hazing the vast and verdant marsh grasses.

Damme if this ain't the best day I've had in months! he happily thought; *And a right-handsome one, t'boot!*

EPILOGUE

"Expulsis piratis—Resituta Commercia"

"He expelled the pirates and restored Commerce"
-Motto of Captain Woodes Rogers,
former Governor of the Bahamas

CHAPTER FORTY-FOUR

I've the fair copies of your reports ready, sir, if you would care to glance them over," Lewrie's clerk, Faulkes said.

"Aye, thankee, Faulkes," Lewrie agreed, seated on the settee to starboard of his great-cabins. *Reliant* and her small squadron were quietly anchored in West Bay below Fort Charlotte in Nassau Harbour, at long last, and he could lounge at ease in his shirtsleeves and a comfortable old pair of white canvas trousers, with a tall glass of cool tea sweetened and lemoned the way he liked it.

The most important of his correspondence was to Admiralty, far off in London, which described all his actions over the last few weeks, the capture of three French privateers, the *Insolent, Otarie,* and the *Furieux,* the amphibious landings his squadron had made, and the raid up the St, Mary's River. Included was his evidence against the late, un-lamented Edward Treadwell and his Tybee Roads Trading Company, and details of the nefarious plan to aid enemy privateers for profit, in violation of American neutrality.

A second set of evidence had to be sent to the British Ambassador at Washington City, with a briefer report that covered his raid, and its results, which proved the existence of Treadwell's plot, and justified his "kind of, sort of" skirting of American neutrality in the narrows of the river, so the ambassador could present the matter to the American government. That would be tit-for-tat and "so there" for American complaints that British forces still garrisoned the upper reaches of the Michigan Territory, *ages* after the peace treaty that had ended the Revolution in 1783!

Despite his distaste for the necessity, Lewrie would have to send a copy of the evidence, the ledgers, account books, and all, to their Consul at Savannah, that "top-lofty" idler, Mr. Hereford, with a cover letter that most carefully disguised Lewrie's loathing of the man and referred to him as a colleague. Hopefully, Hereford would stir up his lazy arse and present the matter to the city officials in Savannah, perhaps to their state government, too, who might lodge accusations and prosecutions against the Tybee Roads Company and all of its subsidiaries. Did they seize the properties and assets, there was a good chance that their seizure and sale, or fines, would make *someone* in state government a tad richer when it was dissolved!

Thud! went his Marine sentry's musket-butt on the deck beyond the door to his cabins. "Midshipman Munsell, SAH!"

"Enter," Lewrie idly said without looking up from his reading.

"My duty, sir, and I am to tell you that a Navy brig-sloop is entering harbour, sir," Munsell reported, hat under his arm. "She's made her number . . . the ah, *Delight,* sir. I believe she is listed as being assigned to the Bahamas Squadron."

"One of Captain Forrester's?" Lewrie asked with his head over to one side in curiosity. "I thought he took both of his brig-sloops South. Hmm. How far off is she, Mister Munsell?"

"She's hull-up at the moment, sir," Munsell informed him, "an hour or more from anchoring, or firing a salute."

"That'll give me time enough t'read all this over before whoever it is comes callin', then," Lewrie decided, yawning. "Thankee, Mister Munsell. Come report to me when I should have t'be up and dressed."

"Aye, sir."

Lewrie quirked his mouth in faint frustration once Munsell had departed. He had planned to finish reading the reports and see them, along with his personal letters, to the packets bound for Savannah, the Chesapeake, and England, then put his head down for a long, lazy nap, but *Delight*'s arrival put paid to that idleness.

Damn! he thought; *I wonder if her captain is important enough for me to put on my bloody star and sash?*

Thankfully, it was a whole two hours before *Delight* came into port, fired her salute . . . a cautious one of twelve guns befitting a Post-Captain of a Fifth Rate frigate . . . and came to anchor. She made a hoist of "Have Despatches", then another of "Permission to Board", which *Reliant* answered with "Captain To Repair Aboard", and a boat made its way to the frigate's starboard entry-port.

Lewrie awaited the newcomer on deck in the warm early-August sun, shoved into his everyday uniform, with the lesser concession of the star of the Order of the Bath pinned to his coat breast.

Bosun Sprague and his Mate, Wheeler, did the ship proud with their welcoming calls, the fully-uniformed Marines and sailors of the side-party saluted smartly, and the on-watch hands doffed hats as the officer, a Commander with a lone gilt and fringed epaulet perched on his left shoulder, doffed his hat in reply.

Midshipman Rossyngton saw him from the entry-port to the quarterdeck where Lewrie stood, whispering to the new arrival.

"Captain, sir," Rossyngton glibly said, making the introduction, "allow me to name to you Commander Isaac Gilpin of the *Delight* sloop. Commander Gilpin, allow me to name to you Captain Sir Alan Lewrie, Baronet, of the *Reliant* frigate."

"Your servant, Sir Alan," Gilpin said with a slight bow as he doffed his hat once more.

"Good t'make your acquaintance, Commander Gilpin," Lewrie said in turn. "At long last, that is, since your ship was out on patrol whenever I came in to Nassau, and our paths never crossed 'til now."

"It is my honour to make yours, Sir Alan," Gilpin declared.

"Join me in my cabins, sir," Lewrie invited, "for a glass of something cool."

"Sounds grand, sir," Gilpin agreed.

"Rhenish, Commander Gilpin, or cool tea?" Lewrie offered once they were seated on the starboard side. "Mind the cats, they're just curious," he cautioned as Toulon and Chalky came slinking.

"Tea, sir, if you please," Gilpin decided, wary of the cats, who found any new visitor worthy of sniffs and inspection. Gilpin had on his best-dress uniform, and the blue coat (so far) was pristine.

"You were down South with Captain Forrester, I take it? Just before he departed, he sent me a letter about it," Lewrie said. "He wished me t'join him, but I had other orders. They're finished now, at last. Did you manage t'catch up with Villeneuve and his fleet?"

"We never did, sorry to say, sir," Gilpin told him as he was presented with lemon juice and *turbinado* sugar to stir into his tea. "We got as far as Antigua and English Harbour, put in to speak with the officer command-ing, and found that the first arrival, that French Admiral Missiessy, had already hared back to France, and there was no clear information as to Villeneuve's whereabouts, so that was as far as we went."

"Then it was best that I kept *Reliant* here, or off Saint Augustine and Spanish Florida," Lewrie said.

Commander Gilpin was a pleasant-looking fellow in his middle thirties, trim and fit, and well-uniformed, with a blunt and honest face. He took a sip of tea, smiled in pleasant appreciation, and gave out a sigh. "Quite re-freshing, sir, thank you. Sir Alan, I—"

Lewrie waved the formality off.

"Ehm . . . I noted quite a few prizes in port, sir," Gilpin said. "Are they your doing?"

"Three French privateers, and a ship and two brigs awaiting return to their owners," Lewrie happily told him, laying a brief sketch of their re-cent doings.

"And you command a squadron of your own, sir?" Gilpin further en-quired. "I note that you fly a 'white-balled' broad pendant."

"A wee one," Lewrie replied. "I brought a sloop with me from Ber-muda, and borrowed Lieutenants Lovett and Darling from your Captain Forrester when I arrived. Damned fine men, full of daring. I shall be sorry to lose them."

Gilpin cocked a brow at that.

"We've fulfilled my orders," Lewrie explained. "The criminal enter-prise is broken up, the French and Spanish are on warning that the Geor-gia coast can't be used for privateering any longer, so I've nothing left to fulfill, but for the minor task of making new charts of the reefs of Ber-muda, so, *Lizard* and I, and her captain, Lieutenant Bury, will soon depart.

Before hurricane season, hopefully, and the climes at Bermuda aren't as sickly as the West Indies, or the Bahamas.

"In point of fact, my First Lieutenant and Lieutenant Bury wish to do a survey of North Ireland Island, and Grassy Bay, with an eye towards its possible use as a naval dockyard. Ever been up to Bermuda, Commander? The one harbour, Saint George's, is close to the sea, but it's bad holding-ground in a blow, and a tight fit did one of our fleets put in there. Whereas Grassy Bay and the Great Sound are hard to get to, for us and any foe, but huge and deep, with what looks t'be a completely impassible set of reefs all round. Only a rowboat could get through, 'assumin' they didn't get lost in the dead-end channels and the maze of coral heads. Soon as Forrester brings *Mersey* back to Nassau, I'm off."

"Captain Forrester will not be coming back, sir," Gilpin said with a quirky look of surpise. Or was it well-hidden glee?

"Oh?" Lewrie rejoined, hoping for the worst. "Why is that?"

"Well sir, once we put into English Harbour, he went ashore to confer with the Admiral commanding, and while I do not know what was said, he returned in some . . . discomforture," Gilpin related.

"Chalky!" Lewrie snapped. "Leave his boot tassels alone! Go on, sir, pray do. Here, puss. Pester me, instead!"

"Soon after, Captain Forrester summoned us aboard the flagship and told us we'd be returning to Nassau, that our services had been deemed un-necessary, and we weighed the next morning," Gilpin went on, "even though there wasn't a breath of wind, and we had to put down our boats to tow us from one warping post to the next out to the channel."

"Well I remember leavin' English Harbour," Lewrie said with a rueful grin. Chalky had come to Lewrie's lap to sniff at the star on his chest whilst Toulon was still on the settee by Gilpin, seated with his tail curled over his paws and staring in curiosity. "Toulon there is safe t'pet, d'ye care for it."

"Ehm . . . thank you, sir," Gilpin said, though making no move to do so. Lewrie gestured him to go on; with his story, he meant, but his guest took it for an order to pet Toulon, so he gave him a tentative pat on the head.

"You were sayin' . . ." Lewrie pleasantly urged, sure that that fubsy toad, Forrester, had come some sort of cropper.

"Aye, sir," Gilpin began again. "The other brig-sloop led out, and found a faint breeze, with a harbour pilot aboard, and I followed in her wake. When *Mersey* got past the last warping post and took her boats back aboard, though, the tide began to carry her astern, and a fluke of wind laid her aback. Before they could cast an anchor free she was driven on the coral and rocks, despite the best efforts of the other harbour pilot and her officers."

Come a real *cropper, has he?* Lewrie thought, feeling like he could laugh out loud like a lunatick; *How bloody wonderful!*

"How awful for him," he said, though, pretending sorrow quite well, if he did say so, himself! "Badly damaged, was she?"

"They finally got her off and fothered the holes in the hull, well enough to tow her back into harbour, sir," Gilpin continued his tale, "but it took half the crew on the pumps and the other half at getting her lightened. They took her down to a gant-line and landed all her guns and carriages ashore, along with all her stores, before getting her into the docks. Whether she is repaired and taken on as a receiving or store ship, or condemned and burned for her fittings, had not been decided when *Fulmar* and *Delight* were ordered to return to Nassau, sir. They were, however, assembling the sufficient number of Post-Captains for a Court-Martial for her loss, and the charge of Captain Forrester abandoning his area of responsibility, sir."

Yes, there is *a God, and He's just, t'boot!* Lewrie gleefully told himself; *They'll "Yellow Squadron" the fool, at long last!*

"Well, hmm," was Lewrie's comment. "Hah! Damn my eyes."

"The Admiral at Antigua sent you a letter, sir," Gilpin went on, reaching into a side-pocket of his coat. "Sorry for being remiss. Evidently, Captain Forrester must have made mention that you and your frigate were on station, or somewhere nearby, under Admiralty orders."

"And a complaint that I refused t'join him," Lewrie freely admitted, recalling the wording of Forrester's last attempt to order him under his flag.

"So . . . both I and Commander Richie of *Fulmar* were ordered to seek you out at once and relay the Admiral's request," Gilpin said as he handed the letter over. "For so long as the strength and the whereabouts of the French fleet under Villeneuve is discovered, and their objective is determined, his verbal orders to me were to tell you that he cannot spare any ships of his squadron to take *Mersey's* place, but . . . as soon as he may safely do so, he will send a ship, or several, to defend the Bahamas. Until then, though, sir, you are in command of the largest ship on-station.

Which makes you the temporary Senior Naval Officer Commanding the Bahamas."

"Mine arse on a band-box!" Lewrie gawped, a reaction that Commander Gilpin did not expect from a Post-Captain, especially one of Lewrie's repute in the Navy; wasn't he the aggressive "Ram-Cat", the bane of the French?

"Well, hmm," Lewrie said after a long moment. "I suppose that Bermuda's out for a good while. I'm glad that I'll have you with me, Commander Gilpin . . . and Commander Richie, is it, of *Fulmar*? I don't know what else we'll have, beyond the two ships of the squadron that I borrowed when I arrived. If Villeneuve comes this way, there's not much we can do to face him, but . . . we can give it a good try."

I s'pose this'll make Bury, Darling, and Lovett happy, Lewrie whimsically thought. They had all dined ashore together a few nights before, and his junior captains had all expressed glum regrets that he would be turning them over to Forrester's control, or for Lt. Bury to sail back to the boring patrols round Bermuda. At least still in his squadron, they could look forward to exciting doings they had assured him!

"Where's *Fulmar*?" Lewrie asked.

"Richie thought to seek you off Spanish Florida, sir," Gilpin said.

"We need t'keep a partial blockade of Saint Augustine. Once you've re-victualled, I'll send a sloop to find him and let him do that for a while," Lewrie decided. "Establish a patrol line down near the Turks and Caicos on the lookout for the French, too."

"I quite look forward to serving under you, sir," Gilpin said with an eager grin.

Once Gilpin had returned to his own ship, Lewrie laid aside his finery and changed back to comfortable clothes once more, ready for a mid-day meal. Yeovill and Cooke had run across a Free Black woman in the Bay Street markets who had been brought as a cook to the islands by a refugee Tory family at the end of the American Revolution. She had been freed years later, and *swore* that she possessed the best receipt for both pecan pie and peach pie, ones that had been her mother's back in Colonial Georgia, and *this* time (perhaps!) they would bake one as good as those he'd tasted in Charleston and Savannah!

Lewrie propped his feet up on the brass tray-table with a fresh glass of tea handy, and mused over, his new duties . . . and over what a well-deserved disaster had befallen Francis Forrester. If he knew the current locations of those few former Midshipmen of old *Desperate*'s cockpit with whom he had served, he would have written them that very instant, sure that all would gloat and shout Hosannahs at the news!

He could "caulk" for half an hour or so; though the windows in the transom were open, and the smaller ones in the coach-top overhead were open, too, it was a warmish day with little breeze reaching him.

Play a little horn-pipe of commiseration? he thought, fingering the holes of his penny-whistle, and putting it to his mouth. He got started on one, but there came a howl and singing wail from above.

"Deck, there!" he bellowed to the Midshipmen who stood harbour watch in lieu of the Commission Officers. "Is Bisquit on the quarter-deck?"

"Ehm . . . aye, sir," Rossyngton called down, kneeling down by the coach-top to show his face in one of the windows. The dog's head appeared in another. "Sorry, sir. I'll shoo him off, directly."

"Oh . . . never mind," Lewrie said with a sigh, laying his musical instrument aside. "Just make sure he doesn't shit on the deck."

"*Really*, sir?" Rossyngton yelped in surprise. "I mean, aye aye, sir. We'll keep an eye on him. Come on, boy!"

For a moment, Bisquit gazed down at Lewrie, matching eyes with him, panting and grinning with what looked like glee, and his triumph of the forbidden territory, at last. Then, he answered to Midshipman Rossyngton's summoning whistles and scampered off.

It's official, and unanimous, Lewrie thought with a shake of his head; *there's* nobody *who cares for my music!*

AFTERWORD

*B*efore privateering was banned by international treaty in 1856, and merchant ships no longer had to be defensively armed, every fresh war between seafaring nations brought hundreds of aspiring rovers from the woodwork with hopes of great profits, and adventure. Near at hand are the examples of the American Revolution and the War of 1812, which saw British trade attacked from the Grand Banks to the West Indies to the Irish Sea and the English Channel by an "auxiliary fleet" larger by far than the nascent Continental Navy or the U.S. Navy.

Privateering companies were formed overnight, investors bought in in anticipation of rich, quick returns, and the fastest and handiest ships were purchased, or offered by their owners as their investment share. Bold and canny sea-captains with good reputations were hired, or promoted themselves, men who could attract sailors on the strength of their reputations and the soundness of their vessels, and younger, fitter, bolder sailors eagerly responded.

Mariners' lives from the times of Sir Francis Drake and those "Bowld English Sea Rovers" of Elizabethan years to the end of the Great Age of Sail were dismal, and consisted of low pay, foul rations, back-breaking physical labour, tyrannical and miserly officers, and a good chance of being cheated at the end of each voyage. Whenever war broke out, common sailors faced the added risk of being 'pressed into a warship, where Navy pay was even lower, and discipline and good order were enforced with physical punishment, and shore liberty was quite out of the question for years on end to prevent desertion.

It was no wonder then that sailors would rather sign articles aboard a privateer and go a'roving in search of riches, loot from any captured ship, and a "lay", or share, in a voyage's profits. In port, they could leave the ship for a good drunk or two, some fresh air away from the typical ship's reek, find "elbow room" and some precious privacy away from their shipmates, and have a run at the whores. To be a privateersman put a swagger in their step, and made seafaring a grand adventure, not a thankless chore.

When captains of any nation at war held recruiting "rondies", they found themselves out-shone by the blandishments of privateers. In those days, there were no organised recruiting establishments, no basic training camps, and no Admiralty department responsible for assigning draughts of men to ships fitting out, or replacing men who had been killed, crippled, discharged, or lost to desertion. A Royal Navy captain had only a limited time to attract *trained*, experienced hands, wide-eyed young volunteers who would be deemed Landsmen, and scour the dregs offered by the Impress Service to complete his ship's complement. If he couldn't, he lost his precious active commission and another officer took his ship, and his place. Some warships had to sail with just enough people aboard to work the ship to sea, perhaps hundreds of men short, to save the captain's full-pay job! God forbid that a warship and a privateer were fitting out in the same port at the same time, for it would be the privateer that would always win!

Privateers operated in every corner of the world where ships of an enemy nation traded, and no seas were immune. Some French privateer captains, mostly from St.-Malo, were spectacularly successful in the Indian Ocean against convoys of the British East India Company, which bore rich cargoes to and from China, India, and the Far East. Some even dared to engage warships, and win, though that was usually the last thing a privateer would risk. If the privateer lost, it was all up, and even if they escaped with damage, that had to be repaired in port, resulting in long down-times with no profit, and a loss of money to pay for the repairs. A fast-sailing privateer's speed was her best defence.

As Falconer noted in his dictionary, privateers sorta-kinda agreed to follow Navy rules when applying for their Letters of Marque and Reprisals, but once at sea it was "Katy bar the door". Or, as it was said in *Pirates of The Caribbean*, the Pirates' Code was not like *real* rules, but more like . . . guidelines, and so was a privateer's behaviour. Indeed, some of the really successful privateers were ex-pirates temporarily made legitimate; conversely, once a war was over, the most successful privateers turned pirate. They swung both ways!

Bermuda, and its mysterious magnetic variations—there is no good explanation for them that I've heard of. I don't know if there really is a Bermuda Triangle, but the latest Admiralty charts I used when writing this book note the swings of several degrees from Magnetic North that are *not* seasonal, have nothing to do with sunspots, and aren't caused by phases of the moon. They caution all mariners to be excrutiatingly cautious when navigating Bermudan waters.

Basil Hall, a Midshipman aboard HMS *Leander* working out of Bermuda during the Peace of Amiens, related several accounts of his time there in *Every Man Will Do His Duty: An Anthology of Firsthand Accounts from the Age of Nelson* (edited by Dean King *et al.*, Owl Books, Henry Holt and Co.), which I found useful. Hall had little good to say of Bermudan pilots, citing a captain who found himself trapped in a maze of reefs and coral heads when putting out to sea. For a huge sum, a pilot offered to conn him free, which the captain paid. The pilot led him and his ship into an even worse spot, then demanded a second large payment. The captain paid again, but once safely free and in deep water, the captain got his own back by threatening to take the pilot to Charleston and sell him for a slave if he didn't get *all* his money back!

From Basil Hall, we also get Bisquit the dog.

Leander's captain and officers had pure-bred hounds aboard for hunting ashore, and the Midshipman's mess found themselves a dog for their own hunts, an incredibly ugly mutt they named Shakings, a term for scrap rope ends and ravellings. Shakings was too friendly, too playful, especially with the officers' pack, and was put ashore several times, but he always mysteriously turned up aboard again after a few days. Shakings sealed his own fate by putting his shore-mudded paws on the First Officer's snow-white breeches. The next day, he was gone forever, drowned by the ship's cook at the officers' behest, dumped overboard tied up in a bread-bag with a 24-pounder shot. That will most definitely *not* be Bisquit's fate!

That xebec that Lewrie's squadron captured in his absence in American ports—in *A Sailor of King George: The Journals of Captain Frederick Hoffman, RN, 1793–1814* (U.S. Naval Institute Press), Hoffman related his early days as a Mid and Lieutenant in the West Indies, chasing French and Spanish privateers in the Florida Straits and on the northern coast of Cuba with its myriad of "pocket harbours". He saw many lateen-rigged xebecs in the coasting trade and some fitted out as very fast, weatherly, and manoeuvrable privateers for short raiding cruises. The Spanish had known of their good qualities since the days of the *Reconquista,* and the depredations of Barbary Corsairs, and brought the type from the Mediterranean, early on in the colonial days. See, I didn't make it up!

Spanish Florida and lower Georgia were very sparsely settled in the early 1800s, and there were no settlements at what is now Miami, or in the Keys. The border country had been a battlefield between the Spanish, English, and French since the 1500s, and if Whites weren't at each others' throats, it was the Indians who raided, and the British colonists who made war on them in return. Governour Oglethorpe lured emigrants to lower Georgia to form a barrier against those raids, to protect his crown jewel, Savannah. Brunswick, Sunbury, Midway, and Darien are real places, and there are many historical sites from the colonial era and the Revolutionary War era to visit, including some restored forts. And, of course there are the Sea Islands. Cumberland Island is pretty-much off-limits for all but day-trippers, unless you're one of the Kennedys, St. Simon's is more touristy, and Jekyll, which I've visited several times, is much more laid back. Good luck, though, if you go in late summer; it's "love bug" season. After driving from I-95 to Jekyll Island, I had to use half a bottle of windshield cleaner and a Dobie scrub pad to see where I was going!

Lewrie's assault up the St. Mary's River is based on an actual event. In July of 1805, HMS *Cambrian* (40) captured a French privateer, the *Matilda*

(10) off Spanish Florida, and put a British crew aboard led by Lt. George Pigot (2)—(not guns, the second of that name on the Navy List!) with orders to enter the St. Mary's in search of a rumoured Spanish privateer. Pigot went much further than Lewrie did, a whole twelve miles, and *way* beyond the edge of my coastal chart, under fire by sharpshooters on both banks, captured the privateer, and brought her out. When I found that incident in Clowes's *The Royal Navy: A History from the Earliest Times to 1900*, Volume Five, near places where I had previously visited, my course was set. I knew where Alan Lewrie would go and knew what he would be doing in the momentous year of 1805 . . . the year of Trafalgar.

News travelled no faster than ships in those days, so rumours of Missiessy and Villeneuve bringing fleets to the West Indies, with Admiral Horatio Nelson in pursuit, came to Lewrie weeks and months after the actual events. He still has no idea whether the French will attack the Bahamas or not. If, Nelson brings them to battle, he also does not know whether to fear for his youngest son, Hugh, now a Midshipman in HMS *Aeneas*, or not, if battle is joined.

All Lewrie can do is to enjoy being temporarily in command of all the smaller warships in the Bahamas, keep his fingers crossed in hopes that the French have bigger fish to fry, and hope that it all blows over so he can return to Bermuda to fulfill the last part of his orders, to survey and chart the reefs and anchorages. He, Lt. Bury, and Lt. Westcott might even have time to sketch out the groundwork for that naval dockyard and fort on North Ireland Island on Grassy Bay and the Great Sound, which was finally begun in 1809. Whilst engaged in that endeavour, might Lewrie take up fish-watching with Lt. Bury, "with a bucket on his head"?

Or, will Dame Fortune decide to serve Lewrie a barricoe of bad turns? He can't be *too* sure that the threat of privateers along the coasts of Georgia and Spanish Florida is well and truly ended, or that Mr. Treadwell's death, and the ruin of his company, will convince other Americans who would connive with his King's enemies in violation of U.S. neutrality to think twice before filling that void.

Since I have a say in such things, after all, rest assured that fresh orders will come, summoning Lewrie to new seas, and new mis-adventures. There is one snag, though: So long as Bisquit is the ship's dog, will Lewrie ever get to play his penny-whistle again?

I will give you one wee hint. Lewrie will find himself and his frigate South of the Equator the next time round, dragged into a bit of glory, followed by a monumental cock-up.

'Til then, I wish ya'll fair winds and calm seas.